The Truth about Leo

KATIE MacALISTER

sourcebooks
casablanca

Published by Sourcebooks Casablanca, an imprint of Sourcebooks,
Inc.
P.O. Box 4410, Naperville, Illinois 60567-4410
(630) 961-3900
Fax: (630) 961-2168
www.sourcebooks.com

Printed and bound in Canada.
MBP 10 9 8 7 6 5 4 3 2 1

Prologue

LEOPOLD ERNST GEORGE MORTIMER, SEVENTH EARL OF March, defender of the crown, spy in the service of the (occasionally insane) king, and sometime rescuer of kittens stuck in trees, was not a happy man.

"I am not a happy man," he informed the kitten as he reached out to pluck it from its leafy bower and received a branch to the mouth for his efforts.

"Why not?"

For one extremely disconcerting moment, Leo thought the kitten had spoken. But since the question originated some distance below him, he quickly discarded that idea. "Why not what?" he asked, removing the branch so he could speak. Barely discernible through the foliage was the slight figure of a girl child, aged about eight and perched with apparent ease on the back of Galahad, his large bay gelding.

"Why aren't you happy? Is it because you're English? My grandmamma was English. Mama says all English are unhappy because they don't live in Denmark. Are you sad because you don't live in Denmark?"

"I'm not sad at all."

"You said you were."

He edged forward along the branch. The kitten, a small hissing bundle of gray-striped fur, appeared to share his general dissatisfaction with life, for not only was it trying to make itself look as large and menacing as possible, but it also appeared to suddenly realize that the sharp things in its mouth and on the ends of its feet might have a use in dissuading its removal from the tree. "I said I was not happy."

"That's the same thing," the girl pointed out, then winced when the kitten took defensive action.

"Damn you!" Leo growled, snatching back his hand from where he had the cat cornered.

"You said a bad thing!" gasped the girl.

"Yes, I did." He made another lunge for the cat and got his hand scratched a second time.

"Mama says that people who say bad words are godless heathens. Are you a godless heathen?"

Leo bit back the urge to expound on what he thought of her mother's teachings and concentrated on capturing the hell-spawn beast without any further damage to life or limb.

"Mama says that people who say the bad thing you said are ignorant because they can't think of anything else to say."

"I can think of a thing or two to say to your mother right now. How is it you speak English so well?" He feigned a move to the left, attempting to catch the kitten off guard, but young though it was, it had a feline wisdom that kept it just beyond his reach.

"Mama taught me. She says that someday, when

my brothers are older, we will go to England and see Grandmamma. Don't hurt Francis!" This last was in reaction to the sight of Leo removing his jacket, waistcoat, and one of his braces.

"Tempting though that thought is, I draw the line at abusing small animals." The kitten spat at him. "No matter how much they might deserve such treatment. I'm simply going to try to snare the beast."

"His name is Francis, after St. Francis of Assisi, who loved all the animals and beasts in the field. He sleeps with me and keeps me warm at night."

Blinking once or twice at the inadvertent imagery, Leo made a rough loop with his brace and attempted to toss it over the cat's head. It fell short by several feet. "You need to watch your pronouns when you make statements like that."

"Do you have family here, like my grandmamma?"

"No. I'm just passing through." He grunted as he slid on his belly along the branch, refusing to think about what the movement was costing his clothing.

The girl's brow wrinkled. "Are you here because of the war?"

"War? What war?" He slid along another foot. He was almost within reach of the monster.

"Papa says the English attacked our ships two days ago. Papa says there are no more ships in the harbor and that the English killed hundreds of sailors. Did you kill any sailors?"

"Not to my knowledge. I'm on my way to Copenhagen from St. Petersburg, and I hope to heaven your father is wrong about the ships." He paused for a moment and thought about what the girl had said, eventually shaking his head. No, he hadn't heard any word of a war intended against the Danish. True, he'd been incommunicado these last three weeks while he traveled from the depths of Russia out to the Danish coast, but surely he would have heard at least a whisper of such a thing had the Admiralty intended on attacking.

Then again, given how unhappy the prime minister and his advisers were with the Scandinavians on the whole—what with their lenient trade attitudes toward that blighter Napoleon—a war wasn't entirely out of the question. But realistically? He shook his head again. The navy would have to be crazy to launch an attack against the Danes. Their navy and army combined were a minute force compared to that of Britain and her allies. "Now then, let's see if we can't end this debacle."

A quick flick of his wrist later and the cat was snared. Gently he held the bucking kitten steady while attempting to wrap a handkerchief around his (now bleeding) hand.

"You caught him!" the child squealed in delight, clapping her hands.

Leo quickly rearranged his hold to avoid all of the kitten's sharp, stabby bits. "Here, you, Anna or whatever your name is—"

"Amadelle."

"No, really? Your mother must be quite inventive. Here's your blasted kitten." He clung to the tree with one arm while leaning down as far as possible, the kitten still hissing and spitting at him. The girl was a brave little thing, for without the slightest hesitation she reached up and accepted the monstrous kitten, removing the loop from around his neck in order to snuggle him. Dewy tracks down her cheeks bore testament to her distress previous to his arrival, but all was forgotten as she beamed up at Leo.

"I'd suggest you keep the vicious brute out of trees in the future," he told her sternly, trying to harden his heart against the look of hero worship that she was bending upon him. Don't get involved with the locals, that had always been his motto, and it had stood him in good stead for the many campaigns he had undertaken across the breadth of Europe. He wasn't about to let a fresh-faced young chit make him break his vow of disinterest, no matter how heroic she made him feel. "You can't count on having a handy rescuer to be lost on the way to Copenhagen, and thus available for service to you, both of which I was."

"Thank you," she cried, her happiness complete. Clutching the hell-spawn cat in one hand, she slid down from the not insubstantial height of Galahad's broad back with an air that bespoke much practice in the art of horse sliding. She continued to beam up at Leo...for about three seconds, after which time shrieking and arm waving commenced, propitiated by the cat's leap from her arms, directly onto Galahad's neck.

His horse was many things—brave, stalwart, and at times, downright stubborn—but when faced with four sets of claws digging into his neck, he protested the offense in the only way he knew: he bolted.

"Francis, no!" the child screamed and dashed after the cat, which had leaped off the horse and turned into a feline streak of gray and white, headed straight for a barn, the roof of which was visible over a copse of leafy trees.

"Galahad!" Leo thundered, but it did no good. The horse leaped over the stone fence that bounded the pasture, and was off down the dirt road before he could do so much as shake his fist and threaten the horse with heinous retribution.

In the short space of three seconds, Leo found himself alone, up a tree, and bleeding from several scratches on both his face and hands.

"There are times," he said, looking upward in case some deity or other might be interested in bending an interested ear his way, "when I firmly believe that I'm the victim of a dread curse. That time in Berlin when I was caught in the countess's bedchamber was one. The recent happenings in St. Petersburg was another. This time, however—stranded in a tree, horseless, and most likely too late to catch the ship sailing for Germany—has to take the top honors." He sighed, considered continuing his self-pity for a bit longer, but decided that wouldn't help him out of his present circumstances. "At the very least, we're having decent weather."

As if on cue, a group of pregnant gray clouds that he would have sworn weren't there five minutes earlier drifted across the sun. The gentle pat, pat, pat sounds on the leaves around him made him sigh again.

"Of course. How silly of me to tempt fate." It took him a good twenty minutes to figure a way out of the tree; without the handy stepping stool that was Galahad or the presence of lower tree limbs, he had a hard time negotiating his descent, but in the end, after much swearing and a little more blood loss thanks to some jagged broken branches, he fell the last few yards to the ground, landing with a heavy thump.

The bones in his left leg, broken a few years past after a leap out of the German countess's bedchamber window, protested but didn't buckle, and for that he was profoundly grateful. He straightened up, made an attempt to brush off the worst of the tree from his clothing, and turned to limp toward the road in hopes of seeing Galahad grazing on the verge.

Three men clad in Danish uniforms, all armed with rifles and sabers, faced him. One of the soldiers held his own sword, which he'd removed to climb the tree.

His shoulders slumped as the men moved forward. "Cursed," he said. "Definitely cursed."

One

A princess strives for modality of both voice and being. Discordant events, such as the refusal by a groom to allow one to ride one's father's stallion, are to be greeted with a slightly elevated eyebrow (no more than one quarter of an inch; anything else is considered mannish), and a slightly aggrieved expression. Under no circumstances should carbolic powder be placed in the groom's underthings so as to ensure unsightly and ceaseless itching of an Unspeakable Body Part.

—*Princess Christian of Sonderburg-Beck's Guide for Her Daughter's Illumination and Betterment*

"PRINCESS!"

Dagmar tapped the end of the quill against her lips and considered best how to answer this latest demand from her cousin.

"Princess Dagmar!"

My very dear cousin Frederick, she wrote, then decided that given the tone in her cousin's letter, the rotter didn't deserve such niceties.

Frederick:

I have received your missive dated today and have to say that I'm shocked that a man who Dearest Papa always insisted had so much potential would use words like "blot on the existence of my life" and "irreverent, mouthy, and in essence, painful to be near" to a lady like me, let alone one of royal blood, but as the good book—and I refer here to my sainted mother's detailed journal— always says, breeding will tell.

"Princ—oh, there you are." A slight form appeared in the open doorway, bobbing a little curtsy before entering the room. "I've been hunting all over for you. There's a drunkard in the garden."

I shouldn't have thought it necessary to point out that the other good book—the Bible—mentions it as a sin to turn one's back on one's destitute and orphaned cousins—

Dagmar paused, glancing over to where her companion stood patiently waiting to be acknowledged. "Oh, hello, Julia. Do you know what the Bible says about cousins?"

The slight, blonde woman of forty-some years looked puzzled. "No. What does it say?"

"That's what I was asking you." Dagmar tapped the quill on her lips again. "Is it a sin to claim that the Bible says something if it really doesn't?"

"I think it is, yes." Julia sat, clasping her hands in a pious gesture that just made Dagmar sigh. It wasn't that she was especially intolerant, or even irreligious, but the truth was that she was forever being taxed with being sinful by her cousin Frederick, who had long claimed that Dearest Papa had let her run wild and had not in the least tiny bit drummed into her how a proper lady should behave.

"Which is ridiculous, because there's no way anyone could mistake me for a man," she muttered, glancing down to where her front was quite obviously not that of a male. "I think they're getting bigger."

Julia considered the offending bosom. "I don't think so, dear. They look just the same to me."

"That's because you're around them all the time." Dagmar gave her front one last dark look. "But my green gown is going to have to be let out again, else I'll pop out of the bodice. Where was I? Oh, yes, the Bible. Well, it may not be in there, but it should be."

"I'm sure you're correct. Did you not hear me mention that there was a drunkard in the garden?"

"Yes, I heard you."

A slight pause followed, ending when Julia said, in a flustered, breathless manner, "Do you not think anything of this?"

"Not particularly. Well, to be honest my first thought was to answer 'When wasn't there a drunkard in the garden' but I realized that we haven't been blighted with over-many garden drunkards in years past, so I decided to keep it to myself."

"But...but..." Julia waved a hand in one of her vague gestures of mild distress.

Dagmar took pity on her. "Is this man doing any harm?"

"No, but he's lying right out in the open, where anyone who ventures into the garden might see him."

Dagmar dismissed him from her thoughts. It wasn't as if she didn't have more pressing concerns than some silly man who had imbibed too much and stumbled into their garden. "Don't let it distress you. He's probably sleeping off a night at the tavern and will leave once he wakes up."

"But he might be injured or worse!"

"What's worse than injured?" Dagmar asked absently, wondering how best to put her situation before her blighter of a cousin.

"Dead!"

"Ah. Excellent point. Why don't you go check and see if he's dead while I finish this?"

A blissful silence followed Julia's departure. Dagmar dipped her quill and continued.

> —*destitute and orphaned cousins who are due your protection, but if you want to spurn God right to his face and damn your eternal soul, then that's your choice. I, as an innocent and did I mention destitute and orphaned young princess of your own blood, albeit one that is somewhat distant relationship-wise if Dearest Papa's genealogical chart is correct, will simply have to throw myself on the mercy of the king, your father, our beloved monarch and supreme ruler. I'm sure he will not turn his back on his own family and throw me out of the only home I've ever known, especially since I am still in mourning for Dearest Papa.*

All too quickly, Julia was back. "He's not dead."

"Good, good."

"He refuses to wake up, however."

"Ah."

Julia wrung her hands for a few seconds. "Oughtn't you to come see him for yourself?"

"I've never really found high entertainment value in gazing upon insensible drunkards, so I believe I will stay here and finish this. How do you spell 'misanthrope'?"

"I would feel better if you did assess the situation for yourself."

"Why?" Dagmar looked up from where she had been adding a word or two to the letter.

More vague hand gestures followed. "Well…he might not meet with your satisfaction."

Dagmar tried very hard not to laugh. "I assure you most sincerely that I will have no undue expectations of this poor soul."

"And then there's the fact that he's just lying out in the garden. He might hurt himself in his stupor. Or someone might trip over him. Or wolves might devour him while he is without his senses. I would feel much better if you were to view the situation."

Dagmar set down the quill. "You're not going to let me finish until I do, are you?"

"I would never presume—"

Dagmar stood, knowing the sooner she went out and viewed the man, the sooner she could return to pleading with her cousin. "Very well, let us view this new addition to the garden."

"Perhaps the crown prince might send a guard

or two to relieve us of his presence," Julia said, trotting beside Dagmar as the latter strode out to the garden. Back behind the roses, at the very edge of the cultivated land, a low hedge marked the boundary of the property. A small shack sat in the corner, ostensibly used for gardening implements, but Dagmar knew well that Julia kept a small bottle of brandy inside it. She'd never let on that she knew her companion used the excuse of a nightly stroll around the garden to have a wee nip since Julia would likely die of mortification should her secret be discovered.

The man lay on his back near the shed, a long, woolen driving coat covering most of his body. He was hatless, his dark hair filthy with dirt, leaves, and a small snail, but he didn't appear to be in harm's way. Dagmar leaned over him and caught a whiff of brandy.

"I doubt if we have anything to worry about," she said a moment later, noting that the man had no weapons on him. "I don't believe he's in any condition to do harm to the garden or anything else to be honest. He'll likely be gone by nightfall."

Dagmar turned and hurried back toward the house. The morning air still held a chill, and although the house wasn't much warmer, at least she could wrap a blanket around herself while she wrote.

"Do you not think we might bring him indoors?"

"Why would we want to do that?"

"If he does not go away by nightfall, he might catch cold."

Dagmar settled herself at the rough table that served

as a desk and dismissed the man from her mind. "He's fine where he is. Now, I shall finish this letter and then take it to Frederick."

Julia fussed around the room for a few minutes. "My dear princess, do you not think that we should be packing rather than writing?"

"No, I do not think that in the least." The quill's scratching on the paper was oddly soothing as Dagmar gave vent to her fears and frustrations of the last thirteen months, since that terrible day when Dearest Papa had succumbed to scarlet fever. "Does 'excrescence' have one *r* or two? Never mind, I'll give it two. It looks better that way."

"Might I be so bold as to inquire to whom you are writing?" Julia asked, rising to peek over Dagmar's shoulder. She gasped when she read the name at the top. "Dagmar! My very dear princess! You cannot speak to your cousin in such a…bold…manner. He is the prince regent, after all."

"He's also a heartless rotter who thinks nothing of throwing you and me out of our home without so much as a warning."

Julia hesitated, then pointed out softly, "I believe that he has spoken of you going to live with your other relatives since shortly after your father's untimely death over a year ago…"

"Pfft."

I've told you before that my German relatives refuse to allow me to visit them, since Dearest Papa angered all of them by marrying my beloved mother, who was, if you recall, English and thus an

enemy of the state of Sonderburg-Beck. Therefore,
your insistence that my companion, Mrs. Julia
Deworthy, and I vacate Yellow House is nothing
short of murder. To be blunt, we have no family
but you, Frederick, to provide us with succor. You
were executor of Dearest Papa's will, so you know
full well that all he retained from his inheritance in
Sonderburg-Beck was a useless and little-known
title. I regret as much as you do that my beloved
mother's modest fortune was lost in bad invest-
ments, but that regret is all I possess.

Julia touched her lightly on the arm. "His Royal
Highness, the crown prince, was most insistent that
we leave dear Yellow House before the fifteenth of
the month, and we are but three days shy of that date.
I do not wish to worry you, my dear princess, but
perhaps another visit to those obliging gentlemen in
town might be in order?"

"I have nothing left to give to the pawnbrokers, so
it would be of little use to speak to them."

You will naturally understand how hard it is for
me to ask...no, beg on dutifully bended knee...that
you either give up your determination to use my
home as guest quarters for official visitors or relocate
Mrs. Deworthy and myself to another of your houses.
You have plenty of them, and we do not require
grand accommodations. We are, in fact, quite used
to shifting for ourselves. A simple cottage would do
nicely for us, even one in the country. Surely you
must have dozens of cottages, Frederick. It cannot

> be a hardship to turn over one to me, your neediest
> of all relatives. Do not fail the Bible and our ties of
> blood by throwing us onto the street.
>
> > Yours in cousinly poverty,
> >
> > Princess Dagmar Marie Sophie
> > of Sonderburg-Beck

Dagmar signed her full name with a defiant flourish. She might have to humble herself to her annoying cousin, but she'd be damned if she disavowed her father's title.

"Perhaps there is something, a little trinket, something you overlooked…" Julia's sentence trailed away as Dagmar set down the quill and sealed the envelope by tipping the nearest candle over the paper.

"I can't even afford proper sealing wax, Julia. Don't you think if there was anything else to sell, I'd sell it?"

Julia's face crumpled into abject despair. "If only I had some means to provide for us—"

"Yes, but you don't." Dagmar immediately felt like a heel. She might have heard that lament numerous times each day, but she didn't have to belittle Julia about it. After all, she was the one who should be supporting them both. She turned in the chair and took her friend's hands in her own. "Sweet Julia, my apologies. I shouldn't have snapped at you like that. Frederick is right: I'm rude and intolerable to be around. You have nothing to feel bad about— your father didn't lose your mother's inheritance through bad investments, after all. Please forgive my bad temper."

Julia threw herself on her knees (she was prone to

such dramatic gestures). "Oh my dearest princess, my very, very dearest Dagmar, do not speak so of yourself. You are everything that is good and generous. I was lost, alone, friendless in a strange country when your sainted mother took me in and gave me a place. Had she not done so, I would have been driven by poverty into that most heinous of all professions."

"Housemaid?"

Julia's gaze dropped and a maidenly blush pinned her cheeks. "You are so innocent, dear Princess. So untouched."

Dagmar thought for a moment. "The night soil collector?"

"Concubine!" Julia said with a gasp, one hand clutching her throat as if speaking the very word choked her.

Dagmar made a little face and addressed the letter. "I've never really seen that as the most heinous profession of all. I mean, most of Frederick's mistresses are quite well off. His children—the baseborn ones—even have titles, and he's given them some lovely houses…" One thought led to another. Dagmar considered the idea of becoming a mistress to a wealthy and generous man, but after a few minutes' thought, gave up the idea. "It's not that I'm morally opposed to such a thing," she said aloud.

"Opposed to what?" Julia, who had picked up her needlework while Dagmar had sat in thought, looked up again.

"Becoming a courtesan."

"Dagmar!"

"Although I do admit that it would probably be

nicer to be married to the man to whom one was intimately involved, what with marriage settlements and such. But I suppose if you were very smart, you could work out all of those business details up front, yes?"

Julia looked as if she was about to fall over. "Do not tell me…you cannot be thinking…dearest Princess! Reassure me that you are not contemplating such a Fatal Step!"

"I've never heard of anyone dying from being a courtesan," Dagmar said phlegmatically but added, "although Mama always said that the French Pox could kill if you had it bad enough. But the point is moot, so you can start breathing again, Julia. You're turning quite blue. I have no intention of becoming a courtesan."

Julia slumped into the one remaining sofa that sat in the nearly empty house. Dagmar knew all too well just how empty it was, since it was she who had sold all but the most essential of furniture. "I thank the Lord for you coming to your senses."

Dagmar picked up a ratty reticule and reached for the rattier-still straw bonnet, plopping it unceremoni-ously upon her head. "It has nothing to do with sense and everything to do with the fact that there's not one man in Copenhagen who I could imagine doing intimate things with. I'm going to the palace now. Wish me luck. If Frederick refuses to see me—which I suspect he will—I shall leave off the letter and stop by the kitchen to see what I can bring home for us."

"Will the crown prince allow you to bring victuals from the palace? He seemed disinclined to have you doing so, even going so far as threatening to have you jailed for sticky bun theft."

Instantly, Dagmar's mouth watered, and her stomach growled. They had been very good sticky buns, well worth both the effort it took to liberate them and the subsequent scolding she received two days past from Frederick. "There's more than one way to raid a kitchen," she said with an enigmatic smile.

"Shall I accompany you?" Julia immediately rose to her feet. "I feel that I should go with you. What your mother would say if she knew I let you go out unescorted…"

"I'll be fine. You stay here and…and…" Dagmar searched her mind for something to keep Julia occupied. Left alone, she'd just fret and worry herself—and ultimately Dagmar. It was far kinder to give her a task to keep her mind busy. "Ah! I know. You shall stay here and watch over the drunkard to make sure he doesn't harm the garden."

Julia blinked. "But you just said that it wasn't likely he would do any damage."

"I have absolutely no memory of saying that," Dagmar lied. "Wrap up well and go watch the man for signs of movement. If he regains his senses, lock yourself in the house."

Catching up a heavy shawl, Dagmar left the dark confines of the run-down mansion that sat on the unfashionable side of town, content to stride along the pitted cobblestones enjoying the weak sunshine and sights of a busy port town.

Copenhagen had been in uproar the last few days following the unexpected attack on the Danes by the British navy. Fortunately, the battle had been short-lived and few civilians suffered by the action, except so far as having one's town filled with sailors in British uniforms. Dagmar didn't know quite how she felt about the attack, other than regretting the loss of Danish life, but upon thought, she decided that attacking a much smaller country was unsporting of the British, and yet she didn't care for the fact that Frederick was looking with favor at Napoleon. She didn't like that particular Frenchman at all. "I pity his mistress a great deal. She must have to put up with the most abominable arrogance…good morning, Jens."

The guard at the door to Amalienborg Palace bowed low and greeted her. "Good morning, Your Serene Highness."

"How is your wife doing? Is her cough better?"

"Much better, thank you for asking."

"And the wee babe? Is he past the worse of his teething?"

"We believe so, Your Highness. My wife told me to thank you for the cure you sent her. She said it was a miracle and that it gave the little fellow the first solid night's sleep he'd had in over a month."

"My mother always swore by rum and lemon for teething babies," she said with a smile and entered the palace.

Courtiers and servants moved around the various halls and rooms without any regard to her. She had a suspicion that it was less because of any sympathetic feelings toward her desperate plight, and more because few of them knew who she was. Other than Jens, who had been a footman in her father's household, she didn't know any of the servants at the palace, and knew few of the courtiers who resided or worked within.

A footman with pimples and a shiny face deposited her in a sitting room, where she encountered two other people.

"Good morning," the man said in stilted Danish, bowing slightly.

"Yes, it is a good morning, if by that you mean it's not raining, and the smoke has cleared from the harbor," she answered in English, looking the pair over. The man was not very tall but had attractive salt-and-pepper hair that curled back from his brow. He appeared to be in his forties, with lines etched across his forehead, attesting to some great worry. His companion likewise bore lines of unhappiness, but hers were centered between her eyebrows. She was tall, taller than Dagmar, and very thin.

"Oh, you speak English?" the woman asked in obvious relief.

"I do."

"It's so nice to find someone who understands us," the woman said, gesturing at the man. "Philip and I haven't heard anything but Danish and French in weeks. Other than three days ago when we saw the ambassador, of course, but even then he seemed inclined to speak in French."

"Indeed." Dagmar wondered briefly who the couple were and what business they had with Frederick. They didn't appear to be political personages, or one of Frederick's equerries would have attended to them. To be parked in the sitting room indicated a guest whose presence wasn't expected or possibly desired. Still, they mentioned the ambassador…

The man must have sensed her reticence to converse, because he gave a little embarrassed laugh and said, "You must forgive our lack of manners, ma'am. My sister and I have been away from home for some time, and it's a pleasure to hear our mother tongue spoken. You will permit me to introduce us. I am Dalton, Philip Dalton, and this is my sister Louisa Hayes."

Dagmar murmured the expected niceties. Being a social person, she wouldn't have minded staying to chat with the couple, but she had an important errand to see to, and the sooner she was allowed into Frederick's presence, the better for her peace of mind.

"And you are?" the woman asked, giving her a pleasant smile.

"Late. Er…my name is Dagmar, but I'm late for a meeting with my cousin. It was a pleasure to meet you, and I hope you enjoy your visit to Copenhagen. If you'll excuse me, I must go find Frederick before he slips out."

Dagmar left the couple in possession of the small sitting room, feeling that more than enough time had passed to inform Frederick that she wanted to see him. As she headed down the hallway, a group of women emerged from a stateroom. At their head was a slight, willowy figure with dark eyes who paused upon passing.

Dagmar sank into a court curtsy, intoning to the floor, "Your Royal Highness."

"Princess Dagmar. I trust you are not here to pester the crown prince again. I believe he was most straightforward in his demand that you do not *ever again* force yourself into his private chambers."

Dagmar had the grace to blush slightly at the reminder, but she'd never been intimidated by her cousin's wife, Marie, and she wasn't about to start now. "Only cowards lock themselves away in their closets."

Marie's dark eyes widened. "He was attending to business of a highly personal nature."

"He was not. He wasn't even near the closestool when I finally managed to get the door open. He was slouched in a large armchair reading a pornographic French book and quite obviously hiding from me because he is so riddled with guilt over his actions. I don't suppose you've talked to him about that?"

The crown princess eyed her coldly, minutely adjusting a silk shawl. "Why should I? I happen to agree that the time has come for you to move on to other relatives."

"I've told you that I don't *have* other relatives—"

Marie held up a hand. "I'm late. I have warned you against bothering Frederick again. If you insist on doing so, it's on your own head." With a sniff and a disparaging glance at Dagmar's gown (mended several times and showing signs of an ill-fought battle with the lye kettle), Marie and her ladies left by a side door to a waiting carriage.

Dagmar looked at the footman standing at attention next to the door and thought of saying a very rude word, but the memory of her mother's strictures ("A princess never refers to anything as a bitch unless it has eight teats") kept her silent.

Until she came up against her cousin's lackeys,

that is. After fifteen minutes of vigorous arguing, pleading, and at one point, threatening, Dagmar had given up hope of being admitted into the crown prince's presence.

Which made it all that much sweeter when she saw that very man while she was loitering around the kitchen, waiting to snatch up a tasty looking loaf of bread, wheel of creamy cheese, and perhaps, if she could arrange her shawl in an unsuspecting manner, the boiled head of a pig. The three kitchen servants suddenly called upon to deal with a badly smoking chimney was her moment of opportunity, and she took it with alacrity before looking up to see the newcomer.

"Speak of the devil." She set down the pig's head and moved over to intercept her cousin on his path to the table containing baked treats. "Good morning, Frederick."

The crown prince spun around, one jammy biscuit in his hand, his eyes (which tended to protrude anyway) bulging out in the manner of a pug dog caught with a pheasant pie in his mouth. "Dahmar!" he said indistinctly, bits of biscuit crumbs spraying out as he spoke. He gave a tremendous gulp, then scowled fiercely at her. "Dammit, what are you doing here? I thought I forbade you to enter the palace."

"No, you forbade me to enter your closet, your bedchamber, the throne room, the grand ballroom, the small ballroom, and most if not all of the rooms on the first through third floors, but you did not forbid me from the kitchen. Thus, here I am. I need to speak to you—"

"If I didn't forbid you, it was merely an oversight.

Out!" he said, pointing a finger at the nearest door before jamming the rest of the biscuit into his mouth.

Dagmar's stomach rumbled ominously. She hadn't eaten in almost twenty-four hours, and the fact that her cousin, her own flesh and blood, could stand there and stuff himself full of sweet biscuits covered in delicious jam while she wasted away to nothing—her mind shied away from the fact that no matter how tight provisions were, she seemed to be gaining flesh rather than losing it—without so much as offering her one little bite goaded her anger in ways that she hadn't anticipated.

"And just where do you expect me to go?" she asked—rash, yes, but she was driven by worry and hunger well past the point of reason. "You're taking my only home away from me while refusing to find me another. Do you expect me to live on the streets like a leper?"

"There are no lepers in Copenhagen," he said dismissively, popping another biscuit in his mouth. Dagmar almost drooled, she was so famished. "And of course I'm not turning you out into the street. You have other relatives. I'm simply insisting that you go blight them with your presence."

"The Sonderburg-Becks won't have me."

"Smart of them," he said, nodding, and eyed the plate of small tarts that a servant held up for his perusal. "What about the English? Your mother was English, wasn't she?"

"Yes, she was, but her only living relative is a church-man of modest means and extremely large family—"

"Good, good, you'll make yourself useful to him, no doubt."

Dagmar fisted her fingers, mostly to keep from snatching one of the tarts, but there was also the need to not throttle the crown prince. "Even if I wanted to go to Cousin Josiah, I couldn't."

"Why not?" Frederick selected a small lemon tart. Dagmar thought she might faint when its pale yellow goodness slipped into the cavernous maw that was Frederick's mouth. He even smacked his lips, the bastard.

"One, I have no money to pay for our passage—"

"Your cousin can send you whatever you need."

"He has no money either. Haven't you listened to me? And two, there are no ships left to take me to England. In case you missed that battle that took place a few days ago"—Dagmar was aware by the shocked silence that settled upon the kitchen that she was speaking very unwisely indeed, but she seemed unable to stop—"in case you missed it, all the ships were destroyed."

Frederick straightened up and looked down his nose at her. "You forget to whom you speak."

"I don't forget," she told him, her gaze holding his. "I simply have nothing to lose. If you imprisoned me, at least I'd have a shelter and occasional meals. Ones hopefully including lemon tarts."

"Don't think I haven't considered it," he said with narrowed eyes before suddenly snapping his fingers. "The solution is quite clear. I don't know why you haven't thought of it yourself. You're half English, and the English are filling the harbor. Go speak to them about your passage to your mother's country."

She stared at him, wondering why God would place such a being in a position of power. If he ate one more lemon tart, she wouldn't be responsible for her actions. "That is wholly impossible."

"Why?" He waved away the treats plate and absently picked up a small bunch of grapes.

Dagmar *loved* grapes.

"Because..." She stopped considering bashing her cousin over his fat head with the nearest tray of pastries and tried to summon up a good reason. "Because I'm not wholly English. They won't want to go to all the trouble of sending home someone who's only half English."

"If you know what's good for you," the crown prince said, dusting off his front and swallowing the last of the grapes, "you'll see to it that they do just that. Because your options otherwise are quite limited."

"Oh really?" Dagmar crossed her arms and allowed a mulish expression to play across her face. "Or what? You'll throw me out onto the streets? You're my nearest living male relative, Frederick. Thus, you are responsible for my well-being, which includes providing shelter for me. Not to mention the fact that if you shirk that responsibility by casting me aside, you will prove to the citizens of Denmark that you are a heartless tyrant who preys on innocent cousins."

The servants gasped en masse.

Frederick looked as if she'd kicked him in an extremely sensitive location, an expression that quickly changed to one of calculating fury. "Oh, I wouldn't let you starve on the street."

Dagmar smiled, feeling a sudden sense of smugness. She had a feeling that he wouldn't like the idea of all the notoriety that would come of such a callous action.

"Although there are times when I feel you deserve it, especially after last month when you attempted to murder my wig in front of the French ambassador."

"I thought it was a rabid poodle!" she protested, trying very hard to keep from smiling at the memory.

"You ripped it from my head and used my ceremonial sword to gut it!"

Dagmar strove for a dignified mien. "I was attempting to save your life."

"You weren't. You were trying to shame me in front of important visitors, and it was the last straw, do you hear me? The last straw! If you refuse to take yourself off to your family as I have repeatedly requested you do, then I shall have no recourse but to send you to a convent. There you will learn humility and the wisdom of treating your superiors with the respect due to them."

"A convent?" Dagmar shook her head. "But... we're not Catholic."

He waved a hand. "That matters not. I will find a convent, and you will go to it. If not here, then somewhere else. I have connections. Perhaps life in a French convent would teach you some meekness."

Dagmar didn't like the sound of that at all. She was not, by nature, a meek or humble person, and she had no intentions of changing her ways now. "You can't do that!"

"I can." Frederick considered his fingernails, then delicately brushed them against the soft velvet of his waistcoat. "You yourself said that I am responsible for you, thus I have the right to dispose of you as I desire. You may hie yourself to a convent or go plague another family member. The choice is yours."

"But, Frederick—"

"No!" The word was snapped with the velocity of a musket ball. It served to startle Dagmar enough that she stopped her protest. "Hear me, Dagmar: I am at the end of my patience with regards to you. You will leave in the next few days of your own volition, or you will leave by mine, and that is the end of the matter. I care not where you go—either your Sonderburg-Beck relations or your mother's family or to a convent in France—but go you will. Upon that, I will brook no further debate."

Without so much as a good-bye, he turned on his heel and strolled out of the kitchen. Dagmar fumed for a few seconds, wanting to hurl at his head all the naughty words that she'd learned from the stable boys, but she knew that doing so would have no benefit.

"Fabulous. Just fabulous," she snarled, her scowl of such a quality that the kitchen maids scurried out of her way. "A convent! Of all the ridiculous ideas."

She stomped over to the table where the boiled pig's head sat, picked it up by an ear, and glared at the cook when he opened his mouth to protest. "Meekness! Me! He doesn't have a single thought for others."

She kicked a small, three-legged stool out of her way.

"And he blatantly goes against the Bible's strictures on cousinly treatment. I just hope he enjoys his days in hell for this!"

One of the scullery maids burst into tears and ran out of the kitchen.

Dagmar struck a dramatic pose for three seconds. "Well, I'm not going to a convent! I'd sooner starve to death on the streets than become a submissive, pious creature. I just hope that when Julia and I fall over in the square outside of the palace and die of starvation and lack of home, the people of Copenhagen know Frederick for what he is!" On her way out, she snagged a basket of freshly gathered eggs, a wheel of cheese the size of her head, and a small brown puppy that had been tied with a bit of twine to a table leg. She didn't know to whom the puppy belonged, but she didn't approve of animals being tied up, and in her present belligerent mood, she didn't particularly care that it wasn't hers to take.

As she left the palace, she began to have second thoughts about the puppy. Not only did he squirm in such a way as to make him difficult to hold, but he also seemed to have a fondness for the boiled pig's head. It was a bit of a struggle, but at last she managed to pry him off the head, although he did claim one of the pig's ears. She paused when she reached the guards at the door. "Jens."

The guard in question bowed low. "Yes, Your Serene Highness?"

"Do your boys have a dog?"

He looked startled for a moment, his gaze dropping to the puppy where it chomped happily on the disattached ear. "Er…no, Your Highness."

"Would they like one?"

Jens hesitated, then gave a weak smile. "As a matter of fact, the wife and I have spoken on the subject. We thought we'd wait a few years until the littlest was a bit older…"

Dagmar considered him. "Will you treat him right?"

"My youngest?" Jens looked surprised. "Aye, the lad's a bit lively, but—"

"No, the puppy. If I gave you this puppy for your sons, would you treat him right?"

Jens blinked.

"Would you love him and cherish him and not strike him just because he has a propensity toward boiled pigs' heads?"

His gaze shifted to the head clutched in Dagmar's left arm. He pursed his lips.

"Would you let him sleep on your boys' beds, and take him for walks even when it was snowing, and give him things to chew on because you understand that dogs need to chew sometimes?"

Jens glanced over to the other guard, who shrugged. "Aye?" he said hesitantly, more of a question than a statement.

Dagmar nodded to herself and shoved the puppy/ear bundle into his arms. "Good. I can go to my death by starvation and lack of home with an easy heart. I have named him Beelzebub. You may call him Bub if you like. Good day."

Two

Under no circumstances should a princess lower herself to the sin of telling falsehoods. Likewise indulging in blasphemy, stealing, and thinking impure thoughts about the new head groom who may or may not spend an inordinate amount of time sans shirt while grooming the horses.

—*Princess Christian of Sonderburg-Beck's Guide for Her Daughter's Illumination and Betterment*

THE WALK TO THE HARBOR WASN'T A LONG ONE, NO matter how slowly her steps dragged. Truly, she didn't want to talk to some strange British captain. She didn't want to be sent to her cousin's over-crowded vicarage where she'd be a glorified—and unpaid—slave, but the steely look in her cousin's eyes warned that her choice was that or life in a French convent.

She shivered. "All I want is a quiet little cottage somewhere, where Julia and I can live out our days in quiet companionship."

The fisherman she was passing looked up from mending his net.

"That," she told him, "or lots of money. Great, huge wads of money, and a grand house and a hand-some man to dote on me. Of the two, the latter seems more attractive, don't you think?"

"Aye," he agreed amiably and continued his mending.

"Alas, neither is likely to be found here." She continued on, stopping some yards away in the middle of the dock and gazing out at the ships anchored in the harbor. She'd garnered some pretty curious looks as she marched through the busy crowds of sailors, merchants, and salvage men who were attempting to reclaim bits and pieces from the two Danish ships that had been sunk.

Dagmar could still smell the smoky tang of the ships that the British had captured (and subsequently burned since they could not spare the men to sail them back to England). Rumor had it that they had kept one ship, though, and it was upon that ship her hopes were pinned.

The harbor buzzed with life, shouts, and cries of both Danes and Englishmen alike filling the air. Small rowboats zipped back and forth between the dock and English ships, ferrying several important-looking men past her into waiting carriages. No doubt they were off to visit Frederick. "I'd wager he serves them those lemon tarts," she said under her breath and hefted her wheel of cheese a bit higher before approaching a man in a blue uniform who appeared to be directing others. "Excuse me," she said in English, "can you tell me who is in charge?"

"In charge?" The man eyed her curiously.

"Yes, I wish to go to England. I would like to engage passage for myself and a companion. Can you tell me to whom I should apply?"

At the sound of her clipped British accent, the man straightened up. She silently blessed her mother for teaching her English and for her own natural ability to mimic. She had to admit that even to her own ears she sounded every inch the British aristocrat.

"Yes, ma'am. The man in charge is Sir Hyde Parker, but he's off to Karlskrona. Admiral Nelson is his next in command, but he's unavailable. Would you be an English lady, then?"

As a rule, Dagmar hated to lie. She'd found through past experience that any lie she told usually ended badly. Therefore, she'd do her best to tell the truth—or a respectable version of it.

With a lift of her chin and a hoist of the boiled pig's head, she replied, "Of course I am an English lady. I am English through and through. No more, no less." Well...that wasn't strictly the truth, although being half English was better than nothing.

"It's just that I haven't seen any English ladies here other than the wife of the ambassador."

"Ah. As for that, I have been stranded in Copenhagen by the death of my father. Naturally, I now wish to go to England." All that was certainly true enough. She would enjoy visiting England if her cousin Josiah hadn't a hundred children packed into what was sure to be a squalid little rectory. "In fact, the crown prince suggested that I speak to one of Lord Parker's men about this."

"Sir Hyde, ma'am."

She blinked at him.

"It's Sir Hyde Parker, not Lord Parker."

"Ah." She waved the cheese at him. "My mistake. I have been away from England for some time, you understand. If Sir Hyde is unavailable, where will I find this Admiral Nelson?"

The man sucked his teeth for a moment while rocking back on his heels, clearly deep in thought, although Dagmar didn't like the glint of doubt in his eyes. "The admiral is likely busy on matters of state, ma'am. Er…might I have your name?"

She opened her mouth to tell him, remembered she was supposed to be English through and through, and settled on using her mother's maiden name. "It's Wentworth. Dag…er…Marie Wentworth. I'm named for my mother, who was the only child of the Duke of Leesbury."

The sailor looked impressed at her late grandfather's title. She didn't have the heart to mention that the dukedom was now extinct and her mother's only living relative was the destitute Josiah. "As for transportation Miss…er…Lady Marie, you might speak with Colonel Stewart."

"And where might I find him?"

"*The Elephant*, normally. That's the Admiral's flagship. But I happen to know that the colonel came into town to oversee the parole of the prisoners. You'll find them at Holmen."

Dagmar's shoulder's slumped. Holmen was a group of small islands that formed the Royal Naval Base. She'd have to hire someone to take her out there, but with no money and nothing she could barter for a ride out, she stood little chance of achieving that goal.

"However, I did hear tell that they were coming into the town proper this afternoon."

"Indeed? That is excellent news." She glanced around the dock, and deciding that there was no sense in dragging herself and her filched goods to the Yellow House only to have to turn around immediately and trek back to the dock, she planted herself and her bounty on the nearest crate. "I shall await his arrival here."

The man looked scandalized. "But, ma'am...my lady...this is no place for the granddaughter of a duke."

She gave a delicate shrug and turned her attention to the busy comings and goings of the English, who, she recalled hearing, had been given the freedom to come and go in Copenhagen as part of the armistice treaty. "I have no pressing engagements today. It suits me to sit here and watch the activity."

What she didn't say was that she'd be keeping an eagle eye out for an opportunity to speak with the admiral or to anyone else who had the potential to help her.

To that end, she spent an hour formulating and discarding any number of plans of what she would do once the British navy transported her and Julia to England.

"I will most definitely not go to Cousin Josiah. His circumstances sound entirely too mean and uncomfortable," she said aloud, watching absently as two small lads in dirty uniforms stopped to gawk at her. She frowned at them until they scampered off upon their business, her gaze moving beyond their slight figures to the rows of storefronts that lined the harbor. "Hmm. Perhaps Julia and I should open up a shop of some type. The trouble is that it takes capital to open a shop. Hmm."

She wrestled with various ways of finding that capital during the second hour that it took the colonel to arrive. By the time his small dinghy docked and the friendly sailor informed her of his arrival, her bottom was going numb, the pig's head was attracting more flies than she thought reasonable, and her cheese was beginning to give off a pungent odor that made her growling stomach want to roar with hunger. She swatted the flies, promised her stomach dinner just as soon as she got it home, and stood up to allow the blood back into her numb backside.

"Colonel Stewart?"

A group of four men approached. One of them paused, giving her a curious look. "Yes?"

Dagmar phrased her statement carefully. "I am a young, innocent maiden stranded here in Copenhagen without family or resource. My father died last year, and although I have appealed to the crown prince for help, he has told me to contact you about seeking transportation to England. My mother, you see, was the only child of the Duke of Leesbury, both of whom I regret to say are also no longer with us. I would like to find a place for myself and my companion on whatever ship is leaving the soonest, so if you could direct me to that ship, I will see to it that our things are brought to it immediately."

She was quite proud of that speech because it didn't include any outright lies.

Unfortunately, Colonel Stewart wasn't as appreciative as she hoped. "I regret to inform you, madam, that although you have my sympathies on the deaths of your parents and grandfather, the crown prince is mistaken in directing you to us for help. The navy has a strict policy regarding the transportation of individuals who are neither a member of its ranks nor a spouse thereof, and you fall outside that policy."

She gawked at him for a moment or two. "What do you mean I fall outside of the policy? I don't care about the policy. Did you not hear the part about me being young and innocent and stranded?"

"I heard it." The man, blast his hide, looked faintly amused.

"Do you not understand that I have no means, no means whatsoever, to get to England, especially as you've destroyed so many of our ships?"

The colonel's brows drew together. "Madam—"

"Does my plight, my desperate and potentially life-threatening plight, not tug on your heartstrings? Can you be so cruel as to refuse to save me just because of some silly rules?"

A hunted look crept across his face. "I assure you, madam, that if it was within my power to help you, I would, but unless you are the daughter or wife of one of our officers, I am unable to do so."

"You would leave me here, helpless and destitute," she almost shouted, gesturing with the cheese, "to a fate worse than death? Yes, I'm talking about *that*, sir! That most heinous of fates!"

He looked startled.

"If that which is most sacred to a young and

innocent maiden such as I is torn from her"—Dagmar leaned forward, pressing home her point—"then the blame shall fall on you and no one but you. Your soul will be condemned for all eternity, besmirched by nothing less than my descent into outright harlotry!"

"Madam!"

She didn't think that officers were supposed to be so easily shocked, but the expression on his face said otherwise.

"I assure you that I do not wish for any such fate to befall you, but unfortunately, the decision is not up to me. If you were the wife of one of our officers, then I could assist you, but in the circumstances of a stranded citizen, my hands are tied. I can refer you to the British ambassador, who I know will be most anxious to give you the aid that you seek."

Dagmar shied away from that suggestion. She'd thought of it herself two months ago, but upon consultation of that individual, had been informed that her mother's birthplace notwithstanding, she was not a British citizen, and thus they had no obligation to assist her.

"You are a cruel, cruel man," she said, gathering up her pig's head and the eggs and sundry other things she'd managed to acquire during the two hours she'd been waiting. "I just hope you will be able to sleep at night knowing the fate to which you have damned me. Good day, sir."

She marched away, fuming with frustration. Now what was she going to do? She was shivering by the time she returned home, her fingers numb with both cold and the strain of holding all her acquisitions.

"Dearest Princess!" Julia gasped when Dagmar stumbled into the two rooms that were all that remained in Yellow House even remotely approaching a habitable state. "You've been gone so long, I was most worried. I have something very important to tell…is that a pig's head?"

"It is. And there are other things, but you'll have to take them from me because my hands are a bit cramped from carrying them home."

"And no wonder! Merciful heavens, let me help you off with your things, and then I'll make us both a nice cup of tea. But first, you must be wanting an update about the drunkard…oooh, cheese too? And is that a chicken?"

"Oh, do I still have that?" Dagmar allowed Julia to remove all the things she had covertly managed to stuff into her pelisse while waiting on the dock, along with her haul from the palace. "One of the fisherman left the chicken unattended while he fetched several of his newly mended nets that I happened to stumble over and knock into the harbor, and I didn't want anyone to steal the poor man's chicken, so I took it to keep it safe. I should walk all the way back into town to return it, although the chicken has evidently been deceased for some time, and it might not last. What do you think?"

"I think it would be a shame for you to go to all that trouble over a chicken. Surely the fisherman will understand. Now, please, do let me tell you about the man in the garden."

Dagmar rubbed her stiff, cold fingers. "Did he suddenly appear at the door offering food or a new home?"

"No, but I really think you will want to know—"

She lifted a hand, and obediently, Julia stopped talking.

"Later. Right now I'm so tired I could fall over and go to sleep for a week."

"Of course. You're exhausted, and here I am trying to chat your ear off. But it really is most extraordinary—"

"Put the kettle on, would you? I need something hot to bring back life to my depressed soul. I think one of those packages has tea in it. At least I hope so. One of the sailors dropped it when I bumped into him coming out of the tea shop, and he didn't seem to hear me when later I called to him that the packet had fallen from his grasp."

Julia cooed and squealed with pleasure as she opened a small brown package, allowing Dagmar to sink into a moth-eaten chair next to the stove.

"So many good things," Julia murmured, touching the cheese reverently. "What will we do with them? Soup for the pig's head, do you think?"

"I don't know. I'm too exhausted to contemplate doing anything with food that doesn't involve stuffing it into my mouth. I just knew we had to have something or we'd starve. And speaking of that, if you look in my bonnet, there's a half loaf of bread. I think we're due some bread and cheese. Do we have any berries or early apples?"

"No, but once you have eaten, I really must tell you something of much importance." Julia bustled around the small, cold room, fetching a cutting board and their sole knife.

"At this moment, there is nothing more important than that cheese."

Dagmar watched Julia hack away ineffectually at the cheese until she could stand it no longer and took charge of making a meal from the bread and cheese.

"I'm sorry I'm such a failure," Julia said a few minutes later, handing Dagmar a cup of weak tea. "Here you brought home a veritable feast, and all I have to show for my day is a hole in my boots and an Englishman."

"We'll have to get you a new pair," Dagmar said when she had consumed enough bread and cheese to subdue the ever-growling beast in her stomach. She paused, looking up. "An Englishman? What Englishman?"

"The man in the garden. He's English. Or at least I believe him to be. He's not exactly speaking coherently."

"He woke up, did he? Is he still in the garden?" Dagmar ate the last of her bread and eyed another piece, knowing she should save it but mightily tempted nonetheless.

"Yes, but dearest Princess, I begin to suspect that he's not the drunkard that we first believed him to be. There is blood seeping through his coat, and he appears to be delirious. I think the two of us together should be able to carry him."

"Why on earth would we want to carry some strange, wounded man?" Dagmar set down her cup and delicately sniffed the air. There was a faint, familiar aroma. "You didn't happen to visit the small shed near the man, did you?"

"No, Princess, I assure you that I was most attentive to your wishes that I watch the man. It's true that I discovered a bottle of brandy...er...it must have been the Englishman's, since I found it near him...but I took only the tiniest of sips from it, just a medicinal amount to warm my blood. You know how my blood suffers in this climate."

Dagmar continued chewing, having no doubt at all that Julia found the bottle where she had last left it in the shed. "Yes, I know how you suffer. What did the man say to you?"

"Nothing that I understood. It was more feverish rambling than anything else. Thus, as soon as you have contented yourself with this delicious meal, I will assist you in bringing him inside the house."

"I don't need an injured man in the house. What I need is passage for us to England, and then some capital with which we can open a shop."

"What sort of shop?" Julia asked, clearly sidetracked.

"I'm not sure. Obviously it should be a shop for something we know a good deal about. What sorts of things do you know about?"

Julia's face wore its usual slightly vacant, vaguely worried expression. "My father always said I was quite capable at darning socks."

"Socks. Hmm." Dagmar allowed herself to relax against the chair, wondering if there was good money to be had in sock darning.

Julia cast an anxious glance toward the dirty window. "Dearest Dagmar, don't you think we should commence to rescuing the wounded Englishman? The sun will be setting soon, and I'm sure he'd be more comfortable inside than out."

"Allow me to state right here and now that I have absolutely no intention of fetching any man to the house, wounded or not," Dagmar said, closing her eyes and allowing the exhaustion to sweep over her. Hopefully, Julia would sleep off her intoxication. "Not unless he comes bearing large quantities of money or passage on a ship. Preferably both."

"But, Princess—"

Clearly, she was going to have to adopt a practical line of objection. "No, Julia. We are not bringing home a stray, wounded man. We haven't enough food to feed ourselves, let alone shelter two days from now, and although it might be entertaining to see Frederick's face when he has to ship a man along with us to a French convent, that amusement palls when accounted with the trouble we'd have to acquire said man. No more mention of wounded people of either sex, please. I'm sure if we leave him alone, he'll go away on his own."

"But—"

Dagmar opened her eyes and gave her companion a very firm look. She didn't like to have to do such things, but Julia was like a terrier once she got her teeth into a subject, and if one didn't take control, she'd run amok. "I shall tell you about my conversation with the British colonel, and after that you will not be able to think of such petty things as wounded men in our back garden."

Julia's eyes widened as Dagmar did exactly that, filling her in as well with Frederick's threat of a convent.

"But we're not Catholic," Julia protested.

"You see? That is exactly what I said to him, and he just threatened to send us to France where they have convents."

"I don't want to go to France!"

"Nor do I, but unless we can change that stupid colonel's mind, I'm afraid we're doomed." Dagmar absently tickled her mouth with the fringe of her shawl while her brain, charged up by the consumption of foodstuffs, whirled around busily.

"It's too bad that you don't know one of the officers," Julia said forlornly. She wrapped her shawl tighter around her arms. "You could marry him, and then the colonel would have to send us to England."

"Mmm. I don't know any English officers. And I highly doubt if I were to meet one that he'd offer to marry me in the next two days."

Silence fell over the house. Dagmar continued to worry away at the problem, thinking all sorts of thoughts of daring escapes from Frederick's men en route to the French convent, but sadly resigning them all to the rubbish bin when she realized that she was responsible for Julia, the least daring person she knew.

"I wonder if he could be an officer."

Dagmar dragged herself from a dark reverie. "Hmm? He who?"

"The person you told me not to mention again." Julia was barely visible in the gathering twilight, but Dagmar could see the silhouette of her arm as she gestured toward the door, adding in a whisper, "The wounded man."

"Oh, him. I'm sure he's just some merchant."

"He didn't look like a merchant. He had documents written in English in his boot."

Dagmar sat up and stared into the deepening shadows. It was one thing for Julia to have a few nips of brandy and become overly concerned about a drunkard in the garden, but another for her to create such an odd detail. "How do you know what he had in his boot?"

"One of them was partially off, and I saw a bit of paper, and naturally, I thought it might give some insight into who he was, so I peeked at it. It appeared to be something about the Czar in Russia, but it was most definitely written in English. And no merchant would have that, would he?"

Dagmar sat silent for a minute, considering this. "The English navy attacked four days ago…I suppose it's possible that he might be one of them. But he wasn't wearing a uniform."

"No, but his clothes were very nice. Dirty and torn and bloody, but you could tell they were of a good quality."

Dagmar gave in to the inevitable. She hadn't at first believed the man could truly be wounded, since she hadn't seen any signs of injuries, but Julia's tale was beginning to cast an ominous light on things. She couldn't leave a wounded man to lurk about her garden. Directly on the heels of that thought came another, one that had so much potential, she allowed it to dance in her brain, illuminating all sorts of very interesting possibilities. "His driving coat did seem to be made of nice cloth. And you say the rest of his clothing was similar?"

"Very nice quality, yes. As nice as the crown prince's garments, I would say."

"He might be someone visiting the ambassador. Or one of the ambassador's staff, itself. How very interesting." Dagmar sat indecisive for a moment, then got to her weary feet. There was no avoiding the fact that she needed to go see if this man was as injured as Julia said. Her sainted mother had brought her up to take care of those less fortunate, and she knew full well that Mama would haunt her to the end of her days if she shirked that responsibility. There was no reason she shouldn't benefit from such generosity, however. "It's entirely possible that he's English and of some worth, and if that's so, then he must have family somewhere who would pay good money to have him back."

"Princess!" Julia gasped as Dagmar scrabbled around under the stove until she found a length of tattered rope. "What are you saying?"

"Were you never taught history as a girl? Dearest Papa used to tell wonderful tales about knights of yore and how they were always capturing each other and then ransoming their captors back to their families for massive mounds of gold and jewels."

Julia weaved a little. "You don't mean…you can't really intend to hold that poor man hostage, can you?"

"Of course I can. It's the most logical thing ever." Dagmar ticked the items off on her fingers. "It will allow us to get the money we will need once we get to England. It will allow us to save that man without draining our meager resources to the point where we might as well march down to the dock this very evening and begin harlotting, and it may very well force that annoying ambassador into sending us to England."

Julia gawked at her. "But…what you suggest is illegal, surely."

"There is a time and place for nice morals, Julia, neither of which is here and now." Dagmar, invigorated by the mouthwatering thought of a veritable mountain of gold, flung open the kitchen door. "Now let's go fetch our captive."

"No."

Dagmar was halfway down the path through the kitchen garden before the softly spoken word attracted her notice. She marched back to where her companion stood in the doorway. "What do you mean, no?"

"No, I will not help you commit a sin so great as holding a poor, injured man prisoner and selling him to his family."

Dagmar slapped her hands on her legs in a most unprincessly manner. "But Dearest Papa's knights of yore did it!"

"What was right for a knight then isn't right for a princess now," Julia said primly, her hands folded as tight as her lips.

"We aren't going to hurt him. If anything, we'll be saving him, since his family won't want to pay for a corpse."

"It's wrong, and you well know it." Julia's stubborn expression, barely visible in the gloaming, softened as she laid a hand on Dagmar's arm. "My dear, you know yourself that it is wrong. You are simply grasping at the idea of salvation because the crown prince put you into a temper."

"What I am grasping at is the only avenue we have open to us." Dagmar took a deep, calming breath, and tried to reason with her friend. "It's this or harlotry, Julia. I cannot go to the French convent. I'm not at all the sort of person who would thrive in such a strict environment, and if you had any love for me, any love at all, you would help me ransom that hurt man!"

"There are always other options. You said yourself that if you were married to an officer—"

"But I don't know any officers!" Dagmar rubbed her forehead. They were arguing around and around in a circle, and it was starting to give her a headache. "I've explained to you already that I don't know any Englishmen, let alone officers."

"You could know the wounded Englishman. Perhaps he would marry you out of gratitude for saving him."

"Oh, come now. That's not very likely."

"But it's a possibility, and you said we had no other possibilities."

Dagmar made a face and snatched up a lantern near the door, quickly lighting it. "*If* he wasn't already married, and *if* he survives whatever wounds he has, and *if* he is, in fact, English, not to mention an officer in their navy, then yes, that might be a possibility, but those are an awful lot of ifs, and I don't intend to hang my future on anything so nebulous."

Julia slid her arm through Dagmar's and beamed at her. "If he is English and unmarried, then you would agree to marry him?"

"If it got us to England?" Dagmar thought for a moment. She'd been betrothed from a very early age to a distant cousin who had died some four years before, and hadn't particularly felt the need to encourage her father to find her a replacement. Marriage tended to restrict one's activities, since husbands frequently felt they had the right to tell one how to live, but if Julia's man was indeed English and unmarried, she could do worse than consider him as a suitor.

The mental image of a dark, cold French nun's cell came to mind. She shivered and hurried forward. "Possibly. Come along, turtle! Let's go see if this man of yours is still alive before we start planning a wedding."

Three

A princess does not approach a strange man and ask if she can have what's in his breeches. A princess remembers that not only is it not nice to ask others for things, but also that not every man plays a game wherein he hides sweets in his clothing so his daughter can find them.

—Princess Christian of Sonderburg-Beck's Guide for Her Daughter's Illumination and Betterment

LEO HAD DIED AND GONE TO HELL. HE ACCEPTED THE fact that the men who had set upon him had been right to leave him for dead—obviously, he died from the wounds inflicted by them. He had a vague memory of dragging himself through the woods to the faint glimmer of light flashing off windows, but clearly that was a delusion, a fevered imagining of a brain that had ceased its primary function.

Dammit, there was a root poking up into his spleen. He shifted irritably. It was just his luck to end up in the hell where roots ensured that the dead did not rest easily.

Then there were the harpies. Shrill female voices argued and squabbled over his head, no doubt trying to decide who would get to rend his flesh and commence the torment of his soul.

Blast it all, the harpies had started at his feet. Cold air swept over his toes as his boots were removed. The voices of the harpies shifted and changed to less cacophonous sounds, although they still argued. That irritated him. He was dead, after all, in hell, with a blasted root the size of a small heifer attempting to bore its way through his tender organs, and yet the harpies continued to squabble and fuss at him.

He opened an eye to glare at them. "Can you give a man no rest? Must you strip me of my boots now? I haven't been dead that long, you know. Isn't there some sort of a period of respite before the torment commences?"

One of the harpies was holding a lantern up to a piece of paper. She looked over at him, and he felt a sense of surprise that she wasn't old and hag-like and the bearer of plentiful warts upon her grisly visage, as any proper harpy ought to be. In fact, her visage wasn't grisly in the least. She had an oval face that reminded him of a Botticelli. If she hadn't been a harpy, he would have thought her pretty.

Whoever heard of a pretty harpy? Death must be playing with his ability to reason.

"You are deficient in warts," he told her, closing his eye and waving a hand toward her. "I will have nothing to do with you."

"Warts!"

"Oh, thank the Lord, he is still alive."

"Julia, did you hear that? He told me I had warts!"

"No, dear, I think he said you were deficient in warts, although that was indeed a very odd comment to make. Sir, what is your name?" a soft voice said near his ear. He brushed at his ear, squirming a little to try to find comfort on that damned root. "Are you, as I suspect, English?"

"Of course he's English, Julia," the other harpy snapped, and to his further annoyance, began to tug at his sleeve. Odd that he couldn't feel his arm. He could feel his toes. He wiggled them. They were cold now that the harpies had stripped them bare to his stockings, and he wanted to inform them of that fact, but he figured they would just laugh and tell him that was what happened to men who died and went to hell. Still, he worried a bit at the lack of feeling in his left arm. "He sounds very English. What I want to know is if he's an officer."

"Madam, I was a major in His Majesty's army before I died and arrived at this place," he said stiffly, trying to convey to the harpy through the coldness in his voice just how irritated he was, but she, like all the other heartless beings of hell, paid no mind to his wants or desires and continued to rip the clothing from his poor, naked body.

"Army? Well, hell!"

"Princess!"

"I think I'm allowed to swear in this circumstance, Julia. An army major is no earthly good to me, especially one that thinks I have warts and is under the delusion that he's dead. What I want is a navy major."

"I don't believe they have majors in the navy, dearest. I think they're called something else."

Leo frowned to himself, and before he could think better of it, protested aloud, "There is nothing wrong with the army."

"I didn't say there was, you annoying—oh, no. Julia, you didn't tell me he was bleeding this much."

Cold seemed to leech into his body from the ground, starting at his left arm and slowly radiating outward. He shivered.

"I didn't know since I did not remove his coat. We should move him as quickly as may be. Can you not see that he is feverish? To lie out here in the damp and cold is to court disaster."

He wished he had the strength to open his eyes and look again at the harpies, but at that moment, he felt as drained as a newborn colt.

Still the harpy on the left of him, the wartless one, tugged at him, peeling off his heavy coat and making him aware of the cold and discomfort. He didn't like her one bit, and turned his head to tell her so. "This certainly wasn't evident before. Look: it appears he's taken a saber blade to the arm and I suspect chest, if the blood is any guide. No doubt the attacker thought he had killed him outright. Julia, hand me the blanket. No, the old one. We'll bind his arm and chest tightly before we move him. That might stop some of the bleeding."

"What a most excellent idea. I knew that you would know how to deal with him once you saw him."

"Don't be heaping praise on my head yet. He's lost a lot of blood, and the fever is upon him. He may well die before I can speak with Colonel Stewart again. Ready? Lift on three."

Leo was confused about whom they spoke, but was distracted by the sudden sensation of floating. The root that had been ground into his back drifted away as he lurched along some sort of wind, one that swore and grunted quite a bit, not to mention threatened to drop its burden and let the vultures have at it.

It must be some other soul the harpies had focused on now that he had drifted off out of their reaches. "Don't let them take your boots," he warned. "Your toes will never be warm again."

Odd, that, when you thought about it. He'd always been taught that hell was filled with hellfire and brimstone, not cold and numbness.

The harpies were back, once again arguing. He dragged his attention from where it had wandered, and tried to focus on what they were saying.

"It is utterly out of the question. You are unmarried, and this gentleman is not your relative. What would your mother say to the idea of him occupying your bed?"

"My mother would commend me for trying to save the life of one of her countrymen. Now stop arguing, and let's get him settled so you can fetch the doctor."

"But your sheets! We just washed them two days ago!"

"And we can wash them again. Julia, my hands are getting tired, and if that happens, I'll drop the poor man. Will you please stop arguing over silly points of etiquette and put him down?"

Pain spiked through him suddenly, a dull, cold pain that seemed to nag at him, dragging him downward into a black pit.

The hellfire came at last, burning at him, ripping

away his sinews and flesh with metallic claws. He heard a man screaming, followed by the low rumble of a male voice speaking in Danish that gave way to another, this one female, that seemed to bore into his brain, urging him to be calm so that the doctor could do his work.

"It's too late for a doctor," he argued, moving restlessly, lying in the pit that alternated cold and fire. "I've died and gone to hell."

"I've done what I can, but I'm afraid it's too late. He won't last the night through."

"But…he was talking! And moving his limbs. Are you sure there is nothing we can do for him? Perhaps a draught or some other physic? My sainted mother used to say that if the fever was attended to—"

"I have been physician to His Royal Highness for more years than your mother was alive. I know the look of death when I see it, and I say this man will not last until morning. If, by some miracle of God, he does survive the night, then I will bleed him."

"Over my dead body you will," he heard the first harpy say in a firm voice. "My mother always said that bleeding made people weaker, not stronger."

He wanted to agree with her, but it was too much effort to speak, so he simply nodded his head.

"Your mother was *not* a physician," the man answered. Footsteps and the sound of a door slamming told of his leaving.

Good, thought Leo. He sounded singularly unhelpful.

"Oh, Princess, what will we do now?" one of the harpies asked, wringing her hands as she stood at the foot of his bed.

"Go fetch me what remains of my mother's herbs. I'm going to make him a fever draught."

"But you heard what the doctor said! He won't last the night."

"Perhaps not, but it won't be for the lack of me trying. Go, Julia, and get some water boiling."

The older harpy moved slowly toward the door, casting a worried look back at him. "If he's not going to live long...Princess, you must marry him."

The pretty harpy turned to her, astonishment clearly writ on her face. "Have you taken leave of your senses?"

"Quite the contrary. If you marry him now, and he..." She made a vague gesture. "Then you will be his widow, and the colonel will have to send you to England."

"I'm not so desperate to find a husband that I need to marry a man on his deathbed."

"Aren't you?"

The wartless harpy looked as obstinate as a mule. For some reason, that amused Leo. He wondered vaguely who the poor man was who they wanted to marry.

"All right, I might be that desperate, but really, Julia. He's desperately ill."

"All the more reason to do it now."

"But...it seems so wrong to just marry him while he's not cognizant."

"It won't matter at all to him if he goes to meet his maker wed, while it will mean everything to you and me."

He closed his eyes, waiting to hear the fate of the

poor, unmarried man. At last the first harpy said, "I suppose it wouldn't matter much. Go attend to the water and herbs while I fetch the last of the damson wine."

Leo drifted for a little bit, coming back to awareness at a slight noise.

"Is it ready?" one of the harpies was asking.

"I hope so. His fever is increasing, so we have to get something in him. I just hope this draught helps."

"I don't want to take a draught," Leo said pettishly, trying with every ounce of strength to open his eyes. He managed to get one cracked to see the pretty harpy sniffing at a bottle of dark red liquid. "You can't cure death, madam."

The harpy set the bottle down on a table, giving him a curious look.

"What have you done with my root?" he asked suspiciously. "How dare you take it away from me. It was you who spirited me here, wasn't it? Don't deny it, I can see by the look on your wartless face that it was. First you strip the flesh from my bones, then you take away the spleen root, and now you threaten to dose me with some foul concoction. I won't have it. Return me to the proper hell, the one that wasn't soft and warm and comfortable."

He panted with the effort to speak, so exhausted he couldn't hold open his eye any longer. He wanted to gesture to the harpy, but his arm appeared to be turned to lead, and he didn't have the strength to lift it.

"What a very odd man you are. What's your name?"

"I do not converse with harpies. It's Leo."

"Leo what?"

"Leopold."

"No, I mean what is your surname? I can't call you Leo."

"Why not? Is there some sort of harpy rule that says you are unable to use a Christian name?"

"Will you stop calling me a harpy? I'm a princess, dammit! A gentle, innocent princess, and I swear to heaven above if you don't stop being so annoying, I'm going to clunk you on the head with the chamber pot."

He snorted, wishing he had the wherewithal to open his eyes again, but accepting that now that he was in hell, he wouldn't be granted any wishes. "I'd like to see you try."

The harpy made an irritated noise and asked (in a way that sounded like she was forcing the words through her teeth), "What is your surname?"

"Mortimer. Do harpies have names?"

"I haven't the slightest idea. Are you married?"

"Not at the moment. What is your name, harpy?"

"Stop calling me that! I just told you I was a princess. I am Dagmar Marie Sophie, the daughter of Prince Christian of Sonderburg-Beck, the granddaughter of the Duke of Leesbury, and you, sirrah, may refer to me as 'Her Serene Highness.' Do you understand?"

He smiled to himself, pleased he had tricked her into telling her name. "You need warts if you're going to be a proper harpy."

"Gah!"

He heard the harpy stomp away, muttering to herself and slamming a door behind her. He chuckled silently to himself, feeling oddly contented for a man who had a lead arm and cold toes, and was tucked into a warm, cozy bed deep in the confines of hell. Perhaps he'd take another little nap, just so he was refreshed when the harpy next came to torment him.

Dagmar was worried. She didn't want to tell Julia just how worried she was, because Julia was a world-class worrier and, once started down a path, would worry to the point that Dagmar wanted to scream. But worried she was, and for once, that emotion was centered on something other than her own dire circumstances.

She considered the man who lay in her bed. He had been exceptionally dirty and covered in dried blood since the doctor that Julia had fetched hadn't felt it necessary to wash any of the muck off the Englishman. Dagmar, mindful of her mother's teachings, waited until the doctor left, and the man—Leo, that was his name—had lost consciousness before she fetched a bowl of water and, with Julia's blushing, gaze-averted help, managed to wrestle the man out of his upper garments.

Whereupon Julia promptly swooned at the sight of so much blood, leaving Dagmar to clean him up. She had done so, not particularly bothered by either the man's bare chest or the blood, more concerned that he might die before the sun rose.

"Although why I care is beyond me," she said, sitting on the side of the bed and wiping his sweaty face with a cold, wet rag. "You're not in the navy, and you're argumentative and stubborn and not at all going to help us in any way. I shouldn't give two figs if you die."

And yet she did. There was something about him, perhaps the way he insisted that he was already dead, or maybe it was the glint of humor she'd seen in the one eye he managed to get open, but there was something about him that appealed to her.

She studied his face. In repose, she could see the hard lines that ran from his nose to his mouth. He had a stubborn jaw; a thin, aristocratic nose that had obviously been broken since the lower half of it was slightly off center; and two dark, straight eyebrows that slashed across a high forehead. He wasn't handsome in the strictest sense of the word, and yet he wasn't difficult to look at. Absently, she reached out and brushed back a strand of hair that had glued itself to his damp forehead.

He moaned and turned his face toward her hand.

"You have had a time of it, haven't you?" she murmured, wetting the cloth and wiping his face again. He moaned a second time. "Should I marry you if you live through the night? Would you mind having a widow who you didn't know? But what if you survive? Maybe I won't need to marry you. Maybe you would be so grateful for my care that you'd do anything for me, including sending me to England with a large purse. No, that won't work. It will take you weeks to recover, assuming you don't die as the doctor says you will, and we only have three days left. It's either ransom or marrying, I'm afraid, and a ransom is just too heartless. Ah, well. If we marry in Denmark, I can divorce you later if you turn out to be unbearable."

The hours dragged by with the speed of an elderly caterpillar. The small hours of the morning passed to late hours, and finally the sun rose. With it, Dagmar's hopes sank, for Leo seemed more fevered, if anything.

With Julia's assistance, she managed to get another dose of draught down him, but he was barely able to swallow the foul mixture.

Exhausted though she was, Dagmar gathered up a bonnet and shawl, instructing Julia, who had snatched a few hours' sleep, to watch over their patient. "I must find a clergyman."

"Is he…gone?"

"No." She felt as if the weight of the world was pushing her into the earth. She didn't want to make the decision, but she had to. Leo could die at any time, and if he died before they were wed…she refused to consider what it meant to lose her last hope. "I must have a clergyman marry us before I see Colonel Stewart."

"You are making the right choice, my dear. But I thought you said that an army major would not be suitable?" Julia asked, glancing fearfully at the door, behind which lay the still figure of Leo. "Will the colonel bother himself with a member of the army?"

"I fervently pray he will. If he dies, the British ambassador will have to take responsibility for Leo, and that care will extend to us, as well. If he lives… well, we'll have to deal with that if the situation arises. I'll be back before he's due for the next draught. If he gets restless, wipe his face. He seems to like that."

"I wish you would let me fetch a pastor," Julia said in a plaintive tone. "I'm sure I will not take care of the major nearly so well as you do."

"It's going to be difficult enough to convince one of the clergy to come out at this time of the morning to perform a spontaneous marriage ceremony. I have a feeling that it'll take all my skills of persuasion to bring it off."

And she wasn't wrong. Pastor Anderson, who tended to the flock in Dagmar's area, flatly refused to conduct a ceremony.

"You have not gained the crown prince's approval," the man yelled down to her from an upstairs window. He appeared to be in a nightshirt and cap. "I will not risk angering His Royal Highness simply to gratify one of your whims."

"Fine," Dagmar said, too tired to spend the time it would take to argue the man around to reasonableness. "I'll simply find someone who isn't deathly afraid of Frederick."

"You do that," Anderson replied, then withdrew his head and slammed closed the shutters and window.

"Obstinate old goat." Dagmar wrapped her shawl tighter around herself against the chill of the early morning and hurried down the street to the next church.

Two hours later she was ready to drop, but was no closer to becoming a wife. At last, in desperation, she stumbled into the palace and requested a meeting with Frederick. When that was denied, she scribbled out a brief note and told the footman to take that to the crown prince. Five minutes later she was ushered into his presence.

"If this is another one of your tricks..." Frederick warned, waving the note at her.

"It's not." She sat without waiting for him to indicate she should do so, too tired even to ogle his breakfast remains.

"I don't have time to deal with your petty issues.

As if it wasn't enough that your ambassador demands I help some of your countrymen find a murderer…I'm ready to wash my hands of all the British!"

"I was born in Copenhagen!" Dagmar protested. "I'm not English."

"Your mother was, and that's enough for me. Who is this Englishman who you wish to marry?" Frederick gestured at a manservant, who removed his dressing gown and helped the prince regent into an elaborately embroidered frock coat.

"His name is Leopold Mortimer, and he's a major in the British army."

Frederick grunted and adjusted the lace at his wrists. "A gentleman?"

"Of course," Dagmar said, crossing her fingers and hoping that she wasn't telling a lie. Leo had seemed well-spoken enough, and he understood Danish, which meant he had been educated.

"Nobleman?"

That was a trickier question. She knew full well that even an impoverished, unknown princess was expected to make a marriage with a man who at the very least bore a title. She decided to risk the truth. "No. But he is a major, and they don't let just anyone become majors."

"Why has he not come himself to ask for your hand?"

"He was wounded in the arm. The doctor said he should not move around unduly." That was certainly true enough.

"Wounded, eh? Is he conscious?"

"Of course he is." She coughed delicately. "He might have some nonlucid periods now and again, as to be expected from one who was wounded so gravely."

"So in other words, he's mostly insensible." Frederick was silent for a moment. "Have you considered that the poor man might not want to be married, let alone wed to you?"

"I'm not a monster, no matter what you might think," she said with dignity. "If, after he recovers from his wounds and we are safely in England, he does not wish to be married, I will simply have the marriage annulled. If that is too difficult, there's always divorce."

"I'm told the British don't countenance divorce the way we enlightened people do."

She shrugged. "I'm Danish, and we will have been married here. I will simply divorce him in Denmark if needs be." Really, did he have to focus so much on the idea of the man rejecting her? She was a princess, after all, not to mention a gentlewoman of much distinction. Well, some distinction. Just a little bit.

Frederick grunted again and waved away the perfume pot his man was offering. "Which brings me to the question of why I should command the bishop to marry you when your own clergyman has refused to do the same."

"Well for one, the major spent the night in my bed." Dagmar kept her expression serene, no easy feat when she was on the edge of falling over into a stupor. "If you don't let us marry immediately, there is sure to be a scandal, especially when I tell everyone you refused support."

"Bah," the prince said, waving away the idea as he turned to leave the room. "I've survived worse."

Dagmar played her last card. "More importantly, if Leo and I wed, then I am no longer your responsibility."

Frederick paused at the door, glancing back at her, a thoughtful expression on his face. "And you promise that if you do divorce him, you won't come back to plague me?"

"I promise."

"I will want that in writing. Witnessed."

She managed to smile wanly. "I will sign a statement that, once married, I relinquish all claims upon you."

Frederick thought for a moment then shrugged. "Very well, I give this marriage my blessing. I will instruct the bishop to marry you this afternoon. Be at the church in—"

"No, it has to be at Yellow House," Dagmar interrupted, getting wearily to her feet.

Frederick never liked being interrupted. He scowled at her. "And why is that?"

"I told you that the major was wounded. The bishop will just have to come to my house—your Yellow House—to marry us there. Don't neglect to tell the bishop that the major is slightly feverish and might ramble a little bit."

"I won't neglect to do that," Frederick said, regarding her as one of the more repugnant species of insects. "I pity the poor fellow, but it's nothing to do with me. So long as you're out of Copenhagen in the next few days, I will advise the bishop to marry you no matter what the groom's circumstances."

And so it was that early in the afternoon, Dagmar Marie Sophie, Princess of Sonderburg-Beck became Dagmar Marie Sophie, Princess of Sonderburg-Beck and Mrs. Leo Mortimer.

The bishop hadn't wanted to perform the office,

but blanched when Dagmar, having had less than an hour's sleep, told him in no uncertain terms just what the crown prince would do if he found out that his commands were being ignored. Dagmar's small bedroom was filled with various clergymen, there to act as witnesses to this important event, and all of them stared with varying degrees of pity and disbelief at the raving man who thrashed on the bed.

Leo was in full grip of the fever, his face wet with perspiration, bright red circles high on either cheek. Dagmar, sitting on the bed next to him, wiped his face and leaned down to whisper, "Leo, the bishop has asked if you take me as your wife. You must say yes. Can you do that?"

His eyes opened, but they were glazed and unfocused. "Hrn?"

Dagmar turned to the bishop. "He said yes, he will marry me."

"He did?" The bishop frowned.

"He said it in English. He is an Englishman. Thus, he speaks in English when he's feeling out of sorts."

"Out of sorts? *Out of sorts?* The man's about to expire from fever," the bishop said, pointing.

The other clergymen backed hastily out of the room, several of them holding up their robes to cover their mouths lest they catch the infection.

"I ought to be reading the office of the dead over him, not marrying him to you."

"He'll be fine," Dagmar reassured him and sent up a little prayer that she spoke the truth. "And Frederick will be most unhappy if we aren't wed today."

The bishop looked like he was going to refuse, but

in the end, decided that he couldn't be blamed if the groom later claimed he had been wed against his will. After all, the crown prince had told him distinctly to see that the princess was married no matter what the man's state. With a clear conscience, the bishop hurried through the rest of the ceremony, ignoring the fact that the groom's statements were neither understandable nor coherent.

At the conclusion of the ceremony, the bride swiftly kissed the groom's damp brow, then with a business-like manner wholly at odds with such a romantic moment, forcibly administered fever medicine to him.

Four

Princesses who hide in an unused carriage solely in order to watch the new head groom disrobe will find themselves confined to their bedchamber for an entire week. Without any of the dreadful novels they so love!

—*Princess Christian of Sonderburg-Beck's Guide for Her Daughter's Illumination and Betterment*

LEO SWAM IN A SEA OF HELLFIRE, NOW AND AGAIN drifting into a dense black cloud that seemed to swallow up all thought and time, only to later reemerge into the red mist consisting of heat and pain and a dreadful, all-consuming thirst.

Awareness of another being ebbed over him occasionally, and he assumed it was the harpy named Dagmar who initiated the torments that racked his body. She also fed him repulsive poisonous liquids, later torturing him by allowing him only the smallest sips of water rather than the gallons that his thirst demanded.

"Just a little, Leo," she would whisper in his ear. "Too much and your stomach will rebel again. Just a sip or two, and I will give you more if that stays down."

He wanted to tell her that he was onto her ways and knew that she was masking her cruelty behind a false face of concern, but it all seemed like so much of a bother.

Later, the demons came, men in brusque voices who prodded and jostled him until they finally lifted him away and carried him over rough ground, the pain of the movement making him grit his teeth against the need to cry out in agony. He wouldn't give the devils the satisfaction of knowing how much they hurt him. The black pit swallowed him then, and it was only later when the Dagmar harpy washed his face that he realized the demons had left.

"Where did they go?" he asked her, glancing around an unfamiliar room. It was small and dark, paneled in wood, and smelling of foul odors. He appeared to be in some sort of small bunk.

"Where did who go?" Dagmar harpy asked.

"The demons. Open the window. I want cool air."

She blinked at him, then dipped a rag into a small bowl of water and gently wiped one side of his bare torso with it. The cool wetness of it felt so good, his fingers curled into soft blankets. "The sailors, you mean? They are above decks sailing the ship. I didn't know you were awake when they moved you. I can't open the porthole because the doctor said you were to stay out of drafts until you were well past the fevers. How do you feel?"

"Thirsty. Will you cease this endless torment and give me something to drink?"

"Yes, but only a little at a time. Your body doesn't like it if you drink too much at once. Here is some barley water. No, don't try to move. I will help you."

She slipped an arm behind his head and propped him up enough to take a few sips at the cup. He wanted to snatch the cup away from her and gulp it down but was asleep before he could fully formulate the thought.

He spent two more days wandering the land of fevered imagination, waking one night to find himself utterly drenched in sweat but feeling remarkably cool nonetheless. He lifted his head. Near the foot of his bunk, a swarthy, bull-chested man sat whistling tunelessly while whittling a piece of polished bone.

"Hello," Leo said in a conversational tone of voice. He tried to sit up but was too weak to do more than make a vague swimming motion with his limbs.

"Eh? Oh, yers awake." The man contemplated him for a moment, then with a grunt and accompanying rude noise, lurched to his feet and flung open the door near him. "Oy! Get orf yer arse and wake the princess and tell her that his nibs is awake."

Princess? Leo wondered if he was feverish. It was obvious from his physical state that he had been. Even the nightshirt he wore was glued to his body with sweat. He sat up, swinging his legs over the edge of the bunk, and reached up to rub his face, but a sudden sharp jab of pain in his arm left him gasping, his head swimming with pain.

"Here now, don't ye go blacking out again. Yer wife'll have my stones for supper if'n she thinks I let harm come to ye while she was havin' a wee nap. Put yer head down betwixt yer knees."

The burly man put one giant hand on Leo's head and forced it downward. Leo fought both nausea and the feeling of standing on the edge of an abyss.

"What's wrong? What has happened? Is he ranting again?" A female voice reached his ears, allowing him to focus on it rather than the need to swoon. He frowned at the floor. The voice sounded familiar. The woman spoke in perfectly correct English, but it was softly accented, as if she wasn't a native speaker. Where had he heard her before?

"Thank you, Mr. Murphy. Can you help me get him back into the bunk? And if you could have one of the cabin boys bring me a fresh bucket of water, I'd be very grateful."

Leo straightened up, at least feeling like he had a grasp on consciousness. A woman bustled toward him, clad in some gauzy white garment that was clearly intended to titillate a male of her acquaintance, although the shawl she had wrapped around herself hid most of the good parts from view. She had brown hair and hazel eyes, and an oval face that he felt he should know, but studying her, he had to admit he'd never seen her before that moment.

"Madam," he said with dignity as the burly man complied with her orders without a word of protest, "I don't know who you are, but I must ask that you leave my room."

"Don't be silly, Leo. If I leave, I can't get you back into bed. Ugh. Your bedding is soaked. Oh! Your fever has broken!"

Her thick woolen shawl slipped down her arms, falling to the floor with a soft whoosh as she clasped one hand to the back of his neck. He found himself staring at a pair of plump breasts barely visible through the thin lawn material of her nightdress.

She had pink nipples. He *loved* pink nipples on a woman.

"Thank heavens those fever draughts worked at last. Now you just sit there, and I'll get your bunk made more comfortable. Oh, Calvin, there you are. You can set the bucket down next to the wall, where it's out of the way while we strip Mr. Mortimer's bed."

The woman fit word to deed as she pulled bedding out from around him, the lad of about nine who was evidently named Calvin complying just as wordlessly as had the other man.

"Who are you?" he asked, frowning as she fussed around him. "And what are you doing in my bed-chamber in that advanced state of undress? Are you, by chance, a lightskirt come in hopes of earning a few bob? If so, I must disabuse you of that idea. Although your nipples are quite nice, I have evidently been ill recently, and doubt if I could perform to either of our satisfaction."

The woman looked down at her chest. The lad looked startled, accepted the bundle of sodden linen that she had shoved at him, and backed out the door without a word.

"I'm not in an advanced state of undress. I'm glad you like my nipples, although I don't see what they have to do with anything in particular. And I don't know what a lightskirt is. My name is Dagmar. I am your wife."

"Ha ha," he said, shifting to the side when she dug out of a sea chest another armful of bedding. She spread it out on the bunk, holding on to his arm when he tried to stand. He weaved when he did so. "Ha ha ha ha ha. That was very funny. Even I, previously ill but now well, can appreciate that joke."

She got him settled on the bunk and returned to the sea chest, pulling out a small package wrapped in red silk. From it, she withdrew a large paper.

He plucked fretfully at the nightshirt, wishing to remove its dampness but unwilling to expose himself to the lightskirt. She'd no doubt attempt to charge him if he did, and although he was a bit confused about just where he was and why his arm was sore, he was fairly confident that in time, memory would return to him. "I hate to ruin such a fine attempt of amusing me, but I can assure you that I'm not married."

"You are."

"You are mistaken. I would remember something like being married, especially to a Danish woman named Dagmar. I take it you are Danish?"

"Half. My mother was English. And I assure you that we *are* married."

"I am very much not mar—" She shoved the paper under his nose. It took him a minute to focus his eyes on the writing, and then another minute to translate the Danish document, but once the pertinent points became clear to him, he felt a cold wave wash over him, making his skin prickle. "Damnation. I *am* married."

"Yes."

He squinted at the paper.

"To a woman named Dagmar."

She folded the paper up and put it away in the chest. "That is indeed so."

"*You* are named Dagmar."

"I have been ever since I was a week old, or so Dearest Papa once told me."

He thought for a moment. Even his mind felt a bit slow and feeble. "I'm married to a woman named Dagmar who is also a princess."

"Congratulations, Leo. You have evidently recovered well enough to reason and understand basic facts. This pleases me. I wouldn't wish to be married to an ignorant man. Shall I fetch you some broth? Or would you like more barley water? I understand from the ship's surgeon that people who have recovered from lengthy fevers shouldn't eat solid food for a few days, but I'm sure some broth or gruel would be perfectly suitable."

Leo sat there, damp, uncomfortable, and with a head that reeled not due to illness, but to the stark facts that the woman Dagmar had presented him. He was married? To a princess? How had this happened? When had it happened? And more to the point, why had it happened? "I wish to know more about this marriage that I don't remember and a wife I have never set eyes upon before and a title that I don't believe I've ever heard—is there such a place as Sonderburg-Beck? It sounds German, not Danish—but at the moment I desire clean garments."

"Oh." The woman stood in front of him and eyed him in a manner that he would have liked to find offensive but was too tired to work up the necessary emotion. "I suppose that would make you more comfortable. One moment, please."

She left the room and Leo, with a shudder of distaste,

peeled off the offensive nightshirt and tossed it into a corner. As the ground beneath him rolled slightly, several pieces clicked together in his mind. Porthole. Cabin boy. Ship's surgeon...by God, he was on a ship. How had that happened? He sat down abruptly on the bunk when the ship rolled again, hastily grabbing at the bed linen when the door opened and the woman who had somehow managed to marry him while he was unaware appeared. She was followed immediately by two sailors carrying a narrow tin tub, which was set down in front of him.

"I'm afraid you'll have to bathe in seawater, since the captain doesn't seem to be inclined to let anyone have fresh water for bathing, but I've found it's bearable once you get used to it. Thank you, gentlemen." This last was spoken to a line of sailors who carried in wooden buckets of water, which they proceeded to dump into the tin tub. She waited until the last of them unloaded the water before moving over to Leo's side. "It's not very hot, but it's better than nothing."

She stood expectantly next to him. He looked up at her and hugged the linens closer. "What are you doing?"

"Waiting to help you bathe. I've never bathed a man before, not in a tub, but Julia tells me that it's right and proper that I should do so, and she should know. She's a widow, you see."

"No, I don't see, and I don't know that I care to. I do know that I wish for you to leave."

Her forehead wrinkled in a manner that he found wholly adorable, a fact that he stubbornly refused to acknowledge. "Why?"

"Why do I want you to leave?"

"Yes. Julia said that most men like to be waited on, and although I have no intention of doing so in the normal course of events—begin as you mean to go on, my sainted mother used to say—allowances can be made for the fact that you've had a fever for almost ten days and probably feel quite weak."

"Ten days!" He tried to remember what he had last been doing, but his memory was hazy at best. All that came to mind was the image of a fresh-faced girl, an obnoxious cat, and anger at the treachery of his horse.

"Yes. Get up and I'll bathe you."

He pulled the bed linens up to his chin and gave her his most haughty look. "Madam—"

"Dagmar. Or *Your Serene Highness* if you wish to be formal."

"—Madam, I have no intention of arising from this bed with you present. Please take yourself off so that I might cleanse off the effects of ten days' worth of sickness."

She tipped her head to the side. "Are you shy? Do you not wish for me to see your naked form? Do you have some sort of defect that you think will cause me to divorce you?"

He sat up straighter, glaring over the top of the bedsheet. "I am not defective! Nor am I overly modest. I simply balk at the idea of parading my naked self in front of strange women."

Dagmar thought for a moment. "Would it help if I've seen your upper parts without clothing? I even bathed them. Julia wouldn't let me attend to your lower half, since she said it was unseemly for an innocent and gentle maiden such as I to do so, and the captain assigned one of the sailors to attend to those needs of a highly personal nature that occurred now and again—this despite the fact that we are very much legally married by the crown prince's own bishop—but as you are now improving, I think it only right and proper for me to aid you in bathing."

He stared at her for a long moment. "You wish to see me naked, don't you?"

"Yes. My sainted mother told me that there was much I had to be told on the eve of my wedding, but she died a few years ago, and of course, Dearest Papa died a little over a year ago, and Julia, although a widow, was unaware that she would be called upon to discuss such things with me as naked men and what to do with their various bits and pieces, so I'm not entirely sure how everything works."

Leo was well aware that the bathwater, such as it was, was rapidly cooling, but he felt oddly loath to end this bizarre conversation. He wanted to keep Dagmar talking just to see what she'd say next. "Are you referring to sexual congress?"

"No, not particularly." She looked thoughtful. "Although I suppose if you wanted to inform me about how to do it, I would be grateful. People don't talk to me about these things because I am a gentle and innocent maiden."

"So you have mentioned." He had absolutely no doubt that she was anything but a gentle maiden, although the forthright look in her pretty hazel eyes gave proof to her claim of innocence.

"I don't often have the opportunity to see gentlemen without their breeches." There was a wistful note in her voice that had him wondering if her innocence was as great as he first thought. "Copenhagen is so cold in the winter, you see."

There wasn't really much to say to that. Leo contemplated his course of action and decided to throw his trust in the legitimacy of the marriage lines that she'd dangled in front of him, and with a flick of his wrist, stood up, allowing the bedsheet to fall to his feet.

Dagmar's eyes widened. "I see," she said after a few moments' silence, her gaze crawling over him in a way that had he not suffered a fever for ten days, not to mention a grievous injury to his arm and shoulder, he would have acknowledged in a wholly physical manner. As it was, he simply stood there and let her look her fill. "And that bit there…" She waved toward his groin. "Is it supposed to look like that?"

He looked down. "I've been ill."

"Yes, but it's rather unsightly, don't you think?"

He squared his shoulders and looked down his nose at her. How dare she make disparaging comments about his penis? "It is quiescent at the moment, but I assure you that is simply the result of the fever. If you are worrying that I cannot perform my marital duties—not that I intend to perform them anytime soon because I have many questions, many questions indeed regarding this so-called marriage that has taken place—I can assure you that when needs must, it works quite well. Or so I've been given to understand from various ladies."

"Hmm." She gave his groin a doubtful look, then gestured toward the tub. "Well, I must admit that

I don't see what all the fuss is about. If my sainted mother had shown me that years ago, we wouldn't have had that episode where she found me hiding in the stables."

He stepped into the tub, glancing at her before sitting down in the tepid water. "What does a stable have to do with the male form?"

She smiled and handed him a small square of cambric. "We used to have a very handsome groom. His upper parts were exceptionally well formed. I felt that his lower half must match and wished to see for myself. Unfortunately, Mama found me before I could ascertain the truth for myself. Here is some soap. If you lean forward, I will wash your back. Try not to get your arm or shoulder wet."

His body felt so weak, and he was so distracted by the mental image of a gentle and innocent princess hiding in a stable in an attempt to spy on a well-built groom, that he wasn't aware of her touch until some minutes had passed.

"Oh, goodness! You have a drawing on your back."

"It's called a tattoo."

"Why do you have a drawing of a"—there was a pause while she leaned forward to squint at the image—"a bird on your back?"

"It's a firebird, and it is the reason young men on their Grand Tour should not deliberately lose their companions in order to drink themselves blind in a tavern in the seedier part of Marseilles."

"Oh." She touched it with the cloth. "It's rather pretty. I have never seen someone with a drawing on their skin. What is a firebird?"

"A mythical creature, and before you ask, I have no recollection of asking for it, let alone the tattoo, so I'm unable to tell you why I chose that image."

"Ah."

Silence wrapped around them, a warm, steamy silence that seemed oddly charged. A warm tingling along his spine finally caught his attention, and it was at that point that he realized she had spent an inordinately long time soaping his back.

"Are you all right back there?" he inquired politely, trying to look over his shoulder without causing pain.

"Yes, fine. The salt water doesn't let the soap work too well." Her fingers, warm and strong, slid along the flesh of his back, sending little chills of pleasure coursing through him. She made swirling motions, little patterns comprised of swoops and circles and long sweeps of her hands, that made him very aware that he was a man, and she was a woman, and one of them was naked.

"I believe…" He had to stop and clear his throat. "I believe my back is clean now."

"Is it? I suppose that's so." She wrung out another cambric square over his back and moved around to kneel next to him, eyeing his chest doubtfully. "I will wash your left side, but the ship's surgeon was most adamant that we keep your wound as dry as possible."

He took up his cloth. "I have washed my left side already."

"Very well. I shall do your lower half, so you won't have to bend…" She paused, staring with growing astonishment at the water. After a minute, she looked up at him, a question clearly evident in her face.

"Yes, it's supposed to do that," he said without looking down at his lap. "That's how it functions."

"Really?" She returned her attention to his groin. "That seems singularly impractical. How do you walk with that in your breeches?"

"Quite painfully when it's in this state. Luckily, I'm not often called upon to stroll about like this."

She gave it another doubtful look, then proceeded to wash his legs and feet, finally taking up a large linen for him to dry himself upon.

Ten minutes later, with his head swimming from the unaccustomed activity and his groin attempting to impress the princess with its apparent prowess, he was tucked into bed.

"Now, if you please, I should like the exact details of the circumstances of our marriage. I don't recall ever seeing you before."

"That will have to wait until after you've had your broth."

"I want to hear about it now."

"I don't want to go into the explanation until later."

Leo glared at her. "Madam, you seem to be under the delusion that you can naysay me. Please disabuse yourself of that notion immediately, and do as I ask."

"Bossy, aren't you?" She had the nerve to look unimpressed by his dictates as she tidied up the room.

"If I am, it's because it comes with my position. When and where did we meet?"

"I didn't realize that majors were entitled to push innocent and gentle citizens around. In Denmark, officers treat ladies with respect."

"I am entirely respectful to you." He stopped, aware

that the words were coming out in a growl. He cleared his throat again. "And I was referring to my title, not my military rank."

"Your title?" She frowned as she gathered up the nightshirt, pausing as she was about to leave the cabin. "I thought your name was Leo Mortimer?"

"Mortimer is my family name, yes. I am the seventh Earl of March."

"Oh, how nice! Frederick will be relieved to hear that." She beamed at him.

He didn't want to allow the distraction, but he was unable to resist it. "Who's Frederick?"

"The crown prince. He's also a cousin and was, until we were married, responsible for me. But now I have you. Isn't it wonderful how things turned out? I'll go fetch your broth and have the men take away the bath."

She left a smile behind as she bustled out.

Leo lay back on the pillows, feeling incredibly confused.

Without any memory, he'd been wounded.

And married.

And hauled onto a ship going…where?

It was all too much to take in. Perhaps he'd rest his eyes until the princess came back.

He slept for sixteen hours.

Five

We do not ogle Italian dancing masters, no matter how tightly their trousers fit or how muscular their derrieres are. Princesses are above such things, and if they aren't, they will soon find themselves with new dancing masters who don't fill out their trousers in quite such an exciting manner.

—Princess Christian of Sonderburg-Beck's Guide for Her Daughter's Illumination and Betterment

DAGMAR STARTED DOWN A CORRIDOR, SAW A FAMILIAR shadow loom up on the opposite wall, and turning quickly, sped back the way she'd come, racing up the steep wooden stairs to the deck. She paused for a moment, looking around wildly for a hiding spot, and had just chosen the fore of the ship when a hand closed around her arm.

"Princess Dagmar," a male voice said rather breathily in her ear. "I find you at last."

Dagmar's shoulders slumped. Caught!

"If I didn't know that there are few, if any, hiding

spots on a ship this size, I would say you were avoiding me. But that can't be, can it?"

She murmured something inaudible and considered her options. Could she, if she twisted out of her captor's hold, outrun him to the captain's quarters, where she could make a plea for sanctuary?

"Not to mention the unlikely idea of a wife avoiding the company of her very own husband, a man who just two days ago she greeted with enthusiasm and appreciation. And no, you can't make it. I might be a little weak still, but if you run to the captain and demand he shelter you from me, as you did yesterday, I shall simply tell him to confine you to quarters."

Dagmar spun around, frowning fiercely at her husband. "It was entirely unkind of you to tell him that I had a mental deficiency and was not responsible for my actions. Now he thinks I'm simple."

Leo, who she absently noted was looking particularly well, regarded her with a steady gaze. The gaunt lines of his face brought on by the illness were softening as he fleshed out a little. His color had returned as well, although she couldn't help but notice that his right shoulder was held higher than the left, indicating he was still in pain. "You ran to him claiming I was beating you. If that's not the result of a deranged mind, I don't know what is."

"You *were* beating me!"

He just looked at her.

She made an exasperated noise. "All right, you weren't actually touching me. But you yelled quite a bit, and you looked like you wanted to beat me."

"If I did, it was only because you refuse to answer

my quite reasonable questions. You might as well give it up, Dagmar. You've led me on a merry chase for the last two days, but the time is come for the truth."

Her shoulders slumped some more. Even she had to admit that his request was a reasonable one. She'd avoided telling him the events of those last two days in Copenhagen simply because she'd come to realize that there was a very sharp mind behind that mild facade.

It didn't hurt that the facade was extremely charming and had taken to haunting her restless nights.

"Come. Let us sit in your cabin, where it's warm."

"We can't. Julia is sleeping after her night's illness."

"Ah. Is she suffering from *mal de mer*?"

"Still, yes. She's been sick the entire time we've been at sea, and at this point, I don't expect her to feel well again until we land. I managed to get a little brandy down her, so hopefully that and the sleep will keep her from succumbing to her horrible condition."

The wind buffeted them as Leo stood watching her. Without warning, he reached out and brushed back a strand of her loose hair, his thumb gently stroking her cheek. "You have not had a very good time of it lately, have you? The captain says you seldom left me while I raged with the fever, and now you are in attendance of your companion."

"She's my friend. I can't leave her any more than I could have abandoned you." Dagmar suddenly shivered, the thin wool of her coat not doing much to keep out the wind and spray. Luckily, she'd turned out to be quite a sailor, moving with the ship in such a way that she didn't much notice its rolling.

"Then it will have to be my cabin. No balking,

now. I am recovered, have bathed and eaten, so there is no reason you can't tell me what happened in Copenhagen."

He took her hand, his fingers warm around hers despite the chill of the North Sea, and led her back down the stairs to the cabins.

"You still don't have any memory of the time before your fever broke?" My, but he smelled nice. It must have been the soap he used—he smelled warm and masculine, and there was a slight pine scent that pleased her.

"Not of events immediate to that time, no."

Oh, who was she fooling? He pleased her in many more ways than just his scented soap. Dagmar didn't want to face the fact that she was having more and more thoughts about just how sleek his flesh had felt under her hands while she bathed him, but there came a point where one couldn't ignore the fact that one was having extremely erotic thoughts, and that time was now.

"I remember quite well what I was doing before I went to Denmark, but it's my time there that seems to have gone missing."

She eyed him, wondering what it would be like to be married to him—really married to him, not just in name. She had a vague idea of what went on in a marital bed but clearly needed more information to fuel those erotic thoughts that kept pestering her at night—or correct them, since she wasn't sure if she was having feasible erotic thoughts.

"The surgeon said I have suffered a saber slash, but even that I don't remember."

How long would it take him to recover from his wounds? He seemed hearty enough, other than holding his shoulder oddly. Would he need his shoulder in order to fulfill those bedroom duties that she thought about so much in the long, dark hours of the night? If only she knew just what those duties consisted of, she might have a better sense of how close he was to achieving them. If only she knew how he was really feeling. If only she had someone to ask.

"And I certainly don't remember meeting and marrying you, despite the fact that I must have been enough in possession of my wits to speak during the wedding ceremony."

She sighed as she sat down on the edge of his bunk. There, right before her, sitting on a three-legged wooden stool was just such a person. Dearest Papa had always said that the only foolish question was the one that remained unasked. Therefore, she would take her courage in hand and simply ask. "Do you want to bed me?"

Leo, who was in the act of removing a heavy wool coat, paused and gave her a wild-eyed look. "Right now, you mean?"

"No, of course not." She thought for a moment. "Unless you feel able to, that is. Do you?"

He stared openmouthed at her for a few seconds, then tossed the coat onto the bed alongside her, wincing as he did so. "I…I…I don't think I've ever…"

"You've never bedded a woman?" She frowned. "Now, that surprises me. My sainted mother said men were forever trying to bed women, which was why I must never have one in my bedchamber unless he was a king or my husband. But if you haven't…I fear we may be in some trouble, since I haven't bedded a man before either."

"Of course I've bedded a woman." He sat up straight and looked incensed, waving his good arm in a grand gesture. "I've bedded dozens of women. Hundreds. Why a king?"

"Why what? Oh, blackmail, of course." She smiled. "There's nothing like a bedchamber scandal to tighten the screws on a man, is there?"

The look he gave her was one of mingled appreciation and horror. "You're quite the bloodthirsty little thing, aren't you?"

"Not particularly. The Danish court is fraught with bedchamber intrigue, however, and Mama felt I should understand how best to use it to my advantage should someone attempt to bed me without being my lawful husband. Do you want to?"

"We're back to that, are we?"

"You didn't answer my question," she pointed out.

"That I didn't. I was hoping you'd forget it." Leo took a deep breath and, with both hands on his knees, said, "Despite what your sainted mother told you, not every man wants to take every woman he sees to his bed."

"Oh." Disappointment filled her. He didn't want to bed her. She had a horrible feeling she knew why too. "It's my bosom, isn't it? I told Julia that it was getting bigger, but she didn't believe me."

Leo's gaze was locked on her bulging bodice.

"Er…they're getting bigger?"

"It's the sea air." She regarded her chest mournfully. "I don't suppose binding my breasts would help?"

"Most decidedly not. In fact, I forbid you even thinking about it."

"I think there's something you should know about me," Dagmar announced.

"I'm sure there are any number of things I should know, about you and our marriage, and since we're on that subject, I'd like a few answers—"

"I don't take well to being forbidden things," she said calmly. "I never have. Dearest Papa said I got that from my mother, but I believe it's because I had to put up with Frederick bossing me around while Papa was ill. Frederick was forever forbidding me things."

Leo just blinked his eyelashes over those interesting eyes and looked at her as if she were a boiled pig's head.

"If it's not my bosom—which I hope will shrink back to normal once it's out of the sea air—then is it something else about my person that repels you, or is it a general unwillingness to bed me?"

Leo took a deep breath. "I'm neither unwilling nor repelled, but I don't wish to discuss your breasts—which I have to say I find utterly delightful as they are—and would, in fact, like to have an explanation that I have been attempting to seek from you for the last two days. The time has come, *Wife*, for the reckoning."

Dagmar flinched just a little at the emphasis on "wife." He never once questioned the validity of the marriage documents she'd brought with her, although just the day before he demanded to have charge of them, and reluctantly, she'd given them over into his possession.

One thought led to another, and before she could

stop herself, she said, "I don't need the marriage lines to divorce you, you know. They're in the records of both the bishop and Copenhagen. And of course, my cousin sent the bishop to marry us, so he would be able to testify that we were properly wed."

Leo looked confused. "According to the papers, we've only just been married, and you're talking about divorce?"

"Not in the sense you mean. I simply wanted to point out that should I desire it, I could divorce you. I believe it's more difficult in England for a woman to divorce her husband, but in Denmark, it's not at all uncommon."

A wry smile twisted Leo's mouth. "Thank you for the warning. Now then, shall we start at the beginning? Where did we meet?"

"In Copenhagen." She smoothed a hand over the bed linens, wondering what it would be like to burrow into them and cocoon herself with his scent. "I like the way you smell."

"Oh no," he said, waggling a finger. "I'm familiar with your ways now, so there will be no distracting me with talk of your breasts and how large they are, and how perfectly they would fit into my hands and how I would like to rub them all over myself. We are going to stick to the topic at hand. Where in particular did we meet?"

"My back garden." She thought about what he said. This rubbing of her bosom on his person hadn't, at first, seemed an overly attractive thought, but the more she dwelt on it, the more pleasing it became. Should she invite him to take her breasts in his hands? She looked at his hands where they rested on his thighs, then she looked at his thighs and lost all thoughts of anything else.

His brow wrinkled. "Your garden? Was it a party of some sort?"

"You have very nice thighs." She was staring, she knew, but she couldn't stop herself. Through the stretched material, she could make out the heavy thigh muscle that indicated a man who spent a vast amount of time in the saddle. "If I let you take my breasts in your hands, would you let me stroke your thighs?"

He fell off the stool.

Instantly, she was on the ground next to him, checking to make sure he hadn't hurt himself. Somehow, her breasts ended up in his hands, which she took as permission to do as she wanted with his thighs.

"Oh!" she said, startled and pleased not just by the sensation of her bosom, suddenly feeling quite demanding, resting in the warmth of his hands, but also by the sleek lines of thigh muscles that her hands were happily exploring. "Oh!"

"Oh, indeed," he said, his voice sounding strangled at he stared down at his hands, now overflowing with bosom. He flexed his fingers. She moaned and arched her back. "I think we might even go so far as to say, 'good God!' or even, 'bless my garters,' not that I understand why garters enter into the subject. Dagmar, if you continue on that track, you'll end up causing me to burst my trousers, and as they are borrowed from the captain, I'd hate to ruin them."

Dagmar stopped rubbing her breasts against his hands and looked down, somewhat surprised to find both of her hands now stroking a very full front of his trousers. She pursed her lips for a moment at the buttons holding the fall up, then quickly released him.

"That is not flaccid," she accused, her gaze firmly on his erection.

"Not in the least, although you needn't sound so annoyed by the fact."

"My sainted mother told me that men were flaccid by nature, and to be otherwise was dangerous, as you were in the bath, although even then you weren't this…pronounced."

"You weren't stroking my thighs in the bath." He seemed to be having some problem breathing, and Dagmar was about to offer to assist him to his bunk when he shifted her so that she sat astride his legs. "I can't believe I'm even thinking this, although it's perfectly natural given the fact that you are clearly trying to seduce me, but when you said you've never been bedded, did you mean that figuratively or literally?"

She ran a finger down the nonflaccid part of him, marveling that something so silly-looking could be so very velvety. "I try very hard never to lie," she said, dragging her gaze from his interesting parts. Leo, for his part, moaned when she wrapped her fingers around him. "I'm not very good at it, and Mama always said that princesses should never lie because what's the point in being a princess if you can't say exactly what you think?"

"Your mother—to the left a bit, darling—your mother sounds like she was quite the woman."

"She was. I miss her and Papa greatly. You are becoming even stiffer, Leo. You would tell me if something was amiss with your male parts, would you not?"

He groaned again and panted just a little as she let her fingers explore the length and breadth of him. "I would. Answer my question."

"Which one? There've been so many."

"Are you really a virgin, or did you just say you were so that I wouldn't annul the marriage on the spot?" He leaned down as he spoke and brought his mouth to her breasts, which somehow he'd managed to get out of her stays and bodice. His breath was hot on her flesh, and she squirmed against his thighs, wanting more, so much more, but unable to put that need into words. His mouth closing on one of her nipples had her releasing his parts in order to grasp his shoulders. She managed to stop grabbing his bad shoulder just in time, clasping his hip on that side instead and shifting so that he would pay his attentions to her other breast.

"I am a virgin. Would you mind sucking on my other breast? It is out of sorts because you've paid so much attention to the right one."

Leo obliged, but before Dagmar could really throw herself into some quality moaning, he stopped and gently pushed her off his legs. What was even sadder, he tucked himself into his breeches again.

"I was afraid of that. I suppose it's for the best, really, since we shouldn't do anything we might later regret."

Dagmar was having some regrets at that moment, but they had everything to do with the fact that he ceased teasing her nipples with his tongue and nothing to do with thoughts of the future. "You don't wish to consummate me?" she asked forlornly.

"Of course I want to consummate you." He gestured toward his crotch, which was quite bulgy behind the yellow material of the trousers. "I want to consummate you as you've never been consummated, and then continue consummating you until one or possibly both of us expire from sheer, unadulterated pleasure, but that, my fine temptress, is not going to happen until I have made a few decisions. And to that end, let us continue the discussion we were having when you attempted to seduce me by means of your delicious breasts."

Dagmar finished squishing her bosom back into their stays and tugged up the bodice of her gown. She was pleased by the thought that she, the most inexperienced of women, had almost successfully seduced Leo. What might she accomplish when she had all the information at hand about the exact proceedings of the bedding?

"All right," she said, getting to her feet when he rose to his. "But you have to kiss me first."

He looked like he was going to protest, then his expression changed to one of curiosity. "Not that I am opposed to such a thing, but why do you wish for me to kiss you?"

"Because my breasts are hot, and those parts of me that my mother said would someday become very useful are in fact appearing to head in that direction because they are tingling greatly, and also because I've never been kissed."

He stared at her as if she was a giant, tingly female part. "What, never?"

"Oh, I've been kissed. Mama and Papa were very affectionate, and men have kissed my hand, of course. But there is a difference between a man like Frederick slobbering on my knuckles, and a man like you, with all your muscles and your warm flesh, and your hair that I want to touch now that it's clean again, kissing me. That I would very much like to experience, and I see no reason why you couldn't do that now, since it involves your lips and not your shoulder or arm."

His eyes glinted with an amused light. "Darling, you're not doing it right if you believe that."

"That's just the point. I'm not doing it at all."

"Far be it from me to deny a lady a simple request," he said, looking somewhat noble. Dagmar wanted to giggle. "But immediately following the kiss, we are going to have the talk that I've been trying to have for two days now. What are you doing?"

"Giggling," she said, making an effort to stop. "You look like a brave knight about to face a dragon."

"Well, stop it. No man wishes to kiss someone who giggles. And I assure you, madam," he said, putting his good arm around her, easing her forward until she leaned on one side of his chest, "I find the princess a much more daunting foe than the dragon. Tilt your head slightly. Other way. No, there's no need to open your mouth up wide. I'm not going to extract a tooth. There, just like that, with your lips slightly parted."

Dagmar's eyes crossed as she tried to keep him in focus when his mouth descended upon hers. At first, she wasn't overly impressed with the experience, and she told Leo so.

"For one," he said, pulling away enough that she

could see him again. "You're not supposed to speak while I'm kissing you. And for another, we hadn't really started. That was just a little preliminary peck, if you will."

"It was just your lips touching mine in no real exciting manner. To be honest, I found it very underwhelming," she said, frowning slightly at him. What if all the romantic tales she'd read of heroines who swooned upon kissing the hero were fabrications of deranged minds? What if this kissing business was a warning that the bedding was going to be just as disappointing? What if—

At that moment Leo swooped in again, and this time, it was as if an entirely different person was kissing her. Leo didn't just kiss her; he took possession of her mouth, his lips apparently taking charge of hers while his tongue swooped and swirled and teased with wet little touches that by rights should have been disgusting—she hadn't imagined a tongue ever entering into the situation—but in reality, seemed to start a fire deep inside her that quickly spread outward. She clutched his good shoulder, wordlessly urging him on as his tongue swept into her mouth and started doing things there that made her wild with desire.

He was right about one thing: he needed his arms and shoulder to kiss properly. He pulled her tighter against his side, his arms urging her to move against him in a way that seemed both sinful and extremely exciting. And when he finally managed to pry her off him, it was with a real sense of regret that she allowed him to move away a step.

"I take it back," she said some moments later, when

she could remember how to speak again. She stared at his mouth, wanting to kiss him again.

"What?" he asked, looking confused.

"It wasn't underwhelming. I want very much to kiss you again, Leo."

"No," he said sternly even as he reached for her and pulled her against him. "Absolutely not. We have things to discuss. Open your mouth just a tiny bit wider, darling."

And he kissed her again, and again after that, and once more after that even though by that point Dagmar was light-headed from lack of oxygen, and Leo's bad arm was trembling from the strain of use.

"I'm going to swoon if you continue," Dagmar told him when his lips reluctantly parted from hers. "Or vomit."

"That is the singularly most unromantic thing I've ever heard," he said, helping her to the bed where she immediately bent over to put her head between her knees in the approved manner of nearly swooning or vomiting women.

"I'm sorry. I just thought you'd like to know that I no longer was unimpressed by your ability to kiss," she said, her voice somewhat muffled. "It's actually a compliment, because no other man has made my insides knot up the way you did."

"I will wear your nausea as a badge of pride," he reassured her, collapsing onto the three-legged stool opposite, "and hope that in the future, your insides will be pleasantly stirred rather than knotted. Now, my dear, you've done your best to hide from me, insist to the captain that I am too ill to speak, and seduce me away from the subject, but there will be no more of that. I want answers, and I have selected you as the person to provide them. I believe the last question I asked was how we met in your garden. Had you invited me there? Were you having some sort of a party?"

"No," she said, drawing out the word. She didn't really want to tell him the truth but couldn't, despite some rapid and desperate thinking, come up with a viable reason why she shouldn't do so.

Except, of course, for the fact that he would in no way like the circumstances.

"No you didn't invite me there, or no you weren't having a party?"

"Neither. Both." She sat up, her head feeling much clearer, and bit her lower lip as she tried to gauge his response to the truth. Unfortunately, she kept getting distracted by his thighs and mouth and all sorts of wicked thoughts, and in the end, she just decided to cast her worry aside. "You were wounded when Julia found you. We dragged you back to the house and tended to you there. And since I needed an English officer to marry, and you said you weren't married— you didn't lie, did you?"

He shook his head, his eyes losing that hazy, smoky look of passion that she had just decided she really enjoyed. A hard light came into them, instead, one that she felt boded ill for any further action of the kissing nature.

"I don't suppose you'd like to kiss me again? I feel much better now."

He just looked at her.

She sighed loudly, took hold of her courage, and continued with such speed that the words tumbled around each other. "You said you weren't married, so then the bishop came around to marry us, and after that, I went to Colonel Stewart, but an admiral named Nelson was there in his place, and he—the admiral—said that even though you weren't with the navy, you were an officer and thus they'd take you home to England. So Julia and I packed the few things we had, and had you taken to the ship that Admiral Nelson said was leaving the next day. And that was almost two weeks ago, and we should be in England soon. Julia and I were thinking of opening a shop."

A parade of expressions passed across Leo's face: disbelief was followed by confusion, which was sadly chased by horror. He shook his head, wincing when his shoulder inadvertently twitched. "I don't know that I'd ever in my wildest delusions have come up with a scenario such as that. We were married *after* I had been struck down? After?"

Oh, how she wished she wasn't there, but her sainted mother had an extremely annoying saying about making one's bed and then sleeping in it. "Yes, after."

His expression hardened. His jaw tightened. The tight fall of his trousers deflated. "Was I even conscious for the wedding?"

"Yes, of course you were." Dagmar hoped that fib wouldn't matter much. He had been somewhat conscious, after all. "You gave your responses when the bishop read the marriage ceremony."

He passed a hand over his face, shaking his head again. "I don't remember any of it."

"The surgeon said the brain fever can sometimes do that, and you shouldn't try too hard to remember things, or they'll slip away forever." She tried to offer that advice as helpfully as possible, but he shot her a suspicious look before standing and moving over to the porthole, opened just enough to let a little salty air into the close confines of the cabin.

"Let me see if I have this straight in my mind: we met and were married on the same day."

"Of course not."

He glanced over his shoulder at her. "Oh?"

"As it happens, we were married the following day." She brushed the wrinkles in her gown, wishing once again that she could be anywhere on earth but that exact spot.

"That makes all the difference."

"I thought so."

"I was being sarcastic, Princess."

Dagmar had never been afraid of a challenge, so despite her desire to run, she deliberately got up and went to his side in order to examine his face as he looked out the porthole. "I know you were. I chose to ignore it. Mama always said one shouldn't acknowledge sarcasm unless it was one's own. And you needn't make it sound as though our wedding was an extraordinary circumstance. It was perfectly normal, if a bit small, but I've never really wanted a state wedding, so it worked out well."

"Not extraordinary?" He turned to her, a flash of anger momentarily visible in his eyes. "You don't call a gentlewoman preying on a wounded, most likely insensible, man an extraordinary circumstance?"

Dagmar stepped back, stung by the unfair accusation. "I did not prey on you."

"Oh no? Tell me, then, why did you marry me, Princess?"

She hesitated, guilt at the selfishness of her plan pushing its way up from where she'd buried it. She tried desperately to think of an altruistic bend she could put on the facts, and failed. "You were wounded," she finally said, wincing at the lameness of the statement.

"And that forced you to marry me?" One of his eyebrows rose. She resented its sardonic tilt.

"You spent the night in my bed. I am, as I believe I've had cause to tell you, a gentle and innocent maiden, and to be closeted alone in my bedchamber with an unmarried man is shocking, quite, quite shocking. If I hadn't married you, my cousin Frederick might have challenged you to a duel."

Now, that was a bald-faced lie, but her pride prompted her to come out with it.

The second of his eyebrows rose to join its brother-in-arms. "I will admit that I am not as *au courant* with the situation in Denmark as I might be, but I had always been under the impression that the crown prince was a reasonable man, much given to thought before action. A duel over an insensible, wounded man in a cousin's bed doesn't strike me as particularly characteristic of such a person."

She picked a stray hair off her sleeve. "You don't know Frederick as I do."

"Granted." He considered her for a long moment. "Why is it that you needed an English officer?"

"Erm." Her brain attempted to come up with a

reasonable explanation and quickly gave up the job. "Did I say that?"

"Yes. I'm interested in knowing the reason behind such an odd statement. Oblige me, please."

He was looking particularly unmovable at the moment. Dagmar hadn't noticed that about him before. Oh, she was well aware that he was very solid, but that was a pleasing sort of solid, the kind of solidity that encouraged her to sport around on his legs, kissing him with every confidence that he wouldn't let her topple over while doing so. But this immovability was something entirely different. It hinted at obstinacy and pigheadedness, and boiled pigs' heads aside, she had never liked porcine beasts in any form. Worse, she had a horrible feeling that this new immovability boded ill for the future. "I am half English, as I mentioned. I wish to visit the homeland of my sainted mother, and since you—the English—destroyed all the ships in Copenhagen, I had to rely on the British navy to transport me."

"And they wouldn't take you without a husband?" His brow wrinkled as he worked out the confusion. "No, that doesn't make sense. They take women all the time on ships, but generally those women work out their passage on their backs." She frowned at him, puzzled until he made an annoyed sound and explained, "Harlots."

"I am gentle," she said, pinching his arm. "And innocent! Most definitely not a harlot."

That damned smug eyebrow rose again. "And yet just a few minutes ago you were sitting on my lap, playing with my penis and trying to suck my tongue out of my head."

"That's because we're married," she protested, suddenly wondering if she had done something that breached an unwritten etiquette. She bit her lip and said more slowly, "I thought that is what married people do. Do they not touch each other and kiss and do all the things that my sainted mother told me was absolutely forbidden with the handsome blond groom who used to wash his naked upper parts in the stable yard?"

He looked back out the window, a muscle in his jaw working. "Yes, married people do those sorts of things."

"Then you take back the statement that I was acting like a harlot!"

"I never said such a thing. I was simply trying to reason out why you felt it vitally necessary to wed me when I was insensible, and I have ruled out the idea that Nelson would aid an unmarried woman. The only other reason must be because you're a German princess, and they wouldn't take you unless you were married to a British citizen."

"I'm Danish, thank you, not German."

"Indeed? My apologies for the incorrect label. Where exactly is Sonderburg-Beck?"

She looked out the small window. "Prussia."

He said nothing, but she could feel him thinking, damn him.

"You needn't adopt that martyred expression, Leo. I might have benefited from a marriage to you, but you also benefit. Not only will you *not* have to duel Frederick, but you are now married to a princess. By our marriage, your third cousin once removed is the King of Denmark."

"That is of great benefit, I'm sure." He tapped his lower lip. "Might I risk being considered material and ask you how big the Sonderburg-Beck holdings are?"

She stared at him, her mind reeling as she repeated, "The holdings?"

"Yes. Is there a castle? A manor house? How many hectares does the land run to? Is it in an agricultural area or industrial?"

Heat swept up from her neck, making her cheeks burn. "I have no idea how big the holdings are, or what the status is of a house or castle. Papa's title was not landed."

"Ah." He continued to look at her, making her feel both irritated (it wasn't her fault that her father had been stripped of his holdings by his family) and embarrassed (she had to admit that Leo had every reason to be angry with her). "I take it that the family fortune went the way of the lands?"

She straightened her shoulders. "Dearest Papa was cut off from his family when he chose to marry my mother, an Englishwoman. Even though she was a duke's daughter, they objected. He refused to give her up, and my grandfather forced him to leave the family home and ensured that he would not inherit anything but the title."

"A sad story."

"Not necessarily. My parents were extremely happy together." Dagmar tried to gather what dignity was left to her. "We were all very happy together until my mother was taken by consumption, and Dearest Papa died a year later."

Leo murmured a platitude that Dagmar acknowledged with an incline of her head.

"So, to recap the situation—" Leo started to say.

"Oh, I really wish you wouldn't."

His expression was filled with disbelief at the interruption.

"Well, I don't want you to recap," she explained with an annoyed gesture. "It's only going to make me blush harder and feel more as though I did take advantage of you, and I didn't, not really. These last few minutes have been painful enough without going over it again, don't you think?"

"On the contrary, I feel the need to make everything absolutely clear. And since the fever has left me a little weak in the thought processes, will you please take pity on me and enlighten me as to exactly how marriage to a penniless, landless Prussian-Danish princess will benefit me? Aside from not having to defend your honor to the crown prince?"

"You are an obnoxious man," she told him, feeling righteously indignant. "Obnoxious, selfish, and ungrateful."

"Selfish!"

"And ungrateful. Don't forget the ungrateful part, because I certainly haven't."

There was a wild glint to his eyes that made her wonder if the fever hadn't affected his brain. "No, we shouldn't forget how ungrateful I am to be married *without my consent* to a woman who was not my choice, solely to provide her a means of passage to a country I had no intention of returning to at this time. We shouldn't forget any of that, should we?"

"I saved your life, you self-centered oaf!" Dagmar yelled, poking him on the non-hurt side of his chest.

"After you married me while I was unconscious."

"You weren't unconscious. You just weren't terribly lucid!"

"Did it ever occur to you to question whether or not I wished to be married?"

Dagmar felt cold and hot at the same time.

"Whether I had a fiancée waiting for me at home?"

Dear God, he had a fiancée? Why hadn't she thought of asking him that before she married him?

"Or a woman whom I loved dearly and wished to spend my life with?"

Her stomach turned over, guilt at her actions making her lash out in return. "I asked you if you were married. You said no. If you were engaged to a woman, you should have said so."

"I was wounded!" he yelled. "Feverish and insensible by all accounts. Do you really expect that I'd enter into a lengthy discussion of my hopes and dreams at that moment?"

He had hopes and dreams? Dagmar wanted to cry. Princesses don't cry, however, at least not where others can see them. Her mother had never cried in front of anyone. "I…I…"

"No, you didn't think of any of that. You simply saw a chance to use me and use me you did."

Leo's eyes were molten with anger, his jaw tight, and his hand clenched where it lay against his hip.

It took a moment of blinking back the pricking in her eyes, but at last she was able to say, in a voice that was much smaller than normal, "I did the best I could at the time. I admit that my actions don't appear in the best light now, but you were not merely a means to an end."

"No?" The word had the velocity of a whip crack. "You married me, used me to get out of Denmark, and now you will expect me to provide for you for the rest of your life. How is that not using me?"

"Julia and I plan to have a shop to support ourselves. I mentioned that."

"A shop." He snorted, his expression telling her without words what he thought of that idea. "Do you have any idea what people would say about my wife being forced to run a shop in order to keep herself?"

The sick feeling in her stomach grew. She swallowed a couple times, wondering if she might not have need of Julia's bucket. "I did mention divorce. I am aware that I was not your choice, and that if it turned out that we couldn't get along amicably, we could divorce. You would then be free to wed the woman of your desire."

"Things may be different in Denmark, but in England we do not get divorces." His voice was as cold as the spray that blew up from the bow of the ship.

"It is illegal? I thought I read of a duke who—"

"It's not illegal, but it is just not done."

The emphasis of his words was unmistakable. "Then I will divorce you in Denmark," she said a bit desperately.

"Denmark or England—so far as society is concerned, it matters not. I would still be divorced, and thus a social pariah. I would effectively be ostracized from all polite society, from my friends and family, and any polite acquaintances. Do you know what society says about a man whose wife has divorced him?"

"No, but I've never been one who cares what society thinks. Do you?"

"Not particularly."

"Then why are you yelling at me about it?" Dagmar asked, relieved and frustrated at the same time.

Leo adopted a righteous tone. "Because you didn't know that I don't care what society thinks when you forced me to wed you!"

She looked at him sadly. "We're back to that, are we?"

"It seems a difficult subject to escape from," he said in a definitely gritty tone of voice.

"Only because you keep harping on it. No," she said, holding up a hand and forestalling the objection he started to make. "You've made it quite clear that divorce, even one conducted in Denmark, is unacceptable to you. That leaves us with two options: an annulment or we remain married, and I support Julia and myself by some method that will not derange your sense of dignity."

"If there's anyone who knows about derangement, it's you," he muttered quietly, but not quietly enough to avoid being heard.

"Then we will simply have to have the marriage annulled."

"Annulments are just as scandalous as a divorce," he snapped.

Dagmar chose to ignore his tone of voice and said, with quiet dignity that bespoke a princessly demeanor, "Since no other option will please you, I will look around when we get to England for some way to support us. You need not worry that I will shame you in any way. I worked too hard and too long to save your life to wish you ill, Leo. Or would you prefer, given your feelings about me, that I call you Lord March?"

"Leo is fine," he answered in a somewhat strangled voice. "Er…I don't believe I thanked you for the fact that you took me in when I was wounded."

"No, you haven't." Dagmar adopted a noble expression and decided that a little appreciation wouldn't go amiss. Leo might be in the right when it came to their unconventional wedding, but it wouldn't hurt him to realize just how close to death he had been. "The doctor told me you wouldn't last the night. He refused even to give you medicine for the fever that consumed you. My mother, however, taught me well, so Julia and I fed you fever draughts for days on end. I was at your side day and night during the worst of your fever, when you kept calling me a harpy and demanding that I let you suffer in peace. Yes, even when the ship's surgeon said he would assign men to watch over you, I left you only to snatch a few hours' sleep when I was about ready to fall to the floor with exhaustion. I did nothing but tend to you, *Lord March*, only so you could get well and become what Mama called the hindquarters of a donkey, which I shall not repeat because she only said that word during times of great stress and afterward always made me promise to forget I'd ever heard her say it. But I can think it, and I assure you that I'm doing so right now."

"I told you to call me Leo." His jaw worked for a few minutes before, to her intense surprise, he took her hand and lifted it to his mouth, pressing his lips to the back of her knuckles. "You can think that word with impunity because you're quite right—I am being an ass. And ungrateful and boorish. You might not think me worth the saving, but I do appreciate the fact that you took care of me so very well. The surgeon said you were a most devoted nursemaid."

Mollified, she withdrew her hand, mostly because her fingers were tingling where his mouth had touched her skin. She wondered if she could tempt him back to the bunk where she could kiss him again. "If we're apologizing, then I should do so as well. The doctor said you would not live through the night, and I thought that it wouldn't matter to you if you died married or unmarried. I never thought of my actions as using you, but I see now how it can appear that way. For that, I am sorry."

He looked silently at her, as if weighing her words. She gazed serenely back at him and was struck again with how pleasing his face was. Not handsome but... interesting. Intelligent. A pleasure to look at. She liked his eyes and his long nose and the way his lips quirked at the edges.

"It would appear we are at a *détente*."

She nodded. "I hope so. I raised my voice, and Mama always said that a princess should never raise her voice unless a wild boar or a bear was attacking."

"How oddly specific."

"Mama had very strong notions on how women should behave," Dagmar said with a little smile that turned into a rueful grimace. "She would have a few things to say to me about wedding you while you were..."

"Unconscious?"

"...not in the best state of mind. She'd expect me to be prostrate before you in penitence."

Leo laughed, a warm, rumbly sound that sent little

shivers of delight down her arms. "I can't imagine you prostrate with penitence before anyone, Princess."

"You may call me Dagmar, you know. What were you doing in Denmark if you weren't on your way from Russia to England?"

He stilled, making her think of a stag freezing as a hunter approached. "What makes you think I was in Russia?"

"You told me so. At least I think you did. It was the first night that we found you. You were raving with your fever, and you said something about being in Russia. Or did you? It seems so long ago. I can ask Julia. She might remember."

"Who exactly is this Julia woman? Is she your maidservant?"

"Not really. Her husband was an equerry with the British ambassador, but he died suddenly, and she was left without anyone in Copenhagen, so my mother took her on as a companion. I more or less inherited her when Dearest Papa died. Julia isn't the least bit sensible, you see, so I have to take care of her. That's why we thought we'd set up a shop in England."

"That, I believe, is a subject we shall set aside for the time being, lest we ruin the *détente*."

"I think," Dagmar said slowly, guiding Leo over to the bed. For some inexplicable reason, she had a need to touch him, and this was the only way she could think to do so without him making reference harlots again. Until she was sure of just how married people were supposed to behave with each other, she'd limit her contact with him to situations that appeared anything but lascivious. "I think that I would like to see to rebandaging your arm, and then we can discuss why you don't want to go back to England." A horrible thought struck her. "Has your father exiled you from your family and stripped you of all your inheritance too?"

"No. My father has been dead since I was four, and my bandages are fine. The surgeon saw to them earlier, while you were sleeping." He eyed her but allowed her to push him gently down onto the bed. "Why did you choose to turn your back on your illustrious connections in Denmark? It seems to me that it would have been far easier to allow the crown prince to see to your welfare than wed a stranger."

"Why were you in Russia but you don't want me to know about it?" she countered.

"Why didn't you apply to your mother's family for aid in getting to England if that's what you wanted so badly?"

"Who's Amadelle, and why did you have her kitten?"

"That was amusing," he said agreeably, crossing one leg over the other and leaning back against the pillow. "Shall we go around again?"

"If you insist. Why did you have a piece of paper in your boot that contains mostly numbers and a few words in English?"

His hand twitched as if he was reaching for his foot.

"It's in the chest," Dagmar said, nodding toward that object. "We put it there with your other belongings, not that you had much with you. What *were* you doing out in my back garden?"

"Being attacked by someone wielding a saber if the surgeon is anyone to go by, and I'm assuming he recognizes a saber wound when he sees one. Why didn't you go to the British ambassador if you needed assistance? Or the king?"

"The king, as you most likely know, is not quite himself, hence Frederick being named the regent. And I did go to the ambassador. He refused to help me because of the Sonderburg-Beck connection. Feelings appear to be running somewhat hot right now between Prussia and England."

"Mmm. So I was your only opportunity for leaving Copenhagen? Why didn't you simply go out to the country if the navy's attack was too much for you?"

"Oh, my need to leave had nothing to do with your navy arriving to sink all the ships."

"I doubt if they sank them all," he said gently.

"No, but they sank enough that I have no doubt the navy will conscript any merchant's ships available until new warships can be built. I thought we were going to forgo recapping the events of the past few weeks?"

He smiled. "You want to avoid it; I have no such desire."

Her lips tightened. She stood before him by turns frustrated, angry, frightened, and guilty, wanting to lash out, but knowing it would do no good. He wasn't to blame for the situation; this was clearly a case of the odious adage about sleeping in a bed she'd made.

She didn't have to like it, though. And since a cranky princess is not a princess whose company is to be enjoyed, she walked out of the cabin without a look or a word.

Six

Docility, humility, and modesty are the princess's bywords. A docile, humble, and modest princess is not a princess who angers the reigning monarch (or his eldest son appointed to rule in his stead) by filling said eldest son's favorite riding gloves with wood lice.

—*Princess Christian of Sonderburg-Beck's Guide for Her Daughter's Illumination and Betterment*

Leo had planned on speaking with the captain after seeing Dagmar, but as irritated as he was, he felt in need of a few minutes to calm his raging emotions. On the one hand, he had a delicious, tempting woman to whom he was legally married, one who fired his blood as no woman had done for a very long time. Just the memory of the heat of her breasts in his hands, the sweetness of her mouth, and the way she touched him had him hard and aching.

And wishing he hadn't been so quick to anger her. Even now, she could be in his bunk kissing him and touching him and allowing him free rein to do all those things that he suddenly wanted to do to her.

But a man had his pride, and she had ruffled his. At least his rage about being used for selfish purposes had passed. Her eyes had been utterly without guile when she admitted the truth behind their marriage. Given that and the evidence of his own body, he was quite prepared to believe that he truly had one foot over death's threshold, and given her desperate situation—what he knew of it—he supposed that were he in her shoes, he might have acted the same way.

"What I know of it," he mused to himself, one arm behind his head as he stretched out on the bunk. "There's something you aren't telling me, my innocent, gentle wife. What could it be, I wonder?"

He had a very good sense when it came to secrets, and Dagmar was clearly trying to conceal something from him. But what could it be? A scandal? That was entirely likely, given her madcap ways and apparently nontraditional upbringing, but it wasn't a thought that particularly distressed him. Whatever scandal there might be would be left behind in Denmark.

Perhaps it was gambling debts? That was also possible, but again, it didn't overly concern him. He had enough wealth to support them both, and he would simply put his foot down about anything above a modest wager.

A word snuck around the edges of his mind.

What if she had to leave town because of a lover?

He sat up, frowning furiously at nothing. "No," he told the empty cabin. "That I will not accept. She didn't know how to kiss at all when we first started."

Although Lord knew she learned fast enough. By the time he had managed to tear himself away from her, she had him shaking with need to possess her. All of her.

The thought that any other man might have stirred the desire he saw in her eyes was unthinkable. Impossible and unthinkable.

He made immediate plans to find someone who would know of all the romantic scuttlebutt in the Danish court, and then instantly felt ashamed of his suspicions. Dagmar had said repeatedly that she was innocent, and he had no reason to disbelieve her.

Which still left unanswered the question of what she was hiding. He was stretched out on his bunk, mulling over that question and what he was going to do upon his unexpected return to England, when the captain tapped on the door, a second man accompanying him.

"Maltheson tells me ye'll live to see another day." The captain, a grizzled man with skin like a tanned hide, eyed him with accurate assessment.

"For which I have the good doctor to thank," Leo answered.

"From what I be understandin', ye should be thankin' your wife more than the doctor. I'm told she refused all help with ye until she knew ye'd survive." The captain gestured to the other man. "This is Mr. Philip Dalton. Thought you might like to have someone to talk to who ain't a woman."

The captain retired from the room before Leo could protest that he wasn't in need of any company.

The man named Dalton looked embarrassed and

rubbed his jaw. "My apologies for intruding on you when I'm sure you'd prefer to be resting, but as we are running out of time, I felt it vital to speak to you before we reach London."

"In what way are we running out of time?" Leo was intrigued despite himself, damn his overdeveloped curiosity. "I don't believe I've had the pleasure of meeting you in Copenhagen, have I?"

"No, although I was told that you were expected to pass that way." Dalton sat in the one available chair at Leo's gesture. "I had no idea that you were going to make an appearance in such a dramatic fashion, however."

"No more so did I," Leo said, grimacing and moving his shoulder slightly to a more comfortable position.

Dalton laughed. "I'm sure not. I simply wanted to speak with you before the ship docked, which I'm told will be very shortly."

"Ah. I'm curious that you were informed that I was in the vicinity," Leo said casually, watching the man out of the corner of his eye. He wanted very much to know just who this man was and how he became privy to knowledge that shouldn't have been bandied about. Leo's business in Russia had been very hush-hush and only a few men outside of England knew of it.

"Lord Salter gave me your name and said that you might be of some service to me should I find you in Copenhagen, where he said you would be stopping en route to Berlin. Alas, I was unable to find you until my sister and I boarded this ship for a return to our home in London."

Leo sat up straight. The man was entirely too

knowledgeable about his business. Just who the devil was he? "You know Lord Salter?"

"He's my godfather." Dalton smiled. "I will say that you are a difficult man to find. I had a hell of a time running you to earth. Lord Bexley, who is acting as ambassador, tried to find you and had no luck. I went to the crown prince, but he'd never heard of you. I realize that this is probably the last thing you wish to hear during your recovery, but Lord Salter urged me to lay my problem at your feet and beg for your help."

Leo felt as if hundreds of ants were crawling over him at the thought of so many people trying to locate him. Dammit, his job frequently depended on him keeping out of the sight of people, not having everyone hunting for him.

"It wasn't until I ran into the admiral that my luck turned."

"The admiral?" Leo scratched at his shoulder. The wound was starting to itch, which he hoped was a good sign and not one that fleas had set up habitation. "Which admiral?"

"Nelson."

"Dagmar mentioned that Nelson was in Copenhagen. What I'd like to know is why I wasn't told of those plans before I arrived in Denmark."

"As to that, I cannot guess. My godfather didn't tell me any of what his plans were. I ran into Nelson at the palace; he was in Copenhagen shortly before we sailed, but last I heard, he was off to Karlskrona to deal with the Swedes."

"I see. And in what manner did Lord Salter wish for me to help you?"

Dalton pulled out a cigar case and offered it to Leo, taking one for himself when the former shook his head. "It has to do with my nephew's death. We are unsatisfied that the person responsible has eluded capture."

"Dalton?" Leo searched his memory for anyone of that name out in Scandinavia or Russia. "I don't believe I know of any Dalton other than you. Was your nephew with the admiralty or the foreign office?"

"Neither." Dalton took a deep breath. "He was a very pious young man, one who desperately wished to take orders and become a priest. Given that a riding accident early on left him unable to sire children, it certainly would have been a good occupation for him, but until his father died, he was unable to pursue that calling."

Ah, it was simply a case of nepotism at work. That he could deal with. "Lord Salter's opinion aside, I'm afraid that I can be of little help in finding out who killed your nephew. I haven't been in England in several months and would be at a loss as to investigating his death. I have a friend, however, who might be able to help you if he's not busy with his own work for the Home Office."

"My godfather was adamant that you were the man to help us," Dalton said quickly. "And I don't need help in finding who murdered Algernon; that, at least, I know. What I need help with is finding her."

"Would it not be easier to simply turn this information over to the authorities?"

"We have. They can do little since the woman disappeared twenty-one years ago."

"I'm sorry, but there's no way I could possibly help with something that occurred so long ago—"

"She was in Copenhagen a few months ago," Dalton interrupted. "A letter from her to a cousin, who is in the employ of a neighbor, was discovered and turned over to me. That is why we made the journey to Denmark. And that is why my godfather thought you could help find her—he knew you were bound to be in the area, and given your area of expertise, you might reasonably be able to find the woman where we could not. Louisa and I set sail immediately for Copenhagen."

"Where I was lying insensible and near death."

"Exactly." Dalton puffed his cigar for a few moments. "When we couldn't find you, or even word of your whereabouts, we gave up hope and convinced Admiral Nelson to allow us to sail home on this ship. We were flabbergasted to find out that you were on board as well."

"Frustrating on all accounts, but I don't see what I can do to help you now," Leo said, his curiosity piqued despite common sense warning him there was little he could do. He had always had a taste for mystery, and tracking down a murderer appealed greatly to his sense of justice.

"I understand that your wife is Danish." Dalton made a gesture with his cigar. "In fact, my sister and I met her briefly at the palace a few weeks ago, but we did not know then who she was. It is our hope that perhaps the princess might be able to tell us something about the woman we seek."

Leo was a little surprised by that. "Is this murderess someone gently born?"

"Not to my knowledge. She was employed as

governess for my two daughters. Her name was Margaret Prothero."

The name meant nothing to Leo, but he made a mental note to ask Dagmar if it was familiar.

He rubbed his chin. "I will speak to my wife, of course, but I hesitate to give you any hope. I gather from what Dagmar has told me of her parents that they did not go out in society much, and she has been in deep mourning for the last year. Then there's the amount of time that's passed—Dagmar would have been a babe in arms when this Prothero woman left England for Copenhagen."

"Unfortunately, I don't know when she fled to Denmark; it could be anytime during the last twenty-one years. The letter handed to me made no mention of her arrival; it simply said that she was quite comfortable in Copenhagen."

"It's not very likely that Dagmar would have met her," Leo answered with gentle regret.

"Perhaps not, but I will appreciate all the help you can give me. And in consideration of that, I will give you a bit of news that should brighten your spirits. The captain told me after we had set sail that your horse had been found just a few days before running wild through the streets of Copenhagen and that the admiral felt you would be happier if he was shipped home with you."

Leo closed his eyes for a moment in order to remember the last time he had seen the beastly animal. He had a vague recollection of Galahad disappearing into the distance but had no idea why the horse had bolted. All things considered, he was pleased Galahad was on board the ship and made a promise to visit him that evening and make sure he was being attended to properly. "That was kindness indeed."

"Would you mind if I ask—I hate to be nosy, but my sister is much fascinated by the admiral's tale that the captain related to us—is it true that you wed Princess Dagmar after you had been so grievously wounded? We were agog to hear the trials your wife went through keeping you alive, and her subsequent bravery in taking on the entire British Royal Navy to get you home to England so that you might die in peace, an eventuality which happily for all did not occur. It's said that the princess found you in her back garden, near to death and unable to speak."

Leo wondered just who the captain was that Nelson felt so chummy as to tell him so much, and added to his mental list of things to do that of having a chat with the captain about telling everyone his business. "Princess Dagmar did indeed find me and evidently married me under the assumption that I was going to die immediately thereafter. Of her bravery in getting me on board the ship, I have no comment save that I'm sure she moved heaven and earth. She is a very single-minded woman, and I have no doubt that Nelson fell like a tower of sugar before her force."

"I haven't had the chance to speak to her, but from our brief meeting in Copenhagen, I agree that the Admiral likely didn't stand a chance against her. You are to be congratulated for making an advantageous marriage out of such a poor beginning."

Leo made a face. "Poor beginning is an understatement. I don't even remember seeing her until I came out of the fever a few days ago."

"Now that is a shame. The princess is quite worth looking upon, and had I been younger, I would have made much of my initial meeting with her."

Leo's gaze shot swiftly to the other man, but it was evident by the amusement on Dalton's face that the latter was teasing him.

"She is a beauty," Leo agreed, spending a few moments thinking over just how pleasing Dagmar was on a physical level. His body had absolutely no trouble appreciating her appearance, but it was her mind that troubled him. The very fact that she'd wed herself to a man who was near death left him floundering between gratitude and annoyance. "What if she is disappointed that she isn't a widow?"

He wasn't aware he had spoken the thought aloud until Dalton, with due consideration, answered, "There's something in that, you know. My own late wife, rest her soul, often told me that there were days when she would have happily pushed me off a cliff. I've always felt that no woman would wish to be on her own without any menfolk to take care of her, but my sister, Louisa, has often declared just the opposite, and in truth, she appears quite contented to be on her own. Perhaps the princess would be happier likewise, although the point is moot now, isn't it? There's not much she can do even if she would have preferred that you not survive the journey home."

Leo shot him another look, a bit startled with how personal a turn the conversation had taken, although he had no one but himself to blame for that. "Er…"

"I'll tell you," Dalton said, setting down his cigar and leaning forward. "You may wish to have a word with your good lady. Louisa heard from the captain that her servant—the princess's servant, not Louisa's—was speaking about ways to end the marriage."

A clammy sensation seemed to grip his vitals. "Dagmar wishes to be rid of me?"

"As to that, I couldn't say." Dalton reclaimed his cigar, gave it a few puffs, and leaned back, adding, "This is only hearsay, mind you, but the princess's maid was overheard talking to the surgeon about how the only honorable thing to do was to divorce you so that you would be none the worse. Dr. Maltheson told Louisa that the maid had other ideas, but that the princess seemed pretty set on that plan of action."

Silence fell in the cabin. Leo struggled with the desire to unburden himself of his worries to this apparently trustworthy man, but a natural tendency to keep his private business close to his chest had him simply saying, "You needn't worry that I'm going to allow Dagmar to do anything so rash as divorce. She has ideas with which I do not necessarily agree."

He was mildly surprised to find that he meant what he said. Divorce was out, no matter how the Danes felt about the idea. Annulment held no attraction for him (and he refused to admit that the interest his body had in Dagmar was most likely responsible for that feeling). "The idea of her running a shop is ludicrous at best."

"She wants to run a shop?" Dalton looked surprised at first but after a few minutes silent smoking said, "I'd be willing to wager that if any woman could make a go of it, she could. She has a purpose of mind that would guarantee success."

"I have a nagging feeling that you're correct. Still, the idea is impossible. I won't have it be said that my wife had to support herself in that manner."

"I'm sure that, given time, you'll work out the problems that the unusual circumstances of your marriage present to you. Now, the captain wanted me to pass along the information that we should be arriving in London tomorrow morning. I hope you won't consider it forward of me to ask if you have a place to stay in town. I'm sure you must, but whether that domicile is suitable for someone of the princess's stature is a question that occurred to Louisa and me. If not, you must allow us to open my home to you and your wife."

Oh Lord, the housing situation. Leo thought over his bachelor digs and immediately discounted them. His landlady had a horror of what she termed "bawdy women" dragging down both her good name and that of her lodging house, and for that reason, never allowed female visitors into the building. Nick, the man he shared lodgings with, once had tried to shelter his half sister overnight until she could be put on a carriage out to the country, and it took some fast talking on both their parts in order to keep all three of them from finding themselves on the street. There was no way that Dagmar could be housed in his rooms, even assuming Nick wasn't around.

"I appreciate the offer, but I assure you that it's not necessary to shelter her in order to gain Dagmar's help. She will, I'm sure, be more than willing to assist you if it's at all within her means."

"No, no, I wasn't motivated by that desire," Dalton

protested. "I am quite confident that the princess will give us what assistance she can. I am simply offering what I know my godfather would wish for me to make available."

Leo almost laughed at the face the older man made at his own words.

"You'd think after all my years, I'd have learned to express myself without insulting the recipient, wouldn't you? I have been too long in the country, I fear. Allow me to redress what injury I have just made and assure you that I am not offering you accommodations solely due to obligations put upon me by Lord Salter. Since my wife's death, I have had few opportunities to indulge in entertaining, and none since Louisa has returned from Italy. We would be delighted to have you stay with us."

"I much appreciate the offer and will consider your kind invitation." Leo took the card that Dalton handed him. "And speaking of Lord Salter, I suppose I should present myself to him immediately upon my arrival to explain why I'm there in London rather than Germany, as I ought to be." Leo didn't relish telling his superior what had happened to send him so far astray, mostly because he didn't know himself. "As for the business with my wife...you won't...er...let it be known that she's been speaking of events which will not be happening? I refer to the dissolution of our marriage. She has the best of intentions but doesn't fully realize that we do things differently in England."

Dalton rose and gave him a reassuring smile. "Naturally, the gossip shall go no further. And now, if you don't mind my impertinence, I should advise you to stay in bed and rest. You look as though you could use a full fortnight of sleep."

"There are moments when I feel that way as well. I will speak to Dagmar at the earliest convenience about your problem. Do you have a description of the individual that I might give her?"

"I'll have Louisa write one up. I never saw the woman myself, but Louisa recalls meeting her once or twice. Good day, Lord March."

Leo lay back on his pillows and thought of the tangled mess that was an unexpected marriage, his wounded arm, the mysterious murderess, and the manner in which his job had veered off course.

He had an uncanny feeling that unraveling that tangle would tax his every ability, including that concerning Dagmar.

Especially Dagmar.

Seven

A royal Tabernacle of Aphrodite is not open to all. Visitations should be limited to husbands only or, in dire circumstances of great need, a physician. It should be also noted that if the crown prince's new and quite handsome young physician continues to appear daily with the intention of applying a soothing balm to a princess's tabernacle, this privilege will be revoked.

—Princess Christian of Sonderburg-Beck's Guide for Her Daughter's Illumination and Betterment

DAGMAR TOOK TO LONDON IMMEDIATELY. PERHAPS IT was the thrilling knowledge that she was returning to her mother's homeland. Perhaps it was a spirit of adventure that she'd be hard-pressed to ignore. Perhaps it was the fact that she was no longer beholden to Frederick for every little thing.

Perhaps it was the man to whom she was now legally bound. She slid a sidelong look at him as Julia bustled up beside her, saying a bit breathlessly,

"London at last! Oh, my dear princess, I cannot tell you how happy I am to be gazing upon its dear old sights again."

Leo stood with his arm held stiffly at his side, one shoulder slightly higher than the other as he watched the gangway being moved into place. He was hatless and clad in a loose blue coat and black trousers, both of which had been provided by the admiral responsible for the destruction of all the Danish ships. Leo's expression was inscrutable, but his face made for pleasant viewing nonetheless. Dagmar found she liked watching him. She liked how interested he was in something so mundane as the moving of a gangway.

"Ah, the beloved scents of London!"

She liked how his hair ruffled in the wind. She hadn't really appreciated just how nice his hair was, but now she did, and just the thought of running her fingers through it gave her odd little tingles.

"Look! A hackney carriage! How dear it all seems after having been gone for so very long."

She also liked his hands. She hadn't ever thought about a man's hands before, but Leo had very nice ones, with long, sensitive fingers. She imagined those fingers touching her in places that only she had ever touched, and grew simultaneously hot and chilled.

"How I have missed the embrace of a vital city bursting with life!"

Dagmar had heard that men like touching women in such places. Would Leo be like other men and wish to touch her in those intimate spots? She was in the middle of framing the question in such a way as to appear neither a shameless hussy with needy personal parts nor an overly coy maiden who may not know exactly the way of such things but didn't wish to appear ignorant, when a thought struck her. Would Leo expect her to reciprocate such touches? She considered the memory of Leo in his bath. Men, she thought to herself, were singularly unlucky to have their plumbing parts external rather than tucked away neatly as women did. Still, she supposed it was only fair that if he saw fit to use those long, long fingers in ways that she was even now planning, then she should be prepared to do the same for him.

"The ebb and flow of London life, sweeping me up and sending me spinning, giddy with delight!"

Dagmar stopped thinking about Leo and his interesting hands and turned to gaze with astonishment at her companion. Julia was leaning against the railing of the ship, her eyes glazed with some emotion. "Julia, are you feeling quite well?"

"Yes, my dearest princess, I feel wonderful! We are in England again!"

"So I gathered."

Her dry tone was lost on the other woman. Julia flung wide her arms and said, "It has been so long… not that I haven't been grateful for Her Highness, your esteemed mama, for taking me in at my time of need…but oh, this blessed plot, this earth, this realm, this England!"

"*King Richard the Second*," Dagmar said absently, having been no stranger to Shakespeare while her mother lived.

"Act two, scene one," Julia said with a happy sigh.

"To be returned to the land of my birth—words fail me, my dearest princess. They fail me!"

Dagmar kindly did not point out the falsity of such a statement and instead returned to contemplating Leo as he stood waiting patiently for the gangway to be tied down.

"And what of you, dearest one? Surely you must feel something having arrived at the birthplace of half of your ancestors? Does your heart quicken? Do you wish to sing out your praises for all that is English? Are you gazing down upon these simple folk and feeling with them a kinship of the most primal sort?"

"No, I'm watching Leo," Dagmar answered with honesty. "Although I am indulging in some pretty primal thoughts about his hands. Do you know, I think he must be feeling better. His appearance is so much improved. I remarked to myself when he was ill that he wasn't at all a handsome man, but now he's quite changed that opinion. He's very dashing, don't you think?"

"Oh, yes, very dashing, very dashing indeed. It's just a shame about his shoulder."

"I like his shoulders!" Dagmar said, a bit startled by how defensively the words were spoken.

"But do you not regret the one being higher than the other? It ruins the balance of his figure."

"Bah on balance. His shoulders are very nice. They're suitably broad to make me feel delicate and tiny, and as you know—" She straightened up, which had the effect of hoisting upward her substantial bosom. She was ready to swear that said bosom was even larger today than it had been a few days before. Drat that sea air! "As you know, I am anything but tiny."

"I apologize if you think I've said anything to belittle Lord Marsh's figure—" Julia started to say, but Dagmar interrupted her when Leo gestured at them. The gangway had finally been moved into place.

"At last! Come, Julia, let us sally forth and see this precious London of yours."

"Is that all the luggage you have?" Leo asked, frowning when Dagmar and Julia each picked up their respective bandboxes and moved forward. "Where are your trunks?"

"We don't have any trunks, and yes, this is all that we possess other than a boiled pig's head and half a cheese wheel, but I left those with one of Frederick's guards who has a puppy."

"The dear princess had to sell so many lovely gowns just so we might eat," Julia lamented, following when Leo took Dagmar's arm and helped her down the rough gangway. "It broke my heart to know that her dearest mama's jewels and gowns had to go in such a manner, but alas, I was unable to stop her from doing so."

"You didn't tell me that you were destitute," Leo said softly, setting Dagmar's bandbox on top of a small leather satchel that held the few items of clothing he'd been given by the captain.

She made a little face of distaste while he helped Julia down. "I believe I told you that I would have to borrow a little money to set up our shop. I will repay it, naturally."

"We'll talk about that at a later time. Here, you!" Leo strode off to one of the men lounging around the dock, scattering orders as he went. Within a very short space of time, Leo had engaged two hackney carriages, one small and barely able to contain two people, and the other larger, into which Leo placed Julia and their small amount of luggage.

"I can't wait to see your house," Dagmar said when she and Leo squished into the remaining carriage.

"What house?"

"The house we're going to."

"We aren't going to a house."

Dagmar turned to look at him, icy fingers (not nearly so long and sensitive as Leo's) gripping her stomach. "You're not letting me see your house? You're going to annul me right away?"

Leo gave a sigh that was tinged with more than a little bit of exasperation. "I do not intend to apply for an annulment today, no."

A bit of the fear eased, but hurt promptly filled the void. "Then why won't you take me to your house? Is it because you're ashamed of me?"

"No—"

"I am a princess, you know," Dagmar said, straightening her shoulders again. Leo's eyes dropped to her bosom when it thrust forward. "And I can't help that."

"Help what?" he asked, a puzzled look on his face when he managed (finally) to pull his gaze from her upper story.

"My bosom. I told you that the sea air made it grow. I think it's very mean of you to not let me even stay one night in your house, Leo. I realize that you don't want to be married to me, but I *am* a princess and the granddaughter of one of your English dukes, so I'm not someone about whom you should be so embarrassed that you can't let your servants see."

"It's not that at all—"

"Then you'll take me to your house?"

"No."

Dagmar felt a sudden need to throttle him but fought down that emotion as being unworthy of a princess. "Why not?"

"Because I don't have a house in town."

She gawked at him. "But you're an earl."

"And a viscount and a baron." He grimaced and tugged at the borrowed neckcloth that was wound around his neck in an intricate manner. "But none of those titles comes with a house in London."

Dagmar was slightly incensed by his breezy manner. "How can you have three titles but no house?"

"You have a title and don't have a house," he pointed out in a maddening manner.

"That's one title. You have three."

"Your title outweighs mine. I'm just a lowly earl, viscount, and baron. You're a bona fide princess. You merit a *serene* in front of your name. That makes your title worth at least two and a half times all of mine combined."

"Your math is faulty," Dagmar said dismissively but spent a few minutes in mental arithmetic. Drat the man; he was right. Her title was more prestigious than his. Even penniless, landless, and a hair's breadth away from being forced into a French convent, her title was the weightier. "Damn," she said.

His eyebrows waggled at her.

"Fine. I shan't cast aspersions at your title for not coming with a house in London, but I would like to

point out that until Dearest Papa died, we had Yellow
House, which is really a small palace."

"Point duly noted." Leo shifted uncomfortably, and
Dagmar was suddenly worried that he was doing too
much too soon after having recovered.

"If you aren't taking me to your house, where are
we going?"

"To my rooms in Whitehall. You can't stay there—
they are strictly bachelor lodgings—but until I can look
around and find a house for us to take, it's that or a hotel,
and you can't stay at a hotel without proper servants."

She didn't like the faint white lines that appeared
alongside his mouth. They told of a gritted determination not to acknowledge pain. He *was* doing too
much, drat him. "Are they far?"

"Servants? I'm sure we could engage a few
quickly enough."

"No, your rooms. Are they far? You need to rest. I
can see your shoulder is hurting, which means you've
overextended yourself. The surgeon was most adamant that you use your left arm as little as possible—"

"I know what he said," Leo interrupted. "I was
right there when he said it. No, my rooms aren't far,
but you need not concern yourself with my health. I
assure you I'm quite over the worst. My arm doesn't
hurt at all now."

Dagmar gently pressed his shoulder.

Leo yelped and swore, jerking to the side.

Dagmar raised her left eyebrow just as he'd done to
her the day before.

"Well, it's going to hurt if you beat on me like
that," he said indignantly.

"I am all things contrite," she apologized. "But it does prove my point that you have overdone it, and you need to restrict your activities until such time as you really are better. For now, we just need to get you into bed."

"That will have to be later as well. Once I drop you and your friend at my rooms, I must go into the city to meet with my employers. They will want to know why I am in London rather than where I should be."

"You can do that later. You should rest first."

"No, I need to do it right away. They won't have heard what happened to me, and I will need to explain it myself—assuming I can do so when I can't remember what happened to me."

"You're tired and hurting. The explanation can no doubt wait until tomorrow."

Leo turned as best he could in the cramped interior of the carriage and frowned at her. "Stop giving me orders. I don't like it."

"I'm a princess. You yourself pointed out that I outrank you. Therefore, you have to do what I say."

"I'm also your husband, and thus the head of the family, in addition to which I don't like being told what to do."

She could be as annoyed as he could. "And you think I do?"

"You're a female," he pointed out, evidently feeling that explained it all.

"You must be extremely ill indeed if you think that has anything to do with the discussion."

By the time they arrived at a tan stone building set in a street of similar tan stone buildings, Dagmar had stated her determination to have her (even more distant than the Danish king) cousin George behead him if he didn't heed her wisdom and rest before attempting any action so foolish as going out into the damp spring air, and Leo was threatening to go out and purchase the first scold's bridle he could, which then led to a heated discussion about exactly what a scold's bridle was, how it was used, and what she (Dagmar) would do to him (Leo) should he ever come within a three-mile radius of her with such a vile contraption.

"And if you were to so much as even wave that thing in my face, you would be a very sorry individual, because it would not be me who was wearing it!" Dagmar finished as Leo handed her out of the carriage.

"A scold's bridle would be too small to fit on a man's head," Leo answered with a slight twitch of his lips.

"You wouldn't be wearing it on your head," she answered darkly.

"Oh, really?"

Julia hurried over to them, her face alight with pleasure, an expression that faded into confusion when Leo added in a tone that matched Dagmar's, "Just how exactly would you intend to silence me if the bridle is not used on my face?"

"You have *other* orifices on your body than your mouth," she said with a toss of her head before marching up the five steps to the door.

"Princess!" Julia gasped, casting a scandalized look at her. "Ladies do not mention gentlemen's fundaments in such a manner!"

To Dagmar's surprise, Leo met her statement with a laugh. "If anyone told me that one day a princess would threaten to shove a medieval metal implement up my—" He stopped, eyed Julia, and with a twist of his lips, turned to pay the two carriage drivers.

The door behind Dagmar opened to reveal an unwashed servant in dirty, stained clothing. "Aye?" he asked, giving her a leering once-over that instantly made Dagmar feel itchy.

"Entrance without the opportunity of catching body vermin would be welcome, but I suspect not entirely possible," she answered coldly, not appreciating the leer or the way the man moved to stand closer to her. She turned to look over her shoulder, calling out, "Leo, on what floor are your rooms?"

"Second," he answered, evidently in the middle of an argument with one of the carriage drivers. "But don't go up yet. I'm not sure if the man who shares my lodgings is in or not."

The repulsive man at the door sucked his teeth, continuing to eye her with a speculative glint that faded into a knowing half smile. Dagmar waited as patiently as she could until Leo returned, allowing him to escort her up three flights of narrow, ill-lit stairs until arriving at a small suite of rooms.

The rooms appeared to be empty and bore an uninhabited air that had Leo sighing in relief. "Looks like Nick is out of the country too."

"Nick is the man with whom you share your rooms?"

"Yes. He also does some work for the government."

"Does he do the same thing as you?" Dagmar asked, more because she wanted to keep Leo there than because she was interested in his friends. The way he was standing clearly indicated he was in pain.

Leo's gaze flickered briefly to Julia. "Something like that. Well, it looks like you ladies will have the place to yourself. Set the bags there, Jacob. I won't need you any further today, although you can check with the ladies later to see if they want tea or food. This, as you can see, is the sitting room. Stay here while I see the landlady. She is very strict about visitors and doesn't allow females at all."

"That's going to make living here a little awkward," Dagmar said, looking around, her eyes widening as she did so. The room was done in astonishing shades of pink-and-green plaid, not at all what she thought of as a gentleman's decor.

"She won't let you live here," Leo said from the door, the white lines around his mouth etching a bit deeper.

Dagmar wanted desperately to make him rest but was at a loss as to how to go about doing that. He seemed disinclined to obey any orders given him, and she doubted whether tears would be effective, assuming she managed to summon them up.

"Then why are you seeing her?" she asked.

"I'm going to tell her that you're both here just a few hours while I find some sort of accommodation. Ring for Jacob if you need anything, and stay put and out of trouble. And don't wander around the rest of the house. Mrs. Lovelily wouldn't like that at all."

"I have the feeling that we've been dumped just as summarily as our luggage," Dagmar told Julia as the door closed behind Leo. "And I don't like that feeling one little bit."

"I think it was a kindness of Lord March to bring us to his private lodgings rather than making us bounce around in those horrid carriages while he finds us a place to live," Julia said, rubbing her arms against the chill in the room. "Do you think we might ask that man for a fire?"

Dagmar glanced at the fireplace but saw no coal. "We could, or we could warm up by means of a brisk walk around town. I'm anxious to see London after you've sung its praises so much, and Leo will probably be away for a few hours."

"But dearest Dagmar, Lord March specifically said for us to stay here." Julia looked horrified at the thought of disobeying Leo's strictures.

Oddly, that made Dagmar want to do so even more than before. She strolled over to the window and looked down on the street below. One of the carriages remained, obviously waiting for Leo. "We've been cooped up on a ship for endless months—"

"It wasn't really more than two weeks, my dear—"

Leo dashed out of the door and jumped into the carriage. The driver flicked his whip, and the carriage lurched forward. Drat the man for casting aside Julia and her as though they were a pair of dirty boots. "And now that we're able to move around again, you want to stay trapped inside these horrible, dusty rooms? Not me. I'd rather get some exercise and see the sights. At least the ones local to this area."

"But his lordship—"

She turned her back to the window and patted her hip to make sure her funds (the few coins and banknotes that Leo had on his person when they found him) were secure in the pocket buttoned to the inside of her gown. "His lordship is gone, and I have no intention of moldering in this room. Stay here if you wish. I'll tell that repulsive man to build a fire so you won't take chill."

"My dear, I think this is most unwise—"

Dagmar closed the door on Julia's protests, jumping slightly when a man loomed out of the shadows at her. She thought at first it was Jacob, but this man, although clad in clothes of equal repugnance, appeared less filthy. He was slightly taller than Leo and had thick, curly black hair. He paused when he saw her.

"Mrs. Deworthy would like a fire," Dagmar told him, assuming he was another servant.

The man raised his eyebrows. "She would?"

"Yes, she is chilled. I happen to think it's rather balmy out, but Julia has always been rather thin blooded."

"I'm sorry to hear that."

"I'm going out," Dagmar continued, pulling on the pair of gloves that had more holes than doeskin remaining. "I realize that Lord March said to stay put, but he is sadly mistaken if he thinks I have nothing better to do with my time than to wait around for his return."

"Ah, you are one of Leo's...er..." The man, who seemed nicely spoken for a servant, nodded toward the door.

"Yes." The more Dagmar thought about it, the more annoyed she was with Leo simply parking them at his room and leaving. Clearly he was going to find some hotel or other in which he could lodge them and conveniently forget their existence. To be honest, she didn't blame him for that, since he hadn't asked for the responsibility of Julia and her to be thrust upon him. Well, her mother had raised her better than to be a burden. She was a princess, and she had all of ten pounds hidden in her underthings; she'd go out and find a shop she could take over, preferably one with lodgings attached. Then Leo would be absolved of all responsibilities toward them. "If he comes back before I return, you may tell him that I am seeking alternate means of support."

"Alternate means…" The man blinked a few times as she brushed past him. "Here, I don't think Leo is going to like it if you're off looking for another protector while you're with him. And just who is Mrs. Deworthy?"

"She's my companion."

The man shot a startled look at the door. "Leo has…he arranged for *both* of you?"

He sounded oddly scandalized. Clearly he wasn't used to ladies of their quality. "Yes, of course. I couldn't leave Julia behind, and Leo said she must stay with us."

The man, who appeared to be in his middle twenties, frowned. "You are German?"

"Danish. Julia's English, though."

"And you and Leo and this Julia…" He made a vague stirring gesture. "All three of you? At the same time?"

What a very odd man. She didn't understand why he was so confused by the idea of Julia living with Leo and her, but evidently he was. Before she could explain that it wasn't necessarily going to happen—thus her going out to seek a shop and lodgings—the man continued on.

"No, never mind, it's none of my business what Leo does."

"Exactly so," Dagmar said, approving of that sentiment. She passed him and started down the stairs, calling after her, "Don't forget Julia's fire."

She emerged into the late spring morning, took a deep breath of coal-scented air tinged with horse manure, and set off to set off at a brisk walk to see what sort of a future was available to her.

Eight

It is right and proper for a princess to revere her family. It is wrong for her to call her cousin a fat-headed ignorant son of a puss-filled weasel.

—*Princess Christian of Sonderburg-Beck's Guide for Her Daughter's Illumination and Betterment*

LEO'S SHOULDER WAS ON FIRE, HIS CHEST ACHED, AND his head felt hot, all of which contributed to the general horrible nature of the day. He'd had no luck finding a hotel suitable for a gentlewoman, and his only relation who had a house in town had let it for the spring and summer and was off enjoying himself in sunnier climes.

Leo climbed back into the hired hack, wanting nothing more than to go home and crawl into bed for a year or two, but his ears still rang with the words that his landlady had hurled at him. "I run a decent house, I do! Have yer hussies out by teatime, or ye can find yerself new rooms!" He had to find somewhere Dagmar and her maid could stay, and he had to find it soon.

"Where to now?" the carriage driver asked as he hauled his aching body into the carriage.

He racked his brain. Who did he know who was in town? That was hard to answer since he'd been away from England for almost six months. There were Nick's parents—Leo had gone to Oxford with Nick and spent his holidays in the Britton household—but Noble and Gillian were usually in the country at this time of year.

Perhaps they had come up to town for the season? Nick's younger sisters had to be about ready to enter society. "Warwick Square," he told the driver and sat back exhaustedly, praying the Earl of Weston and his family were in town.

They weren't.

"Damn and blast," he snarled when a scared-looking servant informed him that the earl was at his country residence.

A giggle from a woman strolling past him had him absently doffing his hat and murmuring an apology for his language. Now what was he going to do? Who on earth could he trust with Dagmar? Philip Dalton's offer floated tantalizingly in front of him, but he hesitated to unload his wife on two people he barely knew. No, he had to find someone else of his acquaintance, someone who would not only keep Dagmar safe, but could discourage her from mingling with society, at least until he'd had time to figure out what they were going to do with their lives.

"Leo?"

He stopped staring at nothing and focused on the woman who had giggled at his outburst. She was a tall, slender woman in her early twenties, with short, curly brown hair, and three spotted dogs that twined around her, tangling their leashes around her legs.

"Yes? Er…do I have the pleasure—"

"I'm Thom," she said, smiling and holding out her hand.

He shook her hand gravely, searching his memory for her. "Er…"

"I haven't seen you in…oh, it must be four years. Do you remember? You and Nick came to stay with Harry and my Aunt Plum that summer."

"Thom!" he said, a sudden memory returning of that idyllic summer. Thom was the niece by marriage of Nick's godfather, the Marquis of Rosse. "You had just come home from a finishing school, as I recall. In Switzerland?"

"Germany, and it was a school of animal medicine, actually." She gestured toward the dogs. "I've always loved animals, you see, and when Aunt Plum said my rough edges needed smoothing in order to be unleashed on society, I was doomed to be sent to a finishing school. Luckily, Harry suggested that all I needed was a little foreign polish, so we settled on a school in Heidelberg that teaches animal medicine. How have you been? You went to the Continent a few months ago, didn't you? Did you fight Napoleon? You look like you've been kicked backward by a left-handed mule. Have you seen Nick?"

The barrage of questions attempted to conceal the real one of importance to her, but Leo had been well aware that for the last few years Thom had held a *tendresse* for his friend. He'd rather imagined that they would make a match of it, but Nick evidently had other plans. Then again, Leo supposed that even the most ardent of lovers would find it difficult to woo a girl when he was more often out of the country than in it.

"I'll live, yes, not directly, I feel that way, and not in several months. I rather thought he was in Spain. It's a pleasure to see you again. How are your aunt and uncle?"

"Good, although Aunt Plum is being driven mad by Harry's eldest daughter, India. She's coming out this year, you know, and Aunt Plum hates society and would rather have red-hot nails driven into her eyeballs than to have to go to balls and routs and all that—a point upon which I wholeheartedly agree, I might say—but she's determined to do right by India, so we're here to get Aunt Plum acclimatized. All except the boys. Digger and MacTavish are in school."

Leo's ears perked up. "Lord Rosse is in town?"

"Yes." Thom gestured across the square, where a pale yellow house with tall, white pillars sat. "I was just taking the dogs for a walk. Aunt Plum had a dressmaker in to work on some gowns for India, and she threatened to have some made for me as well. I thought it better to be out of the house until that particular nightmare is over."

Leo laughed. He'd always thought Thom a peculiar—if charming—young woman, and he could see that she hadn't changed in the years that had passed since they last met.

"I don't suppose you're looking for some way in which to fill your time?" he asked, an idea forming even as he spoke.

"Would it keep me out of Aunt Plum's way while she's in full dressmaking mode?" Thom asked.

He considered the question and had to answer honestly, "Not entirely, but I can help divert Lady Rosse's attention to that of a new subject."

"Oh? Who would that be?"

"My wife. She's Danish, needs a new wardrobe, and I suspect would like being shown around town." He held out his arm for Thom, who automatically took it. "Shall we stroll to your house? I'd like to beg an extremely large favor of your aunt and uncle."

"A favor?"

"My wife also requires housing."

"Well, they'll see you, naturally," Thom said with obvious hesitation. "But if you are looking for a place to stay, I should tell you that the twins have chicken pox, and Plum has forbidden anyone to stay with us until the crisis is over."

Leo's hopes were dashed, but perhaps the situation wasn't as bad as Thom made out. "Surely it would be possible for one woman—" He remembered in time the companion. "Two women to be in the house without coming in contact with the poxed children?"

Thom shook her head. "Aunt Plum is very firm on the subject. I had the chicken pox when I was eight, so I'm allowed to stay, but the two youngest were sent away to the country with Lady Weston."

His hopes rose again. Dagmar might very well have had chicken pox when she was a child. In which case, she would pass Plum's immunity test, and be able to stay with the Rosses until such time as Leo could find a house.

It was certainly worth asking her. He had few other options left to him.

"I believe I will return to my rooms and discuss the matter with Dagmar. Would you tell Harry and Plum that we'll call on them this afternoon?"

"All right, but don't expect to go beyond the ground floor," she warned. "Aunt Plum has declared the upper floors to be a battlefield of pox, and none are allowed to venture onto it."

Their arrival at the Marquis of Rosse's house some two hours later was not without drama.

The door was opened by a handsome man of dark complexion and eyes that danced with a wicked light when they alighted upon Dagmar. Leo remembered him from old as being the extremely odd Castilian butler. "Chyes?" the butler inquired, pursing his lips as he eyed Dagmar.

"Would you be so kind as to tell your lord and lady that the Earl of March *and his wife* have arrived?" Leo noted that the emphasis had completely escaped its target.

"And this beauteous lady?" He bowed and took Dagmar's hand to kiss it. Leo took her hand away from him. The butler tried to take it back. Dagmar giggled.

"Is my wife, as I just said. My dear, this is—" Leo poked through dark, dusty memories, and withdrew a name. "Juan."

"Juan Immanuel Savage Torugula Diaz de Arasanto, and I am very at your," the butler said, giving Dagmar a come-hither look that by rights should have steamed the drapes.

"You're at my what?" Dagmar asked, looking

confused. Leo wanted to kiss her for that. It wasn't many women who wouldn't be flattered or at least flustered by such blatant sexuality.

"Chyes," he agreed and, with a sidelong look at Leo, heaved a dramatic sigh. "I shall fetch Harry and Plump."

"You do that. Oh, my apologies, Mrs. Deworthy." Leo realized with a guilty start that he had left Julia out on the front steps. "By all means, come in. I did not mean to neglect you."

"It's quite all right, my lord. I am but a humble companion after all." Her pale blue eyes were large as she scurried over to where Dagmar was standing, glaring at him. "What a very odd man. Is he a servant?"

"The butler, yes."

Julia blinked. "I don't believe I've ever seen a butler who tries to kiss the hands of visitors and refers to the master and mistress by their first names."

Leo smiled at her, then shifted the smile to Dagmar, just to see how she'd like it. He'd been told once that he had a smile that made ladies feel quite flushed, and he had hopes it would thaw the block of ice that had settled around his wife.

Her frown didn't so much as quiver.

"I think you'll find that everything about Lord and Lady Rosse's household is a little eccentric, from the family right down to the servants. But you needn't worry about liking them," he said, addressing the last to Dagmar. "Plum is the epitome of kindness, and Harry is a good friend to have at your back in the time of need."

"Did I hear my name being taken in vain? Leo, you rogue, you look like hell. Have you heard we're under siege from the chicken pox? Thom says you were injured. Is this your good lady? She's clearly far too good for you, you old reprobate. What's your name, my dear? Thom didn't say anything other than Leo had possessed himself of a wife."

The tall, wiry figure of a man with a pair of shiny spectacles hurried down the grand staircase toward them, a smiling woman at his side.

"Harry, you might let them come in and take off their cloaks before you start peppering them with questions. It is a pleasure to see you again, Leo, and of course, your wife and her companion as well."

Dagmar and Plum did the little bobs women did upon meeting each other, while Julia, evidently finding the informality lacking in niceness, performed a full court bow to Plum, murmuring something about it being so kind, so very kind of them to take her in from such dire circumstances.

"My wife's companion, Mrs. Deworthy," Leo introduced them. "And this is Dagmar. My dear, Lord and Lady Rosse, better known as Harry and Plum, whom I have known since I was in short trousers."

"It's such a pleasure to meet you," Plum said, taking Dagmar by the arm. "Normally you would be most welcome to stay as long with us as you like, but as I know Thom told you, we have the most hideous cases of chicken pox in the house. Six of the servants have come down with it, and both twins, and although I thought they were getting better, we had to have the doctor around again this morning. So I'm afraid that we're unable to ask you to stay with us unless you've both had the chicken pox?"

"I'm afraid I haven't. Julia says she has, but I have no memory of ever being ill with it."

"Oh, that's too bad. I should very much have liked to get to know you."

"Perhaps if Dagmar was to promise that she wouldn't go anywhere near the nursery..." Leo stopped when Plum turned a gimlet eye on him.

"No, Leo."

"But if she stayed on the ground floor—"

"No," Plum repeated more firmly. "I will not have others exposed to that disease. It's been a hellish nightmare with the twins and the servants, and no more shall fall to its spotty clutches, I tell you, *no more!*"

"Sorry, old man," Harry said, giving him a consoling buffet to his good shoulder. "Plum has spoken, and upon this, I agree with her. You're welcome to stay with us once the plague has moved on, though."

Leo sighed to himself. He knew any further protests were going to be met with deaf ears.

"What are we to call you?" Harry suddenly asked Dagmar, his brow furrowed as he eyed Dagmar's breasts in a manner that had Leo suddenly wanting to punch him. "Are you a Lady March or a Your Highness sort of person?"

"I am a Your Serene Highness sort of princess, actually, but you will please call me Dagmar." She smiled at Harry.

Leo, on the other hand, stopped wallowing in pity and glared at him. "Harry, I've known you for a very long time, and although I've always viewed you as a respected elder, a man to whom I can come for advice and assistance, if you continue to ogle my wife like that, I will have to knock you down once or twice."

"Ogle her?" Harry dragged his gaze over to Leo. "Me?"

"Ogle her, you. You were staring at her chest." He turned his glare onto Dagmar, who along with everyone else, looked down at her front. He hadn't noticed before just how plump and perfect that gown made her breasts look, but he was noticing now, and he didn't like it one little bit. "Mind you, I'm not saying that Dagmar's gown isn't just about laying it all bare for you, but still, I'd think that you would have the common decency to ignore the fact that she's damn near naked on her upper parts."

That was patently untrue, but Leo had an unreasonable desire to swathe her in the heaviest blanket he could find, and since that wasn't possible, he did the next best thing: he made himself obnoxious.

"Well," said Plum, considering him with an amused glint in her eye. "I think that bodes well for your future. But surely you aren't going to let Leo get away with that sort of behavior, Dagmar?"

"Alas, I am not speaking to him," she replied with lofty disregard.

"No? Why don't you tell me about it," Plum said, taking Dagmar's arm and escorting her toward the sitting room. "You can't stay with us, but you can certainly take tea."

"I'm afraid we don't have time for that," Leo said, a sudden wave of weariness making him stagger slightly. "Thank you, but I must find somewhere for Dagmar and Mrs. Deworthy to stay."

"Don't be silly, Leo. There's always time for tea. Now, Dagmar, tell me what Leo has done to put you on such terms with him."

"His behavior is enough to drive a weasel mad," Dagmar said, yielding to Plum's pressure, and allowing herself to be herded into the sitting room. "If I were speaking to him, naturally I would inform him that my gown is quite suitable for the purpose of covering my bosom and all my other parts, but since I cannot tell him that, then I shall simply alternate between pretending he does not exist, and wishing him to the devil."

"Trouble in paradise already?" Harry asked softly as, reluctantly, Leo followed the ladies. He didn't particularly want a cup of tea, but he also didn't wish to embarrass Dagmar with his bad manners. Besides, Harry was likely to offer him something stronger, which he very much did want.

"He refuses to let me put him to bed," Dagmar said, causing everyone in the room to freeze. "I've begged and pleaded with him, but he refuses."

Leo groaned to himself as all eyes turned to him.

"Having some bedchamber trouble?" Plum asked, her gaze going from Leo to Dagmar. "I have a book that might help."

"If it is large enough that striking him over his head with it would render him insensible so that I could get him in bed, then the book would be most welcome," Dagmar declared.

Harry gave him a sympathetic look. "Listen to Plum, old man. Her books are really quite remarkable."

"I have never met anyone so obstinate as Leo," his

wife continued, appealing to Plum. "Look at him, just look at him. Don't you think he needs to go to bed, Lady Rosse?"

The little companion said softly, "Oh, he does, he very clearly does," before effacing herself on a chair in the corner, observing the proceedings with interest.

"Call me Plum, please, and I quite agree that it's every husband's duty to do as his wife likes in the bedchamber. Let me just fetch you a copy of the latest book."

Leo intercepted Plum as she was about to leave the room. "Dagmar, stop, I beg you. You're just going to embarrass us both."

"Embarrass us!" She spun around and stomped over to him, poking him on his good arm. "I like that. All I'm trying to do is make you well, and you tell me I'm trying to embarrass you. Every other man I know would let me put him to bed, but not you!"

Harry's mouth opened and closed a couple of times, after which he took his wife by the arm and steered her over to a sofa, where they both sat. "This has all the evidence of being an extremely interesting argument."

"Yes, but don't you think I should get the book—"

"Consider Leo, my dumpling. He does not have the air of a man who would be appreciative of the joys of Squirrel Hoarding Nuts."

"I like squirrels," Dagmar told them. Leo wished for a moment that an earthquake would strike and open up a pit at his feet.

"I'm sure you do, my dear," Plum said sympathetically before turning a chastising look on him. "For shame, Leo. Depriving your wife of…squirrels."

Dagmar lifted her chin and looked to be suffering nobly.

"Oh no," he told her, shaking a finger at her. "If anyone gets to wear that long-suffering expression, it's me. Harry, Plum, you have misunderstood the situation. I haven't refused to take Dagmar to my marital bed."

"Well, you haven't, although I've always felt that was because you were delusional with fever," she pointed out. Leo wanted to throttle her. And kiss her—both, although the kissing was leading.

"I'm not going to detail our personal issues here," he said grandly and then ruined the effect by explaining anyway. "I was near death, and Dagmar and Mrs. Deworthy nursed me back to good health, and that left no time for…er…other activities."

"He was very much almost dead," Dagmar agreed, her gaze softening as it rested on him.

"I thought he was dead several times," the companion offered, nodding and accepting the cup of tea handed to her. "Dearest Princess Dagmar worked ceaselessly over Lord March."

Leo felt suddenly warm, too warm, and had an overwhelming desire to get Dagmar alone in a bedchamber, where he would thank her in ways that would surprise her. He started making a list of just how many methods of gratitude he could perform.

"And that is why I want him to go to bed, you see. He is clearly in pain, but he will not let me put him to bed and make him more comfortable. He insists on running around when he should be resting. I've told him that the fever could return, but he scoffed at the idea."

"I did and still do scoff. I'm not so feeble as to be unable to bear up under a little discomfort," he protested, although in reality, he was feeling more than a little miserable. His shoulder throbbed with a growing persistence, the wound on his chest ached, and his limbs felt as if they were encased in lead.

"That's very understandable, my dear," Plum said, patting Dagmar on the arm. "Men can be so stupid about resting so they can get well again and perform to their utmost their squirrel duties."

Harry gave her a long look but said nothing.

"And I'm relieved to know that this interesting story was nothing more than wifely concern for Leo's health, rather than a failure in the connubial department."

Leo weaved slightly and made a gesture toward Dagmar. "My wife's desire for me to recover in bed notwithstanding, I would appreciate any suggestions you have on someone with whom I can trust her welfare. Just for a few days, until I can set up a house."

"Hmm." Plum looked at Harry.

Harry looked at Plum. They both turned their heads and looked at Dagmar. She smiled a beguiling smile that Leo felt to the tips of his toenails.

"I'm afraid I can't think of anyone at the moment," Plum said slowly. "I don't know a great many people who are in town now, at least, no one with whom I would feel comfortable sending Dagmar to stay."

"There's Renfrew, but he's taken to drink, and his wife can't control him," Harry offered. "Noble's in the country. My cousin Althea is about ready to give her husband yet another child, and from the way she complains about intimate details that I would really rather not know, I suspect inhabiting the same house with her would be a highly unpleasant experience, one fraught with the latest update on her piles. What about Salter, Leo? He's in town now."

Leo thought about the whispers involving the head of his department and several young maidservants who were let go after they had become pregnant, and swore to himself. He had much respect for Lord Salter's political acumen, but he'd be damned before he left his attractive, innocent, tantalizing wife within fifty feet of that old reprobate. "Er…no. But that does bring to mind someone else."

"Really? Who?" Dagmar asked, sipping her tea.

"Do you remember the man and his sister on the ship?"

"Oh, them." Dagmar gave a little shrug. "They were pleasant enough. Plum, Leo says I must have clothing and is willing to purchase it for me despite the fact that we might have to be annulled. Can you help me?"

"Certainly." Plum moved over to sit next to Dagmar, obviously settling in for a confidential chat. "I do know of an excellent dressmaker. What exactly do you need to have made, and why would you have your marriage annulled?"

Harry thrust a glass of whiskey into his hands. Leo looked down at the glass, seeking clarity of mind in its amber depths. He really did not want to take up the offer made by Philip Dalton, but there seemed to be little other choice. "What do you know of a man called Dalton?"

"Dalton?" Harry looked thoughtful. "Philip?"

"Yes."

"Cousin to the Duke of Lancaster. Lost his wife a few years ago. Spends most of his time in the country. I understand he's quite the hermit. Bookish. Dabbled in politics in his younger days, but mostly stays busy with an academic interest—Roman architecture or something of that ilk. There's a sister too, if I'm thinking of the right man."

"That sounds like him. Her name is Louisa."

"That's it!" Harry nodded. "Louisa Hayes."

"Her son was killed. Murdered, according to Dalton." Leo gave Harry a sober look. "And he hoped Dagmar would know who she was."

Harry's spectacles glinted in the sunlight. "And did she?"

"I haven't had the opportunity to ask her yet." Leo explained about the connection with Copenhagen, glancing over to Dagmar as he did so. She was chatting quietly with Plum. He had a horrible suspicion that his wife was detailing her reasons for divorcing him, but decided that of all his friends, Plum and Harry would keep his private affairs from public knowledge. "Know if Dalton has any vices?"

"Obvious ones, you mean?" Harry shook his head. "He's chapel and fairly devout, or so I seem to recall. Doubt if he's one to chase skirts, although you never know for sure. You thinking of putting your lady in his house?"

"It's possible. His motivation in seeking my help aside, he knew a hell of a lot more about my business than made me comfortable, but I gather his godfather—Lord Salter—had been bending his ear about me."

Harry removed his spectacles and polished the lenses with his handkerchief. "How long do you think it will take you to find a house?"

"A few days if I'm lucky."

"We'll be happy to help Dagmar if you like. I know Plum is dying to know more about your wife." His eyes twinkled behind the lenses when he added, "As am I."

Leo sighed again, a slow, exhausted sigh. "I'll just have to warn Dagmar to let me know if anything untoward happens in Dalton's home."

Harry started to speak but stopped when they heard, "Leo, I do believe that your wife is correct in her determination to get you into bed."

Leo stared at her while Harry doubled over in laughter.

Plum blushed and added hastily, "That is, you look as though you should be in bed resting. Could you not go to a hotel with Dagmar? Harry, you are the most idiotic of men. Cease laughing or you'll give Dagmar the idea that you're mad."

"I appreciate the thought—both of the thoughts," Leo said, giving his wife a little bow. "But as I can't be by Dagmar's side all day, a hotel is out of the question. I believe I have a solution to the situation, however. Philip Dalton and his sister were on the ship with us, and they extended an invitation to stay with them while we looked about for a house. I will take Dagmar there now."

"What an excellent idea. I seem to recall the Daltons from before I married my first husband—" Plum stopped, gave her husband an odd glance, and cleared her throat before going on. "I don't remember a sister, though. Still, Mrs. Dalton was very kind to me at my coming out. She had a daughter much the same age, and I remember us clinging together for support at the endless round of balls and routs."

It took another twenty minutes before Leo was able to escort his wife out to the carriage, promises by both Plum and Dagmar to pay respective calls being flung between the two ladies.

"And so it is decided that we will go to the house of a friend of Lord March?" the companion was asking when he climbed wearily into the carriage.

"Yes, some people who were on the ship with us," Dagmar murmured, watching him closely.

"And are they quite nice?" Julia fretted with a silk fringe on the edge of her reticule. "I should hate to know what your mother would have to say to me if she knew I had said nothing against you staying with people who weren't quite proper."

"I saw them at Amalienborg waiting to speak with Frederick, so I gather they are perfectly respectable. His name is Dalton, I believe."

Leo leaned back in the carriage, Dagmar at his side, feeling oddly pleased by that fact despite his exhaustion and pain. Across from him sat the companion, her inane chat drifting around the carriage like the incessant twittering of a bird. He closed his eyes, too tired to focus on what she was saying, and instead focused his mind on the two most immediate problems: what to do with a wife he hadn't particularly wanted but who now seemed to hold an erotic sway over him and what sort of a reaction Lord Salter would have to find his mission cut short.

"Leo," Dagmar said, interrupting his musings.

"Hmm?"

"Do you speak German?"

"A little."

"Good. I want to practice saying a few things."

He opened his eyes to look at her. "Why?"

She lifted a hand in a vague gesture. "You never know when you might be called upon to speak to someone German."

He couldn't dispute that, so he closed his eyes again.

"What do you intend to do after you abandon Julia and me at these Daltons'?" she asked in German.

He opened one eye again and rolled it around to look at her. This was no language practice. She glanced toward her companion and gave her a toothy smile.

Ah. That was the way of it. "Abandoned?" he asked in the same language.

"Is that not the correct word?" She thought for a moment.

"Leave is, I believe, the verb you are seeking."

"No, that doesn't convey with it the sense of you dropping us and running away so that you don't have to see me again."

He turned to face her, confused as to whether she was having difficulties with the strange vocabulary, or if she really felt he was abandoning her. "I am not dropping you and running away."

"No?" She picked at a hole in her gloves, and he made a mental note to tell Plum, who was evidently to oversee the acquisition of a new wardrobe, to include such frippery things as gloves and boots that weren't patched and a shawl that didn't show signs of moths. "What do you call a man who throws his wife at virtual strangers and then goes off and does who knows what?"

"If you are implying I'm getting rid of you—"

"You are."

"I'm not. I've explained to you about my landlady. You cannot stay at my rooms, and I won't have you staying by yourself at a hotel. If you have a friend or relation in town, I would be happy to know about it, but otherwise, as you just said yourself, the Daltons appear to be respectable, and they offered to have us."

"Aha!"

"What on earth is that supposed to mean?"

"Aha, you admit you are dumping me so as to get away from me. I don't know why you won't just annul me if you don't want me."

"Who says I don't want you?"

"What man would abandon his wife—"

"I am not abandoning you, dammit!" he thundered, causing the companion to gaze upon him with mingled astonishment and concern. He bared his teeth in what he hoped was a smile before saying in a lower volume, "The Daltons asked us to stay with them."

"Us, Leo, us. Not Julia and me, but us, all three of us."

He frowned, puzzled.

She touched his hand with the tips of her fingers, just a simple little touch, but it sent a streak of fire coursing down his arm and straight to his groin.

He really had been without a woman for too long if the merest brush of a finger was arousing. He thought of going to one of the infamous houses available to gentlemen of means, but the truth was, his body wanted Dagmar.

He was beginning to suspect that his mind wanted her as well, damn her delectable self.

"I have rooms already," he pointed out, trying not to think of her mouth or the way her breasts almost overflowed the bodice of her gown, or how her legs would feel wrapped around him. He needed distance, that's what it was. Trapped with her pressed against his side, her warm, tantalizing scent filling his brain with all sorts of erotic images was clearly wreaking havoc on his ability to reason. Distance would help. He could go back to being a logical individual then.

Dagmar glanced at her companion, but the woman appeared to be dozing. "And just what, might I inquire, do you plan on doing once you fling Julia and me to the wolves?"

He rolled his eyes at her statement. "If you mean what are my plans for the rest of the day, I must see Lord Salter before word of my arrival comes to him by other means. He won't like that at all, and since he's not going to be happy about me being in England when I should be in Prussia, I'd like to keep him from losing what little temper he has. If you are concerned about my well-being, I assure you that once I have spoken with Lord Salter, I will return to my rooms."

"And do what?" Dagmar asked, her lips tight.

Leo had an idea she was very angry, but couldn't muster up the strength needed to placate her. If he could just get away from her tantalizing self, he could stop thinking of her lying in his bed and plan what he was going to say to Salter.

"Rest." What a blissful thought that was. Tantalizing, almost erotic in its attractiveness. He shivered slightly, wanting to feel the coolness of the sheets contrasted by the warmth of Dagmar's silky flesh.

In a desperate attempt to distract himself, he asked her, "Have you ever heard of a woman named Prothero?"

Dagmar frowned. "Not that I can recall. Why?"

"Dalton was in Copenhagen looking for her. He believes she murdered his nephew."

"How horrible!"

Briefly, he gave Dagmar the basics of what Dalton told him.

"There were only a few Englishwomen in Copenhagen that I knew of, and none of them are of the right age or social class." She looked distressed by this fact.

Leo felt a need to comfort her but was too exhausted to do more than to say, "I will tell Dalton. Frankly, I think too much time has passed to ever find the woman. He's just going to have to accept that."

"I suppose that would be for the best." Dagmar was silent for a few minutes, watching him with a worried expression that did odd things to his heart. He was just contemplating one particularly delightful way to repay her for her concern when she asked, "Why don't you stay with Julia and me? I'm sure there is plenty of room, and if not, I will sleep with Julia so that you may have whatever room the Daltons would give to me."

Oh, hell no, his mind told him. *You can't think when she's near you, and you'll need all your wits to cope with whatever Salter throws at you. Distance, that's the key, distance emotionally and physically. Under no circumstances should you be in the same house as Dagmar. Different accommodations are preferable. Different cities, advisable.* Hell, the way his body tingled all down the side that was pressed against her, different continents might not be enough.

"All right," his mouth said, and he had to fight to keep from banging his head against the side of the carriage.

He was doomed now. Doomed, doomed, doomed.

Nine

Princesses who are too young to attend a ball do not perch on the tallest parapet of their cousin's palace in order to throw down cups of wine upon the arriving guests, thereby staining their finery.

—*Princess Christian of Sonderburg-Beck's Guide for Her Daughter's Illumination and Betterment*

DAGMAR SAT AT A SMALL ESCRITOIRE AND TAPPED A quill against her lips while mentally running over the happenings of the last few hours. Before her sat a pristine diary bound in the loveliest calfskin she'd ever seen, its creamy pages as smooth as the silken night-dress that, like the diary, Louisa Hayes had pressed upon her.

"Everyone should have a diary," Louisa had said, presenting it to her. "Always write down the important things that happen to you, and what people say and what they do. That way you'll never forget even the smallest of details."

It was a rather odd thing to say, but then, Dagmar

reflected, Louisa Hayes was a bit of an odd person. Take, for instance, the episode that occurred the moment that they crossed the threshold of the Daltons' town house.

"Lord March! Princess Dagmar!" The tall, gray-haired woman whom Dagmar had last seen the day before, on board the ship, rushed forward, her hands extended in welcome. "I can't tell you how delighted we are that you have so kindly allowed us to shelter you while you are looking around for a house—oh!" She stopped just as she reached Dagmar, one hand clutching her throat while the other shook as it pointed past her. "But you...I saw you in my dream!"

Have arrived at Dalton House, Dagmar wrote on the first page, feeling that since the diary was a gift, she was obliged to do as its giver had commanded. *Upon doing so, Mrs. Hayes almost swooned at the sight of Julia, claiming that she had seen her in a dream. Is she mad? Prescient? Or perhaps just confused?*

She certainly had seemed all three when she babbled something about having a dream where someone resembling Julia had threatened to stab her through the heart. "Which is ridiculous when you think about it," Dagmar said aloud as she set down the quill. "Because why on earth would she dream that someone as sweet as Julia wished to stab her? No, I think she's just a bit off center."

Still, it had been somewhat disconcerting to have their hostess take such an instant—and vehement— dislike to her companion. Julia, naturally, felt the awkward situation the most.

"I shall go away to a hotel," Julia had declared in

a harsh whisper when the two ladies were escorted upstairs to the bedchamber that was to be given over to Dagmar. "I shan't stay where I am not welcome."

"Don't be silly," Dagmar said with more confidence than she felt. She watched Louisa as she puttered around the room with her housekeeper, making sure everything was just so. "Mrs. Hayes is clearly one of those high-strung women who imagines things."

"But she said she *dreamt* about me," Julia had said, tugging at her sleeve. "She said I had *stabbed* her. Me!"

"We both know that there are some women who thrive on drama in their lives," Dagmar said quickly, not wishing to dwell on the fact that the woman clutching her arm was one. "We shall simply forgive her little peculiarities. In all likelihood, we won't be here very long—yes, Mrs. Hayes?"

"I asked if you were sure you would be happy here. If you and Lord March would just agree to take Philip's suite—"

"I'm sure we'll be very comfortable in this room," Dagmar had answered politely, but now that the space of a few hours had passed, she took a moment to consider the implications of sharing a bedchamber with Leo.

For one, she'd get to see his firebird again. She looked forward to that, as well as touching it, and possibly, although who knew where this thought came from, licking it.

Licking men's backs: is it a thing that married people do? Must ask Julia when she's not upset from being accused of wanting to kill our hostess.

*Also, is Leo up to bedding me? Drat. Still don't
know what that entails, so unable to make judg-
ment on whether he's fit for it or not. Wonder if
there's a book on such a thing? Mr. Dalton has a
nice library. Shall check.*

Dagmar blotted the journal entry, decided she might
like keeping a record of the events of the day, and went
to check on Julia before proceeding downstairs.

"Your room seems quite comfortable," she told
her companion a few minutes later, tucking a blanket
around the latter's legs. The bedchamber given to Julia
wasn't nearly as large or nicely decorated as her own,
but Julia didn't seem to notice, what with her repeated
comments that she had no idea why Mrs. Hayes had
taken such an aversion to her. "I wouldn't fuss about
it, Julia, I really wouldn't. She might be a bit peculiar
in the head, and Mr. Dalton won't like you calling
attention to it. Now, have you everything? Excellent."

"Oh, my dear princess, you are kindness personified
to care for me in such a manner," Julia said as Dagmar
took up her candle before blowing out the lamp.
The orange-and-red glow from the fireplace cast long
shadows that seemed to reach inky fingers toward
Julia's bed. "But I cannot help but wish that we were
in our own home, just the two of us, as snug as two
little church mice."

"In a cold, drafty house that never seemed to be
warm?" Dagmar shook her head and opened the door to
leave. "Give me a small room with a cozy fire any day."

"I do hope that Lord March finds us a house very
soon. I cannot like having you live with a woman

who might be"—Julia's voice dropped to a whisper—"quite mad."

"I'm sure she's not that. She seemed fine other than the odd dream. Sleep well!"

Dagmar escaped before Julia could continue, and hurried her way down the stairs and into a room that a brief tour earlier in the evening had shown to be a small library. The fire had been banked for the night, but Dagmar was well used to chilly houses and simply pulled her wool shawl tighter over her arms, holding her candle high in order to peruse the walls of books. She spent a good half hour searching for a book that would offer her some insight, but Mr. Dalton's library was sadly deficient in either erotic literature or smutty stories of the ilk that her father's groom used to leave lying around. Those had never been as helpful as she hoped, but perhaps now that she was older and more worldly, they would be more instructive.

"Although really," she sighed as she put back a book that looked promising but turned out to be a treatise on bizarre animals found in the depths of the ocean, "it would be hard to be any more innocent than I already am. Blast Mama and her insistence that princesses not learn practicalities like how to bed a man."

She exited the library, the whisper of her gown trailing on the stone floor the only sound that followed her. Evidently the household had gone to bed, for there was only one night candle burning in the hall. She started toward the staircase, intending on returning to her bedchamber, when the low rumble of masculine voices reached her ear. Leo must be back from his visit—no amount of logic and sense could persuade him to delay until the following day—to Lord Salter.

She didn't hesitate; she simply went to the room from which the sound emerged and, with a quick glance around to make sure no footman was hidden away, opened the door a crack and put her ear to the gap.

"—can't imagine that he would actually carry through with that threat."

"You have no idea just how enraged your godfather can get when he's crossed," Leo said in a tone that had Dagmar frowning. He sounded exhausted. "Needless to say, I have been ordered back to the Continent to finish what I started. I told him I wouldn't be able to leave until I had the situation with the princess settled, and that's when he threatened to run me through with a dull saber and dump my carcass in the sewer so the rats could finish me off."

Dagmar's frown grew. This Lord Salter person wanted Leo to leave her? She didn't like that idea one bit, although she couldn't for the life of her explain just why. After all, it wasn't as though she was a weak woman who had to have a man handy to take care of her. She'd done just fine on her own since her Dearest Papa had died. So why did it make her stomach feel cold and clammy when she thought about Leo returning to Europe?

"Not without me, he doesn't," she heard a voice growl and was more than a little startled to realize it came from her.

"You look like he's chewed you up and spat you out," Dalton told Leo, which gave Dagmar the impetus she needed.

She opened the door and marched into the room, her candle held before her as she imagined Joan of Arc might have held a sword. "Leo, I insist you come to bed with me right now. No, don't protest that you don't want to. I didn't sit up for countless nights keeping you alive just so you can drop dead now. Don't dawdle. The bed won't stay warm forever."

Mr. Dalton, who was in the middle of taking a sip from a brandy glass, choked and sputtered out a fine spray of amber liquid.

Leo set his glass on the table. "Princess," he said in that way that made Dagmar feel itchy and annoyed.

"My lord," she said in as close an approximation to his drawl as she could.

"I've told you that I don't like being ordered about."

"And I've told you that you need to be in bed. Leo, you are going to do yourself a grievous injury if you don't get some rest. Just look at you." She waved vaguely at him. "I'd wager that it's all swollen and hot and hurting you greatly, and if you would just be sensible and let me attend to it, you'll feel much better."

It was Leo's turn to choke. He did so, hastily taking Dagmar's arm and escorting her from the room without a look back at their host, who was whooping with amusement. "Dear God, woman, you are determined to make everyone think I am a eunuch."

"That would be a false assumption," she told him as they mounted the stairs. "I've seen your testicles. You quite plainly have them. They're too large to miss, in fact, although I will admit I didn't get a really close look at them. But they were most definitely there, so if anyone should accuse you of being gelded, I will put them to right on the matter."

"You are kindness personified," he told her gravely. She shot him a suspicious look, undecided if he was teasing her or just so tired he was speaking in an unguarded manner. "Which room is yours?"

She pointed to the door ahead.

"Since I know you're bound to ask, yes, I will retire for the evening. I assume my room is somewhere along here?"

"Yes." Dagmar opened the door to their bedchamber. "It's right here."

"But that's your room."

"It is."

"Are you saying it's mine, as well?"

"I am."

"Mrs. Hayes put us both in the same room?"

"She did."

"Together? At the same time?"

Dagmar fought the urge to pinch him. He couldn't possibly be so stupid as not to understand the simple concept of the two of them sharing a room, could he? Perhaps the fact that he was so tired was making him slow. That or he just really did not care for the room. "Do you know, I tend to indulge only in conversations where I'm encouraged to do more than simply confirm the validity of your repeated statements, but I shall mark this one down to the fact that you are tired. This is the room given over to us. It is a nice room. You will not dislike it intensely, I promise you."

He stared into the dancing firelight that gilded the

furniture in the room, an odd expression crossing his handsome features. "At this moment, I can't imagine anything more hellish than what lies in there."

"My sainted mother had a saying about those who make their beds must sleep on them," Dagmar said, giving him a gentle push to get him going. The poor man was clearly at his last shreds of strength, which meant that, sadly, she'd have to put off asking him about the bedding process until he had a chance to rest. "And in this case, you chose the house that contained your bed, so now I will see to it that you lie on it. The bed, not the house."

"I could go back to my lodgings..." Leo's protest was feeble at best, and Dagmar dealt with it swiftly.

"You'll be much more comfortable here. There is a nice fire burning, which in itself is a hundred percent improvement from your lodgings, and also, I've had the maids bring up some water so that I might bathe your wounds. If you were at your cold, dusty rooms, I wouldn't be able to take your clothing off and attend to you."

He made a gulping sound that worried her for a moment, but since he didn't fall over in a fit or begin to froth at the mouth, she assumed it was just a minor bubble of wind coming up and proceeded to disrobe him as efficiently as possible.

She had removed everything but his stockings and trousers when he stopped her, one hand on hers as she reached for the buttons of his falls.

"Dagmar, I feel obligated by breeding and a concern for your welfare to warn you that if you continue on the path of stripping me as naked as the day I was born, I will in all likelihood consummate this marriage in a very real and tangible way that would totally eliminate any chances you have of an annulment."

"Oh," she said, blinking once or twice at the sudden rush of warmth to her face and groin. "Good."

"Oh, good?" he repeated, shaking his head, his fingers still keeping her hand from completing that task that she now very much wished to achieve. "Oh, good, Dagmar? Good? Shy and innocent maidens such as you do not embrace the physical acts of marriage. They are repulsed by the physicality of it. They skitter away from the sounds and scents and liquid effusions generated by it. They faint at the thought of the deflowering. They do not greet thoughts of being bedded with cries of joy and overall enthusiasm."

Dagmar pried his hand from hers and unbuttoned his trousers. His penis immediately sprang forward, taking her by surprise. She frowned at its demand for attention for a moment, before affixing Leo with a look that Julia once referred to as "steely." "When have I ever given you the idea that I am like other shy, innocent maidens?"

He thought about that for a moment, then slid his trousers down and tossed them onto a chair. "Fair enough. But I want to make absolutely certain that you understand what will follow if you remain in this bedchamber with me. Specifically if you approach the bed within a five-yard radius. Or remove your clothing. Either action constitutes acceptance of the fact that I will bed you as you've never been bedded before."

"I'm a virgin," she couldn't help but point out, glancing down at his man parts. They were certainly much more robust than they had been back on the ship. That boded well for how quickly his wounds were healing. She felt a moment of pride that her role in his care had restored his parts to such a healthy state. "I believe I've mentioned that. Therefore, I haven't been bedded before."

He took a deep breath. Dagmar fully approved of what that action did to his chest. She liked watching the muscles of it move as he breathed, and even with the angry red line curving down from under the bandage on his shoulder, she couldn't help but admire the breadth of it. How on earth had anyone ever gotten the better of him in order to wound him? He really was magnificent, from the top of his dark head down to the strength of his arms—albeit one now a bit less impressive than the other—across his chest, down to his stomach, which bore an interesting little trail of dark hair that led down to his masculine bits, and farther on, to his thighs and calves. She'd always been one to admire a man's legs, and she couldn't help but feel a little smug that her man would cut a dashing figure in the satin breeches and stockings of court dress, should the opportunity ever arrive of him wearing them.

She was indulging in a little fantasy of him parading around in nothing but very tight fitting satin breeches when her attention was forced back to the present by the sheer sight of him turning around.

"Oh!" she said and then, not having the ability to come up with any other word, said it again. "Oh."

"Oh?" He looked over his shoulder as he peeled back the bed linens. He frowned. "What are you staring at? My tattoo? You've seen it already."

Her gaze, her attention, her every waking thought was wholly and completely focused on the glory that was his behind. "Oh," she said a third time, and unable to bring actual words out, she stepped forward and put both hands on him.

His flesh was warm and inviting and sleek. "Like one of Frederick's horses," she finally managed to say, her entire body tingling as her fingers swept across the heavy muscles of his buttocks, along the dips on either side, and over the ridged muscles that curved forward into his belly.

"My ass?" He tried to look over his shoulder at it. "If it's hairy, I apologize, but there's nothing I can do about that, unless you'd like to shave it each morning for me, and the thought of having someday to explain to a valet why my wife was shaving my ass is too much to contemplate. We won't even speak of the cost of procuring ass soap and special ass razors which would no doubt be needed, not that I think they even have such a thing."

"You are an odd man," Dagmar said, her fingers still caressing this new object of joy and delight. "But one with a truly wonderful behind. I would like to have a bust made of it and place it where I could touch it every day. Do you mind if I cup you just here?"

He made a noise that sounded like a cross between a moan and a gasp. "Not at all, assuming that you have no objections when I reciprocate."

"I just…I had no idea…the groom's behind in his tight breeches was nice, but not like this…" Dagmar continued to fondle him, smooshing the sides together, stroking the heavy curves, and in general, just having a splendid time. "Do you have some tight breeches, Leo? Preferably satin?"

"Right," he said, turning around and taking her hands when she gave a little click of disappointment. "I've been as patient as I can be, because I understand it is the way of shy, innocent maidens to be surprised by the male body, but you go too far when you begin to knead my ass cheeks. There is only so much a man can bear, Dagmar, and you have pushed me past that point. Beyond which, it's my turn."

"Your turn for what?"

"I get to strip you and stare at you and fondle you while touching you with fingers that are apparently made of fire. Turn."

She looked at her hands as he spun her around, his fingers working steadily down the line of hooks on her gown. "Did I hurt you?"

"Not in the way you mean. Arms up."

Obediently, she lifted her arms, a bit taken by surprise when he whisked her gown over her head without waiting to finish unhooking it.

"This is quite a treat, having someone help me with the hooks. I haven't had a maid since Dearest Papa died. Julia offered, but it doesn't feel right to ask her to do something like help me dress. No, the laces are in the front." He turned her, quickly dealing with her stays and tossing them onto the same chair as her gown and his trousers. She stood before him in nothing but her shift. He knelt, and she felt his warm fingers just above her knees, tugging off the garters that held her stockings up. She had to keep from grabbing at his shoulder when he slid off both stockings and shoes, so pleasurable was the touch of his hands on her legs.

Those very same hidden parts of her that had been so aware of him before were even more so now, and she entertained thoughts of just what it would be like to have his hands on them, rather than hers. She was mentally composing a request for him to touch her lady parts when he stood up, taking her shift with him until she stood stark naked.

"Now," he said, a wicked smile curving his lips as his gaze locked onto her breasts. "I have my revenge."

"That doesn't sound right. I thought there was going to be touching, not revenging. Why aren't you going to touch me in pleasurable places like my knees and my breasts and my lady secret? I think there should be touching, Leo. Lots and lots of touching."

Leo laughed when she punched him in his good shoulder, shaking his head as he did so. "Just when I think I know what you're going to say, you surprise me. Rest assured, my well-endowed little squab, there will be much touching. So much touching, your head will spin. But first, we will start with the kissing."

Well, that was all right. She enjoyed kissing him, except…she stopped him when he put his good arm around her, pulling her up to his naked and, she couldn't help but notice, hot and extremely hard body. "I should check your wound first. It might need bathing."

"We will both need bathing by the time we're done, darling. And stop wiggling against me like that or it'll be all over before I get to do all the touching you demand, and then your lady secret will go unattended."

She ceased struggling to remove herself from his

arms so she could peek under the bandage, weighing her need to make sure he wasn't hurting himself further with the desire to have him attend to her private parts. She had no idea what form the attending would take, but she was willing to bet it would be good.

"Very well, but if you hurt yourself, I will have many harsh things to say to you. Oh! Do that again!"

He did. His breath was warm on her breast as he bent and nuzzled each breast before taking each (suddenly demanding) nipple into his mouth and teasing it with his tongue. She thought of pointing out that it wasn't technically kissing, decided it didn't matter in the least, and dug the fingers of one hand into his good shoulder while wallowing in the sensation.

"I think this would be easier to do on the bed," he said a few minutes later. "But first…"

He reached around her with both hands and cupped her behind, giving both cheeks a squeeze. She giggled. "It's not nearly as nice as yours."

"I think it's much nicer."

"I'm serious about the bust of yours. Do you know of any competent sculptors?"

He bent as if he was going to lift her in his arms, made a noise of irritation, and wrapped his good arm around her waist, guiding her to the bed, instead. "That, darling, is another discussion that is best left for another time. Into bed you get."

"This is very exciting," she said, crawling into the tall bed and watching with admiration as he lit all of the candles and lamps in the room. "I've wondered what exactly happens, but there was no informative pornography in Mr. Dalton's library, so I'm afraid you're going to have to tell me just what steps are needed."

"What do you know about pornography?" he asked, looking dumbfounded.

"Not a lot, because what I found in Frederick's study was couched in terms that didn't make much sense, not to mention the fact that there seemed to be a pornography language that I was not privy to."

He pursed his lips. "If I asked nicely, would you forget what you've read and trust me to show you how things are done?"

"If you like. But you'll have to tell it to me without the pornography language."

He did tell her then, in descriptions so clear that she stared at him in disbelief.

"No," she said, her gaze on his penis. It was looking much more than robust, well into the exuberant state. "I'm afraid you've been misled."

"I assure you that I haven't." The bed sagged slightly as he climbed in beside her.

"Leo, I am quite conversant with my body. I knew that the male part must come near the lady part, but to actually venture inside? No." She shook her head. "There's simply no room in there."

"Tell me, how do you think babies are birthed?" He was reclined next to her, not making any sort of move to begin all the promised touching, and Dagmar was a bit unhappy about that state of things.

She thought about his question. She'd seen pregnant woman, of course, but it never seemed to be quite nice to ask them how the baby was removed from their bodies. "Mama always said it had something to do with the navel, and that's why I shouldn't put things in it."

"Your navel or your…lady parts?"

She thinned her lips. "Lady parts are not a purse, Leo. We do not store things in there. For one, as I've just mentioned, there's no room. Fluids come out, yes, but that is the curse of all women, and never have I heard of anyone storing things in theirs."

Leo opened his mouth, closed it, shook his head, then opened it again. "I think we'll just let that go as well. You're just going to have to trust me that I know what I'm doing, and other than the sundering of your maidenhead—you do know about that, yes?"

She stared at him.

He sighed again. "Let me explain about that too."

It was a very eye-opening ten minutes while Leo gave her a basic lesson in anatomy, demonstrating points on both their bodies until she felt that she had a thorough grounding in the subject.

"Very well," she said at the conclusion, lying on her back and spreading her arms. "I will take you at your word that it will work. You may commence sundering me."

He ran a finger down her cheek, to her neck, and then down to her breast, where his hand cupped her. "In good time, my darling, in good time. First, there are other pleasures to explore."

"Touching?" she asked hopefully.

"Much touching. This, for instance." He took her breast in his mouth again while trailing his fingers down her belly until they danced amongst the oft-mentioned lady parts. She squirmed, overwhelmed by the sensation and aware of a deep burn that started in her belly and seemed to spread out to her limbs. "And this."

His breath was hot on her skin as he kissed a path down her belly, swirling his tongue in intricate patterns that moved, inevitably, lower. She was wholly enjoying the experience until she felt his warmth approaching those parts that were still awaiting his fingers.

"Leo?" She sat up, looking down at him. He was propped up on his good arm, stark naked, the dark brown of his hair lying in stark contrast to the pale flesh of her stomach.

"Yes?"

"I believe you're doing it wrong."

He looked down at her pubic bone then back up to her. "I don't think I am. You are just too gentle and innocent to know what it is that I'm doing. You must have faith that I know the way around these things."

"I'm gentle and innocent, but not an ignoramus, and you *are* doing it incorrectly."

A little frown marred his brow. "You do not know the ways of physical pleasure—"

"Who on earth told you that? I know all about the special manner one can touch one's personal and secret lady parts, and thus, I am the perfect person to inform you that you, not possessing said parts, are going about it completely wrong. There must be touching, Leo. Lots of touching."

"I'm going to be touching you. In a way that should make your toes curl, if any of my past whom— never mind. You will please simply trust me that you will enjoy this."

He bent his head, and by heavens, she did enjoy it. She couldn't stop writhing and moaning long enough to pinpoint just what it was about his tongue and fingers and who knew what other parts of him were doing that made it feel as if her body had been gilded in liquid gold and sent flying into the clouds, but they did, and she did, and really, that was all that mattered, until she arched back in the most exquisite moment of pleasure that she'd ever experienced.

"All right," she gasped, struggling for breath as he lifted his head and removed his fingers from her various parts. "I was wrong. You were right. You know what you're doing."

He gave her a smug smile that deepened as he crawled up her body, careful not to put any weight on his bad arm. "I accept your apology for doubting my prowess. And now, my darling, I'm afraid that it's come to the time when I must give you a little pain, because I simply will explode if I don't, and I can't imagine that even your devoted care would allow me to recover from an exploded groin. Tell me you trust me, Dagmar."

"I trust you," she said, worried nonetheless. If everything was put together the way he described, she'd likely be the one who would need care afterward. Still, he wasn't a cruel man, so perhaps he was right and there was a way that they would fit together.

"You are not certain, though," he said, sliding one arm under her knee and spreading her open in a way that left her feeling intensely vulnerable. "Put your other leg around my hip, my darling...yes, like that. Look at me, Dagmar. No, not my cock, my eyes. Look at my eyes."

She dragged her gaze up from where he was poised to pierce her and met his eyes. They were dark and warm and filled with amusement and something else that made her suddenly not quite so concerned. Passion, that was it, his eyes were brimming with passion for her, and seeing as how he had given her great pleasure with his mouth and fingers—she made a mental note to write about that in her new diary—it was only right and fitting that she should do the same for him by allowing him to tear her asunder.

"Oh!" she said a moment later, that exclamation doing duty once again as pretty much the only thing she could think of to say. The sensation of him sliding into her body was one that opened her eyes, so to speak. It wasn't unpleasant at first, but that changed in a flash, and suddenly she was clutching Leo's shoulder (thankfully remembering in time not to harm the injured one) and telling him in no uncertain terms what she thought of him in furious Danish.

"Be patient," he said, interrupting her tirade. "Just…no, don't move, not yet…give it a few minutes. Oh dear God, woman, how on earth can you feel this way? Do you have any idea what you're doing to me? No, you can't know, but I will tell you. It's splendid, Dagmar. It's utterly and completely splendid, and I never want to stop doing this."

Dagmar looked around wildly for something with which she could hit him on the head, some large, blunt object that would knock him silly so that she could remove his person from where it was assaulting hers. And just as she was stretching to the side for an oil lamp, something magical happened. The pain eased—not completely but enough that when she reached for the lamp, a wave of delicious awareness rippled through her.

She blinked and gave a small experimental move to the other side. Another ripple. "Oh," she said for the third time, but this "Oh" came out more like a purr. And by the time Leo, his breath hot on her neck as he began kissing her shoulder, mumbled something that sounded like an apology, she had decided that he hadn't been incorrect about fitting together, and perhaps she had been wrong estimating the amount of space available in her lady secret.

"I'm sorry that I caused you pain," Leo said some minutes later, after he had rolled off her. "I've never been with a virgin before, so I had no idea if it was better to go slowly with a hymen or quickly. I thought quickly might be best."

Dagmar conducted a quick assessment of her body. She had a wonderful sense of languid liquidness, as if she was made up of the molten gold that she had felt coated her earlier. She was still a bit sore, but on the whole, she felt that was a reasonable price to pay for the earlier ecstasy. "Do you swear that it is gone?"

"What is?" Leo raised his head and winced. Dagmar clicked her tongue and rose, making a face as she had a twinge of pain as well. In addition to that, she was unpleasantly messy in areas where she preferred not to be messy.

She used one of the cloths to tidy herself before slipping her nightdress over her head and moving over to check Leo's bandage. "The maidenhair that you said you had to break through and which I assume was the cause of all the pain. Stop moving, and I won't hurt you."

"Maiden*head*, and yes, it's gone now. You are officially a woman." Leo lay back and let her unwind the bandage.

"I have been a woman for many years. Ah, good, your wound hasn't opened up again. You must be more careful, though."

"I couldn't stop myself once I got started," Leo answered, his voice slower and deeper than normal. Dagmar figured he was on the very last bit of strength he possessed and was momentarily pleased that he had saved up enough energy to finally answer all those questions she had. "It'll be better the next…"

"Time," she finished for him. She sat looking down at him, this man who hadn't wanted a wife but who had amazingly seemed to take her in stride. He really was a handsome devil with those dark eyes and the dark curls, and that chin that for some reason made her legs feel wobbly.

She put a hand on his chest and wondered at the little spurt of possessiveness that followed. *He's mine*, she thought and enjoyed the way that sounded. *He's my husband, and I believe I will remain married to him.*

She fell asleep tucked up next to him, the warmth of his body seeping pleasantly into hers, and for the first time in what seemed like an eternity, felt that all was right with the world.

Ten

Needlework is an important skill for any young lady to possess, royal or otherwise. It gives beauty where there is none and is not, as some misguided princesses might claim, a torment put on earth to bring on madness, the vapors, and incontinence. A princess shouldn't even know the word incontinence, let alone charge their needlework instructress with possessing such an unfortunate condition. It is likewise unacceptable for said princess to force several cups of tea upon the instructress with the sole objective of using the poor woman's subsequent retreat to the conveniences as a means of escape to the crown prince's orchard in order to steal his apples.

—*Princess Christian of Sonderburg-Beck's Guide for Her Daughter's Illumination and Betterment*

LEO WHISTLED A CHEERFUL TUNE TO HIMSELF AS HE tripped lightly down the stairs, somewhat amazed that he should feel so very excellent that morning. Oh, there had been the slight disconcerting note when he woke up and discovered that his wife had evidently arisen before him—tradition dictated that the husband be the first to rise on the morning following a wedding night—but he was becoming more comfortable with the knowledge that Dagmar, while many things, was not going to be a wife who followed tradition.

"Wife," he said aloud to himself as he reached the ground floor. The word had a nice ring to it, one that was warm and round and bespoke of many enjoyable activities, both physical and mental. But mostly physical. "I have a wife."

"So I have been given to understand, m'lord," said the slow, somber tones of a man of much dignity. A black, terribly upright figure drifted into Leo's view. "Assuming, that is, that your lordship didn't bring a harlot to your bed, but I feel that eventuality is a remote one." He paused, gave Leo the gimlet eye, and then added, "I have been mistaken in the past, however."

"Your estimation of my character is indeed accurate in that I would never bring a woman of low repute to a home in which I was residing as a guest. My own home is completely another matter, of course."

"Of course," murmured Manfred. "Gentlemen must have their fun."

Leo pondered the conversational ramifications of explaining that he wasn't in the least bit serious about bringing prostitutes to his not-yet-existent home, but decided in the end that he was in too much of a good mood to set the butler straight. "I can assure you that an entertaining night's sleep is always high on my list. You wouldn't know how to turn a handspring, would you?"

"M'lord?" Manfred eyed him with disfavor. Leo could feel the disapproval rolling off him in nearly palpable waves.

"I had a sudden desire to turn a few, but upon reflection, my shoulder is probably not up to it, and my wife would have more than a few things to say should I harm it. Have you seen said female this extraordinarily glorious morning?"

"It is raining outside, m'lord," Manfred said, gesturing toward a rain-splattered window with a sense of gloomy pleasure. "I fear the phrase 'extraordinarily glorious' might be a bit effusive."

"Not if you've spent the night as I did," Leo said with a jaunty wiggle of his head.

Manfred sighed the sigh of the heavily martyred and opened a door for Leo. "The breakfast room, m'lord."

"You might want to stifle your exuberant expressions of jubilation," Leo said in an undertone as he passed the butler. "Such wanton gaiety is unseemly in butlers. Good morning, my dear. Philip. Mrs. Hayes. I see I am the last down to breakfast."

Dagmar looked up from where she was perusing a sheet of newspaper. He paused next to her chair, his body wonderfully aware of hers, and for a brief moment, thought seriously of escorting her upstairs so that he could introduce her to one or two variations of last night's activities that had occurred to him while shaving that morning, but upon reflection, he decided that not only was it rude to act the eager bridegroom in front of his hosts, but also that Dagmar might be a little tender in places he preferred to be hale and hearty.

"You were sleeping so soundly, I hated to wake you up. Will you take me to this?" She held out the paper and tapped on a paragraph.

He squinted at it, mentally bemoaning the fact that it was getting harder and harder to read the fine print of the newspaper. "You wish to go look at a sewer?"

"No, it's what they found while digging the sewer. It's all sorts of Roman artifacts and tiles and possibly a temple or two. Doesn't that sound exciting? Dearest Papa always had an interest in ancient things, and I used to read books to him about Roman invasions. The newspaper says that visitors can see the finds and the remains of Celts and Romans and the possible temple for the next few days before the digging continues. Won't that be wonderful to see?"

She looked so hopeful, Leo didn't have the heart to tell her that he hadn't the slightest interest in matters archaeological. "It's almost too exciting to bear, I agree, but I'm afraid I can't take you there today. As I told Philip last night, Lord Salter was unable to see me for any length of time last night, and I am to return today and make a thorough report, so I will be tied up at the Home Office until after luncheon."

"You must see him again?" Dagmar's shoulders slumped. "I had hopes we'd be able to look for a house today." She glanced down the table and added quickly, "Not that we don't appreciate your generous offer to stay with you and Louisa, Mr. Dalton."

Philip Dalton smiled. "I would wonder if you did not wish to set up your own home, so I assure you that no offense is taken. As it happens, I've always been interested in ancient Roman history as well, so I would be happy to take you to see the archaeological dig, Princess Dagmar."

"That won't be necessary." Leo was startled to find the statement came from his own mouth. Before he could wonder at the sudden need to keep Dagmar from going off alone with men who were not him, he continued, "I will take Dagmar to see the bodies and urns and whatever else they've dug up tomorrow. Will that suit you, my dear?"

"Yes, so long as we aren't delayed much longer than that. Dearest Papa would never rest easy in his grave if he thought I had the opportunity to see a Roman temple and missed it."

"Indeed," the little companion said. Leo hadn't noticed her at first, since she was sitting at the far end of the table. He loaded up a plate with sirloin, potatoes, and kidneys before taking a seat opposite his wife, the better to admire her while he ate. "Indeed, His Serene Highness was most fascinated by all things of the ancient mien. I recall once both Their Serene Highnesses, and of course, Princess Dagmar, going to visit a Viking vessel that had been unearthed in a field that a farmer had tilled. It was most exciting."

"There were sacrifices with the ship," Dagmar said with obvious dark pleasure. "It was loaded with them, fairly dripping with bones and skulls and pots of sacrificial oils and unguents. Papa wanted to keep one of the skeletons, but Mama insisted that it was unclean. Such a shame. I would dearly have loved one for my own."

Silence fell for a few minutes while everyone mulled over Dagmar's somewhat startling appreciation of the macabre. Leo decided it just added to her charm and wondered where the average man about town could acquire a skeleton.

"Why don't we make a party of it?" Louisa suggested, pouring Leo a cup of tea before topping off her own cup. "I should like to see ancient Romans as well, although I own I don't care much about the thought of being near a sewer, and I absolutely will not touch a skeleton."

Dagmar didn't seem to mind having company on her visit to the remains, so they made a plan to set out early the next morning.

"If you like, Philip and I will be happy to show you about London," Louisa Hayes offered as Dagmar sipped at a cup of hot chocolate. "I haven't been back here for more than two decades, so I would enjoy seeing the sights as well."

"I'm afraid I am promised to Lady Rosse and her niece this morning," Dagmar answered, and Leo felt a slight easing around his chest. He gave himself a mental shake, telling himself he would not become one of those men who were so jealous that they couldn't allow other men to be in company with their wives. "We are to meet with her dressmaker, and then Julia promised to give me a little tour of London. She used to live here."

"Many years ago," the companion said quickly. "But I do have such fond memories of growing up in Cheapside, and I yearn to show my dearest Princess Dagmar the site of my beloved old home."

Louisa frowned at Julia and murmured something noncommittal. Leo, having wolfed down his breakfast (a habit that came from too many days spent in battle-scarred Russia), rose and bowed to the company. "I will take my leave then, as Lord Salter was most particular in his request that I present myself promptly this morning. My dear, I will leave you in Plum's capable hands. Don't stint yourself when it comes to ordering gowns and such. Order several of them. And all those underpinning bits you'll need." He leaned down to kiss her cheek, got an eyeful of her cleavage, and added just for her ears, "But make damned sure they cover your breasts. I don't need every man with a pair of eyes in his head ogling you."

Dagmar giggled and, rising, saw him to the door, promising that she would spend as much of his money as humanly possible.

"Within reason," he cautioned, visions of her bedecked in jewels dancing in his head. "Neither one of us would be happy being bankrupted."

"I have spent my entire life giving the appearance of wealth that never existed," she replied complacently. "I am well versed in living in poverty and have no desire to continue that lifestyle. Leo, about last night…" She stopped and, to his delight, blushed.

He leaned close so that the footman on duty couldn't hear. "Last night was splendid. I know you don't have that same opinion, but I promise you that you soon will. Possibly tonight, if your body recovers quickly enough."

She met his gaze despite the blush. "Does the fact that you can't annul me mean that you have forgiven me for marrying you, and you want to remain married? Together? With each other?"

He knew exactly what she was asking but even so,

hesitated. "I certainly don't wish for an annulment nor for you to live over a shop. And if I ever catch you soliciting recommendations for places to live from the random individuals that you encounter while strolling around, you, dear wife, will not like what follows."

She stiffened. "Was that a threat of physical violence?"

"Why?" he asked, curious. "Does that frighten you?"

"On the contrary, it makes me think you are an ogre. Only such a monster would use his strength against someone weaker than he was."

Her nostrils flared in a way that utterly delighted him. She was a hair's breadth away from poking him in the chest, he just knew that, and was sorely tempted to push her over the edge just to see what she'd do, but alas, time was passing and he had things to do. "As it happens, I don't condone violence against anyone, unless it's a matter of life or death, so you can stop looking at me like that. I simply meant to imply that you should not be so trusting of people with whom you haven't an acquaintance, especially where our lodgings are concerned."

"Oh." She relaxed and gave him a sunny smile that he felt down to his toenails. "I didn't really ask that many people if they knew of a house we could take; just one or two nice-looking ladies, and they simply looked scandalized and escaped me as quickly as possible. I noticed that you didn't answer my question, though. Is that because you don't want to be married to me, but you don't wish to hurt my feelings because you took my maidenhead last night?"

"No, it's because here and now is not the time to discuss our future. Enjoy your shopping."

She made a face. "I like being able to have new clothes but dislike standing for hours while being fitted."

"You'll have a good time with Plum and Thom," he predicted, then kissed her swiftly, lest he remain to do the job in a more thorough manner, and left the house with yet another whistle on his lips and a fine appreciation of the evening to come.

He was organizing the packing of his belongings and making arrangements with Mrs. Lovelily for his removal from her premises, when a noise from the room next to his had him striding into the narrow hallway.

"Nick?" A tall figure loomed out of the dim light.

"There you are. I wondered when you would show up. Yes, I'm back from the Continent. Got in a few weeks ago, although I was immediately called to Islington and only just returned yesterday. I expected to see you last night, though, after catching an eyeful of your entertainment. But…you're injured?"

Entertainment? He couldn't mean Dagmar—there was no way she would not inform Nick just who she was. Perhaps Nick took the companion for a woman of ill repute. "Yes, in Copenhagen. I was evidently attacked by a couple soldiers. Did you know that Nelson attacked?"

"Read about it in the papers, but I don't have the contacts that you have, so I didn't know anything but what was reported. Were you caught in that battle? I thought you were off to Germany after St. Petersburg?"

"I was en route when I got caught up." The clock that squatted on the mantelpiece in the sitting room chimed, reminding him that he had a quarter of an hour to make his appointment. "Damn and blast, I have Lord Salter waiting for me and must leave. But I am glad to see you back, Nick. I had no idea you were in town, but I'm glad you are. Harry thought you might be able to help me with a little problem. I'll try to find you once I have Salter settled, and we can discuss the matter."

He shouted for the manservant, who brought him his coat, and gave swift instructions for the packing of his belongings. Nick, frowning, waited until he was done, asked, "You saw Harry? He's in town? Er…just him or the whole family?"

Leo painfully slipped on his coat, wondering when the pain in his shoulder was going to ease, but casting a sympathetic glance at his friend nonetheless. Nick looked like hell. Good. With the satisfaction brought by a wedding night behind him and anticipation of many more nights to come, Leo was full of enthusiasm for the wedded state. It was time that Nick stopped mooning about claiming he wasn't good enough for Thom and settled down to marrying her. "All of them are here, including Thom. Nice girl, Thom."

"Yes, she—"

"Smart as a whip and doesn't waste your time chatting about insipid things like babies and the latest tittle-tattle."

"I know—"

"Nice-looking too. She's not a beauty like Dagmar, but she's easy enough on the eyes. Any man would be lucky to wake up to her each morning."

"Who is Dag—"

Leo made the killing blow with a flourish of his hat.

"Pity no one has married her. Girl like that oughtn't be spending her life living with her aunt and Harry."

Nick looked beyond miserable. Leo congratulated himself on a job well done. "She isn't—"

"Yes, she's very helpful and accommodating. In fact, Plum and Thom will be giving assistance to Dagmar this morning. Blast. I'll have to run for it. Salter can damn near raise welts with the tongue-lashing he gives people who keep him waiting."

He dashed off before Nick could say anything more, and after planning what response he would make when Nick asked him to be best man at his wedding, mentally began constructing an apology for his late arrival that would hopefully appease his superior.

Eleven

Princesses do not—repeat, do not—put toads into their cousins' beds.

—*Princess Christian of Sonderburg-Beck's Guide for Her Daughter's Illumination and Betterment*

"I don't understand, Your Highness—"

"If you wish for me to call you Thom, then you must call me Dagmar without the Highness."

The small, round woman with a heavy Cockney accent said something that Dagmar took to be a request for her to raise her arms, and she did so, averting her eyes at the number on the tape as it encircled her bosom. She didn't care what anyone said; the sea air had made it grow.

"Very well, Dagmar. I don't understand why Mrs. Hayes had such an aversion to your companion. Are you certain that she didn't..." Thom's hands danced in the air in a vague attempt to express a blunt thought, finally resorting to just saying it. "Are you certain that your friend didn't do what Mrs. Hayes said she did?"

"Nonsense! Julia would never attempt to kill her, either by strangling—oh, higher, please. My husband seems to feel that too much of my bosom shows as is—either by stabbing, as Louisa claimed happened in her dream, or by any other means."

"What's this about strangling?" Plum bustled into the room, greeting the seamstress with a cry of pleasure. "Oh, Madame Bentwhistle, how happy I am to see you. You've met our princess, I see. Dagmar, Madame is the most talented modiste I know, and I'm sure she'll have you dressed to the nines in no time at all. Are you almost done with the measuring?"

"We're done now. At least we are if Margaret took down those numbers right." Madame gave a pointed look at the young woman with her, who appeared to be suffering from a perpetual, adenoidal sniff. "I have a few things that I can alter quickly, but the rest will take a few weeks. The shifts I can have done by tonight, and one walking gown that I was making up for a duchess, but as she's not seen fit to pay me for two years, your princess can have her gown."

"That will be excellent, I'm sure," Plum said, examining some fabric samples. "Oh, this would look splendid on you, Dagmar. Now who was strangled?"

Thom looked confused. "I don't know. All I heard about was a threatening note. Was there an attempt on Mrs. Hayes's life?"

"No, there wasn't. I told the story badly. No, no ruffles, Mrs. Bentwhistle. I am very anti-ruffles. My sainted mother said that only very young girls could wear ruffles without looking desperate, and I haven't been a very young girl for ages. I wouldn't be opposed to a touch of lace though. Mama always said you can't go wrong with good lace. Where was I?"

"I'm not sure," Thom said, casting a glance toward Plum, who was perusing a sheaf of fashion drawings. "Maybe you should just tell it all again, since Aunt Plum didn't get to hear it."

"There's not that much to tell, really," Dagmar said, pointing to a pale green velvet when the seamstress held up two pieces of fabric. "That will do nicely for a pelisse. With gold trim. We were in the breakfast room, which faces the street in order to catch the morning sun, and Louisa noticed the post being delivered, so she said something about it always taking her butler so long to bring it in, and Julia offered to run out and fetch it from a footman, and Louisa said that would be nice, and so Julia did. Fetch the post from the footman, that is. No, the russet brown, Mrs. Bentwhistle. My mother told me to avoid deep reds since they make my skin look as green as a toad's. Well, Julia and I were chatting about what sight we might see this afternoon once the fitting is done, not really paying attention to Louisa—Mr. Dalton had left the breakfast room right after Leo departed—and all of a sudden there was a shriek and Louisa collapsed against her chair. We ran to her, naturally, but she started screaming and pointing at Julia, and saying that she had tried to curse her, and then she showed us the handful of salt on her plate that she said came in a letter."

Dagmar paused, reliving the moment again: Julia, clutching her throat and protesting of her innocence, Louisa Hayes sitting at the table, her face red with anger, holding out a letter for Dagmar to see, and before her, a plate with a tiny mound of salt. There was something not right about the whole scene, but she couldn't put her finger on just what.

"Heavens," Plum said, clearly fascinated by the tale. "And did the letter say anything to clear it up?"

Dagmar shook her head. "There were no words on it, just the symbol of a snake twined around a diamond shape. Louisa said it was an old Swiss curse that meant death was coming to the house. She claimed Julia slipped the letter into the stack of mail that had arrived, but she couldn't have. I would have seen a letter if she'd had one."

They discussed the situation for the duration of the session with the dressmaker, but came to no conclusion other than that lace was definitely superior to ruffles and that Louisa might well be a bit round the bend so far as mental stability went.

"Not that I would blame her if she was overly distraught. Not with her son being killed by a deranged Englishwoman." The ladies stared at her in horror. She hastened to add, "Oh, this was many years ago. Evidently the woman ran away to Copenhagen, and they wanted to know if I had ever heard of her. I haven't, sadly."

"An Englishwoman…such as your companion?" Thom asked slowly.

"Good Lord, no! Julia wouldn't kill anyone. She's far too delicate for such a thing."

"It's very curious nonetheless."

"Regardless, I think Louisa is…perhaps overly imaginative is a good description."

"A charitable one, to be sure. I'll be ready to go in a few minutes," Plum said as they were donning their hats and coats a short while later, adding as she trotted up the main staircase, "I just want to check on the twins and make sure they're resting and not playing horse races, as they were this morning."

"They play at horse racing?" Dagmar pulled on her gloves.

"Yes, but not often," Thom said. "You have no idea how hard it is to get two grown horses up the back stairs. I won't be a moment. I just want to fetch my diary so that I can note any houses that you like, in case Leo would like to see them later."

Dagmar emerged from the house to the sunny street, looking around her with pleasure. This was a pleasant neighborhood, with a central square and a few people strolling the streets. One was approaching her now, a familiar man who sped up when he saw her.

"To the very princess a morning most good," the butler Juan said, stopping before her to kiss her hand and waggle his eyebrows. She buttoned her coat when his eyes strayed to her chest. Perhaps Leo was right that her bodices were a bit low. They hadn't seemed that way in Copenhagen, but then, her bosom hadn't appeared to be as large there.

"Good morning. Isn't it a lovely day?"

"Very so, chyes." Juan glanced over at a carriage that stopped, his eyebrows rising at the man who emerged from it. "It is you! Britisher! But it has been the years of many, has it not?"

"My name is Britton, not Britisher. And yes, it's been a few years. How are you, Juan?"

To Dagmar's surprise, the man who exited the carriage was the servant from Leo's lodgings. What on earth was he doing there? He obviously knew Juan; perhaps they were old friends.

"I am excellent fine because I have been seeing my manager of the ladies," he said, smirking at her in a way that made her want to button her coat a second time.

"Manager of the...oh." The servant gave her a thoughtful look that turned to one of dismay when he glanced behind her at the open door. "Dear God, you're...what are you doing here?"

She stared at him in surprise for a few moments before saying, "Leo—"

"For the love of all that's holy, woman," he interrupted, startling her when he took her arm and forcibly marched her down the street. "Leo isn't there! I just met him a short while ago, and he was off to Pall Mall. You must leave immediately. If you need assistance or help in escaping the woman in charge, I can help you, but not here. This is Lord Rosse's house, and his wife would have my balls on a platter if she thought I was bringing pros...er...working ladies around."

"I am not a working lady," Dagmar said indignantly, pulling her arm from his grasp and stopping despite his obvious desire to remove her from the premises. What a very odd servant he was. Then again, Juan the butler was just as odd, and he had disappeared into the house. Perhaps all servants in England behaved in such a curious manner. She would have to ask Leo at the first available opportunity. "Leo won't let me work."

"No, of course he won't. He never was one to share

his women. That's beside the point. If you have a message you wish to get to him, I will take it, but—"

"Nick!"

The servant froze, swearing under his breath before he shoved Dagmar behind him when he turned to face the door of the house. "Oh, hello, Thom."

"Oh, hello, Thom? *Oh, hello, Thom?* Really? Is that how you greet me after four years, seven months, and eleven days since the ball at Britton House, not that I was counting?" An incensed Thom marched down the street to where they stood. She clutched a red Morocco diary in a manner that indicated she might at any moment smack him alongside the head with it.

"I'm sorry that I had to leave without letting you know—" Nick started to stay, but to Dagmar's intense enjoyment, Thom cut him off with jerk of the diary.

"You ran away because you couldn't give me a straight answer to my question. Just like a coward, Nick. A *coward*."

"It wasn't that at all. I had a job—"

"You didn't want to give me an answer, so you ran away to France for seven months, and then when you came back, you were *still* too cowardly to face me!"

"I'm not a coward—"

"That sounds like the actions of a cowardly man to me," Dagmar said, moving to the side to watch Thom, lest she suddenly start beating the odd servant with her diary. Not that the man wouldn't deserve a sharp talking-to after the manner he used while trying to get rid of her, but still, she didn't condone beating people with diaries. "What question was it that he refused to answer?"

"Madam," Nick said, scowling at her. "This is a private conversation, and I will thank you to take yourself off."

"Oh!" Thom said, taking Dagmar's arm and holding her tight. "How dare you speak to my friend like that, you...you..."

"I thought coward was a perfectly good adjective," Dagmar commented. "Men seem to dislike it so very much. Though you might risk being considered repetitive if you use it again."

"Coward!" Thom finished.

"Friend?" Nick's shoulders slumped. "I might have known you would take up with someone the likes of her. No offense intended, madam. It's just that Gillian's influence is reaching further afield than I thought."

"Who's Gillian?" Dagmar asked Thom.

"Nick's stepmother, the countess of Weston. She's very nice and is my aunt's great friend, although you don't want to get into a confined space with her dogs. They tend to be odiferous." Thom turned back to Nick, ire flashing in her eyes. "As for you, sirrah, since you obviously have no excuse for your actions of the last four years, seven months, and eleven days—"

"Not that anyone is counting," Nick said under his breath.

"—then you can just take yourself off."

"I came just to see you!"

"Really? Why?"

Dagmar had to applaud her new friend's straightforward manner. She liked the fact that Thom didn't put on airs or throw grand, dramatic scenes. She watched with interest as Nick's face worked through a variety of emotions: irritation, dismay, embarrassment, and finally, a sort of pathetic resignation that had her stifling a giggle. Clearly there was a history between the two people, and just as clearly, Thom wasn't going to let Nick off the hook.

Nick glanced at Dagmar. "I wanted to explain to you where I've been, and see how you've been and how you are keeping yourself, and…and that sort of thing. Could we possibly discuss this without your *friend*?"

The emphasis on the last word was unmistakable, and Dagmar had a feeling she'd just been insulted somehow.

"Why?" Thom asked again, a little frown between her brows. "Do you have something to say that would embarrass Dagmar?"

"No, but—"

"Nick! What a surprise to see you! Harry told me you were off in the countryside saving fallen women and lost orphans. How have you been? You look horrible." Plum emerged from the house and swept Nick into an embrace that he returned. "Have you been ill?"

He laughed, giving her a squeeze before releasing her. "Not at all, just underfed and overworked as usual. You look as wonderful as ever. Is Harry at home?"

"Not right now, no, and before you ask, you can't stay with us unless you've had the chicken pox. The twins have it and insisted on spreading it to everyone who comes within a ten-yard radius of them. Are you in town for a while, then?"

"Yes." He slid a glance toward Thom, who was still

frowning at him. "I wanted to speak with Thom, but it appears you're going out."

"We are indeed. We promised to show the princess some houses."

"Princess?" He looked puzzled, and at that moment, the penny dropped in Dagmar's brain.

"Oh!" she yelled and, grabbing Thom's diary, whomped him on the chest with it. "You think I'm a harlot!"

"What?" he yelped, rubbing his chest and looking confused. "Me? No. I never! Wait, you *aren't* a prostitute?"

Thom took the diary from her and walloped him again on the chest. "She's a princess, you ignoramus!"

"How the blazes was I supposed to know that? A princess? A real one? Not just...er...she's not just saying she is, is she? You have some proof?"

"Oh!" Dagmar gasped and would have taken the diary again, but Nick snatched it out of Thom's hands.

"Yes, of course she's a real princess. Her cousin is the king of Denmark."

"The *king*," Dagmar enunciated slowly and clearly, "of, as Thom says, *Denmark*."

"Oh, dear," Plum said, her gaze moving from person to person. "It would seem there's been some sort of misunderstanding."

"I believe that is a gross understatement." Nick made Dagmar a little bow. "You have my apologies, madam. Er...Your Highness."

"The correct form of address is Your Serene Highness, not that I ever expect people to address me that way, because my sainted mother said that it was more important to comport yourself as a princess than to expect others to treat you as one; however, for you, I will make an exception."

"She's also Leo's wife," Thom said, suddenly looking a lot more cheerful.

"Yes, I am. We were married in Copenhagen more than a fortnight ago."

Nick looked from Thom to Dagmar then to Plum. He blinked, opened his mouth to say something, shook his head, made yet another bow, and excused himself. Since his carriage had departed, he took himself off down the street and never once looked back.

"Well, that was very odd," Dagmar commented as the three ladies turned to climb into the waiting carriage. "What a very strange man. I take it that he isn't Leo's servant as I first thought?"

"No, he's an old friend. I believe they met in school. They've certainly known each other for most of their lives. Thom, did you know he was in town?" The two younger ladies settled themselves facing the rear. Dagmar wanted badly to ask Thom about her history with the odd Nick, but decided it would be impolite to pry.

"No." Thom looked out the window, her fingers smoothing again and again a pleat in her gown. Plum and Dagmar exchanged looks that she hoped meant that Plum would fill her in on the details at a later time.

Dagmar was returned to her temporary home some six hours later, having seen a great many available homes, but none that she felt would suit Leo. He was an earl, after all, and didn't deserve a home that had stinking drains, unsanitary attics, or walls in imminent threat of tumbling down.

"We'll try again tomorrow," Plum told her as she prepared to leave the Dalton's house, having stopped in just long enough to greet Louisa Hayes and chat politely for a few minutes. "There's sure to be something that's not filled to the window sashes with rats or reeking of cesspits."

Dagmar thanked her for her help, saw her off, and returned with Louisa's arm linked through hers.

"It sounds as though you had an absolutely horrible time. I'm sure a cup of tea would go a long way to restoring your humor—"

A loud crash and muffled shriek stopped them for a moment; then both were running for the library door. Louisa flung it open to display the sight of Julia clasped in Philip Dalton's arms. Dagmar couldn't believe her eyes: Julia was laughing and gazing up at Philip with a delighted coquettishness.

"Philip!" Louisa gasped, her face a contortion of anger and surprise. "What are you doing with that woman?"

Julia's coy manner fled as Philip hastily set her on her feet, his face flushing a dull red. "Ah. There was an accident, you see. Mrs. Deworthy was on the ladder getting a book from the top shelf—"

"A book of sermons," Julia cut in quickly. "By the Bishop of Lansdowne. My father used to love his sermons and read them to us frequently."

"—and when I entered the room, it disturbed her, and she slipped and might have injured herself gravely, but I managed to catch her." Philip Dalton sounded as uncomfortable as he looked, gesturing at Julia even as he put a polite distance between them.

Louisa just stared at him until he took a few more steps away from Julia, repeating, "She could have been gravely injured."

Dagmar smiled, feeling it necessary to defuse the situation since Julia was sure to be the focus of Louisa's irritation. "And we are all grateful that you were there to see to it that she wasn't injured. Julia, my dear, come to my bedchamber with me. I have a slight headache in my temples and know you will soon make it go away."

She took her companion firmly by the arm and hustled her out of the room even though Julia trailed half-finished explanations.

It wasn't until they were alone in her room that she asked, "Honestly, Julia, what were you thinking? No, don't tell me it was an accident; I know full well you didn't throw yourself into his arms, but once you found yourself there, you really should not have been so obviously pleased by the situation. You know that Mrs. Hayes seems to have an unreasonable distrust of you, and such behavior, while innocent on your part, cannot help but fan the flames of her suspicions."

"Oh, my dearest princess!" Julia put her hands to her cheeks, her eyes round with horror. "You can't think that I—that I should lower myself—to act like a common woman—with Mr. Dalton, who has been so kind to Lord March and you—"

"No, no, I know you didn't arrange for it to happen." Dagmar took a deep breath while Julia declared again and again that she was innocent of

all wrongdoing. She was always so emotional and
took slight at any perceived slur upon her character,
whether or not such a slur existed. Dagmar knew
to tread carefully, lest she have a hysterical woman
on her hands, and she very much wanted to spend
some time alone with Leo when he returned from
his duties rather than calming her friend. "Don't
be silly, no one thinks you're throwing yourself at
Mr. Dalton's head. No, I certainly do not think you
behaved incorrectly. No, my mother would not cast
you out from the house for wanton behavior. There
was nothing to be wanton about. Why don't I have
some tea sent up, then you can take a little rest? Your
nerves are clearly not recovered from the seasickness
during the voyage."

It took some doing, but at last she managed to calm
Julia down, although she refused to rest in her room
and took herself off to a small side garden, where she
claimed she would commune with nature and rest her
jagged nerves.

Dagmar considered taking a nap herself, but the
arrival of a man with a packet of mail for her forestalled that event.

"For me?" she asked when Louisa had her fetched.
"Are you sure? No one knows I'm here."

"It looks like a royal seal to me, although I don't read
Danish. Perhaps it's from one of your illustrious cousins?" Louisa asked, handing her the oiled silk packet.

"Possibly, but I don't know why one of them
would wish to contact me. Oh, you're absolutely correct. It is from Frederick."

Although plainly curious, Louisa murmured

something about having some letters to write and moved across the room to a small escritoire, giving Dagmar privacy to read her letter.

You right royal pain in my arse, the letter opened.

Oh, yes, it was from Frederick. The man might have fooled everyone else, but with her he had the manners of a leprous swine.

> *Admiral Nelson has presented me with a bill for the transportation of yourself and a serving woman to England. I thought you said you were going to marry that Englishman who you almost killed in your garden? We have an agreement, Dagmar. You signed it, and my advisors tell me it is legally binding, so don't even think of returning and trying to foist yourself upon me. I have enough grief trying to cope with Papa and the English, and now the French are irritated with us, and I think I'm getting gout in my left foot.*
>
> *Stay away! We have an agreement! Go wed that Englishman and blight him with your presence. Enclosed is the bill for your travel. I wash my hands of you.*

Dagmar fumed silently to herself, thought of several scathing things she could say to Frederick in response, but decided that she was above such things. And besides, she had a feeling he'd burn any letter from her without bothering to read it.

A shadow crossed her as she stood wondering whether or not to show the bill to Leo or whether she should just let Admiral Nelson hound Frederick for the money. She looked up and, to her amazement, saw Philip Dalton carrying Julia up the steps from the garden and through the French doors to the very room she was in.

Louisa twisted around in her chair and watched with tight lips, the quill crushed in her grip. Philip said, as he entered the room, "You won't believe the tremendous run of bad luck this poor lady is having. She was out strolling through the west walk and twisted her ankle in a rabbit hole. She thought she might have broken it, but I've examined it and assured her that it's only wrenched. There, now, you sit quietly on that sofa and I'll have the doctor fetched. Louisa?"

Dagmar tucked her letter into her sleeve and knelt by Julia, giving her ankle a quick look. It wasn't swollen or disfigured in any way, although there was a large smear of dirt on the back of Julia's stocking. For a moment, she was ashamed to find herself considering the idea that Julia might have arranged the accident just so that Philip would have to carry her.

"It was the way she clung to him," she said to her reflection some hours later. She sat in a borrowed nightdress before a small mirror in her bedchamber, absently brushing her hair. Louisa had offered her the loan of a maidservant, but Dagmar had always had a dislike of people touching her hair and had sent the maid away. "She was definitely enjoying it far too much for someone who had twisted her ankle. Or... maybe I'm being influenced by Louisa. Maybe it was just an accident, as Julia claims. Oh, this is ridiculous. Now I'm doubting what I saw with my own eyes.

I'm also talking aloud to myself. Well, at least I'm not answering myself. That would definitely be bad. The Louisa kind of bad where one is prone to scenes accusing guests of throwing themselves at one's brother's head."

She gave her hair another few passes with the brush, musing on the way Louisa had accused Julia of attempting to compromise herself.

"I don't even know if that's possible," she said, setting down the hairbrush.

"What don't you know is possible?" A swirl of cool air around her ankles had her turning to see Leo closing the door behind him. A little shiver of anticipation swept over her. Now that he had recovered from the fevers, he really was quite nice to look at.

"If one can willingly compromise oneself. You look well, Leo. Quite, quite well." Her gaze all but consumed him as she watched him move across the room. Even having been so gravely injured, there was a sense of hidden power about him, an air of coiled strength that both titillated her and made her feel protected. It was a heady mix, one that she realized was the source of the languid arousal that made her skin feel too small for her body.

"Do I?" He looked down at himself, frowning at his boots. "I could have sworn I cleaned that mud off. Why do you wish to compromise yourself?"

"I don't, but I couldn't help but wonder, just for a second—and I'm truly ashamed to admit this, although if I can't bare myself to my husband, I don't know who I can bare myself to—did you say something?"

"No."

His voice was choked, and Dagmar wondered if he was in pain. She hoped not. She was willing to give the lovemaking another try despite the fact that there was some element that had been most painful. She watched with interest as Leo (who also eschewed the use of a servant) began to disrobe. "As I was saying, I am ashamed to think this, but I couldn't help wonder if Julia isn't behaving with less dignity than she should around Mr. Dalton."

"Throwing herself at his head, you mean?" To her surprise, Leo nodded. "I think you're right."

"Just because of the incident in the library and then the one the garden? I'm not so sure. I wondered if I wasn't being affected by Louisa's dark suspicions."

"You are not including into your calculations the incident in the hall."

He carefully peeled off his jacket, waistcoat, and shirt, leaving his upper parts bare. Dagmar mentally applauded this action and waited with bated breath for him to remove his trousers. "What incident in the hall?"

"It was something I saw when I came upstairs just now." Leo moved over to the bootjack and loosened his boot. Dagmar, realizing he had no manservant to help pull it off, obliged, taking advantage of the assistance to admire his thighs in the tight-fitting trousers. They weren't skin tight, as one sometimes read of in sensational literature, but they were very snug, and she wholly approved of Leo's choice in tailors and the tailor's interpretation of how Leo's thighs should be clad. "You know how there's a bend to the left that you have to take to get to this wing?"

Dagmar nodded and pulled off his other boot. She wondered if he'd think her bold if she whipped off his trousers while she was at it.

"Well, just as I came around that bend, I found your companion with her hands on Dalton's shoulders and his nose practically on her leg."

"What?" Dagmar stopped fantasizing about Leo's thighs and stared down at him. "What a very odd position to be in. Were they touching in an inappropriate manner? The way you did last night?"

Leo grinned but shook his head. "No. Mrs. Deworthy said she caught her gown on a nail and couldn't release it. Dalton happened by on his way to bed and was helping her. Or so he said."

"And Louisa?"

"She came down from the floor above, evidently having been called upstairs by the housekeeper, and when she saw Dalton on his knees before your friend, she went into hysterics. I'm surprised you didn't hear her."

"No doubt I would have if I hadn't been too busy talking to myself." With reluctance, Dagmar rose to her feet. Disrobing Leo would have to wait for another time if there was trouble with Julia. "I will go calm down Julia and do what I can to reassure Louisa that her brother is in no danger of being coerced into marriage."

"I doubt if that thought even crossed Louisa's mind," Leo said dryly before catching her hand and stopping her. "No, there is need for you to soothe troubled waters. Your companion, once freed of the nail in question, took herself off to bed. Dalton escorted his sister to her bedchamber, assuring her all the while that he wasn't being taken advantage of. Now, I wish to discuss something of great importance."

"Whether or not we are to have sexual congress?" Dagmar asked, her mind once again focused on the matter that she felt was of the moment.

He gaped at her for a few seconds. "I was going to tell you about a task that Dalton has asked I undertake, but now all I can think about is getting you into bed and having my wicked way with you. Wait—did you mean that you wish to make love, or that after last night's experience, you don't want anything to do with me again, at least so far as lovemaking goes? Because if it's the latter, I can assure you that not only will it be easier now that your maidenhead is no more, but also that my technique is bound to improve with time. I have not had experience with virgins, and thus, was unsure of how best to introduce you to the arts of love, but I believe I have a plan now."

"Plans are good. I have several plans of my own, many of which include your thighs. In fact, the plan uppermost in my mind involves removing your trousers." Dagmar reached for the appropriate buttons. "You look somewhat surprised. Have I not mentioned how much I like your thighs?"

"You have, and I appreciate the compliment. May I be allowed to reciprocate?"

Dagmar, having released Leo from the confines of his lovely tight trousers, spent a moment in appreciation of his legs, his groin, and pretty much all of him. Her stomach tightened and did a little flip-flop that made her just want to fling him onto the bed and lick every inch of him, a thought that simultaneously shocked her to her depths and made her feel like a very wanton woman. "You may, although they can't hold a candle to your thighs."

"You are too kind and very mistaken. Your thighs, however, are splendid. They are glorious. They are sublime in perfection of thigh-ness."

"Really? How odd that we are of one mind concerning our favorite parts."

"Ah, but that's not my favorite of all your bodily delights."

"It isn't? What is, then?"

"Your breasts," he answered promptly, taking them in his hands.

She gave her bosom a swift, startled glance. Even through the white lawn of the nightdress, her breasts were visible, strained against the fabric as they demanded that Leo's hands never leave them. "Even though they're too large?"

"They are in no way too large. I like them excessively. Thoughts of them occur to me at random hours of the day. I remember their shape and feel and the weight of them in my hands, and how your breath gets raspy when I rub my cheeks on them and take them into my mouth. And by then, I usually have an erection of such quality that I could demolish a small brick house with it, so given that painful situation, I figure I might as well go ahead and continue thinking about your breasts, and so I dwell lovingly on how your skin tastes and how I like to feel your breasts against my bare chest, and how very badly I'd like to rub said erection upon them should you allow me to do so."

Dagmar stared at him, all sorts of images running pell-mell through her head. "You wish to rub yourself on my breasts?"

"Yes," he said, nodding quickly. "Yes, I do. Very much so. Does it shock you?"

She thought about that for a few minutes. "No, it doesn't shock me. Surprise, yes, but not shock. I'm also surprised that you like my breasts so large. Julia always said that gentlemen preferred a neat, tidy bosom, not one that overflows one's stays, which is why I was so distraught with the journey here and the way the sea air made them grow larger."

"Julia is not a gentleman, and thus she doesn't know these things. I'm afraid you're not going to find much scientific proof that sea air has any effect on breasts, but if it was so, why then I'd buy a house right at the seaside and you'd stroll the beach every day, and every evening I would put scented oil on your breasts and weigh them in my hands, caressing them and stroking them and rubbing my fingers all over them in an attempt to determine how much larger the sea air had made them grow."

"Goodness," Dagmar said, her mind filled with erotic thoughts and her body ablaze with desire and need and wanting that was not helped in the least little bit by the fact that Leo's fingers were suiting action to word. She arched her back so as to better deliver her breasts to his hands. "Do you happen to have any of that scented oil?"

He laughed and pulled her to her feet, whisking her nightdress over her head and leaving her as bare as he was.

She glanced at his shoulder. The flesh around the bandage looked normal, not at all red or inflamed, and the pale line down his chest where the skin had been stitched together looked every bit as normal as it should. She pursed her lips.

He leaned forward and licked them. "My shoulder is fine. My chest is fine."

"On the contrary, your shoulder is a bit mangled, but your chest..." She drew in a deep breath as her fingers moved upward from his belly to the unmarked pectoral muscle. "Your chest is wonderful. Would you like to rub yourself on me now?"

A little tremor shook him. "May I?"

"Yes, if you like."

"Would you mind if following that, assuming I survive such delights, and I'm not at all sure I will given the ample bounty of your delicious breasts, if I survive, will you mind if I conduct those activities that I performed last night? You seemed to enjoy it then, and I believe that a revisit to the circumstance might make you a bit more comfortable with the idea, as well as prepare you."

"I wouldn't mind, but prepare me for what?"

Leo, who was gently laying her down on the bed, taking a moment to stroke his hands up her legs to her belly, stopped caressing her to sit down and don the same face he wore when he explained the how-tos and whereby of lovemaking the evening before. "Some women find it necessary to be stimulated for a certain amount of time before the man mounts her. To do otherwise would make the experience unpleasant and painful for her."

"But that's how it was for me." She continued quickly when a hurt look flashed in his eyes, "At the end, that is. The first part was utterly lovely."

"That was your maidenhead. I thought I explained that."

"You did, but what if I'm one of those unfortunate women?"

"What women?" He just looked confused now.

"The ones who must have you put your mouth on them to give them pleasure. Well, not you personally, because I feel very strongly that should you do so to another woman, I would get a small gelding knife and—"

"I take your point," he said hastily and kissed her. "You need not have worries about me straying, darling. I'm not that sort of a man. As for women needing time to bring them to pleasure, all women are like that. Men tend to have speedier natures where connubial acts are concerned, and women take longer to arouse." He shrugged with his good shoulder. "It's simply the nature of things."

"So I'm one of those mouth-upon-secret-parts women?" Dagmar was worried about this. While the experience had been very pleasurable, she couldn't help but feel that it was a bit sinful. It had been her experience that anything that felt that good was *always* sinful.

Leo stared at her as if he didn't know what to say. "Does it make you that uncomfortable?"

"No. Not really. Sometimes when I think about it for a long period of time. But it *was* very nice."

"Would you prefer if we proceeded without doing that tonight?"

"If you like. Leo?"

"Hmm?"

"Are you always going to lesson me before we engage in sexual activities?"

He looked so startled she wanted to laugh. He eventually chuckled and leaned down to kiss her again, this time lingering on the process. "I promise you, my darling wife, this is the very last time I bring the schoolmaster into the bedroom."

"Well, I don't know about that. What does the schoolmaster look like?"

Leo gave her a hard look for a second before he realized she was teasing, at which point he swooped down on her and tickled her ribs while nibbling on her neck. "Wench! I'll teach you to torment a wounded soldier."

This business of being a wife—Dagmar decided later as she snuggled against her husband, sated, tired, and very, very pleased with herself—was a lot more complicated than she had first envisioned. She hadn't included in her thoughts of marriage the intimacies of the marriage bed, which did indeed get better with time. She smiled in the darkness, so contented she could almost purr.

Twelve

Those around us know us by the words we use, which is why it's important for any lady, not just one of a royal lineage, to avoid besmirching her character by the use of words better suited to the stable (which location will be banned to a certain princess should the shocking language continue, especially at the dinner table when the company includes the bishop).

—*Princess Christian of Sonderburg-Beck's Guide for*
Her Daughter's Illumination and Betterment

LEO KNEW THE EXACT MOMENT THAT DAGMAR WOKE up, because she stretched her silken legs alongside his and gave a long, happy sigh.

"Good morning. I have a present for you."

Her eyes opened, and he instantly was drawn into their ever-changing depths. "The thing about hazel eyes," he found himself saying aloud, "is that they can look a certain color one day and a different color the next. I don't know how it is scientifically possible, or if it's a false impression that we cherish about our loved ones, but today your eyes are bluish gray, whereas yesterday they were grayish green."

She blinked her bluish-gray eyes and reached up to touch the back of his neck.

"I don't have a fever," he said, smiling at her and catching up her hand in order to press kisses along it. "If I sound giddy, it's simply because I'm quite content with life at the moment."

She slid her foot along his calf, making him remember just how satiny her flesh was. "What is this present you have for me?"

He flipped back the bed linens to reveal his erection.

She made a little face at it. "That's very sweet of you, Leo, but I have no idea where I'd keep such a thing without causing comment from visitors."

"Goose," he said, rolling on his back. "I thought I might show you a new way to indulge our earthier selves. If you would just kindly impale yourself on me, I believe you will enjoy being able to set the pace."

She stared at him. "You mean…you intend for us to…but it's morning."

"All the more reason to greet the day with a smile on our faces," he said, waggling his eyebrows as he gestured toward his crotch. "Hop on and let us get with the smile making."

"But…" Her gaze bobbed between his penis, now waving gently in the cold morning air at her, and his face.

She was hesitating. He didn't like that. Why was she hesitating? One concern occurred to him. "Did you need to use the closestool again? I know you did so a few hours ago, so I assumed you wouldn't need to do so upon awaking."

"No, I don't need to use it again. Did I wake you when I did earlier?"

He smoothed out the wrinkle of concern between the dark sweeps of her eyebrows, allowing his thumb to trace the line of her cheek down to the pink mouth that held such allure for him.

She bit his thumb.

"You did not. Actually, I believe I woke you while returning to bed from the same mission a few minutes before you arose. If you don't need to use the closestool, then what is holding you back from even now riding me like a wet mule?"

"Why would a mule be wet?"

He waved away the question and her look of curiosity. He had to get to the bottom of this blasted hesitation she had. It threatened to ruin all of his wonderful morning plans. "It's just an expression. Are you sore from last night?"

"No. On the contrary, there was no pain at all, just pleasure." The look she gave him was downright seductive, and it heated his blood. Whereas a moment before he was pleasantly anticipating teaching her a new method of lovemaking, one look from those wickedly wonderful eyes and all he could think about was planting himself inside her.

"Then why aren't you driving me insane with all those deliciously hot little muscles you have that grip me and make me deranged with ecstasy?"

She looked thoughtful now. He didn't care for that either. He wanted her back to looking seductive. "Is that how it feels to you? I wondered. Because to me it feels like…well, I don't quite know how to put it into words. If you could imagine a sausage stuffed into a tight glove, and—"

"Dagmar, my darling, would you think me uncouth, unkind, or just downright monstrously selfish if I asked for the sausage-in-glove discussion to be kept for a later time? Because I feel quite strongly that if I'm not allowed to make love to you right this minute, I will burst and then the sausage won't come even close to filling the glove."

"Very well," she said, giving his penis a suspicious look. She rose to her knees and proceeded to straddle his hips. "But I would like to note that I never read anything in the groom's pornographic literature that referred to people conducting sexual activities first thing in the morning. It seems like this must be another one of those sinful things that feels good and yet will probably damn our souls."

Leo was on the verge of saying, "To hell with our souls," but since he hadn't as yet determined just how strictly Dagmar had been raised, he kept that blasphemy to himself and proceeded to explain to her how this new method of lovemaking worked.

She was a fast learner, he'd give her that. She asked a few intelligent questions about why he thought this was something she needed to experience, but the moment she sank down upon him, her eyes widened, and she said in a breathy voice, "Oh, now I see! Yes, yes, you were right to insist I try this…to the left? Really? I can move like that? Goodness! Leo, this is very…you're so right there…what happens if I do this?"

"My eyes cross," he said, suiting action to word when she reached behind her and clasped various dangly parts of his personage. "Good God, woman, don't stop! Eye crossing is encouraged during this sort of engagement. Nay, a necessity! Do that little move to the left again, please. Wrrl!"

"What?" Dagmar asked, stopping the delightful rhythm she'd picked up. She peered down at him, concern writ on her lovely face. "Whirl?"

"No, wrrl. It's a statement of absolute pleasure at the combination of the left-most move and the grasping of my stones. Shall we try it once more?"

"No." Dagmar smiled then, a smile that was filled with the knowledge of women down the centuries. "We will try a move to the right. Thusly."

"That is not a wrrl move," he said, the words coming out more of a moan than conversation. "That is definitely a nnrn."

"You are a silly man, making up words like that." She flexed her hips, and he thought he might just die and go to heaven.

It took him a few minutes to recover enough brain power to actually speak again, and then it was only to say, "You think so? Then I shall have to show you that you are not the only one who can drive a person near unto death with pleasure. Prepare to wrrl and nnrn, madam."

"What—" she started to say, but when he flipped her over and wrapped her legs around his hips, he bent down to bite her gently on the neck just as he plunged deep within her.

"Wrrl!" she said, arching up against him. "Oh, yes, definitely wrrl!"

"And nnrn," he said, making a little hip swivel of his own, not as payback, more as a way to show her that he too could do amazing things with a slight shift to one side. "Do not forget the nnrn."

"Never!" she gasped and tightened all of those wonderful muscles around him. He fervently hoped that she wasn't counting on him to last longer than the time between two seconds, because he knew he was bound to disappoint her if she was.

"Luckily," he said some long minutes later, when he was able to catch his breath. His arm and chest hurt, but he cared little for that as he managed to roll off her and forced air into his lungs. "Luckily, you didn't."

"Do not speak to me," she said from where she lay, a veritable puddle of satisfied woman. She lifted a hand and waggled it at him. "Your nnrns and your wrrls and your hoochas did me in. I die. What didn't I do?"

"Count on me to have any sort of staying power. Hoochas?" He propped himself up on his good arm. "What is a hoocha?"

"It's the name I gave to that little extra push you do that makes my female receptacle want to jump for joy."

"Ah." He lay down again, pleased with her praise. He would have to work on developing the hoocha move if it pleased her that much. "You know, we don't *have* to go to that archaeological dig today. We could remain here and practice all of the moves that you find worthy of improvement."

"The Roman temple!" Dagmar, who had been lying with eyes closed and making little murmurs about never being able to move again, leaped up and ran for the basin of water. "I almost forgot about that in the ecstasy of the sinful morning activities. Get up, Leo! We have ancient Romans to see!"

"They'll still be there tomorrow," he pointed out halfheartedly, but while he did so, he enjoyed the view of Dagmar's ass. It was lovely, round, and pink, and clearly she had grown it just to delight his senses.

"We're promised to go with the Daltons today. Besides, we can wrrl and nnrn later. Right now, dead Romans beckon!"

He was contemplating just how many ways her ass delighted him when she flung a pair of trousers at him and ordered him to get dressed. Her enthusiasm amused him, a state of emotion that lasted through a hurried breakfast—that was only mildly disturbed when Louisa Hayes accused Dagmar's companion of slipping poison into the cup of tea she had passed to her—and into the next hour that it took to arrive at Oxford Street and the scene of what appeared to be utter chaos.

"How thrilling it all is," Dagmar said, her hand holding tight to Leo's as they picked their way across a devilish landscape made up of burnt wood, mud, and crumbled brick walls lying in large blocks. "Do you suppose there is someone we can talk to about what they found?"

Leo surveyed the workmen, obviously going about their business of taking down one building in order to erect a new one. "Doubtful, but we shall see. You there! Can you tell us where the temple has been discovered?"

Before the mud-encrusted workman could reply,

another man hurried forward, pushing a pair of spectacles up his long, beaky nose. His black hair was parted in the middle and slicked down on either side, and he moved with sharp, awkward gestures that reminded Leo for some bizarre reason of a bird. "Sir! You asked about the remains? Might I introduce myself? I am Oliver Buryboots, curate of St. Margaret's—indeed, I am their most devoted curate and, if I may be so forward as to tout myself, an expert on objects Roman, all things Roman, anything Roman. You and your party have come to see the baptistery?"

"It's not a temple? I thought it was a temple. The *Times* said it was a temple," Dagmar protested.

"We have come to see the remains, no matter what they are." Leo introduced them all briefly, helping Dagmar over a jagged piece of stone wall and ignoring the sensation of wetness oozing into his left boot.

The curate gestured them forward, his hands moving in sharp little jabs as he spoke. "I'm flattered that Your Highness and your lordship, and of course, the other ladies and gentleman, take such an interest in things archaeological. Most people haven't the slightest interest, not the slightest interest at all, and even though I've pointed out a hundred times that it would be a shame, the veriest shame of all to lose such an exciting and unique opportunity as presents itself to us, alas, the builder, Mr. Welles, insists on continuing forward with his building in just a few days' time. Such a shame, don't you agree?"

"What exactly is a baptistery?" Dagmar asked Leo, who was loath to admit that his memory of his days in church was long gone.

"Somewhere people are baptized, I assume."

"Indeed you are correct, Lord March, very correct in your assumption." Oliver danced around a piece of stump that had evidently been dug up, and made shooing gestures at the workmen who sat around a small campfire, metal mugs of tea clutched in their hands. The men watched them without the slightest bit of interest.

"It's very muddy here, isn't it?" Julia said to Dagmar in a soft undertone as she picked her way after them. "Is there an odor at the baptistery, Mr. Buryboots?"

"None at all, madam, I can reassure you that there is no odor at all. Shall I tell you how they found this fabulous treasure that is soon to be lost to us? I shall, for I can see the princess is most interested."

"Please do," Dagmar said, and Leo—with now two wet feet—consigned himself to being bored for a good cause. Dagmar's cheeks were pink with excitement, and her hand on his good arm kept squeezing to signal her delight with the muddy pit. They descended a slight slope and came to a stone door set in the floor of what was probably the cellar of the building being replaced.

"As you can see, the workmen uncovered this stone trapdoor in the floor. A trapdoor! No one knew it was there, you know, and it was a great surprise to Mr. Welles, who ordered it opened. Imagine the surprise of all who were present when they found this!"

Mr. Buryboots lifted a lantern that had been resting on a rock, and gestured forward. They all craned to look. Rough stone steps led down into a dim light. Faint noises emerged from the depths, indicating, along with the flicker of light, that people were beneath the surface.

Despite the mud, Leo was interested. Dagmar was beside herself with joy. Philip Dalton peered forward as well, Louisa on his arm. "Is it safe to traverse?"

"Quite safe, I assure you, Mr. Dalton, quite safe indeed. My colleagues are down there now, making what records they can before it is utterly destroyed. If you would follow me?"

The curate bobbed down the stairs, Dagmar at his heels.

"Perhaps I should stay up here," Dagmar's companion started to protest. But Dagmar cut her off with a quick, "Oh, do come, Julia. You know you always loved to hear when Dearest Papa had news of a new artifact."

Reluctantly, the woman brought up the rear.

The air in the chamber to which they descended was, as the curate claimed, surprisingly fresh. It was damp down there, true, but there was no smell of sewage, no odor of mildew or rotting things, just a pleasing earthy smell that reminded Leo of fresh tilled soil under the summer sun.

"As you can see, the sixteen steps lead down into this grand chamber. The walls are of red brick, and my colleague the Reverend Mackleford, who is down at the far end, believes that these eight double arches that span the room originally allowed light in to illuminate the ceremonies held within."

The chamber was of a good size, like that of two large ballrooms put together, and was lit with various lamps and the odd occasional candle set in a dish. Eight graceful arches spanned each side of the room, with a center line of arch columns marching down the middle of the chamber. The lowest parts of the columns were bedecked with painted imagery (most of which had flaked off) and some tiled mosaics that were still visible despite the centuries of dirt and neglect.

"Oooh," Dagmar said, moving to one of the columns and wiping at it with a handkerchief. "This is gorgeous. Julia, do you see the fishes in this tile?"

"How lovely," Mrs. Hayes said as she moved over to the arch column opposite. "Why didn't I bring my sketchbook? Look, Philip, at that exquisite tile work."

"What's that?" Leo asked the curate, gesturing toward a round pit in the center of the room. It was ringed with stone and appeared to have steps leading downward into blackness.

"That is the pool, or bath if you will, for which the chamber is named. If you come closer, you can see that a spring still exists in it."

Leo stood on the edge and looked down into the pool and saw that indeed, water bubbled up out of the ground. The pool itself didn't contain much water, only a few feet, but Leo guessed it must have its source in one of the rivers that flowed through London.

"What is of such interest over there?" Leo asked, nodding toward the far end of the chamber. Some sort of wooden bridge had been created with a few planks, leading up to a small dais of earth and stone. The distance was great enough across the room (and the light suitably dim) as to make it impossible to see what the half-dozen men were doing.

"Ah, that is our big surprise." The curate nodded

several times in succession. "Our very big surprise. Reverend Mackleford discovered the remains of what we believe to be several slaves. Were they sacrificed here, in this holy place, or were they merely left here when the building was abandoned? Who shall know, who shall know?"

"Dagmar," Leo called, holding out a hand for her. She looked up from where she and her companion were examining a half-rotted painted image. Julia had a small journal out and was sketching the image. "Did you wish to see the skeletons?"

"Oh, yes!" She all but ran to him, taking his hand and following as the curate led toward the end of the room.

"Now, I should warn Your Highness and lordship that the going here is quite rough. Part of the floor is gone, as you can see, no doubt the result of a sinkhole. We have had some planks put down in order to cross over, but only one person may cross at a time lest the planks fail. Shall I go across first and allow you to come to me, Your Highness?"

Leo pushed past him and strode across the planks, moving surely but swiftly since he wasn't overly fond of heights. He stopped at the end and nodded to Dagmar. "It's safe. Don't look down, though."

"Whyever not?" Dagmar trod lightly across the board, evidently not feeling the slightest bit bothered by the gaping pit beneath her. Indeed, her gaze was not on it or him, but the people behind him. Leo smiled to himself at the thought of her being so fascinated by something that most people would shun. She really had the most interesting personality traits.

"Dalton? Mrs. Hayes?" he called. "Did you wish to see the skeletons?"

"Absolutely not," Louisa called, moving over to where Philip and Mrs. Deworthy were now studying the bottom of an arch. "I have no desire to see anything dead, let alone a person. I shall content myself with studying this lovely tile work on the arch."

"I've been taking down transcriptions of the inscriptions," Philip said a few minutes later, when he arrived at the plank. He looked at it dubiously before craning his neck to see what it was Dagmar and the others were discussing. "Is that safe?"

"It appears to be so."

"Ah. I suppose in the name of completion I should examine the last arch for inscription as well." He hurried across the plank much as Leo had done, with eyes averted from the pit beneath him. "I shall be sure to send in my translations to the scientific society."

"Not interested in skeletons, then?" Leo watched as Philip made a brief examination of the lower part of the arch pillar, clicking to himself in happiness when he found some engraving.

"What?" Philip asked as he squatted next to the base of the column in order to see it better. He glanced over his shoulder at the group of people on the dais. "Oh, not so much, no. Bones are bones. They can't tell us nearly so much as what our ancestors left behind in written form."

Leo watched with some interest as the gaggle of clergymen and Dagmar all made a thorough study of the heap of brown bones, busily discussing theories of who the people where, why they had been cast upon the dais, and whether or not they had been bound before death.

"I don't see how you can say that they weren't slaves when it's quite evident by that scrap of iron shackle that the poor victims were bound in such a way as to guarantee their immobility," Dagmar argued with a man who had been briefly introduced as the Reverend Mackleford. She was about to continue when a shout from the far end of the chamber had them turning to look.

"Help!" came the cry. "Help me, someone!"

"What on earth?" Dagmar rose to her feet, absently dusting off her gown as she peered along with Leo into the dimness. No one was visible, although a brief flutter of color from behind one of the arch pillars indicated the source of the sound. "Is that Julia?"

"She's trying to kill me! Philip, save me!"

The voice echoed down the long chamber, the horror in it seeming to grow with each reverberation. Leo started toward the plank bridge, Dagmar at his heels, but Philip Dalton sprinted past him, crying, "Louisa!"

He reached the plank first and crossed it quickly, but stumbled just as he was reaching solid ground on the far side, falling and half twisting, frantically scrabbling at the dirt in order to keep from plunging into the pit. His thrashing legs caught the plank, and for one moment, it balanced precariously, then tumbled into the abyss with a dull crash.

"Help!" came a strangled cried from the far end. "Strangling…me…"

"Dear God, can it be?" Dagmar clutched at Leo's arm, instantly releasing it when she realized it was his wounded one. "Has Julia lost her mind and actually attacked Louisa? Leo, we must do something!"

By now the cluster of clergymen were immediately behind them, all demanding to know what was going on. Philip had clawed his way to his feet and dashed down the length of the room, yelling that he was there and all would be well.

"Dalton will see to her," Leo consoled Dagmar, who was now clutching his good arm, the both of them straining to see what was happening behind the first pillar. Just as Philip reached it, a small figure crawled out a few feet and collapsed. He immediately bent over the woman, his shoulders bowing as he clutched her to his chest.

"Oh no, it cannot be, it just cannot be," Dagmar said softly, her words drown out by the demands of the clergymen for someone to do something, for someone to fetch a new plank, more lanterns, and lastly, a doctor, none of which was possible trapped as they were.

Philip stayed where he was for a minute, visibly rocking on his knees before he carefully set down his bundle, pulling off his coat to lay over the woman's head. Dagmar's fingers dug into Leo's arm. He ground his teeth, wanting to be on the opposite side of the pit, desperate to assess the situation. Without glancing back, Philip suddenly disappeared.

"What is he doing?" Dagmar demanded to know.

"I assume he's gone for help."

"You don't think Louisa—" She stopped, unable to say the words.

Leo shook his head. "I don't know what to think. It

would appear that Mrs. Hayes has suffered from some sort of an attack—ah, there is someone."

Around the column that blocked their sight of the stairs leading upward, a handful of men and one woman appeared, Philip Dalton amongst them.

"Bring a plank!" Leo bellowed at them. "We can't get across the chasm without one!"

The workmen had clustered around the fallen woman, but one of them, lifting his head and glancing their way, turned and shoved a youth toward the door.

"That's Julia whose arm Philip is holding," Dagmar said in a whisper. "Do you think—"

"I don't know," Leo repeated, every nerve in his body jumping with the need to be acting. He hated being trapped and unable to offer assistance. "Where the devil is the plank?"

"There!" the curate next to them shouted triumphantly, and all the men around them shouted encouragement as the youth staggered in with a heavy wooden plank. Two of the workmen broke off to help him, while the third took a gesticulating Julia when Philip shoved her at him.

The second the replacement plank was down, Leo was across it, Dagmar right behind him. They bolted down the length of the room, and when they arrived breathless at the fallen woman, Julia gave a glad cry and tried to throw herself on Dagmar, but the workman held her back. She flung out her hands in entreaty, crying as she did so, "Princess, oh my most beloved princess, this is madness! Sheer madness! I couldn't! I just couldn't! What Mr. Dalton says is simply impossible! It is like a nightmare come to pass!"

"Yes, it is a nightmare come to pass," Philip said grimly, striding forward to face Dagmar's companion. "It is my sister's nightmare that you have brought to fruition. Someone fetch a constable! I wish this woman, this murderess, taken into custody!"

"Nooo!" Julia cried, falling to her knees.

"How can this be?" Dagmar asked, looking at the covered body. "I just don't understand how this can be. Julia would never harm Louisa. Never."

"And yet you heard my sister accuse her killer with her own words! Did you not hear her? Did you not hear the damning words issued with her last breath?"

"Yes, we heard, but—"

"Her cries of anguish will live with me until my dying day." Philip Dalton's face was as cold as the marble arch next to him, his eyes blazing with a light that boded ill for the woman keening at his feet. "And I will see to it that justice is done."

"Are you sure she's dead? Perhaps she was only wounded but appears to be no more." Dagmar moved toward the body but was distracted when Julia, with a strangled sound, suddenly leaped to her feet and would have run for the stairs had she not been caught by two of the workmen.

Dalton leaned close to Leo, saying swiftly, "March, take your lady out of here. This is no place for her, and you are better suited to fetching a reliable doctor than one of these ruffians."

Leo frowned, not wishing to leave the scene. "One of the clergymen could bring a doctor, surely."

Dalton glanced toward Dagmar. "It is not solely for that reason that I urge you to take the princess away. It is bound to get unpleasant when the constable comes to take the woman into charge."

There was truth in that, but he well knew that Dagmar would not leave her companion for anything but the most dire of needs.

"My dear," he said, taking Dagmar and leading her past where Julia was struggling against the two workmen, alternating between begging and pleading with them, and protesting her innocence. "We must fetch a doctor immediately, in case Mrs. Hayes is not dead but instead gravely injured."

Dagmar, who was about to protest his method of escorting her from the room, stopped dragging her heels. "You're right, of course you are. I hadn't thought—Philip seemed to be quite certain—but yes, we must find a doctor immediately and have him examine her." She lifted her voice and called to her companion, who had slumped down on a bit of fallen rock, her face in her hands and shoulders heaving, "Julia, my dear, we will be away a few minutes only, then we will return to straighten this out. Do not distress yourself any more than necessary, and have faith. We will clear up this terrible confusion and make it all right."

Her companion's loud sobs followed them up the stairs.

Thirteen

Young ladies do not run away to sea to become sailors, no matter how boring they believe their lives to be or how strict and intractable they consider their parents. Princesses never use the words "pus-filled donkey heads" when referring to their parents and will, indeed, write three hundred times the phrase "An ungrateful child is sharper than an adder's beak."

—*Princess Christian of Sonderburg-Beck's Guide for Her Daughter's Illumination and Betterment*

DAGMAR PRESENTED HER CASE AS SUCCINCTLY AS SHE could. "Our host's sister has been killed, my companion is suspected of murdering her and has been taken by the constable to a prison, and Leo and I can't possibly stay in Philip's house. I know you don't wish us to stay here, but truly, we do not need much space. Just a spare sofa or two and a few blankets would do for us, and I promise we won't leave the ground floor."

Plum stared openmouthed at her, then turned to Thom for verification.

Thom nodded her head vigorously. "Poor Dagmar was in a horrible situation there, Aunt Plum, so rather than going to look at houses, as we had originally planned, I told her to pack her things and come here. I know you don't want visitors while the twins are still down with chicken pox, but really, you can't expect her to stay where she was."

"No, of course not." Plum put a hand to her brow. "I just don't...your hostess was murdered? By Mrs. Deworthy? I think we need some tea for this."

"I think we need something stronger," Thom said, and Dagmar had to agree with her.

"You're absolutely right. Juan!"

"Chyes, my lady Plump?"

The butler appeared seemingly out of nowhere, leered at Thom, ogled Dagmar, then smacked a couple of big wet kisses on the back of Plum's hand while covertly peering down her cleavage. Plum didn't seem to notice his actions as she waved the others into the sitting room. "We need whiskey, Juan."

"Whiskey? Does Harry know you wish to drink his so valuable whiskey?"

"Never mind Harry," Plum said, giving him a push toward the library. "Just go fetch the bottle and three glasses. Dagmar looks like she's about to drop, and I suspect that by the time she's done telling us what happened, we're all going to need a stiff tot."

Dagmar tottered over to a sofa and collapsed on it, feeling boneless and beaten. "I shouldn't be here. Poor Julia is suffering who knows what ghastly torments in prison—prison! My mother would roll in her grave if she knew!—and here I sit in comfort with spirits and friends around me. You are my friends, aren't you?"

The last was plaintively spoken, and Dagmar was vaguely embarrassed by the needy note in her voice, but she suddenly quite desperately felt the need for a friend.

"Of course we're your friends," Thom said quickly, sitting next to her and patting her leg in the age-old manner of one who wishes to provide comfort but is ill equipped to do so by physical means.

"We are indeed, and don't worry about sleeping on the sofas. We'll simply tighten the quarantine on the children and affected servants, and put you and Leo at the farthest possible bedchamber. Where is Leo, speaking of him?"

"He's gone off to see Julia," Dagmar said forlornly. "He wouldn't let me go with him. He said the prison is having an epidemic of gaol fever, and it wasn't safe for me. Although why it would be safe for him is beyond me."

"Men like to think they're invincible," Plum said complacently. "Now, I want to hear the full story of what happened, every last little bit."

"All right, but it's a long story, and really, I should be focusing my brain on what to do for Julia."

"Don't worry. We'll help you figure it all out," Thom told her. "Aunt Plum is a wizard when it comes to making plans of a devious nature, and I bet we could talk that bastard Nick into helping, as well."

"Thom!" Plum said, shock evident on her face.

"Oh, I didn't mean bastard literally, even though he is."

Dagmar, distracted by the turn the conversation had taken, stopped feeling sorry for herself and looked with interest at the younger woman. "That nice man who I thought was Leo's servant is a bastard? But you—" She stopped herself, not knowing how to continue that thought in speech in a way that wouldn't offend.

Thom nodded, evidently not in the least bit bothered. "I want to live with him, yes. It's quite all right, he doesn't mind people knowing he's baseborn. His father, Noble, is the Earl of Weston, and he's always recognized Nick and given him a home and a name, and all of that. Nick dotes on Gillian, his stepmother, and all his younger brothers and sisters revere him. It's quite sickening, really, the way they idolize him. Nick the wonderful, Nick who can do no wrong." Her lips twisted. "Little do they know that he's a coward through and through."

"Oh, Thom, I thought we discussed that," Plum said, giving her niece a squeeze on the shoulder. "Harry explained to you how Nick had agreed to do some work abroad and didn't feel it fair to bind you to him when he might not return."

"Bull droppings! That was just an excuse to run away and not have to deal with the fact that I wanted to become his mistress."

A little smile flitted across Plum's lips but was gone immediately. Her voice, when she spoke, was level and carefully devoid of emotion. "Yes, well, that is an entirely different subject, and not one suited to this moment in time. Poor Dagmar needs our attention now. We must do what we can to help her companion."

"As I said, Aunt Plum is a genius when it comes to

making intricate plans." Thom's expression was back
to pleasant interest. "Just tell her all, and then sit back
and let her craft a plan so cunning that even a fox
would be devastated by its brilliance."

Plum looked modest. Dagmar had her doubts that
anyone but she and Leo could get Julia out of the bind
she was in, but she tried to keep an open mind. "Very
well, but I warn you again that it is a long story if I
am to start at the beginning. It goes all the way back
to Copenhagen."

"How very fascinating. Start there and we'll see
what help we can give. Wait, we'd better have the
whiskey first, just to brace ourselves. Why hasn't
Juan brought it by now? Drat the man. If he's drunk
it all, I will have several severe and cutting things to
say to him…"

Plum marched to the door and was about to throw
it open when the doorknob jerked in her hand, causing her to step back in surprise.

"Plum!" the woman who opened the door said, a
smile lighting up her face.

"Gillian!" Plum responded, likewise with an expression of surprised joy, and the two women embraced.

"Oh this is excellent," Thom commented, giving
Dagmar one last awkward pat before getting to her
feet. "You'll have the very best assistance humanly
possible with Gillian giving Aunt Plum help with her
plans. She's almost as devious, although I must admit,
not quite as inventive in scope. Hello, Gillian. Have
you come to see your bastard of a stepson?"

The woman named Gillian, who had bright red
hair and pronounced freckles, stopped hugging Plum

and turned to Thom with raised eyebrows. "Thom, how delightful to see you again. You are looking well. Bastard? Really? Is it like that?"

"He's a coward," Thom told her simply.

Gillian thought about that for a minute then nodded. "He is. I told him at the time that he should explain to you what he was doing before he left, but he listened to Noble, not me, and we all know the sort of advice men give to each other when it comes to women."

"Incorrect," Plum said, twining her arm through Gillian's and escorting her over to Dagmar.

"Bad," Gillian agreed.

"Stupid to the point of being ignorant," Thom said with more than a touch of acid.

Dagmar pondered for a moment, then added, "*Misguided* is, I believe, a better word for it. Although I suppose that sometimes *stupid* fits too."

"Quite. I don't know you, do I? I've a horrible memory for faces." Gillian smiled, and Dagmar was reminded of a warm, sunny summer day spent lolling around in the hayloft, eating apples and perusing the groom's smutty periodicals.

"You don't know her. Gillian, Lady Weston, may I introduce Her Serene Highness, Princess Dagmar of Sonderburg-Beck, who is also Lady March."

"March?" Bright green eyes examined Dagmar with interest. "I wasn't aware Leo had marr—God's toenails! Princess? A real princess? Leo married a *princess* princess?"

"Are there any other kind?" Dagmar asked.

"Yes, there are." Gillian smiled again. "And because

I know Thom will ask, I'm referring to the sort of woman who has lower morals than she probably should and who calls herself a princess but really isn't entitled to do so."

"What a very odd country this is," Dagmar mused as she took her seat again. "In Denmark, prostitutes don't try to pass themselves off as nobility. They are content to service men and enjoy their sinful lifestyle to the fullest."

"It's a bit different here in England, that's very true. The women of ill repute in this country are far less content, but that is not a subject for the moment. We'll simply agree that the English are very definitely characters."

"You are not English yourself?"

"I'm only half-English."

"As am I!" Dagmar said, feeling quite at home with the older woman. There were a few threads of silver in her red hair, but her *joie de vivre* gave her a sense of timelessness that Dagmar couldn't help but envy. After the drama of the last few days, she was feeling old, ragged, and definitely hag worn.

"Gillian, I'm delighted you've come, but I hope you've opened up your town house, because you simply cannot stay here."

"Chicken pox," Gillian said, nodding. "We got a letter from Nick last night, and he mentioned it. That's why we're in town. We had no idea he was back in the country, and since the boys are at school, we thought we'd come to town for a few weeks, just the two of us, as sort of a holiday from the girls."

"You need a holiday from your daughters?" Dagmar couldn't help but ask.

Gillian sighed. "We have two daughters, one fifteen and one thirteen. They both believe they're in love with the drawing master, who I will admit is a handsome man and Italian to boot. He has the most delicious accent, so I quite understand the attraction. However, the daily drama of living with two love-struck girls is beyond belief. If they're not trying to sneak out of the house to follow the poor man around the little town near where we live, they're arguing about which one of them will marry him first—they're determined that they can both wed him—and in their spare time, they write the most horrible love poems that they will insist on setting to music and singing to us every evening. Noble threatened to wall them up in a tower until they were eighteen, but it does no good. They're determined to drive us both into an early grave."

Plum laughed, and Dagmar joined in politely, although she felt sorry for the two girls. Something in her expression must have shown because Gillian, glancing at her, added, "Truly, they make their own woes. Noble tries desperately to bring order to the chaos that follows them, but you know how it is with girls that age—everything is a life-or-death situation. It's all black and white with no shades of gray; either they're bouncing around the house on a cloud of ecstasy because Signor Cosmo praised their painting, or dragging their moping selves with dire warnings of their imminent deaths due to disappointment and crushed spirits when he failed to notice while they were trailing him about the market."

"They sound like lively girls," Dagmar offered,

not sure what else to say that wouldn't betray her own rather spotted romantic past with her father's groom, two drawing masters, and a traveling vendor who had the greenest eyes she'd ever seen. Then again, she would never have revealed the objects of her passions to her mother, since that lady, while being an estimable woman in general, had an annoying propensity to deliver notes regarding Dagmar's behavior found lacking.

Had Mama ever found out that Dagmar hid in the hayloft in order to watch the groom while he bathed his upper parts, or that she had tried to convince the green-eyed tinker to elope with her (she was all of ten at the time, but quite smitten with him), Dagmar knew she would never have been allowed to leave Yellow House without a full score of maids and footmen to watch her every move.

"Oh, that they are. Plum, I've been on the road since dawn. Would such a thing as several large cups of tea be possible?"

"Yes, of course, what a shameful hostess I am." Plum bustled over to the bellpull and gave it a tug. "I've asked Juan to bring some whiskey, but if you'd prefer tea—"

"Whiskey? At this hour?"

"We need it," Thom said, perching on the arm of a chair and swinging her leg. "We have troubles."

"Nick?" Gillian shook her head. "I can't say that I blame you, the way he's behaved, but you know he's devoted to you. He always has been. He's just…a little overly sensitive because of the circumstances of his birth and the fact that he's always felt he was a burden on us, which is just ridiculous because Noble has enough money for all our children. And heaven knows Nick does so much work for my foundation that he's certainly due the money that Noble settled on him, but he won't touch it. He says he should be able to make his own way and not be dependent on us."

"Gillian has her own foundation," Thom told Dagmar in an undertone. "She redeems harlots."

"They are so often unhappy," Gillian said with a little shrug. "And frequently fall into bad situations where they aren't even allowed the money they earn. We take the ones who wish for a better life and teach them a trade skill. Thus far, we've trained and placed into good employment thirty-seven women who were formerly street bound."

"How very noble," Dagmar said.

A look of consideration crossed Gillian's face. "Not really, no. I mean, he supports it wholeheartedly and never complains about the money we spend—oh, I see what you mean." She shrugged again. "It's what we do. And Nick helps when he can. He has worked tirelessly both rescuing women from dangerous situations and also with the group attempting to enact child labor laws. He's very altruistic."

The last was aimed at Thom, who merely said, "I've never doubted his concern for those in need. It's his lack of concern for those who wish to live with him in a connubial way that I take issue with."

"I don't understand why you are against marrying this man," Dagmar commented. "I know that you said you would do so, but most women *wish* to marry, not just be a mistress."

"I have strong feelings," Thom said complacently. "Sometimes they get me into trouble. Gillian, to answer your question, I don't intend to do anything about Nick. I asked him to be my lover years ago, and he refused. I don't intend to ask him again. If he chooses to continue being an idiot and a coward and a man who can't face a woman who wishes to bed him, then that's his problem, and not mine."

"Oh, I know all about men who don't wish to be bedded," Dagmar told her. "It turns out that most of them are quite willing to do so. It helps if you can take off their trousers."

"I don't think we need to be teaching Thom the ways of seducing a man into a relationship," Plum said quickly, sharing an unreadable look with Gillian. "That's not what she wants, not really."

"No, it isn't," Gillian agreed. "I can't imagine anything worse than trapping a man into marriage by taking advantage of his honorable nature."

Dagmar sat stunned, feeling as if a bolt of lightning had shot out of the sky and straight through the house to where she sat. Had she taken advantage of Leo's good nature by seducing him against his will? It was bad enough she had married him without his express consent, but now had she compounded that sin by seducing him, all the while telling herself it was what he wanted? Was he even now feeling himself bound to her while wishing otherwise?

She felt sick and disoriented, as if the floor had fallen out from under her feet. She wanted desperately to run away, to leave the house, to leave England and return to the safety and comfort of her home in Copenhagen.

But that wish was impossible. She was homeless, and in a strange country full of people who all had their places in society and who had family and friends and loved ones to care for. Her friend was in prison, and her husband, who had repeatedly told her that they would work out some sort of a relationship, clearly did not intend one of the intimate nature they now shared.

She had been a fool. A selfish fool, one who deserved scorn, but there was little that heaping coals upon her head would do but leave her with an insane desire to wash her hair. No, she owed it to Leo to fix the situation. She had saddled him with both a wife and companion that he didn't want, and now he was drawn into Julia's troubles. He deserved better treatment than that, and she swore a silent oath that from that moment on, she would see to it that she would right the wrongs she had done.

The sound of her name pulled her out of her miserable contemplation of her own tarnished soul.

"—not me who needs the help with Nick. It's Dagmar. Her friend has been jailed for murdering her host's sister."

"No, really!" Gillian looked at her with new respect. "It's just like something out of those gothic novels that Noble loves so much. Please tell me that there's a mad monk involved. Or a skeleton!"

"There's no monk," Dagmar said after a few second's thought. "Although a curate and a handful of churchmen are involved with the telling. And two skeletons."

"Capital!" Gillian clapped her hands together with

obvious delight. "I can't wait to hear all about it. I just wish Noble were here so that he could enjoy it as well."

"Where is he?" Plum asked, opening the door and bellowing out into the hall, "Juan, if you don't stop guzzling the whiskey and bring it in here instantly, I'll have all your tight trousers thrown out."

"Noble? He went off to the club to see Harry. I assume he is there?"

"No doubt. The twins were being a bit obstreperous this morning, and Vyvyan is ceaseless in her demand for a new pony, so he sent her and Nurse off to the stable while he escaped to the sanctity of his precious club. I certainly wish I had one to run to now and again. But that's beside the point—oh, there you are."

Juan appeared in the doorway, wobbling slightly as he carefully walked into the room, a tray bearing two large decanters and glasses gripped firmly in his hands. "I have the woes of many, Plump. I need very, very whiskey such to survive the drama of the *diablos*."

Plum opened her mouth, no doubt to tell off the butler for referring to her children as devils in the hearing of guests, when a distant rumble from abovestairs was followed by the crash of pottery. Instead, she winced and hurriedly closed the door to the sitting room. "Yes, yes, just leave the tray and go see whether it was something valuable that broke. And also see if they've let another horse into the long gallery. It sounds like they have."

He left but only after snagging the smaller of the two decanters, and he was in the act of swigging from it as he exited the room. Plum turned the lock on the door after him before facing them all with a bright smile. "There now, we won't be disturbed, so you can tell us everything, Dagmar. Thom, pour us all a tot. Gillian, stop looking up at the ceiling with that worried expression. The twins are very resilient, and that was only a minor scream you just heard, not one that hints of actual dismemberment or maiming, so all is fine. Relatively speaking. Ah, thank you, Thom. Shall we toast to Dagmar and Leo's health?"

They did, and once a few more toasts were made to the distillery that produced the whiskey, the inventor of the door lock, and tailors who made tight trousers (Dagmar's offering on the toast altar), they had all settled in comfortably. By the time she'd told the three women her tale, beginning with a chance meeting in Copenhagen and ending earlier that day, two hours had passed and the decanter was empty.

"That is just about the most bizarre thing I have ever heard, and I've lived with Harry's children for six years now." Plum, who had adopted the position of lying on her back on the floor, with her legs elevated onto a nearby chair, waved a hand at nothing. "And I include in that statement the time that Thom swore the stable was haunted by a deranged cow."

"Distressed mooing could be heard every night at the stroke of ten for a fortnight straight," Thom said from her position on the window seat. She was too long to be able to lie down on it, so had scrunched herself into a huddled position that looked singularly uncomfortable. A pillow lay over her head, making her voice somewhat muffled. "And once the vicar exorcised the entire stable yard, the phantom mooing stopped. If that's not haunted, I don't know what is."

Gillian walked across the room, her path curved and circuitous. She stepped with exaggerated care and twice stopped to giggle at absolutely nothing. "I think the point here is that something must be done. We cannot have the companion Jennifer—"

"Julia," Dagmar said from where she sat on the floor, her back to the wall, her legs straight out before her. She was sitting thus because they—her legs— seemed to have stopped working. They appeared to be made out of some of the India rubber that Frederick had on his desk, and she felt it was wiser to let them stiffen up in a straight position than bent.

"We cannot have the companion Julia rotting away in gaol simply because there's been a gross...gross... what is it that I'm thinking?"

"You are thinking," Plum said from her position on the floor, waving her hand toward Gillian, "that we need more whiskey."

"Misconstrued something. I just can't make the words come out on my tongue. Misconstrued justice?"

"There is no justice at all that I can see," Dagmar said, frowning at her legs and wondering if they had hardened up yet sufficiently that she could stand. "Misconstrued or otherwise. Julia couldn't have killed Louisa. She's not at all the time of person who kills others. I feel it in my India rubber bones."

"Then we must find out who did kill that poor woman, so that your companion will be released," Gillian said, wobbling her way over to a chair where she plunked down with more energy than grace.

"If we all put our minds to it, I'm sure we'll have it figured out in no time."

"Leo is at the gaol now. He will speak with Julia and determine what happened, and then he will tell the officials so that they let her go." Dagmar offered this tidbit with no little amount of pride, feeling quite confident that Leo would do just that, at which point she would strip him naked and then allow him to do all the things that he kept saying he wanted to do.

She frowned, the pleasant thought suddenly stained with darkness. "Oh, but I can't."

"Sure you can. Harry has lots of whiskey. He always says that it's as vital as air when it comes to dealing with the children. I'll just have Juan bring us some more."

"No, I meant that I can't take off Leo's clothes, because I am giving him up. I'm releasing him, like a wee little captured bird, so that he can fly off and be happy without a wife who seduced his person against his will, and I shall live in misery and heartbreak, and will raise haunted cows until I die alone and unloved in a small stable with only a vicar to exorcise me." A few tears welled up in her eyes at the thought of the noble way she had determined to conduct her life from that moment on.

"You know what I think?" Plum, who had been humming to herself, lifted her head and looked at Dagmar. "I think you're tipsy. Why do you want to turn Leo into a bird and let him fly off?"

"I seduced him. Didn't you hear that part? I said that I seduced his person against his will."

Gillian, who had slumped at an angle in the chair, snorted. "There's not a man alive who wouldn't be willing to be seduced by Your Royal Highness."

"My Serene Highness," Dagmar corrected sadly, two fat tears rolling down her cheeks.

A little snore came from under Thom's pillow.

"I still don't understand why you want to let Leo go. Don't you like him?" Plum asked, waggling her feet.

"Yes, I do, but that's the problem. You see, I thought he was going to die, so it was all right to marry him, but then he didn't die, and Julia and I worked so hard to save him, and then he woke up and once I bathed him, I could see he was incredibly handsome."

"Leo? *Handsome?*" Gillian shook her head and fell over sideways. "Has his appearance changed since I last saw him, Plum?"

"No. It's love." Plum waved her hand again. "You know how it makes everything look wonderful."

"Madam," Dagmar said, outrage filling her every morsel. She managed to get to her feet with only a minimum of unladylike grunting. She stood up, one hand on the mantel for balance, the other on her hip as she looked down her nose at Gillian, who had pulled two cushions to the floor and was making a comfortable nest upon them. "Madam, did you just disparage my husband?"

Gillian stopped arranging the cushions. "No."

Dagmar's shoulders slumped. She felt suddenly deflated. "Oh. I thought you did. I was going to call you out for your slur on Leo's handsomeness."

"If you think he's handsome, then that's all the matters." Gillian stopped, giggled, and then continued, "But seriously, what are we going to do about this gross something of justice that I mentioned a bit ago?"

"What we need," Plum said, ceasing the humming

long enough to roll over onto her stomach, so that she could look at the two women. "What we need is Harry. He still has contacts. He'll help Leo."

"Noble has contacts too, you know," Gillian said quickly, evidently feeling her husband was being slighted. "He will help Leo."

"I'm sure any assistance will be greatly welcome," Dagmar said diplomatically, and with an *oomph*, sat down hard on the now cushionless sofa. "Once Julia is freed, then I shall release Leo from his marital vows and go off to live in abject *fortvivlelse*."

Plum propped her head on her hands. "For what?"

"*Fortvivlelse.* It's… I think the rubber has gone to my brain now because I can't think of the word in English. I want words to mean *great sadness*."

"That would be *great sadness*," came a muffled voice from under the pillow.

"Go back to sleep, Thom, you're not being in the least bit helpful." Plum tried to pin back Dagmar with a look but couldn't focus enough to do so. "Dagmar, I don't know why you suddenly feel that Leo isn't wildly ecstatic to have you as his wife, but I do believe that you need to talk to him about it. I think you'll find that he didn't mind at all that you seduced him."

Dagmar slumped uncomfortably against the end of the sofa. She appreciated the advice, but in her heart, she knew that matters went deeper than that. She'd taken away Leo's choice twice, and it was time that she let him live his own life the way he wanted. It would do no good to protest that to the ladies present, though. They'd just tell her that she was crazy. The best thing to do was to refocus their attention on something that would distract them. "I think the most important thing at the moment is to get Julia free. Assuming Leo can't do so, what resources do we have?"

"I think we should go to the scene of the incident," Gillian said after some thought.

Dagmar stopped dwelling on her life of despair without Leo—"Despair! That's what *fortvivlelse* means"—and thought about that suggestion. "What good will that do?"

"It might give us ideas about what happened."

"I suppose—"

The doorknob rattled, followed immediately by a demand for the door to be opened.

"It's locked," Plum yelled at the door. "I don't know where the key is."

Loud orders could be heard, and a minute later, a key scraped in the lock and the door opened. Two men entered the room only to stop and stare at the occupants.

"Oh, hullo, Harry," Plum said, kicking her heels over her behind, totally heedless of the fact that her bestockinged lower legs were exposed by her prone position. "Did Noble find you? He went to look for you."

"That's him, there," Gillian said, pointing.

Dagmar turned to look at the new arrivals. Harry was accompanied by a tall man with dark hair touched with silver at the temples and pale gray eyes. Both men wore identical expressions of surprise.

"Er…had a little tipple, did you?" Harry asked, passing his hand over his lower mouth.

Thom snored loudly.

"Just a little. We needed it. We were facing Gillian's misconstructed thing and needed it."

"Justice. Only we decided it wasn't justice. And don't forget Dagmar's *farfugviggler*."

Both men turned to look at Dagmar. She sniffed sadly at her fate. "*Fortvivlelse*."

"Just so," Harry said, his eyes wide behind the lenses of his spectacles. He slid a glance toward his friend, who was looking askance at Dagmar. "Noble, this is Leo's wife, the Princess Dagmar of Sonderburg-Beck."

"Our Serene Highness," Gillian said, then smiled at her husband with such obvious desire that Dagmar was simultaneously giggly and envious. "Hello, my lord of deliciousness. Kiss me?"

"You are drunk, Wife!" Noble said, trying to look scandalized, but Dagmar saw him waggling his eyebrows at Gillian as he bent to comply with her demand.

"Oh, Juan, there you are." Plum pushed herself up to a sitting position. "We need more whiskey."

"I think coffee would be more the thing," Harry counter-ordered, and Juan, who had evidently been dipping into the reserves, wheeled about smartly and, after crashing into the wall twice, managed to leave the room, a trail of Spanish oaths following after him. "Let's get you ladies up off the floor, shall we?"

A half hour later, after having consumed three lemon cakes and several cups of strong black coffee, Dagmar felt her limbs and brain had returned to their normal state. Her heart, sadly, was still heavy with the knowledge of what she must do once Julia's situation had been resolved. She was made to recount the story again, after which silence filled the room.

Thom woke up at that point, moaned about a

headache, and sat up. She was given cake and coffee, and although she said she wanted neither, she wolfed both down.

"Where's your bastard son?" she asked Noble around a mouthful of cake.

He looked momentarily startled.

"And by that term I mean the son who is a rotter."

"Which rotten son? I have three."

"Noble! Don't call our boys and Nick rotten!"

He grinned. "You've said worse about all three."

"I'm a mother," Gillian said with a lift of her chin. "I'm allowed."

"I was referring to your eldest rotten son, not that I think Dante and Sebastian are rotters in the least. They, I'm sure, wouldn't treat a woman who wished to be their mistress so cruelly."

"Ah," Noble said, blinking once or twice. "Ah. It's that, is it?"

"He is rotten to the core. A cowardly core. One filled with maggots that are so disgusting, his mere presence would sicken a normal human being."

"So the fact that he's on his way here after making himself presentable isn't a good thing, then?" Noble asked, and Dagmar could see a twinkle in his eye.

She was pleased by that, since it hinted that both Gillian and Noble looked upon Thom with favor.

Thom sat up straight for a moment, then slouched back in her chair and took another bite of lemon cake. "It's nothing at all to do with me where that bastard takes his maggoty core."

"Excellent," Noble said and helped himself to the last cake.

"Hey now," Harry objected, glowering at the empty plate. "I was going to have that."

"I'm your guest. Besides, you've put on weight. It won't hurt you one bit to drop a stone or two."

Gillian eyed her husband but said nothing. Plum stifled a giggle, and Harry, after covertly sucking in his stomach—not that he had much of one, since both men looked quite fit to Dagmar's eye—said to her rather breathlessly, "Where's your husband?"

"He's at the gaol trying to free Julia. How long do you think it will take? I don't want him to remain there for any longer than he has to due to the gaol fever."

"Gaol fever? They haven't had gaol fever for years n—" Harry jerked when Plum stomped on his foot. "Ah. Yes. Horrible outbreak they've had of late. Very dangerous to ladies. Might be best if Noble and I went to check on him, hmm?"

"If you're going to the prison, then I'm going as well," Dagmar said, making a snap decision. She was tired of being left out of what was bound to be a delicate situation. Leo didn't know Julia the way she did, and besides, she would feel better knowing everything possible was being done.

"I don't think that would be good—" Harry started to say.

"If Dagmar is going, I shall go too," Thom said quickly, standing up and lurching over to where Dagmar stood next to the fireplace. "I'll show that bastard that he's not the only one who cares about people to the point of ignoring those he loves."

Noble started and was about to say something when Gillian whispered in his ear.

Dagmar looked at her newfound champion. "That doesn't make any sense."

"He's a man," Thom said loftily. "They frequently don't."

"True."

"I suppose if they are going, we should go as well," Plum said slowly, her gaze moving from Harry to Gillian then to Dagmar. "It's not right to let two young girls go to gaol without some sort of supervision."

"No one is going with us. Noble and I will—"

"I'll go fetch my hat and cloak," Dagmar interrupted, not wishing to argue with Harry, especially as now he was going to be her host, but also not prepared to be kept to the side.

"Juan! You will please tell Noble's rotter son that I have gone to be useful and helpful to a woman in need rather than stay here and allow him to grovel before me while begging my pardon, followed by a proposal of marriage, because I know Aunt Plum won't let me live with him in sin as I'd prefer. You'll be sure to tell him that, yes?" Thom asked as she marched out of the room after Dagmar.

"No," Juan said, shaking his head. "You use the words of too many sounds. I tell him you go and he's a *bastardo*."

"That works for me." Thom ran lightly up the stairs while Dagmar gathered her things.

"Would it be asking too much for her not to refer to my son by that sobriquet?" Noble asked mildly over the sound of Harry protesting to no one in particular that prison was no place for a woman and what about that gaol fever?

"I wonder where we should have their wedding," Gillian mused as she too rose and gathered up her things. "Plum, would you be opposed to us having it in the country?"

"Not at all. I think that would probably be best if we all end up with gaol fever. Harry, dear, stop fussing. It'll be all right if we all go to the prison. What can happen with us all there to see that no one gets into any trouble?"

Fourteen

Princesses never question their mother's homilies
that are intended on bettering their character
through proper conduct (and if their mothers
say adders have beaks, then beaks are what they
possess and no amount of questioning the crown
prince's learned men of science about adder faces
will change that fact).

—*Princess Christian of Sonderburg-Beck's Guide for
Her Daughter's Illumination and Betterment*

"THE GOVERNOR SAYS YOU MAY SEE THE PRISONER NOW."

"And about time too," Leo muttered to himself as
he followed the guard out of the waiting room into
the depths of the prison itself. He wasn't an impatient
man as a rule, but having to spend hours first convinc-
ing the governor that he simply wanted to get to the
bottom of the murder and then waiting for permission
to see Dagmar's companion had tried his patience
almost to its limit. He had time, however, to mentally
compose several questions he wanted answers to, and

once delivered to a small, dank stone cell, he wasted no time in getting them.

"Good afternoon, Mrs. Deworthy." He glanced around her cell. It wasn't by any sense of the word comfortable, but he didn't see overt signs of filth or vermin. There was one wooden chair and a metal-framed cot bolted to the floor, upon which had been laid a less-than-clean pallet and horsehair blanket. "I am glad to see that you are unharmed by your trip to the prison."

"Lord March!" She leaped up from where she'd been huddled in a miserable ball at the end of the cot, and rushed toward him. The guard behind him made to check her, but Leo held up a hand to stop him. Luckily, it had the effect of keeping her from leaping upon him in gratitude. "You have come at last! They have set me free, have they not? I am ready to leave this instant!"

"I'm afraid you haven't been released, not just yet that is."

"But—" Her lower lip trembled and tears filled her eyes. "But they can't be serious in believing that I could have done anything so heinous—so sinful and disregarding of all moral values. I assure you, Lord March, that a horrendous mistake has been made! This slur against my character is unbearable! I would not—I *could not* have killed dear Mrs. Hayes!"

"And that is why I am here," he said in a reassuring tone that he was far from feeling. The evidence against Julia was staggering, especially given the eyewitness testimony—his own included. But he owed it to Dagmar to investigate the crime. Until he was easy in his mind that her companion was innocent—or guilty—then he'd do his damnedest to find out the truth. "Be seated, please, and we will discuss the events."

"I don't want to discuss them!" Julia wailed, covering her face with her hands. "I don't want to think about it ever again. I just want out of this terrible place!"

"I understand that, madam, and you can take my word that I shall do my best to see to it that you are released, but in order to do that I must first be in possession of all the facts, and that includes what you saw and did and heard."

"Very well," she said and sat on the extreme edge of the cot, but leaped up a second later when a key sounded in the door.

To Leo's intense surprise, Dagmar flew into the room.

To his pleasure, she went straight to his side.

To his amazement, she wasn't alone.

"Er…" he said a moment later when Plum, Harry, Gillian, and Noble all trooped in after her. The cell wasn't large to begin with, but filled as it was by seven people, space was at a premium.

"Hello, Leo. We've come to help." Dagmar squeezed herself up next to him, which pleased him greatly.

"So I see. All of you?"

"Goodness, it is a little tight in here…Gillian, would you mind moving your elbow? Thank you. Oh, hello again, Mrs. Deworthy. We've come to save you."

"Plum, please," Harry said in an undertone, flashing Leo an apologetic look. "I suppose you're wondering what we're all doing here."

"I understand from Dagmar that you're here to help. Hello, Noble, Gillian. It's been a long time."

"Too long," Gillian called over Plum's shoulder. Both she and Noble had barely fit into the small cell with the others. There was a general jostling of elbows and shuffling of feet, but at last everyone had a modicum of space. "It's a pleasure to see you again. You must come down to Nethercote as soon as you can. And bring Dagmar, of course, assuming she hasn't cut you free by then."

"Cut me free?" He twisted around to look down at his wife, who was murmuring soft, supportive platitudes to her companion. "Why would you want to get rid of me?"

Dagmar stopped murmuring and gave him a sad look. "It's what you deserve."

"Wait…I don't understand—"

The door opened again and smacked up against the back of Noble, who swore and scooted forward just enough to allow Thom entrance.

"Gracious. It's like a pod packed full of peas in here, isn't it?"

"Like a sausage in a glove," Dagmar said forlornly, which just made Leo hard.

"About this cutting me free—"

"Hello, Mrs. Deworthy. I don't know if you remember me, but I'm Plum's niece, Thom. I'm here to be supportive and helpful and put your wishes and needs and desires above those of certain bastard men who wouldn't know a good thing if it came up and bit him on his backside, which sounds like an obnoxious thing to do, when you think about it, but I don't know, there's something somewhat appealing about it as well."

"We really have to get her married off," Plum said in an undertone to Harry.

"I fear for her libido if we don't," he agreed.

"Hello again, Leo," Thom said, her hand visible over the heads as she waved at him. Leo couldn't actually see her through the densely packed bodies, but he acknowledged her with a greeting.

"It's nice to hear you, Thom, and I'm sure Mrs. Deworthy appreciates you supporting and helping her, but perhaps if some of you—the female some of you—wouldn't mind returning to the governor's office, I could actually proceed with ascertaining just what happened earlier today in the baptistery."

Leo had to raise his voice for the last bit, since Plum and Thom started arguing.

"I don't see why you insist on having such a hidebound, rigid attitude. Especially after your experience with your first husband."

"My first husband was an utter and complete abomination—"

"As is Nick."

"Do you think we could go five minutes without slandering my son?" Noble asked.

"Not to mention the fact that my first marriage has nothing to do with the situation, nothing at all."

"I say it does. And Harry wouldn't mind if I just was Nick's mistress, would you, Harry? I mean, you must have had mistresses before you married Aunt Plum."

"About this cutting loose—" Leo said, leaning down to speak in Dagmar's ear.

"Good Lord, I'm not about to discuss that in front

of Plum," Harry said, struggling to get his arms free enough to cover her ears.

Dagmar sniffled quietly and bit her lower lip. He wanted to bite it as well, but a swift calculation of the remaining space—about a spare inch—left him with no room to maneuver himself into position where he could kiss her.

"Well, I don't care what you say. If that blighted, maggoty rotter ever shows his cowardly face and begs my forgiveness, not that it will be swift in coming because I have five long years' worth of anger to vent on him, but if he does, then I shall stand firm on the subject."

The door opened again, and once more smacked Noble on the back. A tall young man squeezed his way in, cracking his shins on the end of the metal cot. Plum, pushed forward, oozed out onto the bed and took up residence on it.

"Hullo," Nick said as the door thumped softly to a close behind him. "Did I hear myself being abused in no uncertain terms?"

"You did," Thom said over her shoulder, being too firmly packed into the room to turn around. "And I would say it to your face if I could do so. Noble, would you mind moving forward just a smidgen so that I can abuse your son to his face?"

"Hullo, Papa," Nick called over her head.

"Hello, Nick. You look well. Gillian, doesn't he look well?"

"He does, very well indeed, although we would have known that if he'd come to see us the instant he got back in England, instead of lounging around London."

"Why are you sniffling in that pathetic manner?"

Leo asked Dagmar. "More importantly, why do you want to leave me?"

"Because I seduced you. I have to let you go."

To Leo's horror, her lower lip quivered for a moment before she sucked it up. He could handle many things in life—being wounded by a saber-wielding maniac, trying to determine the facts behind a bizarre murder, even handling a wife he hadn't known he'd married—but the sight of Dagmar trying so hard to hold back tears melted his insides. He didn't want her sad and crying. He wanted her giggly and giving him come-hither looks that sent him thither with a song on his lips and an erection in his trousers.

"Noble, please."

"Eh? Oh. Gillian, I believe if Plum sits on her heels that you can join her on that repulsive cot, and then we will all be able to breathe a bit easier. We'll have to burn your gown later, because I have no doubt the cot is infested with all sorts of vermin, but the loss of a gown is a small price to pay in order for Thom to be able to face Nick."

Gillian hopped on the cot, and the two ladies did, in fact, sit on their heels, both of them watching with interest as Thom was able to turn to face Nick. Noble, with a wink at the rest of them, jostled her straight into his son's arms.

"My apologies," he murmured.

Leo took advantage of the fact that everyone was focused on Nick and Thom to speak to his wife. "I don't know why you believe you seduced me, because I have no recollection of any such event, but since you evidently wish to, then I'll go along with that. Why, however, does that make you want to leave me?"

"You are a coward," Thom told Nick, her face pink at the fact that she was more or less pressed up against him, his arms loosely around her.

"Yes, I am."

"You are despicably slimy and cruel and heartless."

"And foolish," he said, kissing the tip of her nose. "Don't forget foolish."

"How you could spurn me to go off and do all sorts of good deeds when you knew I would have been happy to do them with you—"

"You wanted to go to that doctoring place in Germany. I knew how much that meant to you, and figured that by the time you were done there, I'd be done doing my work, and we'd both be back in England together. But that didn't quite work out. You stayed in Germany for two years, and then my work took me back to the Continent."

"—is beyond the understanding of any normal human being."

Dagmar, rather than turning toward Leo as he hoped, turned away, her little shoulders tight with anguish. "I don't want to leave you," he heard her say in a very small voice.

"Then why, for the love of God, are you attempting to do so?"

She mumbled something that he didn't hear.

"You didn't even ask me to wait for you!" Thom yelled at Nick.

He looked highly uncomfortable, no doubt partly because, with the exception of Dagmar and Leo, the occupants of the room were all avidly watching him. He tugged at his neckcloth. "I couldn't, Thom. Not without having a fortune. It wasn't fair to you to ask you to wait for a pauper."

Thom managed to shove him in the shoulder. "You *have* a fortune! Your father gave you one! Enough for us to live on, anyway."

"But it's not really mine—"

"And I have a dowry!"

"She does," Harry agreed. "Gave it to her myself."

"We could have lived on either of those, but no, you didn't want to!"

"Thom, you don't understand—"

"No, I don't! Explain it to me!"

Nick opened and closed his mouth a couple of times, finally looking with desperation at his father.

"Don't look at me," Noble said, shaking his head. "I thought you should have wed her before you went."

"Noble!" Gillian protested. "That's not what you told him at the time!"

"I told him what he wanted to hear because he thought he was going to be killed. Do you think I'd send my son off to do dangerous work with an uneasy mind that could distract him at a vital moment?"

"I suppose not," Gillian allowed. "But that was years ago, and now Nick needs to just do what he should have done then and marry Thom."

"That's all right," Thom said, sniffing as she pushed away from Nick's embrace. "It's clear he doesn't want me. I'll just go back to Germany and take care of donkeys and horses and those adorable cows with the pretty eyes and enormously long eyelashes."

Nick glanced heavenward, but his expression of long-suffering martyrdom switched to one of fury when Thom added, "And I'll find a nice goatherd who isn't a bastard and become *his* mistress."

"You'll do no such thing. You'll marry me, and we'll live on my father's money, and you'll like it," Nick said savagely, but immediately began laughing when Thom spun around and punched him in the shoulder.

"We'll live on Harry's money!"

"We'll pool the money together and live on that, all right?" he asked, pulling her back into his arms.

She smiled and leaned up to kiss him. "*After* you've apologized."

"This is so romantic," Gillian whispered to Plum.

"It really is." Plum dabbed at her eyes, then nudged Gillian. "Now we just need to fix Leo."

Leo, who had been distracted by the Nick/Thom scene, was about to demand that his wife tell him what was wrong but paused to glare at the two women. "I don't need fixing!"

"No, of course you don't. Only Dagmar seems to think you do," Plum said quickly, giving him a sympathetic look. "You enjoyed her seducing you, didn't you? Apparently, she thinks that you didn't have a say in the matter."

"We told her that was ridiculous," Gillian added, nodding at Plum. "But she just said something about despair and living by herself, and you being as free as some very free thing, and it all got a bit confusing."

"By then we'd emptied the bottle," Plum admitted. "That probably had something to do with it."

"Did you offer them a copy of your new book?"

"No, no, the new one isn't ready yet." Plum blushed a pleasant shade of pink, sending Harry a quick look under her lashes that he returned with a bawdy grin. "We're still perfecting a few of the more...advanced...positions."

"Wait'll you see Panther Dancing at Newly Dawned Morn. It'll knock your boots right off your feet," Harry told Noble with a wink.

"If you do it correctly, yes, it should. But about you, Leo—"

Leo had enough of Dagmar avoiding his gaze. "What," he asked her, interrupting Plum, "is this nonsense about you seducing me?"

Dagmar shot a look around the room. "This really isn't the place for this conversation."

"I don't know why not," Nick said, looking up from where he had been whispering in Thom's ear. "Lord knows I was made to bare my private affairs in front of everyone. I don't see why you shouldn't as well."

"This is different," Leo said and bodily forced himself past Noble and Harry, dragging a resistant Dagmar behind him. "We'll be back in a minute. Nick, would you mind moving to the side? Thank you."

They managed to squeeze themselves out the door, emerging from the cell with what Leo imagined was a popping noise. Once in the corridor, he took Dagmar with his good arm and bent to kiss her. She turned her face away with another lift of that damned stubborn chin. "All right, we're alone. What's all this business? Why won't you let me kiss you as is my right and duty as a thoughtful husband bent on ensuring your complete and utter satisfaction with all things husbandly?

Why do you think you seduced me, and most of all, why do you want to leave me?"

"I *don't* want to," Dagmar all but wailed, tearing herself away from him to move a few steps away. "Aren't you listening to me? I keep saying I don't want to, but that I have to."

"I apologize," he said, making her a little bow. "It was a bit distracting in there, what with Nick and Thom working out their differences, and Plum going on about panthers. Why, if you do not wish to abandon me, are you insistent on doing so?"

She took a deep breath and turned to face him. He had to admire her pluck—she clearly felt she was performing some horrible but vital chore. "It's because of the way we were married. Don't you see, Leo? I married you when you were less than sensible of your surroundings."

"You did that because you thought I was dying. And I likely would be dead if not for you."

"That's beside the point."

"I don't think it is, no," he said, shaking his head.

"And then I put you on the ship to bring you home, because I thought you were on your way home, but again, you had no choice in the matter. I made the decision for you."

"Ah," he said, light beginning to dawn. "You believe you seduced me into bedding you, thus eliminating the ability to annul the marriage?"

"Yes. I did seduce you, Leo, no matter what you say, and I can see that you're going to protest that I didn't, but that is just your manly pride at being the one in charge of such things. The truth is far less flattering. In every important matter, I have taken your choices away and made the decisions for you, and that is the reason I must now set you free. It's not right that you should have so little say in your own life, although I will say in my own defense that I never meant anything but good for you."

He watched her silently, his heart filled with a sensation that he was hard put to name until it occurred to him that it was love—actual love, not just lust or fondness or even a strong liking, but outright love, romantic, all-consuming love. He loved Dagmar. He loved the way she stood there and argued with him; he loved the way her mind worked, even if it was at the moment going off on a bizarre track that he doubted he'd ever be able to follow; and most of all, he loved the fact that she loved him enough to sacrifice her own happiness for his. What a wonderful, marvelous woman she was.

"You utter idiot," he told her, taking her in his arms before she could bristle at the tenderly spoken words. "You adorable, fascinating, completely and wholly illogical woman. You love me."

"I am not illogical!" Dagmar said, looking duly outraged at the very idea. "And I object strongly to you saying so. I am the most logical person I know. I think things through. I make plans. I consider alternatives. If that's not logical, then I don't know what is!"

He waited until she wound down, then said casually, "Not going to dispute it?"

Her lips thinned. She knew exactly what he was talking about, because she was the person meant to light his life with her delectable self, whether or not she wished to admit it. "I don't know what you're talking about."

"You're not a very good liar, though. Not that I want a wife who lies to me, but there are times when such a skill comes in handy, as I've frequently found. There was a time when the late czar asked me what I thought of his favorite mistress, and if I'd spoken the truth, even a diplomatic version, I wouldn't have seen the next morning. No, on the whole, I think it would be better if you learned how to prevaricate convincingly, especially if one day the local vicar of wherever we end up living asks you to judge flowers. Or babies. Or the many things that ladies of the manor are asked to judge. But never you fear, my darling, I shall teach you. And you will learn because you love me."

"Stop saying that!" She stomped her foot. "I'm letting you go, dammit! You're going to be a free man again. Stop making plans to teach me to lie to a vicar because we aren't going to have a manor house. We aren't going to have a life where I will judge babies and flowers. I am going to live above a small shop, the specifics of which I have not yet ascertained, and you will go about being a highly desirable earl who holds one shoulder just the teensiest bit higher than the other but which doesn't detract from his handsomeness one little bit."

He laughed. "Now I know you're in love with me. No one else has ever called me handsome. Dagmar."

"What?" She frowned at his shoulder, clearly annoyed with him, and that delighted him all the more.

He leaned down to whisper in her ear, "I happen to love you too."

"You don't!" Her eyes were wide with surprise. "You're just saying that because you're suddenly overwhelmed with gratitude for the fact that I, a princess of noble blood, married you and saved your life."

"You're fooling yourself if you think either of those things matters. I'll be eternally grateful to you for saving my wretched hide, but only because it means I get to spend the balance of my life with you. Now kiss me, tell me that you love me, and that you've given up all ideas of abandoning me, because you know I won't let that happen."

"But, Leo—"

"No."

"I took away all your choices—"

"You saved my life and acted in my best interests in bringing me home."

"I seduced—"

"You did no such thing. Darling, do you think I don't have the wherewithal to resist even the most alluring of women if I chose to do so?" He laughed at her outraged expression and laughed even harder when she pinched his good arm. "It was your first time. I wanted you to be comfortable with what was going to happen, so I let you take the initiative that night. You didn't seduce me; if anything, I was guilty of putting you in a position where I knew your curiosity would triumph over what might be considered better sense."

"What better sense?" she said, her cheeks deliciously pink. She didn't turn away when he bent down to kiss her again.

"You've been so focused on how I wasn't worthy

of a wife who took action when it was needed that you never once considered whether or not you should be congratulated or commiserated for having such a lame husband. I'm an odd duck, my darling. I have a title and a suitable fortune to sustain myself, but no family and few close friends. I have fewer connections in polite society and, regrettably, even less of a desire to cultivate the same. I much prefer to live by my wits than to retire to the country and become a squire. In short, my gorgeous bundle of princess, I am not a very good catch. You'd be far better off without me."

She gazed at him with those lovely hazel eyes, now filled with serious consideration. "I don't particularly wish to live in the country and judge babies either. Will you take me with you on your missions?"

He hesitated, thoughts flashing through his mind about keeping her safe, locked away from harm and danger. That balanced with the delightful image of Dagmar at his side as he trod the delicate paths of intrigue at the various foreign courts into which his missions took him. He would conduct all manner of secret arrangements, negotiations, and agreements, while she enthralled and captivated everyone with her unique charm. He grinned. "We'll make an unstop-pable team."

"A team? Do you mean we will work together?"

"Yes. You'll have to leave the more dangerous work to me, but I can see where a wife would be an asset to many of my jobs."

She thought about that for a moment, then gave a little nod. "Very well, I will allow you to love me and remain married to me."

"You allow? I like that." He laughed aloud, pulling her tight against his chest and giving her a loud kiss. "You're incorrigible, madam, which is one of the reasons that I love you so very much. And now, lest my masculine pride take the beating you feared it had earlier, you may tell me just how much you love me."

"Enough that I was willing to let you go, you annoying man," she said, biting the end of his nose before pushing the door open a few inches. "If I don't have to tear out my heart by releasing you from your marriage vows, then we had best save Julia so that we can go off and do secretive things. Will you really teach me how to lie convincingly?"

"I will."

"Excellent! I already know how to shoot a pistol, in case someone attacks you with a saber again and a pistol is at hand. Oh, pardon me, Nick. Was that the back of your head? Perhaps we can get back into the cell? Leo and I have come to an accord."

"Well, that was easier than I expected," Gillian said to Plum.

"Young people these days talk more than people of our generation," Plum answered. "When I was growing up, we were discouraged from ever talking about feelings or emotions or thoughts to men. It just wasn't done."

"Really?" Gillian looked surprised. "I've never kept any of my thoughts from Noble. If I have something to say to him, I say it."

"Which has kept my life interesting if a bit chaotic," Noble said, but the look he gave his wife was one of such heat, her eyes sparkled in return.

Leo squeezed his way back into the cell, his heart swelling with the thought that he had many, many years in which to perfect his own heated looks to Dagmar. "Now then," he said once Dagmar and he were smooshed together at the far end of the cell. Her companion Julia sat with her back against the wall, her feet tucked under her in order to leave room for them. "Now that all the romantic complications have been settled to everyone's satisfaction—"

"Seriously, my lad," Harry told Nick, evidently finishing up a conversation, "you will have to let us give you an early copy of the revised version of Plum's first book, which is to be printed next month. The annotations to Jogging Camel alone are worth a good week's bliss…eh? What? Sorry, Leo. Continue."

Leo eyed Dagmar, who smiled at him. "Put us down for one of those copies as well," he said before turning back to her companion. "Shall we start at the beginning, Mrs. Deworthy?"

Fifteen

There comes a time in every female's life when she passes from girlhood to womanhood. Such times should be greeted with a withdrawal from polite company in order to repose with quietude in her bedchamber. Scenes wherein the afflicted stomps around her home demanding that someone shoot her and put her out of her misery are not appropriate, nor are demands for opium and an entire cask of brandy.

—*Princess Christian of Sonderburg-Beck's Guide for Her Daughter's Illumination and Betterment*

"THERE'S REALLY NO BEGINNING TO BEGIN AT."

Julia looked so pale and frightened that Dagmar stopped wanting to leap on Leo and kiss the breath right out of him, and instead edged forward until she could pat her friend's foot—all she could reach with Leo in the way—in a comforting manner that she hope implied all sorts of moral support.

"One minute I was there, sketching the images that

we saw on the base of the arch—you remember that, don't you, dearest Princess?—and the merest slip of a second past that Mrs. Hayes went deranged, quite, quite deranged! She threw me bodily against the wall, causing me to hit my head very hard. Indeed, I believe I was insensible for a few minutes, for when I came to my senses, I found that I had been dragged halfway up the stairs and left to lie in a patch of dirt and rat droppings. It was horrible but not nearly so horrible as when I regained my feet and went down the stairs to see what had happened. Mrs. Hayes lay on the ground with red ink on her face, and Mr. Dalton kneeling next to her, patting her hand and saying her name over and over again."

"Red ink?" Dagmar glanced at Leo, who had half turned so they could both see Julia. "Was she sketching as well?"

"Yes, but not with red ink. Like me, Mrs. Hayes was using a pencil."

"Are you sure it was red ink?" Leo asked.

"Where did you see this ink?" Nick asked at the same time.

Julia sniffled into her handkerchief for a moment before answering, "Yes, I'm sure, and it was on her face, dribbling from her mouth. There were also a few smears on her gown, but most of it dribbled out the side of her mouth."

Leo glanced down at Dagmar. "That sounds like blood to me."

"I'm sure it was meant to look that way," Julia said calmly. Dagmar wondered at that, since Julia was usually prone to hysterics at the first sign of blood. "There must have been a bit of it on the stone, for when I knelt next to her to ascertain her state of health, I got some on my hand, and it rubbed onto my gown. You can see the stain here." She gestured toward a small red smear on her faded green gown.

Dagmar stared at her. "Julia, I hate to say it, but that is blood."

"No, it's not." Julia shook her head emphatically.

"It looks like blood," Plum said.

"It's not. Blood dries brown, not red." Julia looked at Dagmar with a hint of irritation. "Dearest Princess, is this really necessary? Can you not purchase by some means or other my release from this nightmare?"

"We're trying to do that, Julia," Dagmar said, sliding a quick glance toward Leo. He just looked thoughtful. "But we need to know the events in their entirety first, so that we can figure out why you were assumed to be guilty. What happened once you knelt by Mrs. Hayes's body?"

"Mr. Dalton saw me and said several harsh things to me about killing his sister, and that my crime should not go unpunished. Which is the sheerest folly!" Julia gave a great sobbing cry and clutched her handkerchief to her face. "I did not kill her! I could not have! I was not even near her when she died!"

"My poor Julia, don't distress yourself unduly. It won't do you any good. You must trust that we'll be able to reveal the truth to all," Dagmar murmured, but her mind was busily turning over the image of Mrs. Hayes with ink on her face.

"Then those horrible workmen arrived, and you, my dearest, my oldest friend, came dashing up to save me, but alas, it was too late. Too late." Once again Julia dissolved into sobs, her shoulders moving in jerks.

They stayed another ten minutes, Leo insisting that Julia go over the events again, but by then Julia was near the state of emotions that Dagmar had expected, and little was had from her other than pleas for her release and the declaration that she had not harmed Louisa Hayes. Their parting was not easy; her companion clung to Dagmar and begged her not to go. There were a few unpleasant moments when Julia pled with her not to leave, but in the end, Leo managed to pry Julia off her and hustled her out of the cell.

"None of this makes any sense," Dagmar said a few minutes later when they assembled outside the prison gates. Their respective carriages were lined up farther down the road, and the group began strolling toward them. Dagmar didn't know what to think about Julia's testimony. She believed her friend was innocent— everything about her voice and face declared it, even if she hadn't been closely acquainted with her for years—but there was still something that bothered her, the same sort of little niggle of…something…that occurred when Louisa received the threatening note at breakfast a few days before.

"It really doesn't. Especially that ink on Mrs. Hayes's body," Plum said, her arm through Harry's.

Dagmar, who had been strolling alongside Nick, paused to allow Leo to catch up. For a moment, she allowed herself to enjoy the memory of his declaration of love. He loved her! He had said the words out loud, and the look in his eyes—that warm, slightly wicked look that made her tingle all the way down to her toes—gave proof to his statement. He loved her and didn't mind that she had taken away his choices, and he was happy to spend his days with her. Could life get any better? He smiled at her as she crossed to his other side, happily taking the elbow he stuck out for her.

"Yes, what about that ink? I think it means something," Gillian said.

"It means that Deworthy was mistaken, and Mrs. Hayes must have had a small vial of ink on her person. Perhaps it was opened during the struggle she had with her attacker," Noble offered.

"Hmm," Harry said. "That doesn't seem very likely. First of all, why would she be carrying around a vial of red ink?"

"Whimsy?" Noble suggested.

"Doubtful. No, I tend to put a bit more of a sinister bend on that ink." Harry glanced first at Nick then at Leo.

Both men nodded. "I agree with you that it would behoove us to look into it a bit more closely," Leo said.

"Why?" Dagmar and Thom asked at the same time. Thom had, by that time, claimed Nick's arm and was sending him heated looks that Dagmar thought boded well for their future.

"That ink wasn't there by accident," Nick said.

"It wasn't?" Gillian looked confused. "Then why was it there?"

"Well, now, that's a very interesting question." Plum spoke slowly, stopping next to a carriage with Harry's coat of arms painted on the side. "What I think is more interesting is what Mrs. Deworthy said."

"What did she say that was so interesting? I mean, other than the whole tale. I missed it if she said something odd."

"She said that she was sure the ink was meant to *look* like blood."

Dagmar thought about that, her brow wrinkling with concentration. Julia *had* said that. How very odd. It just made Julia's calm demeanor more confusing than ever.

"You can't mean to say that someone deliberately tried to make it look like Mrs. Hayes was bleeding?" Gillian asked.

"Why else would there be red ink dribbling from her mouth that way?" Plum asked. "If I was writing a scenario where I wanted it to look like someone was bleeding, but that person wasn't doing so, then that is the only way to achieve it."

Dagmar looked at Leo, now utterly confused. "Do you agree with that?"

There was a faint line between his brows, but he met her gaze. "I don't quite know what to think. I believe the situation requires more investigation."

"In what way?"

He hesitated, giving Nick time to answer her question. "I think you're going to have to examine that body, Leo."

"Good Lord, why?" Dagmar asked, aghast.

Neither man answered her. Plum looked thoughtful. Gillian just looked as confused as Dagmar felt. The men wore inscrutable looks that told her that they'd closed ranks and were trying to protect the women from some unsavory fact.

"I think that the ladies might be more comfortable at home," Noble said with an almost imperceptible nod to the others.

"Yes, I'm sure they would," Harry agreed. "Plum, my dear, why don't you take the others home and give them all a restorative beverage? Other than my whiskey, assuming Juan has left any."

Dagmar hated it when men did that. Her father was forever siding with Frederick about all of the things she wanted to do or know, and nothing annoyed her more. There was no way that she was going to allow them to shuffle her off to the side where she would be safe. Safety was boring. She wasn't married to a man who fairly dripped with intrigue only to be kept from all the exciting parts of life.

"Fine," she said decisively and leaped into the carriage that Leo had evidently rented for their use. "Leo and I will pay our respects to Louisa. And if it so happens that we take a little peek into the coffin to see how she looks, why then, no one will be the wiser."

"Dagmar—" Leo started to say.

"It's going to look very suspicious if the four of you arrive at Mr. Dalton's house and demand to see his dead sister," she pointed out. "Whereas it is only decent, common manners for you and me to pay our respects to our late hostess."

Leo grimaced and faced the others. "She has a point."

The men clearly didn't like it but, in the end, had to admit that it was the only way to accomplish an examination of the corpse without causing either comment or distress to Philip Dalton.

They rode in silence through the city, the sun

beginning to grow heavy in the sky. "I wish I could pinpoint what it is that bothers me," Dagmar said after about twenty minutes' silent contemplation.

Leo roused himself from a light doze. "Hrph? What was that?"

"There's something that someone said…no, something not said that should have been said. And that letter at breakfast, the one with the salt. Something has always bothered me about that." She looked up from where her gaze had been fixed on her gloves. "Do you think it's possible that someone really was threatening Louisa? Not Julia, because as I've mentioned repeatedly, she simply isn't that sort of person. But what if someone else was threatening Louisa, and she thought it was Julia? Could that unknown person be responsible for her death too?"

"It's possible," Leo said slowly, rubbing his eyes. "But we heard Louisa Hayes scream the name of her murderer, and she'd hardly do that if it was another person who was throttling her."

"Not unless that person *appeared* to be Julia," Dagmar said, feeling as if a bolt of inspiration had just struck her. "What if someone was masquerading as her? That would explain why Louisa was screaming that Julia was killing her."

"But why put ink at her mouth, then?"

Dagmar opened her mouth to answer but closed it again when she realized she couldn't explain that away. "I don't know," she finally said. "It appears to have been put there for no real reason."

"I've been trying to remember the morning, but I don't…no, I don't remember seeing blood on Mrs. Hayes's mouth. Do you?"

"No, but I didn't get terribly close to her. Mr. Dalton had her in his arms, and then we had to fetch the doctor. And after we did that, I was busy trying to calm Julia and didn't see Louisa when they carried her away. Did you?"

"No. Dalton warned me to get you out of there because he knew the constables would be there shortly to take your companion away." Leo shook his head at a thought. "It doesn't make sense unless…"

"Unless what?"

"That comment your companion made…"

"The one about the ink intended to look like blood?"

"Yes." Leo leaned back against the cushions, wiggling his shoulder until it was comfortable. "No one else was near Mrs. Hayes. If it was ink, and it was placed on her to simulate blood, only one person could have done it."

"Philip Dalton," Dagmar said, shaking her head even as she did so. "But why would he do that? Why would he want to simulate blood on his sister?"

"I don't know, but I'd give a great deal to see his hands," Leo said darkly.

She stared at him. "This is becoming tiresome, but I feel compelled to ask you to explain yet again, although really, you could make an effort to tell me things rather than hint at them with deep distrust, thus making me feel exceptionally stupid because you've seen something or heard something or, worse yet, figured out something that I haven't. Why his hands?"

Leo laughed. "You're not stupid, although you are exceptional. Do you not recall what Mrs. Deworthy said about there being a few drops of red ink on Louisa

Hayes's gown and the stones near her? That implies that the ink was splashed or spilled somewhat, and the likelihood is that whoever had the vial of ink got some of it on his hands."

"Oh. That makes sense. How annoying that I didn't think of it as well. Do you intend to be smarter than me all the time?"

"I doubt if that claim is valid even on my best of days, but if it will make you happy, I promise to be dull witted every other Thursday."

"Excellent. About Mr. Dalton's hands...we can't very well march into his house and ask to see if his hands are stained red. That's assuming they would be; there's no guarantee that they are even if he splashed ink around Louisa."

"No, but at this point, I'm willing to take any slight lead I can find."

"You don't...you don't suspect Philip Dalton of having something to do with Louisa's death, do you?"

"I don't quite know what to suspect. I wish I had more information."

That made her smile to herself. Leo, she was coming to discover, liked things arranged in an orderly fashion, including information. "Is this what you do when you're in Europe?" she asked, suddenly filled with curiosity. She wanted badly to know everything there was to know about him, and hugged to herself the joy of knowing she would have many long years to delve into what made him the way he was.

He shot her a look vaguely filled with question. "You mean when I'm doing work for Lord Salter? Not really. Well, perhaps sometimes. Generally, I am given missions where I'm expected to acquire information that certain individuals would prefer to keep hushed. Sometimes I'm called upon to take action, although now—" His mouth gave a wry twist when he moved his bad shoulder. "Now I suspect that my duties will be purely information gathering. Which is where you will come in most helpful, my dear."

She preened, feeling so happy that she could burst into song. "Because I'm a princess?"

"Because you're a woman, and women talk more to women than they do to men. Unless that man is a lover, but somehow, I have the feeling you won't like me taking on missions where I'm to woo another."

"I feel quite confident that should you ever be required to be another woman's lover, either in name or deed, I will be obliged to geld you." She brushed off a piece of lint from her sleeve when Leo laughed, then added, "And just in case you think I'm not serious, I should add that I'm well versed in gelding techniques. When I was young, I had great regard for my father's groom, as I believe I've mentioned, and he was a master gelder. People used to come from far and wide to bring their stallions to him because he was so quick. A sudden flick with the knife, a dab of ointment that he swore sealed the wound almost immediately, and hey nonny, there were a pair of testicles on the ground. So you see, I feel I learned from the best there was."

Leo crossed his legs, his expression priceless.

She patted his knee, pleased that he took her comments seriously. "I shall be delighted to help you in all ways, Leo. I quite look forward to it. Papa would never take us anywhere because there was no money to be had for trips, so the thought of being able to travel is very exciting. Where will we go first?"

"Nowhere for the moment. I've told Salter that I had to get you settled first. But once we have a house…perhaps Berlin. Perhaps Prague. Or Vienna. It just depends where I am needed."

"Wherever we go, I'm sure it will be wonderful." She dwelled for a few minutes on thoughts that she'd prefer he not know she was thinking, since they involved his naked person and imagining him naked and doing things to her made her feel wonderfully wicked, but eventually, her mind returned to the problem that stumped them both.

"Why did Louisa knock Julia silly and drag her up the stairs? No one else was around that part of the room. It had to be Louisa. But if it was her, then who attacked her? Why can't we figure this out?"

Irritatingly, Leo had no answers. Instead, he took her hand and rubbed his thumb across her knuckles, which served to remind her that she was newly married to the most handsome man on the face of the earth and could expect to enjoy much connubial bliss that evening. She'd never wished so hard for the hours to pass as she did at that moment.

The Dalton house was hushed and suitably swathed in black crepe both inside and out, so as to warn to all passersby that a death had occurred within.

The butler greeted them in subdued tones, nodding when Leo said—with an equally solemn mien—that they were there to pay their respects. The mirrors had been turned to face the wall and draped in black crepe.

White flowers bedecked all the horizontal surfaces, while in the small sitting room, where a bier had been made, upon which the closed casket rested, flames from two dozen tall candlesticks danced and flickered in the draft.

"Thank you, we'd like a few minutes alone with our thoughts," Leo told the butler as he gently shooed the latter out the door.

"Very good, my lord. I will inform Mr. Dalton of your arrival."

Leo waited until the door closed behind him before turning and saying hastily, "We have about two minutes. Let's get the lid open. Er…you're not squeamish, are you, love?"

Dagmar glowed with pleasure at the term of endearment. "No, not at all. Julia's the one who makes huge scenes at the sight of blood."

"Excellent. We'll just…this seems to be screwed down…we'll just have a quick look…damn and blast it. Can you unscrew the bolts on that side? We'll take a fast look and no one will be the…hell."

"I can't seem to loosen these screws," Dagmar said from her position at the far side of the coffin. "They're stuck."

"They aren't stuck. Those are lead seals binding it closed. There's no way to get them off short of cutting them." Leo's face was grim when he glanced to the door before rushing around the casket to where Dagmar stood. "Down on your knees."

"What?" She knelt when he pushed her downward, quickly following suit. It was just in time too. The door opened to find them both apparently in prayer.

Leo rose stiffly. "Dalton, you needn't have come to see us. We know you must be exhausted by the day's tragedy. Dagmar and I thought we'd come offer a few prayers for your late sister. We had no intention of disturbing you."

"It's no disturbance," Philip said, his voice hoarse. He seemed slightly winded, and Dagmar couldn't help but notice the lines of strain fanning out from his eyes. He reminded her of one of Frederick's coursing hounds, held back by a huntsman but dancing and straining every muscle in anticipation of being released. Philip had that same air of controlled frenzy. Could grief for a beloved sister have affected him that way? Or was she allowing Leo's dark suspicions to taint her view of him?

Leo strolled forward, his hand extended. Dagmar held her breath until Philip shook Leo's hand. She had half expected Philip to be wearing gloves, but he wasn't, and as far as she could see, neither hand bore any red stains.

There went Leo's theory. The man himself must have noticed that, because he looked slightly disgruntled as Philip escorted them to the drawing room. "The funeral is arranged for tomorrow," he was saying when they entered it. "I would be honored if you could see your way to attending, although I will understand if it would be too much for your nerves, Princess Dagmar."

Dagmar wanted very much to tell him that she'd back her nerves against his any day, but she bit her lip and simply murmured, "My sainted mother would never let me live a day in peace if she knew I refused to do my duty to a woman who had been considerate and kind to us."

Philip talked for a bit about his sister and what her loss would mean to him. "We had been so close growing up, and then Louisa married and her husband's post took her to Italy. When he was of age, her son Algernon—the one of whom I spoke to you—returned to England and took up residence with me for some years. It was Louisa's fondest wish that she be able to return as well, but after Algernon's untimely death, she hadn't the heart to do so until her husband died of cholera some six months ago. And now my wife is dead, and Louisa is dead, and I shall die a lonely old man."

"You have friends who care for you," Dagmar pointed out with a gentleness that she hoped belied the slight annoyance at his maudlin comments. Grief she understood well, but she had little tolerance for wallowing in self-pity. "You have other family members who will no doubt embrace you in your time of need."

"I am alone in the world," he replied, striking a dramatic pose—one hand on his chest and his head bowed.

"You might travel," Leo suggested. His eyes were bright with some emotion, but Dagmar couldn't tell if it was excitement or curiosity. Perhaps it was both. "Go to Italy. Didn't your sister wish to return there?"

Philip's head jerked up. "Italy? I don't recall her saying that. She was thrilled to be back in England."

Dagmar sensed something not quite truthful in that statement. She glanced at Leo, pleased to the ankles with the thought that she was having her first experience helping him with subterfuge. Did he want her to say the obvious? His expression gave her no warning, but she thought, on the whole, that he had arranged the conversation to lead to just that point. She would speak. "Oh, but don't you remember our first morning here? We were at breakfast, and Louisa was telling both Julia and me about her lovely villa outside of Florence and how she wished very much to return there because she found the weather more conducive to her general health than England. Leo, you remember that conversation, do you not?"

"I do."

Philip looked flustered for a moment. "I stand corrected. Perhaps it was just my wishful thinking that Louisa wanted to stay here. Alas, the point is moot now."

"Is it?" Leo said under his breath. Dagmar heard him, wondering what he meant. There was no disputing the fact that Louisa was dead. They'd both seen her dead body at the baptistery...a thought struck her at that moment, a thought so amazing, she almost blurted it right out but managed to catch herself in time. The partner of a man who practiced covert actions did not speak her thoughts in front of others—not about something as mind-boggling as this.

They stayed for another ten minutes or so, then bade farewell, promising to attend Louisa's funeral the following day.

"Well?" Leo asked once they were safely ensconced in the carriage. It jerked and bumped over the cobbled streets, sending her into his side again and again until he simply wrapped his undamaged arm around her and pulled her up tight against his side. "What do you think?"

"I think this evening isn't going to come soon enough, although I do hope that we are allowed to sleep in a bedchamber rather than on the sofa, as I told Plum we would. We couldn't possibly indulge in all the activities I'd like to indulge in if we are on a sofa."

He grinned at her, more than a little bit of that grin a leer. "You'd be surprised what we can do on a sofa. There are one or two enticing images dancing in my head at this very moment."

"Really? Such as what?"

"Well, for one, there's the thought of you bending over the back of the sofa."

She thought. "I don't see how that would accomplish…oh! Oh, yes, I see now. Hmm. That might be interesting, although I have doubts of my ability to stand while you are going about your business. Have you had the opportunity to see Frederick's chunk of India rubber?"

Leo choked slightly. "I fervently hope that's not a euphemism of any sort."

"It's not, not that I understand why you think so. I was referring to Frederick's chunk of rubber and how it applies to my legs."

"I…it…" Leo stopped, blinked a couple of times, then shook his head. "No, I simply cannot do it. I can't connect the two things without stepping into the land of the risqué. Tell me, my darling, imaginative wife, how do the two things relate?"

"Engaging in lovemaking with you makes my legs feel like Frederick's India rubber."

"Do you think," he said mildly, "that we could leave off the Frederick part of that? It's stopping the function of my brain every time, and it's getting harder to stop imagining things of which you have no familiarity."

"Oh!" Dagmar said, suddenly making the connection. "You mean an India rubber phallus, as described in much detail in Henrik's pornography."

He stared at her in surprise. "Who the hell is Henrik?"

"My father's groom. Didn't I mention him to you? He had wonderful upper parts, which he kept bare during the summer, and like you, he looked exceptionally well in tight breeches, especially when he bent over. He also kept a collection of pornographic periodicals that I found most interesting, although sometimes the words confused me. And of course, I couldn't go to my mother, asking what they meant, and Julia claimed not to know. Maybe you could tell me. Do you know what *back scuttling* means?"

Leo made another choking noise.

"No? How about *blowing the groundsils*?"

Leo gurgled.

"*Spanking a belly ruffian?*"

"Dagmar—"

She dredged through her memory. "*Lobster kettle?*"

"No, I do not know what that—well, yes, actually I do know, but it's nothing you need to know—"

"*Sapphist jig.* Leo, I'd dearly love to know what a *Sapphist jig* is."

"No, you wouldn't, not unless you have the same sort of interest in women as you have in me. Regarding sexual acts, that is."

"Really?" Dagmar thought about that in silence for

a few minutes. "I didn't realize that was possible. How is it done, exactly?"

The following ten minutes were eye-opening, to say the least, but had little to do with the situation at hand. "That's all very well and fine, but I think I prefer you," she said after giving the matter due consideration.

"I'm delighted to hear that. What did you have to promise Plum and Harry that they agreed to put us up despite the infectious state of their children?"

"Nothing. I was suitably pitiful. What are we going to do next?"

"Have a meal, most likely. Then indulge in polite chat for a few hours before we can decently retire, following which, I shall most indecently ravage you from the top of your adorable head to your ten little pink toes, and if you are very good, I will allow you to ravage me in return. Following that, a little restorative sleep and then possibly morning ravaging."

"Could we omit the polite chat and go straight to the indecent ravaging directly after supper?"

He grinned at her. "I like the way your mind works. Have I told you that? Well, it's true, I do. I like that you're just as willing to engage in mutual ravaging as I am and also that you say what you think. Few women I know do that."

"Thom does," Dagmar pointed out.

"Yes, but I have no desire to be married to her. You wouldn't let me, even if I did."

"Nick would probably have something to say about that too."

"Indeed he would." Leo took her hand. Dagmar wasn't sure why such a simple gesture warmed her heart the way it did, but the touch of his fingers against hers made her want to burst into a lusty song that Henrik was wont to sing after a visit to the local harlot. "I assume your original question referred to the situation with Philip Dalton?"

"Yes. You have suspicions about him, grave suspicions that I can't even put into words because they seem so outrageous."

"More outrageous than the idea that your friend murdered our hostess in an act of sheer cold blood?"

"No. But still very unlikely. Plus, I don't see how it could be done."

"That is why the few hours of polite chat that we will be obligated to make with Plum and Harry will feature the subject at hand." Leo's expression shifted from lighthearted to one of a darker mien. "I'd like to get Nick's and Harry's opinion just in case we are both sniffing down a false path."

The evening passed just as Leo suggested. When they arrived at the Rosses' house, Dagmar was shown to a first-floor bedchamber, having promised most faithfully not to venture into the floor above, where the children and the stricken servants were quarantined.

"This isn't the best room by any stretch of the imagination, but it will do in a pinch, and a pinch is exactly what you and Leo are in," Plum told her, waving a vague hand around the room. "How are you set for clothing? You're slighter than I am, and not as tall as Thom, but if you are in need of some garments until your wardrobe is finished, we'd be happy to lend you what you need."

"I'm fine, thank you. Louisa gave me a couple of

gowns, and I won't need anything more before the seamstress is done. Plum." Dagmar glanced at the open door. "I should warn you that I believe Leo is going to attempt to do something quite dangerous tonight."

"Really?" Plum's eyes opened wide. "What would that be?"

"I think he's going to try to break into a coffin, and most likely engage Nick and possibly Harry to help him."

Plum gazed at her with an O of surprise on her lips for a few seconds before she raised her eyebrows and said, "So it's like that, is it?"

Dagmar nodded. "Naturally, I won't let him risk himself in that manner. If he were caught, he'd have absolutely no excuse to offer, and if what he thinks is true, he might also be in grave danger."

"Well then," Plum said, slipping her arm through Dagmar's as the two women left the room and started down the stairs to the floor below. "We'll just have to see to it that no harm comes to him, won't we?"

"I really do like you," Dagmar told the older woman. "I'm so glad that you are Leo's friend."

"Your friend too now, my dear," Plum told her with a laugh and pressed her hand.

Supper was a merry affair since Noble and Gillian were present to celebrate the engagement of Nick and Thom, although Leo thought it would have been much merrier if Thom and Nick were actually speaking to each other, but since they had had one of their disagreements over where they would reside and whether Thom would stay safely out of Nick's sometimes dangerous employment, Nick spent the meal alternating a glower at his plate and Thom, all the while Thom spoke archly about the possibilities of marrying some goatherd in Germany.

By common consent, conversation was confined to mundane topics, and it wasn't until the men joined the ladies for coffee that Leo addressed them all. Judging by the look of exasperation that Dagmar shot him when he entered the room, he took it that the ladies had been peppering her with questions that she couldn't—or wouldn't, bless her delectable hide—answer.

He took a stand in front of the fireplace and faced them all. "I'd like to preface what I am about to say with the statement that I have no actual proof of anything. You were all present at the interview with Dagmar's companion, and you heard the broad hints she made and no doubt have little difficulty in interpreting them. At the time, I thought they were a wild attempt at dragging attention away from herself and onto the nearest scapegoat, but after seeing Philip Dalton a few hours ago, I have changed my mind."

"You saw the body?" Nick asked, momentarily distracted from mouthing silent things to Thom, who was pointedly perusing a book about Germany. "Was red ink present on the mouth?"

"No, we didn't see the body." Leo's gaze touched Dagmar for a moment before returning to the room in general. She smiled at him, and he thought longingly of the bed that must even now be waiting for them. "Not for the lack of trying, however. Dalton has had the coffin sealed."

"That's easy enough to get around," Harry said with a dismissive shrug. "Simply unbolt it."

"We did, but he's also seen fit to use lead seals on the coffin."

The company as a whole stared at him. "Lead *seals*?" Noble asked. "I don't believe I've ever seen that on a coffin."

"It's not unknown in Eastern Europe," Leo told them. "Usually in cases of plague. I have never seen the like in England, however, but the seals are present. They're about the size of a plate, three on either side of the coffin."

"Well, that proves that something is wrong," Gillian said, her brow wrinkled with thought. "Who would seal a coffin in such a way unless he had something to hide? The question is, what exactly is that something? Surely there can't be anything amiss with the body of his sister?"

"I think, my dear, Leo is hinting that perhaps what's amiss is the lack of a body," Noble said thoughtfully.

Leo nodded. "That is exactly what I've come to suspect."

"But where is it then?" Plum asked, looking confused. "What did Philip do with her?"

"Nothing."

"Nothing?" Plum's expression was almost comically shocked. "You don't mean he just dumped her out in the wilds for the animals to scavenge?"

"No, I mean there wasn't a body to be disposed of."

"Leo," Plum said firmly, giving him a sympathetic look. "There is a body. You saw it. Dagmar saw it. For heaven's sake, you witnessed the poor woman's murder! How can you say there isn't a body when there must be?"

"Because what we saw was a cleverly planned, and exquisitely performed, farce." Leo smiled at Dagmar and let a little of his lustful thoughts show in his eyes, enough so that she suddenly sat up straight and blushed adorably.

"Louisa Hayes isn't dead?" Thom asked, clearly drawn into the conversation despite her better intentions. "Why did she pretend to be so?"

"That is something I have yet to understand," Leo admitted. "But given what Dagmar's companion said, and the fact that Philip Dalton must have come close to straining a muscle getting to the room where Dagmar and I were closeted with the coffin as quickly as he did, as well as the fact that the coffin itself is sealed against any and all prying eyes, leads me to believe that what we witnessed was one giant, elaborate hoax. For some yet unknown reason, Philip Dalton and his sister wanted to make us believe that she was killed by Dagmar's companion."

"That makes even less sense than Mrs. Deworthy wanting to kill her," Plum protested. Dagmar looked thoughtful and opened her mouth to speak, but hesitated and frowned at her hands instead.

"Why would they do that? What would they have to gain by such a conspiracy?" Harry asked.

"They must have had a reason for doing so," Gillian said, glancing at her husband. "But I will admit to being a few steps behind everyone else and confused about just how they pulled this wool over your eyes. Dagmar was very detailed when she told us about the events, and it seemed quite clear that Mrs. Hayes was dead."

"She looked dead," Dagmar agreed.

"Ah, but looks can be deceiving. And if you recall, Dalton made very certain that neither you or I were allowed to get close to her."

"That's true," Dagmar said, her lips pursing. Leo had to fight with the urge to scoop her up in his arms and carry her off to bed where he would sate himself upon her lovely body until they were both exhausted…but then he remembered his bad arm, which forced him to amend the urge to simply sweeping her along with one arm, but even that idea was fraught with difficulties, because Dagmar was sure to insist on seeing to his wound before he could get down to the sating, and might even refuse to let him do all the things that he planned to do because it might hurt his shoulder. He smiled at her again, trying to indicate the fact that he was simultaneously warmed by the thought that she put his welfare so high, and confident that he knew his own limitations and wouldn't push past them on his quest to make her the most sexually satisfied woman who had ever lived. He put all of that and more into his smile.

"Leo, are you feeling all right? You look as if you're about to have a fit," was the response to all that effort. Dagmar rose and came to his side, placing one cool hand on the back of his neck. "Is your fever back?"

"No, and I am not about to have a fit. Really, woman! That is not the sort of thing a man likes to have said in front of his friends. Besides, I'm not the sort of person to have a fit. I've never had a fit. I never will have a fit. And stop feeling my head. I don't have a fever either. Go sit down and await the satiation to come."

She blinked, cocked her head to the side, and said, "Did you just chastise me in front of *my* friends?"

"Yes. We're even—my humiliation for your chastisement. Sit." He leaned over and kissed her loudly, adding in a softer voice, "Please."

"You're a very odd man sometimes, Leo. I find that I like that about you." She patted him on the cheek, beamed at the interested audience, and resumed her seat.

"My German goatherd will never chastise me in front of others," Thom said to no one.

Nick growled to himself, then suddenly leaped to his feet, stomped over to where Thom was sitting in an armless chair, pulled her to her feet, gave her a kiss almost identical in audible levels to the one Leo had just bestowed in Dagmar, then sat down, pulling Thom onto his lap.

Leo decided to ignore them and continued on with his summation of the situation. "Dagmar and I have come to the agreement that it would be wise to look in that coffin. I believe that the proof we seek will be in there—or rather, not in there. To that end, I propose that a small group of us do something quite reprehensible."

"Excellent!" Harry said, rubbing his hands, his eyes alight behind his spectacles. "I am at your service."

"You don't know what it is Leo wishes to do," Plum pointed out.

"It doesn't matter. I haven't done anything reprehensible in a very long time."

"I will be available for assistance, as well," Noble offered. "I assume Nick will be happy to lend his aid too, which he'd probably tell you except he's busy kissing my soon-to-be daughter-in-law."

"I'm your man," Nick managed to say before Thom grabbed his ears and kissed him for all she was worth.

"Very good," Dagmar said, standing and brushing her skirts. "I'm sure the other ladies will be just as thrilled to join you as I am. Eight people makes a good number for the breaking in of coffins, don't you think?"

"No!" Leo was filled with a desperate knowledge that Dagmar would forever leave him feeling as if the floor had suddenly dropped out from under him. "Eight is far, far too many. Four is good. Four is the right number for breaking into a coffin. Isn't it, Nick? Er…Harry?"

"It is, it is indeed the requisite number," Harry said, nodding. Plum pinched him. "Plum, you're going to leave a bruise if you continue with that sort of behavior. And if you do that, I won't be able to perform Conquistador in Sandstorm Seeking Shelter as you demanded I do this evening."

Plum turned bright red and smacked him on the arm. "There are times, Harry, when I see exactly where your boys get their manners. Stop deliberately embarrassing me and help Leo come to the point where he graciously agrees that we will accompany him."

"You know full well that we're not going to let you men go off and have adventures without us," Gillian said, patting Noble on the leg. He gave her a long, slow look that had her cheeks turning a little pink too.

"That's right. Leo said I was his partner in covert activities, and if there is anything more covert than breaking into a man's home and rifling through his coffin,

I don't know what is." Dagmar gave him a look that warmed him like the sun in the middle of an August day.

Leo made a few more protests, but in his heart, he knew the cause was a lost one. He could no more deny Dagmar a desire than he could cut off his own arm, and besides, he had a plan in mind that would guarantee the safety of the ladies.

"If we're going to do this," he said after a moment's thought and mental shrug at his lack of common sense, "we might as well do it in the proper style. Nick, if you could tear yourself away from your bride-to-be for a short while, I'd like your company. Harry, I have a job for you too. Dagmar, my darling, if I asked you to stay here while I left you for an hour or two at most, would you do so?"

"Yes," she said without hesitation.

"He's going to go peek in that coffin!" Gillian exclaimed.

"No, he isn't," Dagmar told her. "He knows that we all want to help. He must have some other task in mind that we can't help with, and so, yes, I will stay here with the ladies. I trust you, Leo."

He honestly couldn't love her more than he did at that moment in time. She was everything he could ever have wanted in a woman—large breasts, a slightly warped sense of wit, a fine appreciation of pornographic literature, and most of all, a brain that worked day and night to keep him on his toes. He loved that brain. "Quite right, my adorable one. We will be back as soon as possible. In the meantime, you ladies can do a few things to help ensure that our visit to Chez Dalton is the success we hope it to be."

Sixteen

It is important for a princess to remember that she is held to higher standards than other women, and in particular, her dealing with people; she must endeavor with all her being to be gracious to everyone, no matter how trying she believes they are. It need not be mentioned that a gracious princess is not a princess who puts an irritating powder into her cousin's wigs and clothing, and then tells his entire court that he has leprosy.

—Princess Christian of Sonderburg-Beck's Guide for
Her Daughter's Illumination and Betterment

SOMETIME LATER, THREE BLACK CLOSED CARRIAGES came to a stop a block away from Philip Dalton's house. Two of the carriages disgorged the conspirators from Plum and Harry's library, while the third unburdened itself of two large men, and one shrinking, small woman who gave a muffled shriek of happiness as soon as her feet touched the ground.

"Oh, my dearest, my most dearest Princess Dagmar!

You have worked a miracle, a veritable miracle! I cannot ever hope to make you understand just how happy I am to see you and how grateful I am that you have made the authorities see reason at long last."

Dagmar was as pleased to see her friend as the latter was to be released. She met Julia's hug with a tight one of her own. "And we are delighted to see you too, although all the gratitude must go to Leo since it was he who went to Lord Salter and had the governor persuaded that you would be safe enough in our care until you have to return to gaol."

Julia jerked in her embrace and turned her face away, but not before Dagmar caught a look of fury in her friend's eyes. Before she could point out that an outright release, rather than the parole Leo had arranged, was out of the question without proof of just who did kill Louisa Hayes—assuming she was actually dead—Julia's expression was back to her normal vapid look, and she was gushing her thanks to Leo.

It was all very curious and made her feel uneasy. Was Julia just distressed by her recent incarceration, and thus annoyed that she hadn't been released outright as she evidently believed, or was there a more sinister explanation? Dagmar pulled her cloak tighter, trying to convince herself that it was nothing but the moody environment around them.

Moody, she decided a moment later while glancing around them, was an understatement. *Downright eerie* worked better as a description. The street was silent now that two of the three coaches had moved off, the clip-clopping echoes of the horses' hooves on cobblestone fading into nothing. A few torn bits of paper whispered along the street, driven by the odd eddy of wind, but Dagmar could almost imagine a ghostly hand lifting and tossing the paper about.

Gas lighting had reached this section of town, but the lampposts were scarce, and their light, a sickly yellow, did little to chase away the darkness.

Dagmar shook her head at her fancies, taking Leo's good hand and huddling next to him with the others while he gave explanations.

"Mrs. Deworthy and the two Runners will stay here at the carriages. If all goes as we think it will, we'll send for you once we are ready to confront Dalton."

"Please don't part me from my dearest princess," Julia begged, tugging at his sleeve. "Can you not see your way clear to including me in your party? I will be as quiet as a church mouse and will behave in no way that would justify the hire of these two men."

Dagmar glanced at the two Bow Street Runners that Lord Salter had insisted Leo engage to watch over Julia. Both men looked bored, and she couldn't blame them.

Leo hesitated. Dagmar leaned into him and said softly, "I appreciate the fact that you are merely complying with Lord Salter's terms for Julia's release to our custody, but I don't think those gentlemen are needed. She's not going to run away, if that's what he fears, and will certainly be safe enough with all of us."

Leo continued to hesitate, his eyes moving from her to Julia before he agreed, gesturing the two Runners to the side for a brief consultation. The men nodded and returned to the carriage, leaving them in the silent darkness of the wee hours of the morning.

"Thank you," Julia said breathily and clutched at Dagmar's free arm.

"Does everyone understand what they are to do?" Leo asked in a whisper. The street was as silent as a tomb, and even the whisper seemed to skitter along it, gathering volume. Dagmar shivered, more from nerves and excitement than from the cold, and pressed closer to her husband. What a nice man she had found. When she considered that anyone could have turned up in her back garden, she was doubly thankful that it was Leo who had found his way there. She smiled at him, causing him to check in mid-sentence and give her a warning look that was more than a little tinged with desire.

"As you know," he continued, squeezing her hand in acknowledgment of the little skitter of attraction between them, "stealth is going to be uppermost in importance. I don't even want to contemplate what I would say should Dalton discover us in his sitting room tampering with his sister's coffin, so above all else, be quiet. Do not speak unless necessary. Do you all have your candles?"

There was a rustle of clothing as several hands were pushed into pockets to pull out various candles and small lamps.

"Very well. Nick and I have our tinderboxes, and we'll light the candles once we get into the room. You all know your parts, yes?"

"Plum and I are guards," Gillian said softly. "We will be stationed at the door leading into the house, listening for sounds of any approach."

"I am to hold the tools and pass them out as

needed," Dagmar said with a little fillip of pride that Leo had chosen her to assist him, rather than the more mundane task of waiting by the door. She held up a small cloth sack that thunked suggestively until she put a controlling hand on its body.

"Thom and I will help cut off the seals," Nick said.

"And Noble and I will lift off the lid and examine the remains, assuming there is something to see," Harry finished. "We are also ready to engage in fisticuffs, should the need arise."

Plum stared at him. "Why would you need to do so?"

Harry shrugged. "It's been my experience that just when you think you have a good, solid grip on life, it goes off down a path you didn't anticipate. Fisticuffs fixes many of the problems that arise when that happens."

"Personal philosophy aside, I doubt we'll have need for you and Noble to engage in battle, but your offer is duly noted. Mrs. Deworthy, I have your word that you will remain in the background?"

"Oh, yes, yes you do, you most certainly do," Julia said eagerly, her eyes bright with excitement. Dagmar felt foolish for imagining that Julia could be anything but the woman she had always been.

"Very well, then we will proceed. Nick, if you would bring up the rear, we'll go in single file, with the ladies in the middle. Remember! Stealth is key."

Getting to the window that opened into the sitting room where the coffin resided was no trouble. They were as stealthy as their number of people could be, with only tiny little outbreaks of stifled giggles that ended as soon as Leo manipulated the large multipaned window to swing open; however, the sight of the coffin glinting in the light of the lantern that Nick held up sobered them all. One by one, the ladies were lifted over the windowsill, the men following until they all huddled together in a corner of the sitting room, their faces white and strained in the dim light of Nick's lamp.

Dagmar had only a vague memory of the room, since most of her attention had been focused on the casket during her visit there earlier in the day. But she had a sketchy memory of the coffin being supported by two small octagonal tables, flanked by a couple chairs and a sofa in gold-and-green brocade, and two medium-sized Chinese vases on wooden plinths stationed on either side of the marble fireplace. As Leo lit his candle from Nick's lamp, he lifted it to cast light on the room. The shadows from the bulky vases were thick and impenetrable. Dagmar shivered again, wondering if it was possible for someone to hide in those shadows, remaining unseen until an unwary person stepped within reach.

Then there was the coffin. She'd never been one to be afraid of the dead, but at that moment, she eyed the solid, hulking mass of the coffin with the perfect memory of every horrific gothic novel she'd ever read. What would she do if the lid slowly opened and a skeletal hand darted out to clutch at her? What if the body of Louisa, bloody and rotting, suddenly sat up and shrieked? What if some unnamed terror lurked within, just waiting for them to release it?

"Right," Leo said, taking a deep breath and luckily breaking the spell of terror that Dagmar was quickly wrapping around herself. His voice sounded as if it had been stretched thin, but Dagmar greeted it with a shaky laugh to herself. "Light your candles, and then to your posts."

"Aye aye, Captain," Gillian said from the doorway, giving Leo a brief salute.

"Gillian!" Plum said, outrage evident in her whisper. A sniffing noise followed. "You've been drinking!"

"No I haven't."

"I can smell it on you!"

"Oh, that. It was just a little nip from Noble's flask. I was chilly."

"You're inebriated!"

"Hush, I am not. I'm just pleasantly warm."

"You're going to get us in trouble, that's what you are," Plum snapped, then added, "Do you still have the flask?"

Gillian giggled. Dagmar ignored the rustling of clothing that indicated that Gillian did, in fact, have possession of the flask and concentrated on laying out her tools. Leo had given her a long oilcloth wrap filled with assorted knives, awls, and blunt objects that she assumed were meant to pry up the heavy coffin lid. She knelt on the floor, arranging them next to her candle, ready to hand one off to whoever needed it.

"Can you give me that curved knife, my love?"

She scooted over to Leo, giving him the object in question. Nick perused her selection, picked one out, and went to work on the far side of the casket. Noble, having heard giggling from the door patrol, marched over to see what was going on and instantly (although quietly) demanded possession of his flask.

"I might as well help cut off those seals, since no one thus far seems to need to be beaten soundly," Harry said softly and accepted the remaining knife that Dagmar handed him. She watched with interest as the three men, setting their respective candles on the coffin, worked at cutting off the lead seals.

"Luckily," Leo said, grunting slightly as he pried up a section of the seal with the curved bladed dagger, "whoever sealed this didn't know his job very well. He just plopped the lead on the wood of the coffin. Ah, there it goes. Nick?"

"Almost done with mine."

"This one came off quite easily," Harry whispered, picking off large flat strips of metal.

"I believe I shall look out the window," Julia whispered as the men rose prefatory to lifting off the lid. "May God have mercy on our souls for disturbing the dead."

Dagmar frowned, momentarily annoyed with her companion for making it sound as though they were the very worst kind of grave robbers, but she was too interested to see who, if anyone, was in the coffin to say anything.

She pressed close to Leo as he counted to three, then the men lifted the lid off the coffin.

The rotten smell of death immediately filled the room, making her cover her mouth to keep from gagging. A handful of flies arose, buzzing around in a sated manner that indicated they'd been feeding well. Leo swore softly. Harry choked and stumbled toward the window. The ladies at the door made gasping noises.

"That is the most disgusting thing I have ever seen, and less than a month ago I carried around a boiled pig's head for an entire day, so I *know* disgusting."

"Why on earth did you carry around a boiled pig's head?" Gillian asked, her voice muffled because she had her handkerchief to her face.

"I'd just stolen it from my cousin, the prince regent." Dagmar studied the repulsiveness in the coffin. "It seemed wasteful to go to all the trouble of stealing it and then leaving it where anyone could take it. Is that a foot?"

Leo, standing next to Nick as the two of them stared in horror at the bloody mass, glanced where Dagmar pointed. "Hard to tell."

"That's…" Dagmar squinted. Maggots squirmed around the mass. "That's…"

"A horse," Thom said, peering over Nick's shoulder.

"Parts of a horse, yes," Leo said.

"Here's his head," Nick said from where he had moved to the foot of the coffin. "Oh look, Thom found his tail."

"I think it's actually two tails," Thom said, looking with interest at the objects she held in both hands.

"Whoever heard of a horse with two tails? This is definitely a foot."

"Hoof," Leo corrected. "There are two hooves over here. And the rest…" He eyed the repulsive mass in the middle. "Perhaps it's better if we don't catalog the parts that are contained."

"Much better," Plum said hurriedly.

"Tell me," Gillian asked her husband in a slower than normal cadence. "If you were called upon to steal a boiled pig's head from a crown prince, where would you hide it?"

"No more flask for you," Noble told her, taking the flask from her hand and kissing her on her nose.

"Nick, help me with the lid…" Harry, Nick, and Leo sealed the coffin again, and while Gillian tried to persuade her husband to hand over his flask again, the three men screwed the bolts back into place.

"A horse," Dagmar repeated, trying to come to grips with that idea.

"They're not going to allow that monstrosity to be given a Christian burial, are they?" Julia asked, moving a few feet from the window in order to watch the men.

"I don't see why not. The poor horse…or horses, given the two tails…died, so there's no reason why they shouldn't be buried."

"It's blasphemy!"

"Oh, hardly that, do you think?" Thom asked as she came around to stand with Dagmar.

"She's the daughter of a vicar," Dagmar told Thom under her breath. "She was raised to believe that one should never take the Lord's name in vain, that you should give unto others, and that horses shouldn't be buried."

Thom looked thoughtful. "Equine burials are a bit unusual, but I don't see anything ungodly about it."

"Nor do I," Dagmar said, thinking more about the subject. "The question is, who would want to kill a horse and put it in Louisa's coffin?"

"I doubt very much that the horse was sacrificed for this purpose." Leo, who had been conferring quietly with Harry and Nick, glanced her way. "It appeared to be deceased for some time, so I suspect that whoever put it there simply paid a visit to the nearest knacker's yard and...er...acquired a suitable substitute for an actual human body."

"At least now you have proof that Louisa didn't die," Thom said, waving her hand in front of her. The air still reeked with the odor of the deceased horse.

"Indeed we do. And I believe it will be best for us to confront Dalton in the morning, before the burial takes place. We should leave now before someone starts singing bawdy tavern songs." Leo's look at where Noble and Gillian were engaged in a passionate embrace was very pointed. "Or indulges in acts better suited to the bedchamber."

Noble broke off the kiss and grinned at him. "We've yet to wake up an entire household with our antics, but I take your point. It's a wonder Gillian hasn't knocked down one of those vases over there."

"I am not clumsy like that," Gillian protested.

Noble just stared at her.

"All right, I am, but I've been very careful not to get near them. Besides, Plum is watching me. She wouldn't let me do something that would stir the house."

"It's just a matter of time," Noble said, taking her arm and escorting her toward the window. "Sooner or later, fate would catch up to you."

Dagmar, who was wondering if Leo would kiss her with that much enthusiasm after they'd been married as long as Gillian and Noble, was about to ask him just that when suddenly Julia appeared to be struck with a fit of madness.

That was Dagmar's first thought when her companion let loose with a blood-curdling shriek from the window.

"It's the devil! The devil has come for us! He's come to punish us for our sins!" Julia screamed, rushing past Thom and Dagmar with her arms flailing in the air.

Everyone in the room froze at the sudden noise, too startled to move.

Behind Julia, a pale golden streak flashed, heading straight for her but veering at the last moment into the corner hidden by a small sofa. Julia screamed in horror and, in her desperate attempt to get away, spun around and ran right into Leo.

"What—" he started to say but was knocked off balance. Julia, her face a mask of terror, leaped over him, tripped, and clutched his arm to steady herself.

"No—" Dagmar managed to get out, watching helplessly as Leo, now seriously off balance, careened headfirst into the nearest of the two vases.

Time seemed to slow down to a standstill. Dagmar knew even before Leo's head connected with the vase that not only would it crash to the ground in an explosion of fine china, but that the impact would send Leo into the second vase as well.

Even as she opened her mouth to tell Julia that it was only a cat that had come in the window, no doubt drawn by the odor of the dead horse, Leo hit the vase with a painful crack, then half stumbled and half fell into the second one before hitting the ground himself. He rolled away, covering his head to protect it from the resulting shower of smashed china.

The noise was deafening. A cannon going off couldn't have pierced the slumbering house more effectively than the sound of two vases being smashed against the tile fireplace.

Dagmar started toward Leo even as the last few shards of shattered ceramics pinged on the tile. "Are you all right? Did you hurt your head? Oh, Leo, tell me you didn't hurt your poor shoulder."

Leo groaned. "No, I'm not hurt, not seriously."

"Well that's good," she said, sighing as she carefully knelt next to him. "I won't worry, then."

The look Leo shot her when he uncurled was more than a little wild. "No, you don't have anything to worry about. Mind you, the whole house—no, the entire neighborhood—is now alerted to our presence, but that's hardly anything to concern you."

"Don't be rude," Dagmar said, swatting him on his uninjured arm. "I meant regarding your wounds, as you well know. Julia, for heaven's sake, stop making that noise. No one is blaming you for making Leo crash into the vases and waking the whole house, not that I've heard anything, so perhaps they didn't hear—"

Just as the words left her mouth, a muted shout came from abovestairs, followed by an answering call from below them.

Dagmar sighed. "It was a good thought. Julia, please!"

"I didn't mean to!" Julia was babbling at Noble and Gillian, both of whom had caught her before she could run out of the room. "I never thought that Lord March would fall—but the devil was after me—my father was a vicar, and he'd never forgive me for being here tonight—if I'd known this was why dear Princess Dagmar had me released—but I never thought he'd fall. Those lovely, lovely vases!"

"Run!" Harry suddenly yelled, shoving Plum toward the window.

"What? Harry, what are you—"

"Run, woman, run! There's no need for you to be caught. Escape while you can!"

Noble looked thoughtfully at Gillian. She smiled. He offered his flask, and the two retired to the small sofa which was currently bearing the form of the golden cat.

"I am not going anywhere, you deranged man. Unhand me!"

"Maybe you should go with your aunt," Nick said hesitantly to Thom. The look she gave him in return was filled with scorn. He shrugged. "I thought it was worth a try."

"Hardly."

"I don't suppose—" Leo started to say to Dagmar.

"No. We're partners, remember? Partners don't run away and leave their other half to face irate men who are bound to wonder why a bunch of people are standing around a coffin at three in the morning." That gave Dagmar a moment's pause, and by the time Philip Dalton, armed with a dueling pistol and accompanied by two footmen and the butler, flung open the door to the sitting room, all of the room's occupants were on their knees, surrounding the coffin.

Philip Dalton stopped in the doorway, holding a candle high and staring in utter surprise.

Seventeen

I fear this will be the last time I am able to write to you, my beloved Dagmar. I know you will take excellent care of your dear father, and I trust that you will heed the words of wisdom I have shared with you. You have grown into a woman of intelligence, wit, and personal charm, and I am very proud to call you my daughter. Just remember that although I may not always be near you, I will watch you from above with a loving and indulgent eye. I love you, my dearest one. Be happy in all that you do.

—Your devoted mama

"Ah. Dalton."

Leo rose from where he had been kneeling next to Dagmar. He decided quickly to brazen his way through the incident in hopes that Dalton would hesitate to make a scene in front of so many men of importance. "I'm sorry that the cat woke you."

"Cat?" Dalton's face was without expression as he gazed from one person to another.

Leo held out his hand for Dagmar, who rose as graceful as a butterfly, her hand warm in his and that delicious sent of warm, willing woman—*his* warm, willing woman—wrapping itself around him in a way that guaranteed he'd have an erection for at least the next hour.

"Yes, the cat. A yellow one. I believe it's currently behind the corner sofa. It came in and knocked over your vases."

"I do hope they weren't valuable," Plum said, looking ruefully at the remains.

Dalton stared at her. "And you are?"

"My wife." Harry helped Plum to her feet, then made a perfunctory bow as Leo introduced everyone.

"You're no doubt wondering what we're doing here," Gillian said, then gave a little giggle. "I'd better let Plum tell you. Noble insists I'm a bit tipsy, which is ridiculous because I hold my liquor better than anyone I know. Besides, Plum is an author, so her explanation will be far more entertaining than anything I could come up with. Noble, stop squeezing me. I am not a rag doll."

Leo felt a surge of pride in his wife. Not only was she *not* slightly inebriated, but she also kept her wits about her in time of need. She would be very helpful to his future missions, and more, she'd keep him entertained and enthralled with her quicksilver mind. "We came to pay our respects to your sister," Leo said quickly, before Gillian could continue.

"You did that last evening," Dalton answered and gestured at the people behind him. Most of them dispersed, leaving the butler and a footman, who, at a nod from his master, lit the candles in the room.

"Our friends wish to pay their respects, as well," Leo said, trying to think of a reason for them to do so at three in the morning.

"Yes, we did. We heard so much about your late sister from Dagmar and Leo, we couldn't help but wish to offer up a few prayers of our own on her passing," Plum said smoothly, elbowing Harry. "Didn't we?"

"Yes, yes, it's just as my wife says. Respects. Prayers." Harry stifled a huge yawn. "Thought we'd get it over with sooner rather than later."

"I am flattered, naturally," Dalton said slowly, his gaze darting from person to person. "I will admit, however, to being curious about the time of day you chose to pay me such an honor. Would not later in the morning have sufficed?"

"No, it wouldn't," Dagmar said just as Leo was about to babble something inane. She gave Dalton a long, placid look. "I'm a princess. Those of royal birth are, by nature, an eccentric people. My dearest father used to work all night on his scholarly pursuits and sleep during the day. He said his humors were in better alignment at night, and with that, I am in agreement. You wouldn't want me going about with disaligned humors, would you?"

Dalton stared at her for a moment. "Er…"

"No, of course he doesn't want that," Leo said smoothly, giving her a grin and a conspiratorial squeeze around her waist. "No one would want you disaligned in any manner. I do apologize for waking the house, though. Our intentions were purely to pay our respects and depart without anyone being the wiser."

Dalton's pale eyes settled on him, and in them, Leo read equal parts awareness, suspicion, and anger.

"You may leave," Dalton said, dismissing his remaining servants. "We won't have any further need of you tonight." He waited until the door closed behind the two men, then strode over to the fireplace, casually examining the remains of the vases before leaning an elbow on the mantel and saying in a drawl, "It would appear that you have gained some knowledge that I would rather have kept private. Shall we discuss the situation, or would it throw the princess's humors into disarray?"

"I think you'll find that Dagmar's humors are up to such a conversation." Leo held out a chair for his wife, who sat with an air of controlled excitement. He gave her an approving squeeze of the shoulder before facing Dalton. Thom, Plum, and Gillian took a seat on the cat sofa, while Dagmar's companion huddled in the corner. The men lined up behind the women. The room had the air of a courtroom, something that Dalton was evidently aware of because he glanced at the six others with a wry little smile. "I see we have jury and crown's prosecutor. But no judge?"

"I am a princess," Dagmar repeated, giving him a beatific smile. "I am above such petty things in life as prejudice or untoward bias."

Leo choked. Dagmar punched him in the thigh and held on to her smile.

"Then by all means, Your Highness—"

"Your Serene Highness," Plum, Thom, and Gillian said together.

Dagmar beamed at them.

"I beg your pardon. *Your Serene Highness* will naturally be ideally suited for the role of judge." Dalton made her a bow.

"He does sarcasm very well, don't you think?" Dagmar asked Leo. "I don't do it at all well. Is that something you can teach me, along with prevarication?"

"I shall endeavor to do so. I live in anticipation of hearing you be sarcastic." He faced Dalton. "Would you mind telling us why there is a dead horse—"

"Parts of a dead horse. Or rather, parts of multiple dead horses," Thom interrupted.

"—in the coffin supposed to contain the remains of your sister?"

"And just why did you kill two innocent horses?" Thom demanded, getting to her feet. Nick said something in her ear.

"No, I will not sit down and let Leo handle this. I've always had a great love for horses, and two of them, two beautiful, noble creatures were ruthlessly murdered because of this man. I don't hold with that sort of thing, and I'm certainly not going to let it pass without protest and a demand for justice."

"Hear, hear," Plum said, nodding.

"As it happens, madam, I am also quite fond of horses," Dalton said, taking them all by surprise. "There is a farmer near my estate who does nothing but tend to the mounts of my youth who are now in their elder years. I can assure you that although the coffin does, in fact, contain the remains of two unfortunate animals, their deaths were not by my doing or command. I simply purchased them from a knacker, along with two horses still alive who were doomed to a similar fate. The horses were past their prime but had great expression in their eyes, and I couldn't bear to think of their future as wallpaper glue."

"Really?" Thom stared at him for a moment, then flung herself forward and gave him a swift hug. "Oh, I'm so glad to know you saved those poor horses. I used to do the same, until Harry told me the stables were full and I couldn't rescue any more until one of the former rescuees passed on."

"At last count, we have eighteen broken-down nags eating their heads off at Rosse Abbey," Harry said. "As well as seven donkeys, a mule that is in love with Plum, and a vast herd of canines of every shape and form."

"The monkey Thom found died last summer," Plum said sadly. "But the rest of the animal colony thrives. Except the cats keep eating the mice that Thom saves."

"The nature of the universe is the nature of things that are," Thom murmured before adding, "Marcus Aurelius. I always did like the Romans."

"Leo…" Dagmar started to say, giving him a look that was all too easy to read.

"No monkeys," he told her.

She pursed her lips, then reluctantly nodded. "I suppose it wouldn't be an effective use of subterfuge."

"I'll get you a lapdog if you like. All ladies of station have lapdogs."

"I have three," Gillian said. "Although they're all massive and would crush you if they sat on your lap. Also, they emit odors. We've not been very successful in quelling that aspect of their personalities."

"I have four," Plum offered.

"Thirty-six," Thom said.

Nick groaned.

"They don't emit odors," she reassured him. "Well, not frequently. Perhaps daily, but not like Gillian's hounds."

"Nothing emits like my hounds," Gillian said with a touch of pride. "In a confined space they can take down a man in his prime."

"As fascinating as this accounting is, might we return to the subject at hand?" Dalton glanced at the clock next to him. "I would like to get a little sleep before I have to attend my sister's funeral."

"One of her dogs might come in handy should we need to torture information from someone," Dagmar told Leo in an undertone.

"I try to stay away from torturing people, but I will remember that as an option." He eyed Dalton. "Now that the matter of the deceased horses is settled, would you mind telling us just why you wish people to believe your sister is dead? I take it she is not in that unfortunate state."

"No, she is alive." Dalton's gaze slid around the room. "At the moment she's on a ship on her way back to Italy."

"She said she wanted to go back there," Dagmar murmured, then shook her head and asked Dalton, "But why the pretense? Does Louisa not know that Julia has been confined, suspected of her murder? It took every ounce of energy Leo had in order to get the governor of the gaol to release Julia into our custody for a few hours. They insist that she is guilty, and without proof, we cannot prove her innocence. Louisa must return or, at the very least, make a statement that she is alive and well, so that Julia's name will be cleared."

Dalton's eyes met Leo's for a few moments. Leo understood the message in them and moved closer to his wife, his hand resting on her shoulder.

"We thought Louisa's murder a fitting example of justice," Dalton said slowly. "More specifically, the imprisonment of the woman who took from us the life of a very dear young man."

Before the last word left his mouth, there was a flurry, and Julia rushed across the room, a wickedly long dagger glinting in her hands. Leo, who had been expecting a response of some form, leaped forward to intercept Julia before she could reach Dalton, and the two of them went down in a tangle of arms and legs and shiny, sharp dagger. Pain burst through him, radiating from his wounded shoulder in hot, sickening waves. He lay insensible for a moment, stunned by the impact, distantly aware of the sound of Julia screaming obscenities at him, his eyes focused on the blade of the dagger where it wavered over his face. He knew he was in danger, knew he had to move, knew without a doubt that in the next second, Julia would plunge that dagger into his neck and he'd never see Dagmar again, but before his brain could command his sluggish limbs to move, another cry sounded, this one higher and filled with righteous rage.

Julia was suddenly torn from him, and the dagger sent flying. Leo blinked up at the sight of Dagmar standing over him, panting with fury as she roared,

"Are you mad? If you've harmed Leo, so help me, Julia, no bonds in the world will be strong enough to keep me from wreaking vengeance upon you!"

Nick and Dalton rushed forward when the companion lunged toward Dagmar, but they weren't quick enough.

Leo was on his feet and in front of his wife before his brain could even process what was happening. Julia snarled something rude and would have stabbed him in the chest, but Leo's training stood him in good stead. He snatched the dagger while jerking Julia forward, effectively throwing her off balance and straight into the arms of Nick and Dalton.

"That will be quite enough of that," he said calmly, wondering all the while if his heart would ever slow down to a normal rhythm. It was pounding so loud he could hardly hear the others exclaim as they circled Julia.

He looked down at Dagmar. "That's the second time you've saved my life."

"I'm a princess," she said loftily, as if he needed reminding. "Saving handsome men from certain death is what we do best. That and waving gracefully to crowds. Have you ever seen me wave? My mother taught me. I'll wave for you sometime, but right now, I'm thinking seriously of swooning."

He put his arm around her, swiftly searching her for signs of injury. "Did Julia strike you while I was befuddled? I didn't think she got close enough to you to touch you, but I was knocked silly for a few seconds—"

"I don't wish to swoon for my own sake, Leo. When I saw Julia with that dagger over your head, the thought that she might kill you flashed through my mind, and I just knew I'd never survive such an event. My heart would break, and I'd die right there with you. At least then we'd be together in spirit."

Her eyes were misty with tears and love, and he thought he'd never seen anyone so beautiful in all his days.

"I prefer to be together in body and soul," he said against her lips, taking advantage of an aborted attempt by Julia to escape out the window to kiss Dagmar the way he'd been wanting to kiss her for the last half hour.

"Plum gave me a copy of her book," she said five minutes later, when she managed to catch enough breath to speak. He was light-headed with desire and need and overwhelming love for the woman in his arms, and couldn't stir his brain to actual speech, so he contented himself with simply holding her and listening to her lovely voice. "Do you know that there's a connubial calisthenic in it entitled 'The Princess and the Jouster'? It involves a man who stands with, as Plum puts it, his lance couched, and the princess seated on the edge of a balcony—or small table, in this case— and a judicious use of a neckcloth. It sounded very interesting, and as I am a princess, and you could well be a valiant knight since you are an earl, I thought—"

"Yes," he said, kissing her, both of them oblivious to the hissing and screaming Julia as Nick, Harry, and Dalton hauled her from the room. "We'll try it tonight. Or later this morning. Or perhaps in five minutes if you keep looking at me like that."

She laughed and kissed the side of his mouth. "You

do know you're going to have to explain how you knew that Julia was mad."

A little pinch of sadness marred the perfect moment, but he simply gave her a pat on her delicious ass and said, "I didn't think you'd let me off that easily. Oh, hell, she's loose again. If you will excuse me, my darling?"

"Go and catch her," Dagmar said, releasing her hold on him. "But be gentle, Leo. She's obviously not quite right in the head."

Leo had a feeling that truer words had never been spoken.

Eighteen

"THE CHOICE IS YOURS. I CAN MAKE LONG, VIGOROUS, and inventive—if you wish for me to look at that book Plum gave you—love to you, or I can answer your questions."

Leo stood in the doorway to the bedroom that Plum had given them, having first exacted promises that they would only visit that room and no others on the floor, lest they encounter infected children or servants.

"And even then," Plum had said at the time, plumping up a pillow absently as she glanced around the room, "I have dire suspicions that you'll come down with the chicken pox, so I've made sure that there are marigolds next to your bed and sandalwood oil at hand. Just rub it on your exposed surfaces."

Dagmar had been confused by such orders. "Will it keep us from becoming infected?"

"I assume so. The doctor has us rubbing the oil on the children's rashes, and marigolds are said to be a good protection against such things. It certainly can't hurt!"

There wasn't much she could say to that, so she

promised Plum that they wouldn't so much as touch any other door on that floor, and unpacked her meager belongings.

An hour after that, the sun had risen, and she was tucked into bed, exhausted from the night's activities but not wishing to go to sleep without Leo. As if summoned by her thoughts, the door opened and Leo entered, looking just as tired but so incredibly wonderful that Dagmar flung back the bed linens and was halfway out of the bed before she realize that she couldn't just leap on him.

"You waited up for me?" Leo looked surprised. "You should have gone to sleep."

"Of course I waited for you. For one, I wish to hear what happened to Julia, but also, I wish to seduce you again, and I can't do that if I'm asleep."

That's when Leo gave her the choice: lovemaking or answers to her questions.

"Could you not answer my questions while I seduce you?" she asked hopefully, sitting on her heels while he began to disrobe. She very much liked watching him do so. There was an elegance about him, a grace despite the stifled movements of his wounded shoulder that never failed to send little shivers of delight down her back.

He stood on one leg while pulling off a boot, giving her a long look. "My darling wife, the second you touch me, all thoughts but what I'd like to do to your soft, silken flesh leave my mind. The answer is no, I would not be able to tell you what happened and make love to you. I'm lucky my brain works at all when you are unclothed. Speaking of which, what is that monstrosity you are wearing?"

She looked down at the linen night rail. "It's the same one I've worn every night, Leo. I don't see what you find so monstrous about it now."

"The monstrous part is that you haven't taken it off yet, and you did so on other nights. Do so promptly, please."

She started to remove the night rail, but deep knowledge of herself had her hesitating then retying the ribbon at the neck before sliding off the bed to pad over to one of the two chairs before the fire. "You're right, I don't think we can combine answers with connubial experiences. You'd better answer my questions first, then I will be a princess in a balcony, and you can be a jouster with a couched lance, and we will both enjoy ourselves so well that we'll forget how to speak."

"Agreed," Leo said, stripping off his clothes.

Dagmar stared. Merciful heavens, he was a fine, fine man. And he was hers! All hers. No other woman could have him. Until the end of her days, he would be available for her to seduce and try out things from Plum's book and make hoarse with shouting out her name while he climaxed. That thought filled her with great satisfaction and no little amount of sexual anticipation.

"Fair warning my equally fair damsel: if you continue to stare at me in that manner, I won't be able to stop from scooping you up and taking you over to that bed where I will acquaint you with a few connubial calisthenics of my own design."

She reached out and wrapped one hand around his penis, while caressing his testicles with the other.

Leo made a gargled noise.

"It really is such a strange body part. So hot and hard, yet the skin covering it is very smooth and silky, and slides delightfully. Do you enjoy the sliding, Leo? I much enjoy it. Look, I can do this with that bit right there."

Leo sucked in a vast quantity of air, probably half of what was available in the room. "Yes," he said in a strained voice that had an odd squeaking tone to it. "Yes, I enjoy the sliding."

"I'm so pleased to know that. Now, about Julia—oh, are you sensitive there? My apologies—you suspected her, didn't you? I can tell you did because you weren't at all surprised when Mr. Dalton accused her of being the woman he was looking for."

"Dagmar."

"Hmm?"

"You're holding my balls."

"Yes, I know. They're very soft and warm too, although not at all hard." She gave them a friendly little squeeze, not enough to hurt, but enough to let them know she approved of them. "I think they're rather charming, although I still feel that they must get in your way at times. How do you sit in a saddle without them being squished?"

"Very carefully. If you don't release me in the next two seconds, I will strip that repugnant garment from your delightfully wanton body and allow my lustful plans free rein, and I can assure you that I have many, many lustful plans."

Dagmar weighed her desire to indulge his lustful plans with her need for answers and decided that as much as she wanted to seduce Leo—and by turn, allow him to seduce her—she really did want to know how it was that Julia could be the person that Leo thought she was.

She released his testicles and gave a fond pat to his penis before sitting in the chair opposite. "Very well, we shall delay my seduction of you until after you have explained how Julia can be someone that I'm quite sure she isn't."

"That makes no sense."

"Really?" Dagmar thought for a moment. "There are times when I am convinced that English is the most awkward language ever. What I meant is that I don't understand how Julia can be an evil woman when she's been Mama's companion—and then mine—for as long as I can recall."

Leo took a deep breath but managed to bring his obviously rampant desires under control. He sat in the chair opposite her. "I will never understand how your mind works," he told her.

"Good. Proceed."

Leo sat, looking perfectly at ease despite the fact that he was naked and very erect in the genital department. "Where do you wish me to start?"

"Philip Dalton. He wanted Julia blamed for Louisa's death, but how did he make us think it happened when it really didn't?"

"The key, as I mentioned earlier, was the way he separated us from Louisa and kept us away from her supposed corpse. I don't know if he investigated the Roman remains the day before we visited it, but I suspect he did. He knew you would be drawn to the bodies, and no doubt realized that it offered a perfect stage to perform his drama. Louisa was left with your companion, since neither woman wanted to see skeletons, while the rest of us were at the opposite end of the room. He managed to conveniently kick the plank aside so that we couldn't accompany him to rescue his sister. Then he covered her up so that no one could see her and insisted that I get you away from the scene before we could examine the body. I am in little doubt that the doctor we were sent to find had either no chance to see Louisa's body or his silence was bought."

"That was very clever of Mr. Dalton," Dagmar said thoughtfully, remembering the scene. It all fit. "You know, I think they knew who Julia was from the very start. There's no other way to explain why Louisa took such a dislike to her from the very start, and the claims of dreams and of being attacked could be manufactured. Oh!"

"Oh?"

Insight flooded her. "The salt! I know what was wrong with it. Louisa claimed that morning that Julia had written a threatening note to her and included a bit of salt inside the letter, but there was no salt on the paper. None whatsoever, and you know that at least a few grains would have remained clinging to the paper."

Leo nodded. "I didn't think of that, but you're absolutely right."

"So all the rest of Louisa's claims about Julia—"

"Manufactured to set the scene wherein we'd believe that Julia had a grudge against her."

"It's so cold-blooded." Dagmar thought for a moment. "And Julia setting her cap at Philip Dalton?"

"You know her better than I do. Is that something she would do?"

Dagmar found it painful to consider her friend with such suspicion, but she couldn't help but feeling it likely. "Perhaps. If she truly is the person you say she is, then perhaps she thought she could engage his affections in order to better her station, although I'm not convinced, Leo."

"I know you're not. I think, however, once you hear what I have to say, you may change your mind."

"Very well." Dagmar sat back, her hands clasped together. "We have dispensed with Philip Dalton and can now turn our attention to Julia. When was it that you came to suspect that my Julia was Margaret Prothero?"

"A few days ago. It just seemed to make sense."

"Not even in the least little bit does it make sense," Dagmar argued. "She isn't at all the sort of person to kill someone."

"What proof do you have of that?" Leo asked her.

She frowned. "What proof do I have? I've known her for most of my life."

"It's not inconceivable that she normally has a very placid nature, but one that can turn deadly given the right circumstances." He took another deep breath and leaned forward to take her hand. "I regret having to tell you this because I know it will cause you pain, but you deserve to know the truth. I spoke with Julia Deworthy at the gaol and told her I was sending off for her marriage records. She knew what I'd find, and at last admitted that she was Margaret

Julia Prothero. She claims that she had no hand in the death of young Hayes, that it was all her cousin's doing, and she was merely a bystander, but I doubt she is speaking the truth."

"I don't know what to say, Leo. It's all so shocking. Are you sure she was not suddenly deranged and making it up?" Dagmar tried to readjust the mental image of an old friend who was in truth a stranger.

"She wasn't deranged, not in the sense you mean." Leo's fingers stroked hers with a gentleness that touched her. "I know it is hard for you to understand how a trusted friend can have such a dark secret, but it does not tarnish the affection she holds for you."

He stopped, but Dagmar couldn't leave the obvious unsaid. "That affection only goes so far, though, doesn't it? She didn't let it stand in her way when she felt threatened by you."

"No, but that has no bearing on all the good years you had together."

Dagmar curled her fingers around his. "It's so difficult to believe that someone I grew up with could be such a monster."

"I don't think she ever meant you any harm, if that makes you feel better. She clearly was beholden to you not only for her livelihood, but also as a way to hide from her past identity. No one would think twice about the companion of a princess, after all."

"No." Dagmar stared at their hands for a moment, marveling at the strength of Leo's fingers. "Did she say what happened to Louisa's son?"

"A little. She claims that he forced himself on her cousin and then turned his attentions to her. While he was attempting to assault her, her cousin struck him down, apparently with more force than she realized. She says she had nothing to do with the attack other than to conceal what had been done."

Dagmar looked into his eyes and saw the truth in them. "You don't believe that, do you?"

"No." His fingers tightened on hers. "There are several things wrong with her story. For one, her description of the attack doesn't fit what Dalton and Mrs. Hayes said of the boy. Julia claimed he was drunk and lascivious, and yet he was evidently a gentle, pious young man with a dislike of drink and an abhorrence of violence."

"Pious young men have been known to force themselves on women before," Dagmar pointed out.

"Agreed, but in this case, there's another fact that effectively eliminates the possibility. Young Hayes had suffered an injury when he was a boy. He was incapable of sexual activity."

"Incapable? He couldn't...not any of it?"

"No. He was gored by a bull when he was a young lad, and the resulting operation ended up leaving him more or less a eunuch. It's one reason why the Hayes family went abroad and stayed there."

"But if he wasn't attempting to rape them, why kill him?"

Leo scratched his chest, distracting her for a moment. She really did love his chest, even scarred. "She won't admit that he didn't attack them because it would damn her beyond all hope of freedom, but I suspect that she and her cousin had hoped to compromise the young man in a blackmail attempt. They'd simply claim he had attempted to rape them both, and his parents would pay to hush up the scandal. They hadn't counted on the fact that he was physically incapable of assaulting them, and I imagine that while attempting to coerce him into that act, he struggled, and most likely fell back against an object that sufficiently wounded him as to leave him near death."

"If it was an accident, why didn't Julia just say that?"

"Because she wanted the blame thrown onto her cousin. To admit that he fell while struggling with them means they are both guilty. Your companion is trying very hard to disassociate herself from any wrongdoing."

"That's quite a bit of supposition," Dagmar said quietly, overwhelmed with sadness for the loss of an innocent young man, as well as her own belief in her friend.

"It is, and I will do everything I can to aid Dalton in uncovering more proof of exactly what happened that night, but given her attacks against Dalton, you, and me, I believe her guilt is established sufficiently to keep her in gaol."

"But she's in there for killing Louisa, not Louisa's son."

Leo shrugged one shoulder. "Does it matter whose death she is imprisoned for, so long as she pays the price of her actions?"

"I suppose not, although I am not easy in my mind about it. Leo, are all your missions going to be as sad as this? Because I feel as if I've lost a dear friend, and I don't know if I could go through this on a regular basis."

He pulled her forward onto his naked lap, his penis

(now in repose), nestled warmly against her hip. "I'm sorry that this had to happen, darling. I know you feel nothing but affection for your companion, but the truth is that she has taken part in the murder of an innocent young man and attempted to attack three other people. Think of her as she was, if it helps. Think of all the years you had together in happiness, and not the sad creature she's become."

"Is there any way we could get her released? Can we tell the police what you have deduced?"

"We can try, but without Louisa Hayes, they may not believe us."

"Mr. Dalton—"

"Is convinced that his actions are just, and will do nothing to aid the release of Julia Deworthy."

"I don't like her being in prison for a crime she didn't commit."

"She did have a hand in the death of the young Dalton boy."

"But she didn't kill Louisa." Dagmar thought for a moment. "Although she would have killed you if we weren't there to save you. Oh, I don't know what to think. My emotions are so confused."

"I understand your dilemma, and I assure you that I will tell the authorities what I know about Louisa."

Dagmar kissed him on the very corner of his mouth and leaned against him, drawing strength from the warm solidness of him. "Thank you. I suppose there is nothing more we can do for her than stand by her. Which means I may now seduce you."

"I believe it's my turn to seduce you."

"Perhaps, but I am a princess."

He tipped his head back and laughed, the noise rumbling around in his chest in a way that made Dagmar feel warm and tingly. "That doesn't mean you are always going to get your way."

"Of course it does. What is the good in being a princess otherwise? Besides, I wish very much to try out this connubial calisthenic that Plum describes on page seventy-three of her book."

"The princess and the jouster?"

"That's the one. I believe that desk over there would be suitable as a balcony."

He glanced down at his lap. "I'm afraid that my lance is no longer couched."

She gave him a dazzling smile, one that had every ounce of love she felt for him. "There are instructions on how to equip the lance. I believe it begins like this…"

Epilogue

Dearest Thom,

I pen these words in a great hurry, as Leo and I have to make a quick escape from Vienna. It appears that the grand duke who we were quite covertly investigating has discovered our identities via a very stupid distant Prussian cousin who wandered into the ball where we were expertly grilling the grand duke about something I can't possibly mention here because Leo says that the mails aren't safe and someone might read it. But you can assume it was on a subject of Great Importance and Much Delicacy, and possibly involving a certain Frenchman who I think really should be taken down a peg or two. But I will say no more on that subject lest prying eyes were to fall upon this letter.

Fritz, the stupid cousin, recognized me as soon as he saw me at the ball, and the grand duke made a huge fuss about us being spies who were determined to engineer his downfall, as well as that of the emperor, and indeed, the Austro-Hungarian empire itself, which is simply ridiculous, but that's how these people think. The grand duke demanded that we be imprisoned, which of course meant that Leo had to fight him off as well as the guards that came running when the grand duke created such a big scene, but luckily, Leo had reconnoitered the palace beforehand, and we were able to escape by climbing down some ivy, which isn't nearly as easy as you might think it is. Regardless of that, we made it back to our lodgings, where even now Leo is hastily thrusting our belongings into a carriage for our hurried leave.

So don't plan on meeting us in Vienna for your honeymoon trip; we simply won't be here. I can't say where we're going, but I'll write once we've reached safety. Oh, and many congratulations on the wedding. I wish we could have been with you for it, but we'll celebrate properly when we see you again. Best wishes to Plum, Harry, and Nick's parents as well, and thank Harry for doing what he could to get Julia free. I'm saddened beyond words that no one will believe Leo's statements and conjectures, but perhaps, with time, we can convince Mr. Dalton to admit the truth. Or Louisa might return to England. We can hope. Until then, pass along my appreciation for your aunt's visits to Julia in my stead. I'm sure Julia is deeply grateful for her visits, as am I.

No, I haven't met any goatherds, but really, I don't think Nick is being unreasonable by demanding that you leave at least some of the thirty-six dogs at home. They can't all fit into one carriage, and besides, you won't be able to indulge yourself in Rocking Horse Derby if the carriage is laden with dogs. Leo and I tried it on a very well-sprung carriage in Paris, and it's definitely one of your aunt's better calisthenics. Just make sure the carriage blinds are drawn before you begin the Derby. Also, a riding crop can be used very effectively if you gently apply it to...oh, there's Leo. Must dash. Much love to you both.

Dagmar

In case you missed them, read on for excerpts
from the first three books in the series that launched
Katie MacAlister's career:

Noble Intentions

Noble Destiny

The Trouble with Harry

Now available from Sourcebooks Casablanca

From Noble Intentions

GILLIAN LEIGH'S FIRST SOCIAL EVENT OF THE SEASON began with what many in the *ton* later labeled as an uncanny warning of Things To Come.

"Well, bloody hell. This isn't going to endear me to the duchess."

Gillian watched with dismay as flames licked up the gold velvet curtains despite her attempts to beat them out with a tasseled silk cushion. Shrieks of horror and shrill voices behind her indicated that others had spotted her activities, which she had hoped would escape their notice until she had the fire under control.

Two footmen raced past her with buckets of water and soon had the fire extinguished, but it was too late, the damage was done. The duchess's acclaimed Gold Drawing Room would never be the same again. Gillian stood clutching the sooty cushion to her chest and watched mournfully as the blackened curtains were hastily bundled past the small clutches of people who stood talking intently, looking everywhere but at her.

"Sealing my fate as a social pariah, no doubt," she muttered to herself.

"Who is? And what on earth happened in here? Lady Dell said something about you burning down the house, but you know how she exag…oh, my!"

Gillian heaved a deep sigh and turned to smile ruefully as her cousin, and dearest friend, caught sight of the damp, smoke-stained wall.

"I'm afraid it's true, Charlotte, although I wasn't trying to burn down the house. It was just another of my Unfortunate Accidents."

Charlotte gave the formerly gilt-paneled wall a considering look, pursed her lips, then turned her gaze on her cousin. "Mmm. Well, you have certainly made sure everyone will be talking about your debut. Just look at you! You've got soot all over—your gloves are a complete loss, but I think you can brush the worst off your bodice."

Gillian gave in to the urge and snorted while Charlotte effected repairs to the sooty green muslin gown. "My debut—as if I wanted one. The only reason I'm here is because your mother insisted it would look odd if I remained at home while you had your Season. I'm five and twenty, Charlotte, not a young girl like you. And as for setting the *ton* talking—I'm sure they are, but it will no doubt be to label me a clumsy Colonial who can't even be a wallflower without wreaking havoc."

Charlotte rolled her eyes as she clasped her hand around her cousin's wrist and dragged her past the excited groups of people and out the door. "You're only half American and not clumsy. You're… well, you're just enthusiastic. And slightly prone to Unfortunate Accidents. But all's well that ends happily, as Mama always says. The curtains can be replaced, and I'm sure the duchess will realize the fire was simply one of those unavoidable events. Come, you must return to the ballroom. The most exciting thing has happened—the Black Earl is here."

"The black who?"

"The Black Earl. Lord Weston. It's rumored he's going to take a bride again."

"No, truly? And this is an event we must not fail to witness? Is he going to take her right there in the ballroom?"

"Gillian!" Charlotte stopped dead in the hallway, blocking people from either direction. Her china-blue eyes were round and sparkling with faux horror. "You really cannot say such things in polite company! It's shocking, simply shocking, and I cannot allow you to sully my delicate, maidenly ears in such a manner!"

Gillian grinned at her cousin and gave her a little push to get her moving again. "Honestly, Charlotte, I don't see how you can tell such awful whoppers without being struck down with shame."

"Practice, Gilly, it's because I pay the proper attention to perfecting a shy, demure look for an hour each morning. If you would do the same, it would do wonders for your personality. You might even catch a husband, which you certainly won't do if you continue to be so...so..."

"Honest?"

"No."

"Forthright?"

"No."

Gillian chewed on her lip for a moment. "Unassuming? Unpretentious? Veracious?"

"No, no, no. Green, that's what you are. Utterly green and without any sense of *ton* whatsoever. You simply cannot continue to say what you think. It's just not done in polite circles."

"Some people like honesty."

"Not in society, they don't. Now stop dawdling and fix a pleasant expression on your face."

Gillian heaved a little sigh and tried to adopt the demure look that spinsters of her age were expected to wear.

"Now you're looking mulish," Charlotte pointed out with a frown, then gave in to a sudden impish grin. She linked her arm through her cousin's and tugged her along the hall. "Never mind, your face doesn't matter in the least. Come, we don't want to miss Lord Weston. Mama says he is a terrible rake and isn't welcomed into polite circles anymore. I can't wait to see how depraved he looks."

"What has he done to make him unacceptable to the jades, rakes, and rogues who populate the *ton*?"

Charlotte's eyes sparkled with excitement. "Lady Dell says he murdered his first wife after he found her in the arms of her true love. He is said to have shot her in the head, but missed when he tried to murder her lover."

"Truly? How fascinating! He must be a terribly emotional and uncontrolled man if he didn't tolerate his wife having an *inamorato*. I thought that sort of behavior was *de rigueur* in the *ton*."

Gillian and Charlotte slipped past small groups of elegantly clad people and paused before the double doors leading to the ballroom. The heat generated by so many people inhabiting the confined space left the room stifling and airless.

Charlotte fanned herself vigorously as she continued to tell Gillian what she knew of the infamous earl. "He doesn't wear anything but black—'tis said to be a sign of his guilt that he's never been out of mourning even though he killed his wife more than five years ago. She cursed him, you know, and that's another reason he wears black. And then there are rumors of a child…"

Charlotte's voice dropped to an intimate whisper that Gillian had a hard time hearing above the noise of several chattering matrons standing nearby. "…and was born on the wrong side of the blanket."

"Someone is a bastard?" Gillian asked, confused.

"Gillian!" Charlotte shrieked and, with an appalled look toward the matrons, pulled her cousin closer to the ballroom doors. "God's teeth, you're as uncivilized as a Red Indian. It must be living among them as you did that makes you so unconventional. Do try to curb your tongue!"

Gillian muttered an insincere apology and prodded her cousin. "Who is illegitimate? The earl?"

"Gilly, really! Don't be such an idiot. How can he be illegitimate and an earl? Make an effort to pay attention, do—I was just telling you how Lord Weston murdered his first wife because she refused to bear him a son and turned to her lover for comfort. Isn't that thrilling? It's said she pleaded with him to give her a divorce so she could marry her lover, but he told her that if he could not have her, no man would. Then he shot her while her lover looked on." She sighed. "It's so romantic."

"Your idea of romantic and mine are most definitely not the same," Gillian said, looking around at the dandies, macaronis, fops, elderly gentlemen in silk breeches, and other assorted members of that small, elite group who possessed the combination of fortune, rank, and reputation to admit them as members of the *ton*. "And this man is here tonight? Which one is he? Does he look evil? Does he have a hump on his back and a squint and walk with a limp? Will he ogle the ladies?"

Charlotte frowned. "Don't be ridiculous, Gilly. The earl is not a monster; at least, not to look at. He is quite handsome if you like large, brooding men, which I most definitely do. When they're earls, of course. And perhaps viscounts. But nothing lower than a viscount, you understand." She forestalled Gillian's questions by turning toward the doors. "Come stand with me and we will watch to see if the rumor is true."

"Which rumor—that the earl killed his wife or that he is looking for a new one?"

"The latter. I will know soon enough if he is—men cannot keep a thing like that secret for very long."

"Mmm, no, I imagine not. If their intentions are not clear in the speculative gazes they impart on every marriageable female who can still draw breath, it's in the way they check the bride-to-be's teeth and make sure her movement is sound."

Charlotte tried to stifle a giggle. "Mama says I am not to listen to a thing you say, that you are incorrigible and a bad influence."

Gillian laughed with her cousin as they entered the ballroom arm-in-arm. "It's a good thing she doesn't know I've learned it all from you, my dear Char. Now, after we view this rogue of the first water, tell me who has caught your fancy. As I told Aunt Honoria, I'm determined you will end your Season with a stunning match, but I cannot help you become deliriously happy if you do not tell me who your intended victim is."

"Oh, that's simple," Charlotte replied with a beatific expression of innocence that was spoiled only by a perfectly wicked smile. "Everyone knows rakes make the best husbands. I shall simply pick out the worst of the bunch—one riddled with vices, bad habits, and a reputation that will make Mama swoon and Papa rail—then I shall reform him."

"That seems like a terrible amount of work to go to just to find a suitable husband."

"Not really." Charlotte whipped open her fan and adopted a coy look. "After all, you know what they say."

"No, what do they say?"

"Necessity is the mother of intention."

Gillian stopped. "Invention, Charlotte."

"What?"

"Necessity is the mother of *invention*."

Charlotte stared at her for a moment, then rapped her cousin on the wrist with her fan. "Don't be ridiculous, where would I come up with an invention? Intentions I have aplenty, and that's quite enough for me, thank you. Now let's go find this delicious rake of an earl. If he's as bad as Mama says, he might just suit."

From Noble Destiny

"You can't leave me now! Not when I need you! How selfish is it to leave just when I need you most? I forbid you to leave! I absolutely forbid you to leave me in my time of Great Distress!"

"I have no choice. I must leave now."

"Widdle, Mama."

"Stop just where you are, Gillian. Don't you dare take another step toward this door!"

"Charlotte, give me the key."

"Shan't!"

"Mama, want to widdle!"

"Char, Dante needs to use the necessary before we leave. Now please, if you have any love for me, hand over the key. Noble's going to be in a terrible fury if he finds out you're holding us prisoner in his library, and I can assure you from experience that Dante does not announce his intention to widdle unless that event is nigh on imminent."

The petite blonde blocking the two oak doors cast a hesitant glance toward the figure of a three-year-old child doing an urgent dance before her. Two thin furrows appeared between her dark blond brows.

"It's a trick. You've taught him to say that. You're using your own child's plumbing as a weapon against me, cousin, and I find that a completely nebulous act."

"The word is *nefarious*, Charlotte." Gillian, Lady Weston, picked up her son and pointed him toward her cousin. "If you do not unlock the door and release us, I shall allow him to widdle upon you."

The child giggled in delight. Lady Charlotte di Abalongia *nee* Collins, sucked in a horrified breath and leveled a defiant glare at her cousin. "You wouldn't!"

"Gillian? Wife, where are you hiding? This is no time for play, woman. We should have left an hour ago!" The doorknob rattled ineffectually.

"Papa, have to widdle!" Dante squirmed in his mother's arms.

"Now you've done it." Gillian nodded, stepping backwards. "Now you've annoyed Noble. I would advise you to move away from the doorway since he is sure to—"

Three sudden bangs against the door at her back caused Charlotte to jump a good foot off the ground.

"—want in. We're in here, my love," Gillian called. "Charlotte seems to have misplaced the key. We won't be a moment finding it."

"WANT TO WIDDLE!"

"What's that? Charlotte? What the devil is she doing here? I thought she ran off to be some Italian's mistress years ago."

"I didn't run off, we eloped!" Charlotte bellowed at the door. "We were married in Paris. It was *romantic*!"

"It doesn't matter. Open the door! Gillian, we have to leave. *Now!*"

"*WIDDLE!*"

"Charlotte," Gillian said, her voice low and urgent. Charlotte eyed the door with alarm as the Black Earl pounded on it, demanding immediate entrance, but she paid heed to the steely note in her closest friend and relative's voice. "I understand you're terribly upset," Gillian continued, "and I know you've had a horrible time returning to England from what sounds like a perfectly ghastly old ruins in Italy, but my dear, I have a son full of widdle, two impatient children in the carriage with Nurse, and a husband who"—she paused as a particularly loud barrage of swearing accented the increased pounding on the door—"is fast losing a temper that has been extremely tried today. Please, please, Char, give me the key before Noble is forced to take drastic measures."

Charlotte glanced from the squirming child to the look of concern in Gillian's emerald eyes. Tears had always worked well for her in the past. Perhaps if she could work up a few, her cousin would see how serious she was. She waited for the peculiar prickling sensation to indicate that her cornflower-blue eyes would soon be becomingly framed in a pool of tears, and allowed a note of raw desperation to creep into her voice. "Gilly, I need you. I truly do. You're all I have left. There's no one else left who will receive me. Papa saw to that. I have nowhere to go and no money. I sold what remained of Mama's jewels just to buy a few traveling gowns and passage to England on a merchant ship. You're the only one in the family who will acknowledge me, and now you are sailing to the West Indies…" Her voice cracked as she brushed at the wetness on her cheeks, surprised to find her crocodile tears had suddenly become real. "Oh, Gilly, please stay. Please help me. I've never been alone. I don't know what to do."

Gillian shifted the child in her arms and squeezed Charlotte's hand. "You know I will do everything I can to help you—"

Charlotte shrieked in joy and hugged her cousin, widdly child and all. "I knew you wouldn't leave me!"

A tremendous splintering noise reverberated through the room as Noble Britton, known by the (in Charlotte's mind, understated) sobriquet of the Black Earl, burst through the doors, followed by a tall, bewigged man with a hook where his left hand should have been, and two smaller footmen in livery.

"Are you all right?" the earl asked his countess, rushing to her side.

She smiled reassuringly. "Of course we are. Charlotte just needs a moment or two of my time, and then I will be ready to be off." She forestalled protests on both her husband's and cousin's lips by thrusting the squirming child into his father's arms just before she grasped Charlotte firmly and tugged her toward a nearby emerald-and-gold damask couch. "While you're taking Dante for his widdle, I'll speak with Char. Crouch, please take Lady Charlotte's things up to the Blue Suite. She'll be staying here for a time. Dickon, Charles, tell the other carriages to start, we'll be along directly."

Noble shot his wife a questioning look before settling a glare on Charlotte, who was profoundly thankful it was a short glare, as she never could stand up to one of the earl's scowls. Both father and child hastened away when the latter announced his intention to widdle right there in the library.

"You have five minutes until I must leave," Gillian told her cousin sternly. "You are welcome to stay here for as long as you like. Now, what else can I do to help you?"

Charlotte's heart underwent a peculiar motion that felt suspiciously as though it had dropped into her jean half-boots. "You're leaving? You're still leaving me?"

"I have no choice," was the calm reply. A burst of pain flared to life within Charlotte's breast at her cousin's defection, but a moment's consideration led her to admit that Gillian really could not remain behind while her husband and children sailed to their coffee plantation. She shoved down the pain of abandonment and focused her energies on explaining what a shambles her life had become.

"Very well. You received my letter that mentioned Antonio died of sweating sickness in November?"

Gillian nodded. "And you wanted to leave Villa Abalongia because you had a difficult time with his family, but you mentioned going to Paris, not home to England."

Charlotte's eyes threatened to fill once more with scalding tears that she suspected would leave her with unattractive, swollen, red eyes and a nose that would require much attention with a handkerchief. "And I don't even have a handkerchief anymore," she wailed, unable to stop the tears. Charlotte seldom had recourse to real tears, but they were just as uncomfortable as she recalled. "Everything's gone, everything! The contessa took it all for her two horrid, fat daughters. She said I wouldn't need my fine gowns when I was in mourning for Antonio. She said I'd have to go live on a tiny little farm in the mountains and tend a bunch of smelly goats, that I wasn't welcome to stay in Florence as I wasn't truly a member of the family, all because I hadn't given Antonio an heir!"

"That was very cruel of her."

"Yes." Charlotte sniffed. "It was. Especially since it wasn't my fault. I wouldn't have minded a child—you seem to enjoy yours so much—but Antonio refused to do his husbandly duty by me."

Gillian's eyes widened. "He…he refused?"

Charlotte nodded, her eyes filling again at the memory of such a grave injustice. "It was all he could do to consummate the marriage. After that…oh, Gilly, he wouldn't even try. And the contessa was forever making nasty remarks that I was not doing *my* duty properly! I tried, I honestly tried! I wore naughty nightwear, I allowed him to catch me *en dishabille* on many occasions, and I even sought advice from the local strumpet as to how to arouse the passion of Antonio's manly instrument, but to no avail. His instrument resisted all my efforts. I think it hated me," she added darkly.

"Oh, I'm sure that wasn't—"

"It wouldn't even twitch for me!"

"Well, really, Charlotte." Gillian looked a bit embarrassed. "It's not as if it were an animal trained to jump on your command."

"I know that, but the strumpet said it should at the very least twitch once in a while, and not lie limp and flaccid like a week-old bit of blancmange. It wouldn't make even the slightest effort on my behalf. If that's not cruel and petty-minded of a manly instrument, well, I just don't know what is!"

Gillian blinked once or twice before patting her cousin's arm and handing her a lace-edged handkerchief. Charlotte viewed it with sorrow. "I used to have handkerchiefs like this," she cried, mopping at her eyes and blowing her nose in a less-than-dainty manner. "But that evil woman took them away from me, just as she took everything else, even my husband!"

"Oh, surely she couldn't have taken Antonio's affection from you—"

"Not his affection." Charlotte sniffled loudly. "He was fond enough of me, although he never dared act so before the contessa. No, she took him away and sent him to a nasty little town on the Mediterranean for his weak lungs. And he died there!"

"Char, I'm sorry about Antonio. I know you must have loved him greatly..."

Charlotte stopped dabbing at her eyes, a look of utter astonishment on her face. "Love him greatly? Where did you get that idea?"

Gillian stopped patting her cousin's hand. "Well... that is...you eloped with him! You dismissed all your suitors and eloped with the son of a minor Italian nobleman. Why else would you sacrifice everything you held dear if you didn't love him greatly?"

"Oh, that," Charlotte responded dismissively, gently prodding the region below her eyes to ascertain whether they were swollen from her recent tears. "It was my third Season, and I didn't care for that year's suitors. Antonio was just like the hero in *Castle Moldavia, Or, The Dancing Master's Ghost.* He was so very romantic, but Papa was being stiff-rumped about my marrying him, threatening to cut me off without a shilling if I didn't marry someone suitable instead. Papa became ever so tiresome, and the Season was really quite boring, so I did the only sensible thing."

"Sensible?" Gillian stared at her cousin in disbelief. "Are you telling me you ran off to marry knowing that your father disapproved of your husband, knowing he would disinherit you, knowing that such an elopement would cause a scandal that would even now keep all of the doors of Society closed to you, and yet you did it not for love, but because you were *bored*?"

Charlotte frowned. "Most of the doors of Society, not all, and I don't see what that has to do with anything. You said you would help me. I really don't think spending my five minutes discussing the past four years is helping me. I don't see how chastising me for actions viewed by some as romantic and daring—"

From The Trouble with Harry

HARRY WISHED HE WAS DEAD. WELL, PERHAPS DEATH was an exaggeration, although St. Peter alone knew how long he'd be able to stand up to this sort of continued torture.

"And then what happens?" His tormentor stared at him with eyes that were very familiar to him, eyes that he saw every morning in his shaving mirror, a mixture of brown, gray, and green that was pleasant enough on him, but when surrounded by the lush brown eyelashes of his inquisitor looked particularly charming. And innocent. And innocuous…something the possessor of the eyes was most decidedly not. "Well? Then what happens? Aren't you going to tell me?"

Harry ran his finger between his neckcloth and his neck, tugging on the cloth to loosen its constricting grasp on his windpipe, wishing for the fifteenth time in the last ten minutes that he had been able to escape capture.

"I want to know!"

Or found another victim to throw to the one who held him prisoner.

"You have to tell me!"

Perhaps death wasn't such a wild thought after all. Surely if he were to die at that exact moment, he would be admitted into heaven. Surely St. Peter would look upon the deeds he had done for the benefit of others—deeds such as spending fifteen years working as a spy for the Home Office—and grant him asylum. Surely he wouldn't be turned away from his rightful reward, damned to eternal torment, left to an eternity of hell such as he was in now, a hell dominated by—

"Papa! Then…what…happens?"

Harry sighed and pushed his spectacles high onto the bridge of his nose, bowing his head in acknowledgment of defeat. "After the hen and the rooster are…er…married, they will naturally wish to produce chicks."

"You already said that," his thirteen-year-old inquisitor said with the narrowed eyes and impatient tone of one who is through being reasonable. "What happens after that? And what do chickens have to do with my unpleasantness?"

"It's the process of producing offspring that is related to your unpleasantness. When a mother hen wishes to have chicks, she and the rooster must…er… perhaps chickens aren't the best example to explain the situation."

Lady India Haversham, eldest daughter of the Marquis Rosse, tapped her fingers on the table at her side and glared at her father. "You said you were going to explain the unpleasantness! George says I'm not going to die despite the fact that I'm bleeding, and that it's a very special time for girls, although I do not see what's special about having pains in my stomach, and *you* said you'd tell me and now you're talking about bees and flowers, and chickens, and fish in the river. What do they have to do with *me*?"

No, Harry decided as he looked at the earnest, if stormy, eyes of his oldest child, death was distinctly preferable to having to explain the whys and hows of reproduction—particularly the female's role in reproduction, with a specific emphasis on their monthly indispositions—to India. He decided that although he had been three times commended by the prime minister for bravery, he was at heart a coward, because he simply could not stand the torture any longer.

"Ask Gertie. She'll explain it all to you," he said hastily as he jumped up from a narrow pink chair and fled the sunny room given over to his children, shamelessly ignoring the cries of "Papa! You *said* you'd tell me!"

"You haven't seen me," Harry said as he raced through a small, windowless room that served as an antechamber to his estate office. "You haven't seen me, you don't know where I am, in fact, you might just decry knowledge of me altogether. It's safer that way. Throw the bolt on the door, would you, Temple? And perhaps you should put a chair in front of it. Or the desk. I wouldn't put it past the little devils to find a way in with only the door bolted."

Templeton Harris, secretary and man of affairs, pursed his lips as his noble employer raced into the adjacent room.

"What was it this time, sir?" Temple asked as he followed Harry. Weak sunlight filtered through the dingy windows, lighting motes of dust sent dancing in the air by Harry's rush through the room. "Did

McTavish present you with another of his finds? Has Lord Marston decided he wishes to become a blacksmith rather than inherit your title? Are the twins trying to fly from the stable roof again?"

Harry shuddered visibly as he gulped down a healthy swig of brandy. "Nothing so benign. India wished to know certain facts. *Woman things.*"

Temple's pale blue eyes widened considerably. "But...but Lady India is only a child. Surely such concepts are beyond her?"

Harry took a deep, shaky breath and leaned toward a window thick with grime. Using his elbow he cleaned a small patch, just enough to peer out into the wilderness that once was a garden. "She might be a child to our minds, Temple, but according to nature, she's trembling on the brink of womanhood."

"Oh, *those* sorts of woman things."

Harry held out the empty brandy snifter silently, and just as silently Temple poured a judicious amount of smoky amber liquid into it. "Have one yourself. It's not every day a man can say his daughter has...er...trembled."

Temple poured himself a small amount and silently toasted his employer.

"I can remember when she was born," Harry said as he stared out through the clean patch of glass, enjoying the burn of the brandy as it warmed its way down his throat. "Beatrice was disappointed that she was a girl, but I thought she was perfect with her tiny little nose, and a mop of brown curls, and eyes that used to watch me so seriously. It was like she was an angel, sent down to grace our lives, a ray of light, a beam of sunshine, a joy to behold." He took another deep breath as three quicksilver shadows flickered across the dirty window, the high, carefree laughter of children up to some devilment trailing after them. Harry flung himself backward, against the wall, clutching his glass with fingers gone white with strain. "And then she grew up and had her woman's time, and demanded that I explain everything to her. What's next, Temple, I ask you, what's next?"

Temple set his glass down in the same spot it had previously occupied and wiped his fingers on his handkerchief, trying not to grimace at the dust and decay rampant in the room. It disturbed his tidy nature immensely to know that the room had not seen a maid's hand since they had arrived some three weeks before. "I assume, my lord, that as Lady Anne is now eight years old, in some five years' time she will be demanding the very same information. Would you not allow a maid to just clean around your books? I can promise you that none of your important papers or items will be touched during the cleaning process. Indeed, I would be happy to tend to the cleaning myself if you would just give me leave—"

Harry, caught up in the hellish thought of having to repeat with his youngest daughter the scene he'd just—barely—escaped, shook his head. "No. This is my room, the one room in the whole house that is my sanctuary. No one but you is permitted in it, not the children, not the maids, no one. I must have someplace that is wholly mine, Temple, somewhere sacred, somewhere that I can just be myself."

Temple glanced around the room. He knew the

contents well enough; he'd had to carry in the boxes
of Harry's books, his estate papers, the small bureau of
curios, the horribly muddied watercolors that graced
the walls. "Perhaps if I had the curtains washed—"

"No," Harry repeated, sliding a quick glance
toward the window before daring to cross the room
to a large rosewood desk covered in papers, scattered
quills, stands of ink, books, a large statue of Pan, and
other assorted items too numerous to catalog. "I have
something else for you to do than wash my curtains."

Temple, about to admit that he hadn't intended on
washing the drapery himself, decided that information
wasn't relevant to his employer's happiness, and settled
with a sigh into the comfortable leather chair to one
side of the desk. He withdrew a memorandum note-
pad and pencil from his inner pocket. "Sir?"

Harry paced from the desk to the unlit fireplace.
"How long have you been with me, Temple?"

"Fourteen years on Midsummer Day," that worthy
replied promptly.

"That's just a fortnight away."

Temple allowed that was so.

"I had married Beatrice the summer before," Harry
continued, staring into the dark emptiness of the fireplace
as if his life were laid out there amid the heap of coal
waiting to be lit should the warm weather turn cold.

"I believe when I came into your service that Lady
Rosse was…er…in expectation of Lady India's arrival."

"Hmm. It's been almost five years since Bea died."

Temple murmured an agreement.

"Five years is a long time," Harry said, his hazel eyes
dark behind the lenses of his spectacles. "The children

are running wild. God knows they don't listen to me, and Gertie and George are hard put to keep up with the twins and McTavish, let alone Digger and India."

Temple's eyebrows rose a fraction of an inch. He had a suspicion of just where the conversation was going, but was clueless to envision what role the marquis felt he could serve in such a delicate matter.

Harry took a deep breath, rubbed his nose, then turned and stalked back to the deep green leather chair behind the desk. He sat and waved his hand toward the paper in Temple's hand. "I've decided the children need the attention of a woman. I want you to help me find one."

"A governess?"

Harry's lips thinned. "No. After Miss Reynauld died in the fire…no. The children must have time to recover from that horror. The woman I speak of"—he glanced over at the miniature that sat in prominence on the corner of his desk—"will be my marchioness. The children need a mother, and I…"

"Need a wife?" Temple said gently as Harry's voice trailed off. Despite his best intentions not to allow himself to become emotionally involved in his employer's life—emotions so often made one uncomfortable and untidy—he had, over the years, developed quite a fondness for Harry and his brood of five hellions. He was well aware that Harry had an affection for his wife that might not have been an all-consuming love, but was strong enough to keep him bound in grief for several years after her death in childbirth.

"Yes," Harry said with a sigh, slouching back into the comfortable embrace of the chair. "I came late to the married state, but must admit that I found it an enjoyable one, Temple. You might not think it possible for someone who is hounded night and day by his rampaging herd of children, but I find myself lonely of late. For a woman. A wife," he corrected quickly, a faint frown creasing his brow. "I have determined that the answer to this natural desire for a companion, and the need for someone to take the children in hand, is a wife. With that thought in mind, I would like you to take down an advertisement I wish you to run in the nearest local newspaper. What is the name of it? The *Dolphin's Derriere Daily?*"

"The *Ram's Bottom Gazette*, sir, so named because the journal originates in the town of Ram's Bottom, which is, I believe, located some eight miles to the west. I must confess, however, to being a bit confused by your determination to advertise for a woman to claim the position of marchioness. I had always assumed that a gentleman of your consequence looked to other members of Society for such a candidate, rather than placing an advertisement in an organ given over to discussions that are primarily agricultural in nature."

Harry waved away that suggestion. "I've thought about that, but I have no wish to go into town until I have to."

"But surely you must have friends, acquaintances who know of eligible women of your own class—"

"No." Harry leaned back in his chair, propping his feet up on the corner of his desk. "I've looked over all my friends' relatives; none of them will suit. Most of them are too young, and the ones who aren't just want me for the title."

Temple was at a loss. "But, sir, the woman will be your marchioness, the mother of your yet unborn children—"

Harry's feet came down with a thump as he sat up and glared at his secretary. "No more children! I'm not going through that again. I won't sacrifice another woman on *that* altar." He rubbed his nose once more and re-propped his feet. "I don't have time to hunt for a wife through conventional means. I mean to acquire one before anyone in the neighborhood knows who I am, before the grasping title-seekers get me in their sights. Cousin Gerard dying suddenly and leaving me this place offers me the perfect opportunity to find a woman who will need a husband as much as I need a wife. I want an honest woman, one gently born and educated, but not necessarily of great family—a solid country gentlewoman, that's what's needed. She must like children, and wish to…er…participate in a physical relationship with me."

"But," Temple said, his hands spreading wide in confusion. "But…ladies who participate in a physical relationship often bear children."

"I shall see to it that my wife will not be stretched upon the rack of childbirth," Harry said carelessly, then visibly flinched when somewhere nearby a door slammed, and what sounded like a hundred elephants thundered down the hallway outside his office. "Take this down, Temple. *Wanted: an honest, educated woman between the ages of thirty-five and fifty, who desires to be joined in the wedded state to a man, forty-five years of age, in good health and with sufficient means to ensure her comfort. Must desire children. Applicants may forward their particulars and references to Mr. T. Harris, Raving-by-the-Sea. Interviews will be scheduled the week following.* That should do it, don't you think? You may screen the applicants for the position, and bring me the ones you think are suitable. I shall interview them and weed out those who won't suit."

"Sir..." Temple said, even more at a loss as to how to counsel his employer from such a ramshackle method of finding a wife. "I...what if...how will I know who you will find suitable?"

Harry frowned over the top of an estate ledger. "I've already told you what I want, man! Someone honest, intelligent, and she must like children. I would prefer it if she possessed a certain charm to her appearance, but that's not absolutely necessary."

Temple swallowed his objections and asked meekly, "Where do you wish to interview the candidates for your hand? Surely not here, at Ashleigh Court?"

Harry ran his finger down a column of figures, his eyes narrowing at the proof of abuse by his late cousin's steward. "The man should be hanged, draining the estate dry like that. What did you say? Oh, no, any woman of sense would take one look at this monstrosity and run screaming in horror. Find somewhere in town, somewhere I can meet with the ladies and have a quiet conversation with them. Individually, of course. Group appointments will not do at all."

"Of course," Temple agreed and staggered from the room, his mind awhirl. The only thing that cheered him up was the thought that Harry's wife, whoever she would turn out to be, would no doubt insist on the house being cleaned from attic to cellars.

About Katie

After writing several boring software books, Katie MacAlister switched to fiction, where she could torment her characters, indulge her penchant for witty dialogue, and fall madly in love with her heroes. *The Truth about Leo* is a brand-new romance continuing the series of delightful Regencies that launched her career (the first being *Noble Intentions*). A regular on the *New York Times*, *USA Today*, and *Publishers Weekly* bestsellers lists, Katie MacAlister has written thirty novels, including unforgettable paranormal, historical, and contemporary romances, which have been translated into numerous languages and recorded as audiobooks. She lives in the Pacific Northwest. Visit katiemacalister.com.